LOVING a SAILOR

JAMIE GRANGIER

For Mom and Dad

Contents

LOVING a SAILOR

Chapter 1. *Rota*

J oel marveled at God's artistry in the clouds as the USS Roland docked at Naval Station Rota at sunrise. Seeing palm trees silhouetted against the morning sky, the captain was eager to hit the streets to explore the Spanish city.

He had light brown hair you could lose a hand in and was a tall and burly man of 28 in a Navy full dress white uniform, so it's no wonder he turned every head in Rota. Tipping his hat to a group of ladies, Joel smiled as he entered a picturesque plaza where the bell tower of a 16th-century Catholic temple caught his eye. He loved visiting religious structures and never missed an opportunity to feel his feet on holy ground, so he walked through the old-fashioned wooden doors to explore the chapels and say a few prayers. After that, he walked along the cobblestone streets until he reached Rota's main gate, where he saw a sign for the Gypsy Market.

As Joel walked through the rows of tents where the gypsies sold olives, spices, nuts, jewelry, clothing, and fabrics, he happened upon a talented flamenco guitarist, so he threw a few euros in the jar and paused to listen for a bit. A gorgeous brunette woman in a pink flamenco dress approached Joel while he enjoyed the baroque melody. A turquoise necklace rested just above her cleavage, and matching earrings and bracelets adorned her ears and wrists. Sunrays illuminated her long, luxurious hair, making her look like a Spanish goddess.

She slowly sauntered up to Joel like a cat getting ready to wiggle its rear before pouncing on its prey. He thought he was hallucinating until she met him eye to eye, then suddenly pushed her heavy chest into his Navy jacket, pressed her lips against his, and cupped his face in her hands. At first, Joel was too stunned to reciprocate. Luckily for him, this sensuous stranger was one heck of a kisser, so he flipped his what-the-hell switch and went for it.

Her body was warm and soft, her kisses were sweet, and she beautifully smelled and tasted like sugared guava, one of Joel's favorite fruits, which always left him wanting more. By the end of the kiss, his hands found her cheeks and then down to her curvy hips.

"Nice to meet you too, sailor," she flirtatiously said with an alluring accent that made Joel melt into a puddle of mush.

The dazzling dame reached inside her dress above her left bosom, pulled out a business card, and handed it to him. He opened his mouth, but she placed her finger across his lips to stop the words from coming. She peered deeply into his emerald eyes, and an enticing smile spread across her face before she turned and walked away.

Bewildered and delighted, Joel watched her vanish into the sea of bustling Gypsy Market shoppers. Once she was no longer in sight, he looked at the business card, which read, *La Cabaña de la Prostituta*, and his eyes almost popped out of his head. He had never had a transaction with a woman in this line of work. That wasn't Joel's style, yet there's always a first time for everything. This exceptionally exotic woman was successful in intriguing him. And the way she had said, "Nice to meet you too, sailor," with her heavy, sexy Spanish accent, kept ringing in his ears, long after she was gone.

Joel couldn't contain his curiosity, so that night at sunset, he went to La Cabaña de la Prostituta, a small cottage along the Atlantic Ocean. Waves slapped the shore, and wind chimes fluttered with the salty ocean breeze, creating the perfect soundtrack for a romantic evening. The dichotomous smells of fried fish and marzipan escaped through the cottage windows, along with the sound of a cork popping off a wine bottle. Growing more intrigued by the moment, Joel inhaled the pleasing aromas as he walked up the steps and rang the doorbell.

Wearing a turquoise-colored negligee, the mystery woman opened the door. "I thought you would've been here sooner."

"I didn't think a prostituta kissed," Joel responded as his eyes feasted on her scantily clad body.

"Well, I don't, but for you, I make excepción," she said as she leaned against the doorway, reached her hand toward him, and ran her fingers down the front of his Navy jacket like she was playing connect the dots with the gold buttons.

"How much?" Joel asked without hesitation as he gently caressed her cheek with the back of his hand.

"Sixty euros para una hora," she breathlessly whispered.

"Okay," Joel replied as he reached into his pocket and then handed her the money, including a nice tip.

The tantalizing courtesan graciously took the euros and motioned for Joel to enter. His heart anxiously pounded as he took off his Navy hat and placed it under his arm as he entered the small but quaint cottage. An eat-in kitchen was connected to a small living room with doors leading to two bedrooms.

She reached for Joel's hand. "I work in the bedroom on the right. Let's go, sailor." With a smile hiding sadness, she turned to open the bedroom door.

Joel's heart pounding accelerated while his feet remained firmly planted on the floor, and a little voice spoke in his mind, saying *Don't do it!* And he knew he couldn't enter the bedroom on the right.

She attempted to pull Joel through the doorway, but his feet wouldn't budge. She looked at him and asked, "¿Qué?"

Joel's heart racing continued as he looked at this stunning woman, noticing wrinkles around her eyes and surmising that she was at least 15 years older than him. Looking at her more intently, he saw that she had a sad expression, and Joel knew he couldn't go through with it. *What woman would enjoy this livelihood? What caused her to become a prostitute?* he wondered as he looked into her sorrowful eyes. Still holding onto her hand, Joel reached his other hand around and closed the door to the bedroom on the right.

"I can't do this. Can we just hang out? I don't even know your name. Please tell me your name," he insisted.

"Mi nombre es Adoncia."

"That's a beautiful name, and it suits you well," Joel replied with a smile. He was an educated man and knew that in the English translation, her name meant *sweet*.

"Gracias. ¿Y usted?" Adoncia responded.

"Joel Layton," he said, then cavalierly kissed the back of her hand. "It's a pleasure to meet you, my dear."

Adoncia blushed and looked at Joel in disbelief. She wasn't used to a man treating her respectfully. "So, you want to talk for your €60?" she asked.

"Sí, but perhaps you could put on some ropas," Joel suggested, even though he would miss the negligee.

Adoncia smiled and blushed at Joel's respectful proposition. She briefly disappeared into the bedroom on the left and came out wearing a blue flamenco dress with a multicolored, handknitted shawl draped over her shoulders.

"You look muy bonita," Joel said with a smile, completely blown away by her beauty.

"Gracias, sailor. Will you please join me for dinner?"

Joel took her hands in his and gently kissed her on the cheek. "It would be an honor to have dinner with you, Adoncia. Thank you."

"No. Thank you, Joel," Adoncia replied.

The ocean played the sand like a piano, wind chimes clinked elegant tones, and the curtains blew in the salty ocean breeze. Adoncia and Joel enjoyed red wine, fried fish, and marzipan as they gabbed across the table like two old friends.

"So, sailor, tell me about yourself. Who exactly is Joel Layton?" Adoncia asked as she refilled their wine glasses for the third time.

He sighed because he knew who Captain Joel Layton of the USS Roland was, but he had yet to define Joel Layton. He hadn't shared his story with anyone, mainly because his past was painful, but he knew he could trust Adoncia. "I grew up on Maryland's Eastern Shore on an island in the Chesapeake Bay. My father was a waterman, and I knew I wanted to be like him. He and my mother were very happy, and I had a wonderful childhood until my parents died in an oystering accident when I was 11 years old. Then I was sent to an orphanage in Baltimore, and that's a time I choose not to remember. As soon as I turned 18, I joined the Navy, hoping to become a captain."

"And here you are, Captain Layton, regal like an eagle," Adoncia replied as she took his hand.

"A lone eagle. Tell me about yourself," Joel began as he gently squeezed her hand. "Tell me how you…" he paused, realizing he shouldn't be asking Adoncia how she became a prostituta.

Not the least bit offended, Adoncia took another sip of wine and then tossed her head back and laughed. "Tell you how I became the CEO of La Cabaña de la Prostituta?"

Joel reciprocated with an alluring grin of his own while looking deeply into her beautiful brown eyes. "Yes, my dear. Do tell."

"Prostitución is a means of survival for me. There's nothing to enjoy about it. You see, Joel, I was in love with a sailor when I was 16. We got married when I was 18. We were muy feliz for several years. He worked on the boat for weeks at a time. Then the weeks turned into months. He sent dinero algunas veces. Then one day, he sent me a letter, saying he was never coming back. I was 23 and never worked. But I knew I could always turn a head. I opened La Cabaña de la Prostituta, and work came to the bedroom on the right. He's been gone for almost veinte años," Adoncia explained as her eyes glistened.

Joel scooted his chair closer to her and put his arm around her, pulling her close and whispering in her ear, "I never would've deserted you."

She laughed in his face. "Sure you would. Every time you go to sea, you would desert me, even if you kept coming back," Adoncia retorted, starting to show her inebriation. "All you sailors are the same. You love the ocean first. You love your woman last."

THESE WORDS RESONATED in the back of Joel's mind for the next decade as he remained the captain of a prestigious warship. A few times a year, the USS Roland went to Rota to be serviced. And that's when Joel saw Adoncia, which was the extent of their relationship. And yes, there was plenty of kissing, but who could blame them?

TEN YEARS AFTER they first met at the Gypsy Market, Joel visited Adoncia for the last time before navigating his final journey across the Atlantic Ocean, for he would be discharged after 20 years of service when he arrived at Naval Station Norfolk. During these two momentous decades, Joel became a well-decorated and revered captain of a guided-missile destroyer, even receiving a Navy Cross for a tremendous act of heroism. He had a career that many people dream about; however, his professional successes had limited his personal life.

Over the last 10 years, he had recalled his first night with Adoncia when she had asked him, "Who exactly is Joel Layton?" He had been pondering that question ever since. Now at age 38, he decided to find the answer, so he chose to retire and start a new life.

Joel was missing a family and the love of a good woman. He had dated some over the years but had never had a long-term love interest since his address was the USS Roland. Joel quickly learned that his uniform was both a blessing and a curse since beautiful and provocative women of all nationalities threw themselves at him. There were plenty of women to sleep with—but none to love. One-night stands weren't his style, and he could spot a gold digger a mile away.

Speaking of beautiful and provocative women, one held an extraordinary place in Joel's heart, and he had to see her one last time. With an extravagant bouquet in his hand, he walked up to the front porch of La Cabaña de la Prostituta as he savored the ocean slapping the shore and the wind chimes fluttering with the salty breeze. Before knocking, he took a deep breath because this would be a bittersweet night.

As if she had read his mind, Adoncia opened the door, and Joel was delighted to see her wearing the infamous pink flamenco dress with turquoise jewelry she had worn the day they met. She was now a gorgeous 53-year-old but didn't look a day over 45. This exotic woman was like a fine wine, and Joel was there for one last sip.

At first, Joel didn't say anything and stared at this beautiful woman with an equally beautiful heart. He reached his hand up to Adoncia's face and gently caressed her cheek before running his fingers through her hair, cradling her head in the palm of his hand while he looked deeply into her eyes. Then he passionately kissed her. For a moment, Adoncia remembered she was a prostituta, and Joel forgot he was a gentleman.

"That kiss was dizzying," he whispered as he pulled her closer. "These are for you," Joel said as he gave her the bouquet.

"Gracias. Las flores son hermosas. I knew you were coming. I saw the USS Roland from the beach today and knew you would be here soon. Entra, marinero. Toma un poco de sangría conmigo," Adoncia sweetly said as she took Joel's hand and led him to the kitchen. She quickly filled a vase with water for the flowers, poured two glasses of sangria, and motioned for Joel to sit.

"This will probably be the last time you see me. I leave tomorrow and will be discharged when I arrive in Virginia. I had to spend my last night with you," Joel explained.

"So, you will start a new life. Do you have any plans?" Adoncia asked as she leaned forward and propped her arm on the table, unwittingly making her cleavage even more noticeable than it already was.

Naturally, Joel was distracted by this. He opened his mouth to speak, but no words came out. Instead, he scrunched up his face like he was trying to conjure up an adequate answer.

"You have no idea where you're going after the discharge ceremony, do you?" Adoncia speculated before downing her glass of sangria and promptly pouring another.

"You know I have no family," Joel quietly responded.

"I remember everything you told me that first night, even your strong dislike of peanut butter," Adoncia retorted with her thick and heavy accent.

Joel shook his head and laughed. "Your English gets better and better each time I see you."

"I have a lot of American clients who love cougars," Adoncia said without missing a beat. "Don't change the subject. We need to make a plan for you. I've got an idea!" she exclaimed, reaching for her laptop on the other side of the table. "I know you will die if you're not working on the water. Maldito marinero. Let's look at the marine job boards and find you a new job. Then maybe you'll meet a pretty chica, settle down, and pop out a few niños." She elbowed him in the ribs and winked.

Adoncia had always read Joel's mind, which was why he adored her so much. Her passionate kisses were merely icing on the cake.

"You're so beautiful and intuitive. How I will miss you," Joel sadly responded. Since he was retiring, he wouldn't return to Rota and would never see Adoncia again. At least, that's what he thought.

"Querido, that's what social media is for!" Adoncia exclaimed.

"Social media?" Joel replied as he choked on a sip of sangria. He didn't do social media. It was a wonder the man had a cell phone, and posting shirtless selfies wasn't his style.

"Vamos, sé moderno. I use social media to find clients."

Joel was perplexed by this, so he downed his glass of sangria and promptly poured another. He was usually a one-drink man, but when it came to Adoncia, he overindulged every time.

Adoncia turned on the laptop, brought up a search engine, typed *fishing jobs*, clicked the first link, and skimmed it. The chandelier caused a glare on the screen, making it hard for Joel to see everything she was doing, so he tried to tilt the laptop to get a better view. Adoncia pulled the computer back toward her and slapped his hand. "¡Estás impaciente! I'll show you when I am ready!" A few minutes elapsed with the sound of the mouse wheel spinning and Adoncia saying, "No," repeatedly as she scrolled the web for Joel's new life. Eventually, she paused when she found something that met her expectations. "Oh, right here! I found it!" She finally turned the laptop for Joel to see.

He scooted his chair closer to Adoncia and put his arm around her as he read the screen, which showed a job advertisement in the *Aleutian Islands Fishing Gazette.*

Position: Deckhand on the Alexandria, deep-sea king crab fishing vessel
Location: Port of Aleutia, Unalaska, Alaska
Start Date: October 15th
Contact: Captain Gunther Alexander

"Alaska? You choose to send me to Alaska? Isn't it cold there?" Joel asked, not taking this seriously whatsoever.

Adoncia leaned toward him, so they were cheek to cheek. She nibbled on his ear before whispering, "I think you should listen to your favorite puta and call the number below the ad."

"If you are trying to persuade me by seduction, it's working," Joel replied, utterly enamored by Adoncia's sensuality as he ran his fingers over her turquoise necklace.

"Call the number," Adoncia whispered before giving him another ear nibble.

Joel laughed and smiled his sexy grin as he went along with another Adoncia impulse. He reached into his pocket for his phone and dialed the captain's number, leaving the phone on speaker.

After the eighth ring, an agitated, raspy male voice yelled, "Hello!" Then the greeting trailed off into a disgusting coughing fit.

Before speaking, Joel politely waited for the hacking to subside. "Hello, I am Captain Joel Layton of the United States Navy," he began as static interrupted his words.

"I didn't do anything with the torpedo," the man snarled, then struggled to clear his junked-up throat.

"I'm calling about the job opening on the Alexandria. I am trying to reach Gunther Alexander," Joel said as he overenunciated his words and spoke louder because of the bad connection.

"This is Gunther. You ain't got to yell. I ain't deaf! Just hungover. The position is for a deckhand. I am the captain," Gunther growled before succumbing to another hack attack.

"Yes, I know that from the ad," Joel snapped.

"Don't get smart with me, boy. I wouldn't care if you were the captain of Noah's ark. Your credentials don't impress me. Only firsthand experience can prepare you for the Bering Sea. I need someone who is up for the challenge. Navy captain, my backside!" Gunther retorted.

Joel was utterly shocked. Anger started in his toes and spread like wildfire until it reached his face.

"What's the matter, boy?" Gunther roared.

"My problem is your lousy attitude, you cigarette-saturated pain in the butt!" Joel fumed while Adoncia's jaw almost hit the floor.

Laughter exploded from the speaker. After the first three cackles, the laugh turned into crackling phlegm that preceded a guttural bark.

Joel stared in disbelief at the phone, then looked at Adoncia. He draped his arm around her and whispered, "He is almost dead. He doesn't need a deckhand. He needs a co-captain in case he dies."

"You're hired! You greenhorn!" Gunther choked out in between several cackles and a nasty gag.

Joel took a deep breath to begin another salty comeback. His retort halted when Gunther's words finally caught up to his brain. "I'm what?"

"Boy, do your ears work?" Gunther asked before once again attempting to clear his throat.

"Quit calling me boy!" Joel seethed.

Meanwhile, Adoncia placed both hands over her mouth to contain her laughter, which became even more of a challenge when the sound of Gunther opening a can came across the speaker loud and clear.

Joel whispered to Adoncia, "He just opened a beer, didn't he?"

Still with her hands over her mouth, she turned toward Joel and nodded yes.

When Gunther didn't get an immediate response, he barked again, "I said you're hired! You meet the only criteria."

"And just what the heck is that?" Joel exclaimed with disgust.

"Well, boy, you are a jerk," Gunther calmly explained in a normal voice, this time without his throat going into convulsions.

"I have your number on my cell phone here. Be in Aleutia on October 15th. Just remember, boy, I am the captain. I am your boss." Then Gunther abruptly ended the call.

"The heck with that lunatic!" Joel huffed as he reached for his sangria.

"Oh, you are so going to Alaska," Adoncia replied as she gently elbowed Joel in the ribs. "You just accepted his offer."

"I did no such thing!" Joel amusedly argued as he turned his head, so his cheek was touching hers.

"Yes, you did. You didn't turn him down. Go enjoy Alaska," Adoncia began as she ran her fingers down the Navy jacket's gold buttons, stopping at Joel's belt buckle. "Please sign up for social media, so we can keep up with each other."

"You are pushy!" Joel sneered as he ran his fingertips down her arm, lifted her hand, and slowly kissed her fingers. "Social media is not my thing."

"Fine! I'll do it for you!" Adoncia snapped as she started typing again. After a while, she reached for Joel's phone.

"What are you doing?" he asked.

"Okay, so I set up an email address for you and then set up your social media profile. I already followed you and had you follow me, so we can see each other's posts. I'm installing the email and social media apps, so you can use them on your phone. I'm also downloading another app we can use to text and make phone calls, so we don't get international charges."

"What's an app?" Joel sarcastically inquired.

"I'm going to pretend you didn't just ask me that. I'll text you the passwords. We may not see each other again, but we can at least talk online. Oh, I made you an oldies playlist and some other music I know you like."

Joel stared at his phone like a monkey trying to do a word problem. He was an intelligent man but had yet to embrace cell phone technology. "Thank you, Adoncia. I'm sure I will figure it out, but I won't be posting any selfies."

"Honestly, I'm surprised you know what a selfie is. So, you will go to Alaska?" Adoncia queried, then took Joel's hand and reciprocated the finger kisses.

Joel caressed her shoulder and the back of her neck before running his fingers through her hair. "It looks like you aren't giving me a choice, and well, I don't have anything better to do."

"You can't stay here with me. You will be bad for business!" Adoncia exclaimed, then kissed his cheek. "Ohhh! ¡Casi lo olvido! I have a present for you. I got it at the Gypsy Market la semana pasada." She reached across the table for a small satin bag and handed it to Joel.

"Come now, you are making me blush," Joel said as he opened the bag and was delighted to see an antique silver identification bracelet with his name engraved in cursive between two eagles.

"I saw it and thought of you. It's from the mid-1900s. I thought you could give it to your true love one day. She can wear it when you're at sea; look at it when she misses you."

"When I desert her?" Joel asked.

"Sí."

"Thank you, Adoncia. I will give this to her, whoever she may be, if I ever find her," Joel replied, then kissed her cheek.

"You will," Adoncia assured as she held his hands. "Spread your wings, sailor. You're an eagle."

Chapter 2. *Williwaw*

J oel's stomach was in his throat. He closed his eyes and placed his hand over his mouth, hoping nothing would come up. Not that there was anything to come up, he hadn't eaten in at least 12 hours. The flight from Anchorage to the Port of Aleutia in the rickety puddle jumper was so bumpy that Joel may as well have been gin in a martini shaker. In addition, the air quality was beyond deplorable, clammy and sticky to the point he broke out in a sweat. No wonder he felt like he was going to yack.

To keep his mind off the dreadful flight, he listened to oldies on his phone, hoping the music would distract him from the nausea. Joel closed his eyes and leaned back against the seat when the playlist ended. "Adoncia, what have you gotten me into?" he muttered as he fought another wave of nausea accompanied by another clammy sweat.

Joel had been looking forward to the flight into Aleutia, which is why he booked a window seat; however, the weather foiled this plan because clouds, fog, wind, and rain concealed the mountainous view and battered the plane until it shook. Despite all this, Joel was proud of himself for not dry heaving while the aircraft abruptly dropped altitude. And if that wasn't bad enough, the landing sounded comparable to a tornado devouring a freight train. Joel was grateful it didn't conclude in a plume of combustion. After exiting the tin can with wings, he restrained himself from dropping to his knees and shouting, "Hallelujah!"

The brisk mountain air slapped him in the face as his foot landed in a puddle of slush, which splashed up the pant leg of his Navy full dress white uniform. A damp wind blew across the tarmac, and water droplets splattered across his face. Thoroughly disgusted with his wet face and muddy pant leg, Joel began walking toward the airport entrance.

Suddenly, sunlight appeared and pierced the fog, creating a spectacular light show and slowly destroying the weightless barrier, blocking the mountainous view. Joel stopped walking while the other passengers hurried by him, and he looked up to the sky and was amazed by nature's performance, which was like the hand of God reaching down from Heaven and pouring gold through the fog, illuminating it with celestial light. At that moment, the nausea and worry dissipated with the mist, and Joel felt a calming peace come over him. He smiled and let out a massive sigh of relief, knowing God was showing him everything would be okay.

Joel remembered being on the workboat on the Chesapeake Bay with his father when Joel was 10 years old. They had just weathered a nasty squall on a humid morning in August, just before sunrise. "Never forsake the sermons God gives us in nature," Joel's father had said as he put his arm around him while they watched the sunlight burn through the storm clouds. Twenty-eight years later, Joel stood over 3,000 miles away from where his love for the water began.

The Alaskan sunlight revealed snow-capped mountain peaks of crystallized beauty. Shimmering clouds hugged the mountaintops like wavy sheets of gold, quickly disappearing as the sunrays burned through the foggy drapery. For a moment, the snow turned pink as if the mountains were blushing, knowing everyone was looking at them because of how beautiful they were. The sun burned brighter and hotter through the clouds as it continued revealing emerald-green mountains, patchy with snow. Blue sky appeared above the peaks as the fog quickly vanished down the mountainsides, and the sunrays burned through the lower layer of fog until they reached the surface of a bay. Reveling in this catharsis, Joel watched the sunlight illuminate the water as it created a bay of rippling gemstones. Above the mountains, a brilliant rainbow appeared, and Joel felt God blessing his new life in Alaska.

Like everything in life, all good things must end, and the azure sky and rainbow vanished as fast as they appeared, succumbing to more clouds and rain, despite the shining sun. Still feeling God's peace, Joel smiled, knowing everything would be all right.

As he entered the small building, Joel was pleasantly surprised to see the baggage claim near the door. Within a few minutes, a buzzer sounded, and the conveyor belt started moving, leading with Joel's duffel bag. He promptly grabbed it and walked toward the front door to catch a taxi to the inn where he would be staying for the next month, giving him ample time to adjust to civilian life and explore the countryside before departing for the Bering Sea on October 15th.

As Joel walked outside to find a taxi, he heard a familiar voice, followed by a gross, familiar cough. "Over here, boy!"

The recognizable utterances belonged to Gunther Alexander, who stood in front of a red and white early 1990s model pickup truck, so Joel waved and walked toward him. In his late 50s and not much on getting regular haircuts, Gunther had unbrushed, chin-length black hair streaked with gray. He was tall and skinny as a post, which only exacerbated his withered face, purple nose, and dark eyes. With an old red flannel shirt with holes in it, dirty jeans with blown-out knees, a jean jacket that was six shades lighter than the pants, and old paint-splattered work boots, Gunther looked like he got dressed in 1990 and hadn't changed his clothes since.

Gunther leaned against the truck with one arm propped up on

the hood and a cigarette in his hand. As Joel approached him, Gunther put the cigarette between his lips and then greeted Joel with a handshake, not saying anything at first, just staring at Joel as if he had seen a ghost. After an awkward moment, Gunther drew deeply on the cigarette and exhaled a cloud of smoke. "I'm Gunther Alexander. Pleased to meet you, boy! Welcome to damn Unalaska, Alaska."

Without asking, Gunther abruptly ripped Joel's duffel bag out of his grasp. He threw it in the truck bed, which was full of old gas cans, coffee cans, buckets, a traffic cone, a busted radio, multiple garbage bags, and whatever else was hiding under the first layer of junk.

"Hop in the chariot, boy, and I'll give you a quick tour of Aleutia before dropping you off wherever you're staying," Gunther instructed.

"Uh, thank you," Joel replied with a cringe.

"It is my pleasure. Now get in the damn truck!" Gunther exclaimed.

Joel took a deep, hesitant breath and then put on his sunglasses. Considering the miscellaneous garbage in the truck bed and Gunther's overly grungy appearance, Joel wondered how messy the inside of the truck would be. He didn't want to offend his captain, so he bit the bullet. He slowly opened the truck door and carefully entered the pig pen on wheels.

As soon as Gunther's skinny bum hit the seat, he immediately reached for an old, disposable coffee cup sitting on the dash. He violently expectorated into the faded cup that needed disposing of months ago. After that, he looked at Joel apologetically. "Sorry, boy."

The truck cab was a disaster, full of crinkled newspapers, greasy fast food bags, and empty cigarette cartons. The ashtray overflowed with cigarette butts. And shockingly, Joel saw something move under the newspapers on the floor. *What the heck is that? A cockroach, a gigantic rat, or worse?* Joel wondered. One thing was for sure, he knew he didn't want either critter crawling up his pant leg, so Joel nonchalantly stomped at it in case it was a giant insect or a disease-carrying rodent.

"Careful! That's my little buddy down there," Gunther admonished.

A small, two-pound monkey crawled out from beneath the garbage and jumped onto the seat. Then it jumped onto the dash and looked inquisitively at Joel.

The monkey's face was black, which perfectly complemented a striking fluffy, white crest that went all the way around his head and down to his shoulders, blending eloquently into white chest and stomach fur. Its back was reddish brown, and its tail and paws were gray.

"Is that a cotton-topped tamarin?" Joel asked in disbelief as he stared at the exotic creature.

"Yeah, a little punk rocker," Gunther said as he rubbed the monkey's chest with his finger. He turned toward Joel with a perplexed look on his face. "Are you a monkey expert? How in the fricking heck did you know that?"

"I spent a lot of time in South America over the years and have always enjoyed visiting zoos in my travels," Joel replied.

"His name is Tiny. Just whatever you do, don't piss him off. Trust me," Gunther warned.

"Hi Tiny," Joel said as he slowly moved his finger toward him to scratch his chest, just like Gunther did. Unfortunately, Tiny didn't see this as an act of affection. Instead, the little punk rocker fluffed his white crest, puckered his lips, scrunched up his face, and made a high-pitched distress call.

Meanwhile, Gunther looked for a new box of cigarettes, acting like Tiny's behavior was nothing out of the ordinary. "Sorry about the mess in here," Gunther said, looking around the cab.

"No worries," Joel responded.

Tiny deflated his crest and unpuckered his face. He looked intently at Joel while slowly turning his head from side to side like it was helping him think. Without warning, Tiny abruptly jumped on Joel's shoulder, grabbed his ear, and stuck his paw and tongue as far into Joel's ear as possible.

"Don't worry. He's just checking for bugs. He does that to everybody he first meets," Gunther explained.

"Is he your monkey?" Joel inquired as his face contorted. Tiny stuck his paw farther into Joel's ear canal.

"Of course not! I'm just monkey sitting," Gunther replied sarcastically, then rolled his eyes. He lit a fresh cigarette and took a long draw, filling the cab with smoke while he started the engine, which sounded like it would blow up instead.

"Oh hey, boy, I wanted to apologize for being grumpy the day you called me. I was as angry as a mouse in a sticky trap," Gunther explained as he finally put the truck in drive and started rolling.

"Don't worry about it," Joel responded as Tiny plopped his fuzzy butt on Joel's shoulder, unsatisfied that he didn't find an afternoon snack inside Joel's ear.

"You see, boy, my wife had just left me and moved into an inn with her friend Tanya, a platinum blonde hussy who tells my wife that she doesn't need me," Gunther lamented as he slammed on the brakes, then took several long draws on the cigarette before putting it in the ashtray. Next, he violently coughed, reached up on the dash for a tobacco tin, and then put a considerable pinch of tobacco into his mouth before continuing, "So understandably, I was hungover about the situation."

Joel was speechless. A monkey had just looked for lunch in his ear, and his new captain, who he barely knew, just shared his sob story. "Sorry, man," was the best response Joel could conjure up.

With a confounded expression, Gunther turned toward Joel, held his arms up, and shrugged his shoulders. Joel reciprocated with a concurring head nod and fought back a cough because of the severely polluted air.

Joel cringed when Gunther reached for the spittoon again but was thankful that the tobacco expectoration had minimal sound effects. Once Gunther put the cup back in its special place, he finally hit the gas. "Okay. Let's go. I'll show you around some. You see, boy, across from us, we have Aleutia Bay, named after the Port of Aleutia where we are now! I should give tours during the summer. I'd make a darn good tour guide. I would, but I hate people," Gunther explained, then laughed and slapped the steering wheel, amused by his own articulations.

Joel glanced at him with a mystified look.

Gunther laughed. "Hey, you seem like an okay kid. You too, Tiny."

Tiny replied with a pleasant-sounding squeak.

As Gunther drove, Joel happily gazed out the window, enjoying the beautiful dichotomy of the majestic rocky elevations and the shimmering bay below. The invisible yet powerful wind blew swirling sheets of fog across Aleutia Bay, and the sun illuminated the pirouetting walls of mist with an impressive celestial hue.

"You see all that wind and fog, boy? That is what we Aleutians call a williwaw. It's beautiful. There is nothing like that fog running like a bat out of hell across the water. Sometimes, the williwaws can be extremely powerful," Gunther expounded as the truck hit a pothole, and Joel almost whacked his head on the window.

Joel reached for the OS handle but grasped air instead since it was missing. Meanwhile, the smoke and tobacco fumes finally burned Joel's eyes and lungs to the point he had to roll down the window. He reached for the handle, but it fell off in his hand. He held it up in front of him, looked up at the missing OS handle, and then looked over at the locks and door handle, wondering if he would make it out alive. Tiny leaned closer to Joel's cheek and let out a cackling shriek like he was laughing at the broken accessories.

"Oh, don't worry about the window handle. It broke 20 years ago. There are pliers in the glove box. Use those to crank the window down," Gunther instructed as he hit another pothole at full speed.

Joel stared at the glove box, thinking, *Do I really want to open that? God only knows what is living in there.* He had a vision of cockroaches, stink bugs, and undiscovered insects flying out of the glove box in every direction. For this reason, he didn't tempt fate. Instead, he put the handle back in place and fiddled with it until he rolled the window down a few inches.

"Well, aren't you resourceful? You'll make a good greenhorn when stuff on the Alexandria breaks," Gunther said before loudly clearing his overly phlegmy throat.

Joel grimaced at the ghastly gurgles. Tiny wasn't impressed either and decided he needed some fresh air too. The monkey crawled behind Joel's neck and over to his right shoulder. Then he reached his paws onto the glass and stuck his nose in the wind. Joel panicked because the monkey wasn't going to jump out on his watch, so he grabbed Tiny and set him down on the seat between him and Gunther.

Unfortunately for Joel, Tiny took this as a sign of aggression. Tiny jumped onto Joel's knee, scrunched up his face, puckered his lips, let out evil shrieks, defecated in his paws, and threw feces at Joel's chest. He repeated the cackling shriek he had just made when the window handle fell off in Joel's hand.

"Come on, little man! How can a monkey so small have poop so big?" Joel exclaimed in a few octaves higher than his normal speaking voice.

"His splatter range is rather large. Don't say that I didn't warn ya!" Gunther laughed until the hilarity turned into a coughing fit.

Joel flinched at the sound of Gunther's sizzling mucus, then frantically looked around for something to clean the monkey dung off his Navy jacket. He knew he was expecting too much to find a clean napkin among the trash piles. With his luck, there would be another poop-hurling monkey hiding down there.

"Just grab some of those papers and used napkins to clean it off. And whatever you do, don't piss him off anymore. I don't want my truck to be full of monkey turds. I mean it!" Gunther admonished as the truck hit another extensive pothole.

Joel reached for an empty grease-stained fast food bag and did his best to wipe the excrement off his well-decorated Navy suit; however, he ended up smearing it, making an even bigger mess. He held the bag in his hand for a moment, knowing that he should throw it away when he got out. However, after looking around the cab, he decided that worse things than monkey poop were hiding there, so he just tossed it on the floor with the rest of the rubbish.

Gunther looked at Joel, started to laugh, and then stopped himself. Joel, however, didn't find humor in this situation.

With his eyes still slightly burning and the scent of monkey muck on his uniform, Joel leaned toward the window to welcome a breath of fresh air as he took in the sights. Along the road, they passed small houses, many needing repairs. These were homes of hardworking people who didn't receive enough monetary reward for their efforts, much like the homes where Joel grew up in the small watermen community on the Chesapeake Bay.

The rickety truck hit another pothole as it drove by a saloon with three old pickup trucks parked out front.

"Is that a popular place?" Joel asked.

"Well, yeah, it used to be. But there is a newer one now that is much more popular. It would be shut down if I could do anything about it. That new place pisses me off!" Gunther agitatedly responded as he reached for another pinch of tobacco.

Joel thought that was a weird response, but most of Gunther's remarks were unusual.

"Anyway, boy. Back to being your tour guide. Now, where was I? Oh yes. You are in the Port of Aleutia, a city on Unalaska Island."

"I know," Joel replied sarcastically. He was feeling exhausted, breathing polluted air, and smelling of monkey ordure. His tolerance level for crap had reached its maximum.

Gunther hit the brakes hard, so the truck slammed Joel's back against the seat. "Boy, let me talk."

"Yes, sir," Joel said.

"Never call me sir. Always Captain. I am not preppy. I am a real man. I have dirt under my nails," Gunther instructed as he waved his index finger at Joel like a father scolding a son.

Oddly enough, Joel wasn't offended by this and couldn't help but laugh.

"Okay, boy, I will give you a quick history lesson. There will be a test," Gunther said before reaching for the spittoon and ejecting the second serving of tobacco. "Aleutia is in the Pacific Ring of Fire. That means volcanoes, 109 to be exact."

I am not a dummy, Joel thought as he stared straight ahead.

Gunther continued, "*Aleut* from Aleutia means *community*. We don't always get along, but we always help each other. This is a small town. You can't always get away from the people who are pissing you off, like your wife. Or her friends." Gunther paused and swallowed hard. Then he coughed and grabbed the spittoon again. Instead of getting a cigarette or more tobacco, Gunther reached into his shirt pocket, pulled out a vape pen, and took a big draw. "Don't worry, boy. It's legal. I have my card."

The skunky stench hit Joel's nose intensely. *This keeps getting better and better,* Joel thought as he tried not to inhale the secondhand vapors. Being a Navy man, he never partook of it.

Feeling a little more mellow, Gunther drove at a turtle's pace. "That's still Aleutia Bay over there, boy. Ain't she pretty? Over here, we have the Aleutian Diner and the Aleutian Grocery Store. We've got a lot of good eats around here, especially at the saloon and Port House. Okay, boy, now follow me on this one. The language is Unangam Tunuu, and there are a few dialects; I don't recommend you learn it. We don't need no come here's screwing up our native tongue. That's not directed at you, boy. People come here and study us, and it pisses us off. At least, it pisses me off," Gunther pontificated.

"That would piss me off too," Joel agreed.

Gunther smiled. "I forgot to ask. Where are you staying, boy?"

"At an inn." Joel winced, hoping it wasn't the one where Gunther's wife was.

Gunther squinted his eyes. "Which one? There are only two in Aleutia."

Joel grimaced. He had survived boot camp with people screaming at him, which didn't faze him, but he didn't want to give the wrong answer to this question. "The Harbor Inn," Joel said as he closed his left eye as if Gunther was going to take a swing at him.

"Oh no, boy! No!" Gunther cried as he hit the palm of his hand on the top of the steering wheel. He paused, shaking his head and pursing his lips together. "Ah, it's okay; I won't hold it against you. You didn't know," Gunther said as he promptly retrieved the vape from his pocket again. "He didn't know; he didn't know," he said as if he were getting ready to have a mental breakdown. Gunther slammed on the brakes, sighed heavily, and took four more draws on the vape before hitting the gas again.

Joel wanted to say, "Vaping cannabis while driving is illegal, ya know?" Instead, he kept his mouth shut and looked out the window, not acknowledging Gunther's outburst.

A few moments passed while Gunther collected himself.

Thankfully, he kept his eyes on the road and didn't drive into the drink. Instead, he flipped on the blinker and turned onto Salmon Road, where they passed a sign for the Aleutian Resort.

"Glad you're not staying there. It's real snooty and fancy. That's where all the darn tourists who want to study us stay. And, over there, that's the Aleutian Corporation; they own most of the land around here. Don't go hiking without getting a land use permit from them." He looked at Joel and furrowed his eyebrows. "I mean it. We take that stuff seriously here."

Meanwhile, Tiny had recovered from the poop incident, climbed back up on Joel's leg, and squeaked at him.

"Tiny, are you making a new friend? I think you should apologize to your new friend," Gunther said in a calm, pleasant voice like he was talking to a little kid.

Tiny turned his head from side to side as he stared at Gunther. He then turned toward Joel and did the same thing before cutely squeaking at him. Joel reached his finger toward him and gently scratched his stomach, and Tiny cooed like he was purring.

"The inn is down Captain's Way, right down there," Gunther explained, motioning out the window. We'll come back; I want to show you the rest of Aleutia first. Over here, we have Aleutia Ship Supply, a two-hour clinic, a pharmacy, a chiropractor's office, city hall, the public library, the visitors' bureau, a community center, and another grocery store. Don't go to that store; they got roaches! Only go to the Aleutian Grocery Store. Anywho, you are in for a real treat!" Gunther said as they entered a narrow road along the water's edge. "That's Eagle Bay. Soon, you will see why. We got bald eagles here. The tourists are obsessed with them. They defecate all over the Alexandria and piss me right the heck off!" Gunther exclaimed as he attempted to roll down his window, but the handle fell off in his hand. "Shoot!"

Joel did his best not to laugh. Instead, he looked out the window at the glimmering ripples on Eagle Bay. "It's absolutely beautiful."

"Oh boy, you just wait! Now, I am getting ready to show you a spectacular view. This view is why I will never leave Aleutia," Gunther said.

"AND HERE SHE IS, the Aleutian Russian Orthodox Cathedral, which we are very proud of," Gunther said as he turned into a parking lot.

Joel fiddled with the window handle to roll the window back up, so Tiny wouldn't climb out. Then Joel and Gunther got out of the truck quickly, so the monkey couldn't escape.

Gunther paused when they walked up to a small white fence surrounding the cathedral and a rather extensive cemetery where Russian Orthodox crosses, some wooden and some stone, marked graves. For a moment, Joel thought that he was standing inside a painting of a place too beautiful to be real. The surrounding mountains and sparkling bay provided the perfect backdrop for this place of worship. The cathedral had white walls, a red roof, and two magnificent green domes, known as the Domes of Heaven. A gold Russian Orthodox cross topped each dome.

A refreshing breeze filled Joel's lungs as he and Gunther stood by the fence, neither of them speaking; they silently appreciated being on holy ground as the brisk mountain air whirled around them and the bay kissed the rocky shoreline. The sun made another celestial appearance, burning through the fog and illuminating the cathedral walls and the bay. Feeling God's omnipresence, Joel looked up to the sky and was so pleased to see two eagles fly out of the clouds and into the sunlight, where they perched on the crosses on the Domes of Heaven. Suddenly feeling a connection with the regal birds, Joel was amazed by this magnificent performance of God and nature.

"Have you ever seen a cross like that before, boy? With three crossbars?" Gunther asked, like a father quizzing his son.

"Yes, Captain," Joel replied.

"Well then, enlighten me."

"The top bar on the cross refers to Jesus as the King of the Jews. The second is where Jesus's arms were nailed. The third tilted bar is where Jesus's feet were," Joel explained.

Gunther smiled and nodded. Then he patted Joel's shoulder, just as a father would to a son.

Joel smiled in return. Oddly enough, he felt pleased that he had Gunther's approval. Then Joel recalled a day, many years ago, when he was young, working with his father on the workboat. It was a vivid memory, an afternoon in late August out on the Tangier Sound, where his father quizzed him on the books of the Bible. "List them for me in order," his father had said as he fished up a crab pot. Joel listed all 66 Bible books in perfect order as he sorted crabs, measuring them for keepers and throwing the small ones overboard. Like Gunther, Joel's father smiled, nodded his head, and patted Joel on the shoulder.

While Joel's mind drifted off to this memory, Gunther was traversed in his own private thoughts as he stared at the far-left corner of the cemetery. Suddenly, loud screeching sounds pulled Joel away from his thoughts. He looked up to see the two eagles take flight and then fly off into the sunlight together. Once the eagles were specs in the distance, Joel looked over in the same direction where Gunther was motionlessly staring at a white stone wall with a Russian Orthodox cross in the center and a plaque beneath it.

"Is that a memorial?" Joel asked.

"Yes. That is our watermen's memorial, where the names of those who died at sea are etched in bronze," Gunther replied as he turned and walked back toward the truck.

Having grown up in a watermen's community and losing his parents in an accident, Joel knew the pain of losing loved ones at sea. *He must know a lot of people on that plaque,* Joel sadly thought as he took another look at the glowing white cathedral, then went back to the truck where Tiny was stretched out full length on the dash, enjoying a sunbath.

Gunther remained quiet as he and Joel got back in the smelly truck and then left on the same road in which they came, before eventually turning on Captain's Way. Once again, Joel fiddled with the handle to slightly lower the window for fresh air. Meanwhile, Tiny curled up on Joel's lap to continue his afternoon nap as Joel took in the sights.

Several vehicles that weren't in use were along the roadside. Gunther and Joel rode by many sturdy metal buildings and heavy-duty equipment, such as tractors, bulldozers, and trucks. They also passed shacks, portable toilets, piles of concrete, and above-ground gas tanks, some new and some old. Joel was incredibly intrigued when they went by massive stacks of king crab fishing pots, which were enormous, so much bigger than the crab pots Joel had used to fish up blue crabs in the Chesapeake Bay. Beyond the stacks of crab pots, Joel was pleased to see several large fishing vessels along the docks.

As he looked out the window, Joel felt like an excited little boy going somewhere new for the first time. Even during his travels overseas as a Navy captain, he felt the same way when he entered a new port and city to explore. It didn't matter where he was or what language the people spoke; Joel loved harbor towns.

As Captain's Way turned into undisturbed nature, Joel grew even more intrigued with his new surroundings. They came up on steep, rocky mountains and a sparkling bay with gorgeous snowcapped peaks in the distance.

"That right there, boy, is Captain's Bay," Gunther said, speaking for the first time since they had left the cathedral.

"It's beautiful," Joel replied as he peered across the bay and saw two eagles flying toward the snowy mountains in the distance.

"And here we are," Gunther said as he pointed to the inn's glimmering sign next to the mailbox. He turned into the driveway, and The Harbor Inn stood in all its glory, a vast two-story white house with several prominent French windows.

"Wow, look at the new truck!" Gunther exclaimed as he eyeballed a brand-new pickup in front of the garage.

"That's my retirement present to myself," Joel explained as he happily stared at his new ride. "It was delivered yesterday."

"I like your style," Gunther said approvingly. "Well, Tiny, let's get you home. Joel, it was nice to meet you. Please don't be offended if I drop you off and don't go inside with you," he said as he scooped up the monkey and put him on his shoulder.

"No problem," Joel responded, unsure if he was ready to experience Gunther and his wife.

"Oh phooey, I didn't show you where the harbor is. It's on Port Road; it's not hard to find. If you can't find it, you're an idiot, and I won't let you on my vessel!" Gunther pontificated.

"I'll find it," Joel replied, then chuckled.

"Come by around half-past six tonight, and I'll introduce you to the Alexandria, a lady you must get acquainted with. The crew will also be there."

"Looking forward to it. Thanks for the ride," Joel said as he fiddled with the window handle until he got the window rolled back up. He got out of the truck and cringed as he reached into the littered truck bed for his duffel bag.

"No problem! Now, shut the darn door, and I will see you later," Gunther commanded.

Joel stood at ease and sarcastically saluted Gunther.

"Boy, you'll fit in just fine!" Gunther exclaimed.

Joel shut the door, and Gunther hit the gas way too hard for reverse, squealing the tires as he drove away like a maniac.

Chapter 3. *The Harbor Inn*

The sound of Gunther's juddering truck engine faded into the distance as Joel slowly walked up the driveway while admiring The Harbor Inn and its gorgeous view of Captain's Bay, which shimmered like a sea of crystals corralled by an array of snowcapped mountains. Joel smiled and inhaled a deep breath of refreshing Alaskan air as he walked over to his brand-new truck.

Beaming sunrays illuminated the dark green metallic paint, which perfectly complemented the shiny chrome grill, bumpers, and running boards. The extensive crew cab was embellished with vinyl flooring and light brown leather seats, and the eight-cylinder diesel engine was most certainly the salt on that margarita. With a massive grin, Joel swaggered around the truck, ogling over all the eye candy that this power-machine had to offer. *If Adoncia was a truck, this would be her,* he thought. After walking around the pickup a couple more times to reconfirm his satisfaction, Joel realized that he needed to pry himself away from it long enough to check into the inn and get settled into his room before taking this metallic beauty on her first spin to the harbor.

As Joel approached the front door, he took off his captain's hat and placed it under his arm before ringing the doorbell. Then he patiently waited for a couple of minutes before the door was opened by a woman who looked at him like she had seen a ghost. The color left her face, making her paler than she already was. As the wrinkles around her hazel eyes foretold, she was a beautiful and slender woman in her late 50s, yet her curly, fiery-red hair erased at least five years off her age, especially from a distance.

She continued staring at Joel with the same expression that Gunther had had on his face at the airport, leaving Joel wondering why he kept freaking these people out when they first saw him.

To break the uncomfortable silence, he introduced himself. "Hi, I am Joel Layton. You must be Gertrude."

"Oh yes, Joel. I am Gertrude Alexander, but everybody calls me Gert," she replied as she shook his hand, still staring at him inquisitively.

Sheesh. Gert and Gunther. These people have terrible names, Joel thought.

"Come on in, darling," Gert said as she motioned for Joel to enter. "Was that Gunther's rat trap I heard? I can't say that I approve of your choice of chauffeur."

"I had no idea that he was picking me up. He surprised me at the airport."

"Oh, it's no problem. As small as this place is, we run into each other all the time. I ignore the drunk punk. Oh, correction, the stinky drunk punk!" Suddenly, Gert scrunched up her face and sniffed the air. "Is that monkey scat on your jacket, boy?" She stepped closer to examine the splatters. "Yes, I have seen this scat before."

"Tiny got offended when I wouldn't let him look out the window," Joel explained, still in disbelief that monkey excrement was on his Navy uniform.

"He's a little fluffy jerk!" Gert exclaimed as she closed the door.

They stood in a beautiful, long hallway with stunning hardwood floors and cream-colored walls, accessorized with a mixture of maritime and mountain décor. An elaborate staircase was on the left, and immediately to the right, an open doorway showcased a comfortable living room with a large television and extremely inviting furniture. Farther down the hall was a spacious dining room across from the kitchen, with a swinging door where a thin, middle-aged woman with platinum blonde hair exited.

She flitted down the hallway and strolled up to Joel. "I thought I heard a masculine voice," the fake blonde said while eyeballing Joel like he was a fresh piece of meat.

Joel wasn't impressed by her at all. She was one of those women who looked like a bimbo no matter what she wore. Plastic surgery was her friend because she had an all-too-perfect nose and huge knockers. Even her crystal blue eyes, along with her unusually plump lips, looked manufactured.

She stared inappropriately into Joel's eyes, making him uncomfortable. "I'm Tanya Hastings. I own the inn," she said as she casually stuck out her heavy chest and puckered her lips like she was going to plant a big juicy one on him.

Joel tried to contain his disgust. "Uh, I'm Joel Layton," he replied as he extended his hand to shake hers.

Of course, Tanya didn't let this opportunity pass her by, for she snatched up Joel's hand like a bullfrog going after a fly.

Gert gave Tanya a disapproving look. Then she picked up a key on a console table along the wall and handed it to Joel. "Here's the key to that stylish new truck you got out there."

Joel chuckled. "Thank you so much," he replied as he glanced down at the table perfectly decorated with a large lighthouse lamp, a few maritime books, and three framed photographs.

In the first picture, a beautiful young woman with long blonde hair, wearing a graduation cap and gown, stood between Gunther, another man close to his age, and a younger man who looked strikingly like Joel. They stood next to the Aleutian High School sign, and from Gunther's youthful appearance with clean-cut, black hair, Joel guessed that the picture was 20 years old. The following picture looked recent; Gunther and the same two men were older and stood in front of the Alexandria. The last photograph looked recent as well. The man resembling Joel stood in front of the cathedral with one arm around his wife and the other holding a baby boy. Joel smiled and hoped he would be in a similar photo one day with a family of his own.

Joel's hand felt hot and clammy, and he realized that Tanya was still holding it. He didn't want to be rude or continue the hand-holding madness, so he quickly pulled his hand away from the fake blonde's grasp. To divert attention from this, he motioned toward the picture of the Alexandria and asked, "Is this the crew I will be joining?"

Once again, all the color drained out of Gert's face. Instead of answering, she changed the subject. "Come on. I will show you to your room. I am sure that you would want to shower and change," Gert said as she walked ahead, then motioned for Joel to follow her up the staircase. Joel felt Tanya's eyes glued to his posterior as he went up the steps.

Upstairs had a big open sitting area in front of a large window, providing a spectacular view of Captain's Bay.

"Wow! This is beautiful!" Joel exclaimed.

"Feel free to sit up here or anywhere downstairs. The house is yours to enjoy. Your room is here, on the right," Gert explained as she opened the door.

Joel chuckled and thought about Adoncia, for their friendship began the night he refused to enter the bedroom on the right. Ten years later, he was in Unalaska, Alaska, starting his new life in the bedroom on the right.

"Thank you, Miss Gert," Joel said as he set his duffel bag and hat on the bed.

"Oh, it's just Gert, my dear. You're such a gentleman," she said as she stepped closer to reexamine Joel's monkey-poop-covered jacket and then looked down and noticed his muddy pant leg. "Honey, please don't be offended, but you smell—badly. Look, why don't you set your jacket and pants outside the door, and I'll wash them up for you. You smell like the inside of Gunther's truck, which is synonymous with a poopy ashtray. That man is a filthy hacking slob! Anyway, take a hot shower and get settled in while I wash this up for you. Hey, are you hungry? I could fix you a sandwich."

"You don't have to go to all that trouble," Joel answered.

"Oh honey, it's no trouble at all. When was the last time you ate?" Gert inquired.

"At the discharge ceremony in Norfolk," Joel said. He had so much adrenaline going from the ceremony and saying goodbye to the Navy that he hadn't even thought about food.

"I thought so. Your life has changed in a very short amount of time. It's okay to take time to let it all settle in."

Joel smiled because these were the exact words that he needed to hear.

"I'll wait in the sitting area until you put your clothes out. When they are clean, I'll leave them for you on the hook outside your door. Then I'll bring you a sammie too."

"Thank you so much," Joel gratefully replied.

"You got it, darling!" Gert winked and grinned before leaving the room and closing the door behind her.

Joel promptly emptied his pockets and then took off his jacket and pants, so the only items covering his hot bod were an undershirt and boxers. As instructed, he set his clothes on the floor outside the door.

Then the quietness of the house filled Joel's ears. "Now what?" he muttered as he sighed and looked around the room. The house was dead silent, except for a clock loudly ticking, making his current situation sink in; he was now a retired Navy captain who had to rebuild his life in a new place. Ticktock. Ticktock. Tick freaking tock.

Well, this is simply unacceptable, Joel thought as he rushed over to the wall, grabbed the clock, and removed the batteries, so it couldn't ticktock anymore. Then he hung it back up as if nothing had happened.

The new silence was beyond deafening. Joel stood with his hands on his hips as he looked around the room, which followed the same color scheme and décor as downstairs. Two extra soft accent chairs sat in front of two large windows overlooking the bay, and a painting of a historic Alaskan fishing vessel hung above the bed, reminding Joel of why he came to this corner of the world.

He took a breather and sat in the accent chair on the right, where he enjoyed a brilliant view of Captain's Bay, sparkling beneath the raging sun. He looked at the empty chair across from him, wondering what it would be like to have someone with whom to share this view. Joel smiled as he recalled his parents spending their evenings side by side in their matching chairs in front of the fireplace. And he remembered his mother constantly rearranging the furniture in their tiny house. At least every two months, she had to completely reconfigure the rooms and reorganize all the drawers and cabinets. Joel's father would get annoyed with her because he would go to get something and then couldn't find it. "She did it again," he had always said. Joel's parents were so in love that arguments never lasted beyond the moment; they often made up before the squabble was over. Joel smiled at these sweet memories and hoped to have a marriage like that one day.

Meanwhile, the silence of the empty room drilled holes in Joel's eardrums. "Okay, it's way too quiet in here!" He sprang out of the chair. "It's shower time. I can't be smelling like a poopy ashtray for another minute!" He grabbed the duffel bag and went into the bathroom.

The spacious bathroom with white walls and floor tiles gave off a bright and calming aurora. In the center of the room, the artistic focal point was a small table with a replica of an 1800s fishing vessel. A dresser provided everything a guest would need, and a large mirror hung over a double sink vanity. The commode was in a private room across from an old-fashioned porcelain bathtub that sparkled beneath a clear skylight. Joel chuckled because he had never been in a tub like this before, and honestly, the handheld showerhead looked like more trouble than it was worth.

Joel took off the rest of his clothes, got what he needed from the dresser, and went to the tub. He turned on the faucet, adjusted the temperature, plugged the drain, and listened to the soothing sound of the water flowing peacefully like a waterfall. "I really can't believe I'm doing this," he muttered as he climbed inside the antique tub.

The hot water caressed Joel's body as the muscle tension from his travels melted away. Once the water level reached his chest, he turned the water off and immersed himself back into the intense muteness of the house. Joel rested his head against the tub, trying to relax his thoughts, but he was unsuccessful. Despite the hot water feeling fantastic on his exhausted body, he still couldn't calm his mind.

Joel took several deep breaths and immediately got mad at himself for subconsciously doing a deep breathing exercise. He grunted before holding his breath and sinking beneath the water to wet his hair. "Enough of this monkey dung!" Joel exclaimed as he released the tub drain, shampooed his hair, and lathered up his body with a bar of lavender-rose soap. He picked up the fancy showerhead and laughed at it before rinsing the shampoo and smelly soap off his body. "Who invented this ridiculous contraption? It's made for two people, like everything else in this house," Joel muttered. He lathered his face and shaved before rinsing for the final time. "Finally!" he exclaimed as he climbed out of the tub, almost slipping. "Whoops!" he yelped as he reached for a towel and promptly dried off. Then he got a clean undershirt, boxers, and socks from his duffel bag and put them on before brushing his teeth and combing his hair.

Joel slowly opened the bedroom door and peeked around the corner to make sure no one was nearby to catch a glimpse of him in his skivvies. As promised, the clean uniform was hanging on the door for him, so Joel brought it in and laid it on the bed. He smiled as he looked at the pure white, well-decorated Navy captain's suit with shiny gold buttons and medals, which reminded him of Sunday mornings when he was a child when his mother laid out his suit and tie for him before they went to church. Smiling at this little memory, Joel pulled on his pants and then tied his shoes before putting on his Navy jacket.

Just as Joel fastened the last button, he heard a knock at the door. He opened it, and there stood Gert with a tray of food and drinks for him. She set the tray on a small table in the right corner of the room. "I hope you like Italian sandwiches."

"I do. Very much. Thank you. Thank you so much for the clean suit. You really didn't have to do all this for me," Joel said gratefully.

"Oh, sweetheart, it's no trouble at all! This was my son's favorite sandwich: sourdough bread, salami, pepperoni, turkey, roast beef, ham, provolone cheese, spinach, and my secret mayo, of course. You can't have a sandwich without kettle chips, a glass of water, a cup of milk, and an oatmeal cookie."

"Was?" Joel asked, immediately feeling bad for asking about her son. "I'm sorry. I don't mean to pry."

"Oh, my dear, don't you be sorry about anything," Gert began, then sadly sighed. "There was an accident during the opilio season last January."

"I'm sorry to hear that. My parents died in a workboat accident when I was 11." Joel paused for a moment before continuing,

"Thank you so much for the sandwich. My mom used to make one just like it."

"Oh, you are so welcome, my dear. I do not doubt that your parents would be very proud of your accomplishments," Gert said with a sad smile.

"Thank you," Joel quietly replied.

"Well, enjoy your sammie. Let me know if you need anything. Breakfast is served at 7 a.m. on Sundays. What would you like?" Gert asked as she walked toward the door.

"Surprise me." Joel chuckled.

"You shouldn't have said that." Gert laughed as she left the room.

Joel sat down at the table to devour his sandwich, but first, he paused to say grace. When he opened his eyes, he began piecing the puzzle together. Gert and Gunther had a son who died at sea last season. He was probably the young man in the photos downstairs because Gert had gotten so wild-eyed when Joel had asked if this was the crew he would be joining. Gunther didn't look unkempt in the pictures, so Joel surmised that Gert and Gunther separated because of the toll losing their son had on them. Joel wished there was something he could do to take their pain away. But he knew this pain never leaves; Joel still had a large hole in his heart from losing his parents 27 years ago.

Joel's stomach growled, reminding him it was time to finally put some food in there, so he picked up the sandwich and smelled it. Oh, it smelled like home! Joel took a large bite, and more memories from his childhood flooded his mind. He recalled his mother making sandwiches for him and his father to take out on the workboat. Joel's father loved rye bread, and so did Joel. His mom always made her sandwiches on rye bread with lettuce instead of sourdough and spinach. But other than that, Gert's sandwich was the same. Even the secret mayo mix was right on point. For a moment, Joel almost felt like he was standing on the boat deck with his father as the gentle Chesapeake Bay waves moved the boat gently from side to side as seagulls flew over, begging for a free crumb. Joel's father always fussed at Joel for not eating the crust, which Joel always tossed to the feathered moochers when his father was fishing up pots. His father had said, "I don't want seagull fecal matter on my boat." But little Joel did it anyway, every day, and for the most part, his father laughed and looked the other way.

Joel took his time enjoying the tasty sandwich with potato chips, something he wouldn't normally eat but decided that he thoroughly enjoyed. He pounded the glass of water and savored the homemade oatmeal cookie and cup of whole milk. Then he checked the time on his phone and saw that he needed to get to the harbor soon to meet Gunther and the crew.

Joel grabbed his Navy hat, sunglasses, and truck key, then quietly walked down the staircase, hoping that Tanya wasn't lurking about, waiting down there to climb him like a tree. Luckily, she wasn't there. He noticed that the picture of the young man with his wife and baby was missing from the console table. Joel heard the television in the living room where Gert sat motionlessly on the sofa, holding the picture, and sadly staring at it.

"That's a beautiful picture, Miss Gert. Thank you so much for cleaning my suit and for the wonderful sandwich. You were right. A hot shower and a sandwich were just what I needed. I am going out to take the new truck for a spin," Joel said.

"You are so welcome. Enjoy that new truck," Gert replied as she looked up from the photo.

"Thank you. See you soon," Joel said before opening the front door.

He swaggered over to the brand-new diesel-engine truck. Joel unlocked the driver's side door, and the new truck smell hit his nose. "Oh yeah!" he exclaimed as he climbed in and sat on the expensive leather seat. When he started the engine, it roared like a panther on steroids. Joel lost his composure momentarily, revving the engine way more times than necessary, basking in the masculinity of his new ride. "Oh yeah! Oh yeah!" he grunted like a warrior.

Suddenly, he felt uncomfortable. He looked toward the window on the side of the house where Gert was laughing and waving at him. Joel immediately stopped revving the engine, blushed with awkwardness, and waved back at her, happy that he made her laugh but still embarrassed over his display.

Chapter 4. *The Alexandria*

J oel searched the radio stations until he found a familiar oldie song. Thoroughly enjoying the first drive in his tricked-out truck, he cranked up the heat, rolled down the window, and turned up the music as he cruised along the narrow roads of Aleutia, waving to the smiling townsfolk like he had been there his entire life.

When he turned on Port Road, a bright light caught his eye. A vintage-style lighted letter sign shimmered the words *Portia's Port House* on top of a striking two-story building. Joel had a few minutes to kill, so he stopped the truck and admired the impressive establishment.

The entire lower level was glass, no doubt providing exquisite views of Eagle Bay and Port Road. On the left side of the building, a staircase led up to the second level where a bald eagle was perched, and Joel could've sworn he saw a large-bodied animal, maybe an elk or a moose, lurking around near the dumpster fence. Joel didn't get a good look at the critter because another truck came up behind him, so he took his foot off the brake and hit the gas.

The harbor was just a thousand feet from Portia's Port House. Five deep-sea fishing vessels floated along the roadside docks. But the Alexandria stood out from the others—like a planet shining brighter than the surrounding stars. Joel kept his eyes on the prize as he drove closer and parked next to Gunther's red and white rat trap. Four other trucks were also parked nearby.

Joel turned off the engine and stepped out of the truck as he admired the incredible fishing vessel. The Alexandria had royal blue paint with a white accent line below the railing. She was magnificent and deserved respect, and Joel gave it to her wholeheartedly.

A nasty cough announced Gunther's presence. "She's 390 gross tons of welded steel and iron."

"She is commendable, even more beautiful than I imagined," Joel replied.

"I thought you would be impressed," Gunther said as he patted Joel on the shoulder. The two captains stood side by side, drooling over the Alexandria like she was a lingerie-runway model with a perky set of double Ds. "Boy, this vessel has a 250-pot limit and a king crab capacity of 251,000 pounds, which is more than the Aleutian Hero, Mariah Leigh, and the Windswept Belle, just down the dock here from us. The Alexandria was built down in the lower 48 in Washington State two years ago, so she is a youngster. She was built by my brother Ralph at Alexander Enterprises. Ralph, our brother Kyle, and I started the company fresh out of high school. Kyle and I couldn't stand working in the factory every day, so Ralph oversees it. And Kyle and I... Oh, darn it!" Gunther paused and sadly sighed before continuing, "I mean, I go down there during the off-season to work in the factory and spend time with Ralph. But the Port of Aleutia is home. This is where I stay and crab," Gunther said, then took a hit from the cannabis vape.

Joel wondered if Kyle was the other guy in the photographs he saw at the inn, but considering how visibly shaken Gunther was by mentioning him, Joel didn't press for details. "I understand why you'd rather be working on the sea than in a factory. I can't wait to be on the water again."

Gunther burst out laughing. "I hope you like throwing up, boy."

"Huh?"

"You'll see." Gunther cackled.

"How much fuel does she hold?" Joel asked.

"The fuel system holds 60,000 gallons. We also have two freshwater tanks at 1500 gallons each. She also has a 1500-pound Alexander-style deck anchor. She's hardy."

"And the engines?" Joel inquired.

"Boy, she has twin-diesel Alexander engines," Gunther replied with a huge smile, enjoying the question-and-answer session.

"RPMs?" Joel asked.

"1800," Gunther answered as he lit a cigarette.

"Sweet. The love of the water runs in your blood. I can relate."

"You grow up on the water, boy?" Gunther asked, then took a long, cough-inducing draw on his ciggy.

"Yes, on the Chesapeake Bay," Joel answered, holding his breath and trying not to inhale the smoke.

"Where the heck is that?"

"I grew up on Maryland's Eastern Shore fishing for blue crab in the summer and oysters in the winter," Joel explained.

"Hmm," Gunther replied like he had failed geography. He shrugged his shoulders, took a few more cigarette puffs, and coughed loudly. "Well, shall we? Follow me to my vessel."

"Do you own the Alexandria?" Joel queried.

"Uh, well, not exactly," Gunther responded.

The Alexandria was next to the dock, so they climbed over the railing and stepped onto the main deck. Suddenly, a loud shriek pierced Joel's eardrums, a dark blur flew by his head, and he felt the wind from the monstrous wings of a large bird. Then a bald eagle landed on the stern, and Joel couldn't believe he was standing only a few feet away from this majestic creature. Meanwhile, Gunther kept talking, but Joel didn't hear a word because he was so mesmerized by the eagle.

"Boy, I'm talking to you," Gunther said, acting like the eagle was nothing out of the ordinary.

"Sorry, man. I can't get over how close this eagle is," Joel replied as he pulled out his cell phone. "I think there is a camera in here somewhere," he said as he stared at it confusedly.

"Boy, are you telling me that you don't know how to use a camera phone?" Gunther asked as he squinted his dark beady eyes, accentuating his wrinkles, making them even more noticeable than they already were.

"You didn't know where the Chesapeake Bay is," Joel retorted.

"Eh, touché," Gunther replied, then laughed, pleased with Joel's snippy response. "I'm surprised you didn't call me a cigarette-saturated pain in the butt again."

Joel laughed and fiddled with his phone until he finally found the camera. Then he victoriously snapped his first cell phone photo.

"Well, aren't you techie," Gunther smirked as he tapped Joel on the shoulder. "How about that other eagle sitting on the engine room vent?"

Joel took a photo of that eagle as well. "Wow, two eagles."

Suddenly, they flew away together, just like the eagles did at the cathedral. The regal birds distracted Joel, and he didn't notice the three men on the opposite side of the deck.

"Hey jerks!" Gunther exclaimed before loudly clearing his junked-up throat. "This is Joel Layton, one of our greenhorns this season."

The three men stopped working and stared at Joel like they had seen a ghost. Gunther noted this but kept the conversation going as he motioned to each crew member while doing the introductions. "This is Kirk Henderson, engineer and relief captain. Hank Morozov, backup engineer and deckhand. And Nick Peterson, deckhand. Bubba is the deck boss and just completed first aid training through the Coast Guard. He is in the wheelhouse. By the way, Kirk's father owns Aleutian Apparel & Gear across the road, so go there when it's time to get your gear."

Kirk was in his late 40s and had wavy black hair and cold dark eyes that could cut you with a glance. With a muscular frame, he wasn't the least bit ugly, but Joel was much better looking. Also with a pleasing physique, Hank wasn't a bad-looking man in his mid-40s, yet his rather extensive mullet made him look like he never let the 1980s go. While on the other hand, Nick was in his mid-20s, and a toque covered his bald head. He was tall and muscular, so those were his bonus attributes.

Hank was inconvenienced by meeting the newest greenhorn, but he did muster up the nerve to at least shake Joel's hand, unlike Kirk, who scowled at Joel's Navy uniform with no intentions of making him feel welcome. Meanwhile, Nick smiled and respectfully initiated a handshake.

"Come on, Joel. Let's head up to the wheelhouse to meet Bubba. Lord give us the strength we need," Gunther said with a chuckle, then looked at Kirk and Hank disapprovingly.

Kirk trailed Joel and Gunther like a dog as they entered the gear room, then climbed a set of stairs leading to the wheelhouse where Bubba was bent over, busting a colossal sag, so the first thing they saw was the crack of his semi-chunky butt.

"Don't you own a belt?" Gunther shrieked as if the sight of Bubba's butt crack was going to blind them all.

"Oh, golly! I am sorry!" Bubba stood up quickly, yanking up his britches. He was a pudgy man of 40 with short, reddish-brown hair.

"The least you could do is hold your pants up with a darn tie wrap! Here!" Gunther pontificated as he pulled one from his back pocket, slapped Bubba on the cheek with it, and then gave it to him.

"Oh, Gunther, you're so clever!" Bubba said enthusiastically as he graciously took the tie wrap and corrected his wardrobe problem. Then he looked up and grinned like a little boy who had just won pin the tail on the pony.

Gunther laughed. "Bubba, this is Joel Layton, one of our new greenhorns."

Bubba grinned like he was meeting a real-life superhero. "It's a pleasure to meet you, Captain Layton. Wow! A real Navy captain. I bet you have so many stories to tell. I hope you feel comfortable sharing them with us!" he exclaimed as he stepped closer to Joel.

Joel figured Bubba was stepping closer for a handshake; however, he gave Joel a Chubby Bubba hug instead.

"I should've thrown him overboard when I had the chance," Kirk muttered.

"Uh, it's nice to meet you too, Bubba," Joel politely said, even though he was baffled by the unnecessary hug.

"Next time, step to the side. It's what I do," Gunther whispered.

Eventually, Bubba relinquished the embrace. "My name is Jonathan Timber, but everybody calls me Bubba. Just don't call me Bob." He stood at ease, assuming the respectful militant stance for meeting a Navy captain.

"I will make a note of it," Joel replied.

"So, tell us about the ship you were on!" Bubba exclaimed like a schoolboy excited for story time.

"For 10 years, I had the privilege of being captain of the USS Roland, a Jagger James-Class guided-missile destroyer," Joel said.

"Alcazar Battle System?" Kirk snidely asked.

Joel furrowed his brow because the average person wouldn't know this. "Alcazar Missile Armament Protection System. The USS Roland had missiles, guns, and torpedoes," he explained.

"That is so awesome! What kinds of missiles and guns?" Bubba asked.

"Tomahawks and harpoons. We had a ballistic system with vertical launch, JG-84 TMGs, and Tarantula Boss Cannons," Joel expounded.

"Squid," Kirk muttered offensively.

At that moment, Joel knew Kirk also had a military background and that his demeaning and disrespectful comment was interservice rivalry, something Joel detested. This time, however, he turned the other cheek.

Gunther promptly shifted the conversation. "How's the sonar, Bubba?"

"Everything looks good, Captain," Bubba jovially replied as he stepped closer like he was going in for a hug, but Gunther was quick and stepped to the side.

"Not that we need it. The captain's intuition is always best," Gunther said.

"The new EPIRB is registered and on board too!" Bubba eagerly added.

"Awesome. Thanks, man," Gunther responded as he slapped Bubba on the shoulder like he had Joel earlier, the only difference being that Bubba almost fell over.

"You didn't cross any wires, did you, Bob?" Kirk callously inquired.

"Don't you have somebody's wife to screw? Get out of my wheelhouse!" Gunther roared.

Kirk looked at Gunther like he was shooting a death ray from his eyes. Then he grudgingly obeyed and left the wheelhouse. After that, Gunther's phone rang, so he left to take the call in private.

Joel noticed a small perch next to the captain's seat. "Bubba, is that for a bird?"

"No, that perch was for Captain Kyle's monkey, Tiny. He won't be joining us at sea anymore," Bubba said sadly.

Joel received more pieces to the puzzle. *If Kyle is the Alexandria's captain, why is Gunther captain this season, and where is Kyle now?* he wondered. Then Joel remembered the conversation with Gert when she told him about the accident last season when she and Gunther lost their son. *Did something happen to Kyle too?* Joel speculated as he continued looking around the wheelhouse and noticed two pictures, one of the blonde woman with the guy close to Gunther's age and the other of Gert, Gunther, and their son's family.

"Bubba, what happened last season to Gunther's son? Where is Captain Kyle?" Joel asked.

Bubba's jovial smile melted away. "I have a sad story to tell. Captain Kyle was Gunther's brother. He died along with Gunther's son Chris during last January's opilio season," Bubba explained as he pointed to the pictures. "The beautiful blonde woman is Captain Kyle's daughter, Katerina. She loved her father and cousin very much. Joel, you closely resemble Chris. You have probably been getting many strange looks since you got here. I mean it, Joel. Looking at you makes me think of Chris. It's a shame he's gone. You would've been great friends. He was my best friend. I miss him."

"I'm so sorry to hear this, Bubba. What type of accident was it?"

"Last year, we had a horrible red king crab season. When you depend on those crabs, and you have empty pots, it's not a good place to be. Captain Kyle was determined to make the opilio season a success, so he chose to take a huge risk and go much farther northwest into the center of Satan's Expanse. This is the most dangerous area of the Bering Sea to fish in. Rogue waves come out of nowhere, especially during storms. But it's the best place to catch crabs, especially after not catching any. We all agreed to go there for the opilios. We had calm seas until the worst arctic storm in 25 years hit. It was in the middle of the night. Pelting rain unlike anything I have ever experienced in 20 years of working on the Bering Sea. The wind was forceful. But guess what? We were catching crabs. Then 25-foot swells started crashing over the deck, knocking us over, but we didn't care 'coz of all those dang crabs.

"To make matters worse, we were dealing with the worst icy buildup I had ever seen. It was 10 degrees out, and the ice was a few inches thick on the railing. We were going on three hours of sleep a day. But, like I said, we didn't care because we were catching so many crabs out there. We were making history.

"Captain Kyle had pneumonia, had been awake for two days straight, and went to rest. Kirk was the relief captain on duty, but Captain Kyle returned to the wheelhouse after a few hours. By this point, the conditions had deteriorated in a short amount of time to 45-foot swells. Captain Kyle looked out the wheelhouse window just in time to see a pot being brought over the railing when a huge wave crashed, knocking the deckhands down. Gunther, Nick, Chris, and I were all out there. Captain Kyle rushed down to help. Kyle and Chris tried to get the swinging pot and secure it. Kyle pushed Chris out of the way as another huge wave came crashing on deck.

"The cable snapped; the pot came crashing down—a fully loaded, 800-pound pot. The pot landed on Kyle and crushed him to death. The cable struck Chris in his cervical spinal cord, killing him instantly. The rest of us were all washed to the other side of the deck. I broke my leg, and Nick broke his arm. Hank was down in the engine room and was safe. Then Kirk, of course, was in the wheelhouse and didn't have a scratch on him. Gunther had a mild concussion, but seeing his brother and son die in front of him caused him more harm than the blow to the head. We couldn't move the pot right away. It was bad. Gunther took Chris inside, and it took a while for the rest of us to get Captain Kyle. Something you will never forget. Chris was my best friend since childhood. I don't know why any of us want to go back out there," Bubba said as his eyes filled.

"I understand that more than you know, Bubba. The love of working on the water is in your DNA. Even a tragedy such as this doesn't take that love away. When you're at sea, you feel close to those you lost out there," Joel said as he patted him on the shoulder.

Bubba took a hanky out of his pocket. "Well said, Captain

Layton. I think you and I will be very, very good friends."

"I think so too, Bubba," Joel replied with a smile as he continued looking around the wheelhouse, and his eyes led him back to the photos on the wall. "What happened to Katerina?"

"She was the most beautiful woman I ever laid eyes on. I really wanted her to have my babies. She said I was like an older brother, and she could never see me that way. Unfortunately, since her daddy and cousin died, she went crazy. I am afraid we will never see Katerina Alexander again," Bubba explained with a heavy sigh. "Have you ever been in love, Joel?"

The wheelhouse door flung open, Gunther stormed in, and Joel didn't have to answer Bubba's question.

Gunther frantically puffed on his cannabis vape. "I don't know how many doggone times I have to tell my divorce lawyer that I don't want a doggone divorce!" Gunther bellowed.

"Then why do you have a divorce lawyer?" Bubba boldly asked.

"Because you look like an idiot if you don't have one! Duh!" Gunther retorted.

"Oh, okay," Bubba said, then shrugged his shoulders.

Meanwhile, Gunther whipped out another ciggy and lit it.

"Hey Gunther, how about we take Joel for a full tour of the Alexandria?" Bubba suggested.

"Yes, good idea," Gunther concurred as he exhaled a huge smoke cloud.

Now that Gunther's nerves were under control, he and Bubba gave Joel a thorough tour of the main deck, including showing him the hatch that led to the crab holds. They went inside and showed Joel the engine room, crew accommodations, and galley, where they found Kirk, Hank, and Nick enjoying a coffee break.

"Gunther, we were just talking about going to the Port House tonight to see a little show," Hank said sarcastically, going out of his way to push Gunther's buttons.

"Oh yeah! I'm down for some of that," Kirk concurred.

Gunther growled at them and did his best to control his fuming rage.

"Gentleman, can we please show some respect?" Bubba asked as he put his hand on Gunther's shoulder.

"Why don't you go back to finishing school with the other little girls?" Kirk snapped.

"Your words can't hurt me, Kirk. I surround myself with an impenetrable barrier of confidence that you can't pierce. That—and I could kick your butt in karate!" Bubba countered, then made the downward block move, accompanied by a high-pitched shriek.

Nick promptly jumped up from the table and grabbed Gunther and Bubba by the arms. "Come on. Let's go to the Port House and have a drink to celebrate our newest crew member."

How in the world do these guys not kill each other at sea? Joel wondered as he followed Nick, Gunther, and Bubba to the main deck.

"Joel, please join us over at Portia's. We go there often to hang out and listen to some great music," Nick said as he climbed over the railing and stepped onto the dock.

"Yeah, she said she would debut a couple of new songs tonight. I told her I wouldn't miss it for the world!" Bubba exclaimed as his cheeks blushed beet red.

Meanwhile, a perplexed look spread across Gunther's face. He grumpily huffed as he went to his truck.

"Come on Joel; let's go. Come meet us up there," Bubba insisted.

"Thanks, guys. Sounds like a plan," Joel replied.

Chapter 5. *Portia's Port House*

The Port House parking lot was filling up, indicating that the party was getting started. Joel pulled into the left side of the lot and parked next to a jacked-up, hot pink pickup truck with a chrome roll bar in front of an owner's sign. If only the truck wasn't screaming pink, it would've given Joel's truck a run for its money on toughness. Joel walked around the pink truck and chuckled before meeting up with Gunther, Bubba, and Nick on the front sidewalk. Then the four of them walked toward the right side of the building to the bar entrance, and Gunther looked even more pissed off than he did earlier. For some reason, Gunther abhorred Portia's Port House. To further his irritation, Kirk and Hank drove into the parking lot like racecar drivers and quickly walked up behind the rest of the Alexandria's crew members, trailing them like a pair of hounds.

The tantalizing scent of gourmet food greeted guests as they entered the Port House. Familiar oldies songs played lightly beneath the townsfolks' chitter chatter while they enjoyed drinks and appetizers. Even though Joel wasn't hungry, entering Portia's Port House made him develop an appetite because the food smell so good.

Next to the door, Joel noticed a framed newspaper article titled, "Captain and Deckhand on F/V Alexandria Killed during Arctic Storm." The article accompanied a family photo of Gert, Gunther, Katerina, Kyle, Chris, and his wife and son in front of the Alexandria. Joel took off his Navy captain's hat and tucked it under his arm as he read the sad article. Then his eyes found their way back to Katerina in the family photo. *She is beautiful,* he thought.

As Joel walked farther into the room, he was awestruck by the breathtaking view of Eagle Bay through floor-to-ceiling windows. The Port House wasn't fancy, but the décor was very nice. Shellac on the dark cherry hardwood floors and bar area shimmered beneath a mixture of bronze track lighting and pendant chandeliers suspended from wooden ceiling beams. Everything in the room sparkled and shined, including dancing poles on each end of the bar, leading Joel to wonder what type of establishment this truly was—and if there would be bar dancers making an entrance at some point in the evening.

Along the windows facing the bay, a double row of high-topped tables provided an immaculate view of fishing vessels coming into port for the evening. On the roadside, the bar was on the left. To the right, a stage was fully set with a keyboard and drum set along with bass, electric, and acoustic guitars. With stage lights and speakers suspended from the ceiling next to a mirrored disco ball hanging above the dancefloor, the Port House was fully loaded to pull the trigger on a bang-up performance. And to add the finishing touch to the Port House experience, light emanated from an old-fashioned jukebox in the far-right corner of the room.

Bubba walked over to the stage and motioned for Gunther, Nick, and Joel to join him. With folded arms and an agitated expression accentuating the wrinkles on his withered face, Gunther grudgingly followed the younger men to the front row. At any moment, Joel expected Gunther to fire up a cigarette or take a hit on the cannabis vape. Meanwhile, Kirk and Hank skulked behind Joel and let out several ear-piercing catcalls.

Suddenly, a reverberating gong sound blasted the room, and all the lights went out. The loud, intense noise sent shivering vibrations throughout Joel's body. After the boom subsided, the room quieted down as the stage lights flickered on.

The musicians took their places. The bass player was a young, skinny guy with no hair. While on the other hand, the drummer was a middle-aged, overweight bald guy with a long gray beard. The keyboard player was a middle-aged woman, who had short brown hair; she wasn't beautiful but wasn't one to be considered ugly. The three of them were in position, waiting for a lead guitar player and singer, as suggested by the unoccupied microphone at center stage.

Once again, the lights dramatically dimmed. Then the stimulating sound of high heels hammered the floor as the silhouette of a curvaceous woman took the stage. She picked up the electric guitar and stepped in front of the microphone as a center stage light illuminated the Port House queen. Her brunette hair had a fake reddish-purple tint. She had sensually teased her long, flowy hair to perfection and painted her large, puffy lips provocatively red, flaming brightly above her porcelain-white skin. Her thin, toned body had curves that would put most supermodels to shame.

She wore a tight black midriff leather vest with a matching high-waisted mini skirt and thigh-high leather boots that would make a stripper envious. Aviator sunglasses hid her eyes, no smile adorned her face, and her black fingernails matched her demeanor. She was one decked-out chick who wore sorrow well.

Joel looked her up and down as his stomach somersaulted. *My God, she is gorgeous!* he thought, never seeing such a beautiful woman in all his life.

Bubba sighed, took off his hat, and held it over his heart as he looked up at the sensual woman and quietly said, "I love you, Portia."

Joel looked at Bubba and cracked a slight grin. Then he glanced over at Gunther. The sight of Portia pissed Gunther off. He wasn't googly-eyed over her like every other male in the room.

The remaining stage lights blasted on, making Portia's sparkling silver electric guitar shimmer. She stepped closer to the microphone and sang as the band lightly played.

You lied
You didn't tell me you lied
You had me hanging on your words
When you walked through the door

The vibrato in Portia's voice was so powerful that Joel's entire body got goosebumps. Her talent utterly bedazzled him as he watched her play a booming guitar solo and then sing the rest of the first verse.

You lied
You didn't tell me the truth
Told me that you needed space
Not that you found somebody new

The drummer hit the gas, playing without restraint, shifting the gears, and putting the tempo into overdrive. Portia swayed her hips while pounding the electric guitar with a wild rock star modulation. Sashaying to the music while wearing those thigh-high leather boots, Portia redefined sexy.

Portia's guitar playing halted long enough for her to remove the aviator sunglasses and toss them to the side—revealing sad overly green eyes with perfectly long lashes, accentuated by thick, black eyeliner. Once again, Joel's stomach somersaulted, making his heart pound while goosebumps covered his body. Portia's eyes were so green that they looked artificial, but he didn't care. At that moment, she looked at the front row and made eye contact with Joel, making him feel like the luckiest man alive. Portia kept her eyes on him as she powerfully sang the chorus.

And you would come
And you would go
And hold her hand
And I would be alone
You lied
You didn't tell me you lied
Why did you marry me
Then you left me here alone
You lied

Portia flipped her hair around and shimmied her hips and boots from side to side as she rocked a squealing guitar solo before showcasing her kick-butt vocals for the remainder of the chorus.

You held me then you shut me out
The flame was hot
The flame was out
Am I just a sweet memory
What about the years you spent with me
Oh, you lied
You lied
You lied
Oh, you lied

The tempo slowed for the second verse as the bass, electric guitar, keyboard, and drums thundered with intensity, driving home the sorrow behind the lyrics. Once again, Portia's eyes locked onto Joel's as she sang.

You lied
Why did you tell me I'm loved
I was so sure that we would last

But you held another girl
You lied
So I will tell you the truth
Now I'm the one needing space
And I will find somebody new

The song continued as Portia sang the chorus wilder and crazier than before, infusing each note with melancholic vibrato. Meanwhile, Gunther grew more agitated with each sashay of Portia's hips.

Even over the loud music, Joel heard someone sniffle. Then he saw Bubba wipe his eyes with an overused hanky. Portia's scantily clad body had an emotional effect on him. There was no way in hell that Portia would have Chubby Bubba's babies. Gunther looked at Bubba and made a terrible face. He irately ran his fingers through his scraggly hair while Kirk and Hank hooted and hollered like a couple of Neanderthals. While on the other hand, Nick and Joel enjoyed the music but remained respectful gentlemen.

Portia concluded the song with another impressive guitar solo. Even though the lyrics weren't his cup of tea, Joel was blown away by her talented performance. Once again, Portia's fake green eyes locked onto his as she dramatically strummed the final chord, and the crowd went wild. "Thank you. I hope you keep coming back to hear my music. Welcome to Portia's Port House."

As she took off the guitar and set it on the stand, the Alexandria's crew huddled in front of the stage. They watched her turn around and bend over, enjoying the view of her tight derriere in that provocative mini skirt.

Portia stepped off the stage directly in front of Joel. Her eyes grazed down his Navy full dress white uniform then back up again, as she smiled seductively with those flaming red lips. "So, you're one of the new greenhorns, eh?"

"That's right," Joel replied.

"I'm Portia," the bar queen said as she extended her hand.

"Joel Layton," he said as he took Portia's hand, pulled it up to his lips, and kissed it.

Meanwhile, Gunther rolled his eyes.

"Great song, Portia!" Bubba exclaimed as he put his arms out for a hug.

Portia tossed her head back and laughed before giving Bubba a sideways hug. Then she hugged the rest of the crew members. Nick, of course, was a gentleman who gave her a respectful side hug while Kirk and Hank went in for full frontal hugs.

Portia saved Gunther for last. Instead of hugging her like the others, Gunther waved his pointer finger in her face like he was scolding her. "You piss me off!" After the sixth finger admonishment, Gunther resumed his stance from earlier with his arms folded across his chest and an agitated expression on his wrinkled face. Portia thought this was humorous because she tossed her head back and laughed again before grabbing Gunther's face and kissing him on the cheek, stamping him with a kiss mark. She spun on her thigh-high leather boot heels, then skipped back up on stage. This time, she picked up the sparkling silver acoustic guitar and returned to her place in front of the microphone. "Would you mind if I sang one more new song for you?"

The crowd went crazy. The fine folks of Aleutia were all too willing to indulge in a second helping of Portia. Bubba reached for his hanky while Kirk and Hank howled like a pair of rabid wolves. Gunther abruptly flung his arms into the air, grunted until he gagged, and then threw his arms back across his chest.

As Portia stood under the spotlight, her porcelain skin glowed like she was an angel dressed in black garb. Joel watched her intently. *My God, she is beautiful*, he thought.

Portia lightly picked the guitar strings. "This song is called 'On and Off,'" she said. Then ever so delicately, the electric piano, bass guitar, and drum brushes chimed in beneath Portia's fancy finger work. The audience swayed from side to side, and Bubba even lit up his cell phone and waved it in the air like it was a candle. Gunther didn't sway with the melody like the other happy spectators. He shook his head in disgust, acting like he would rather be anywhere but Portia's Port House.

In a soft and wounded voice, Portia sang as Joel watched every word fall from those perfectly pouty red lips.

I am getting tired
I've been waiting here all night
Hoping that you might
Come back in and change your mind
Oh, how you loved
Oh, how you lied
Just like a lightbulb
From dark to bright

While "You Lied" was a wild Rock & Roll song, "On and Off" was country at its finest, for Portia's versatile voice presented an eloquent twang that tugged at the heartstrings. Joel listened carefully, feeling a connection to every word pouring forth from Portia's soul. Where the first song evoked anger, this song evoked pain, and the people listening felt like the pain was theirs.

Transitioning to the chorus, all the instruments picked up intensity, playing a little louder and a little more complex, but still maintaining that wounded country inflection. Portia's voice grew more robust with each line of the chorus.

How did you turn it on and off
You said you loved me

Then you turned and walked away
How did you make up in your mind
What you're thinking
And what you really meant to say
You are a thief in the night
An awesome swindler
With a con artist's appetite
How did you turn it on and off
I've heard your lies all before
Don't come back through my door
Goodbye on and off

Joel didn't know Portia, and he didn't know the man who was the impetus for this song. However, the one thing Joel did know was that he wanted to snap that jerk's neck for causing this gorgeous woman to write such dark and depressing music.

Gunther shook his head for the umpteenth time, wishing he was somewhere else. Meanwhile, the slowness and sadness of this song provoked more tears from Bubba, who looked like he was getting ready to hug everyone in the room.

Portia gracefully swayed with the melody like a weeping willow flowing with the wind. As she sang the second verse, her voice projected even more anguish than it did in the first one.

Funny how the sun
And the moon they seem to fight
The sun hurts my eyes
And the moon it fills them up
Oh, how you cried
Oh, when you lied
You'll be a trickster
For all of your life

Portia powerfully sang the chorus two more times before the tempo slowed, and the song ended the way it began, with soft musical accompaniment. "Thank you so much for coming tonight. Please make yourselves at home," she said before taking off the guitar and placing it on the stand. Portia hopped off the stage and clinked her thigh-high leather boots as she sashayed her way over to the bar to wait on customers.

"OH, WHAT A BLESSED DAY THIS IS!" Bubba exclaimed at the top of his lungs. "Come on team. Let's drink together at the bar. Come on Joel. We have so much to celebrate!"

Gunther rolled his eyes and grunted as he and Joel followed Bubba to the bar, where Joel had the privilege of sitting between them.

As soon as Portia walked behind the counter, Tiny leapt onto her shoulder, and she scratched his back as she leaned her cheek into him. She hugged the little punk rocker, holding him close to her heart, but the wee lad took advantage of the situation by sticking his paws down her chest. "Behave yourself, young man!" Portia admonished. Then she set him near the cash register, where Tiny had an antique wooden ship replica that included a perch, feeding station, and bed. Tiny squeaked at Portia when she went to the other end of the bar to take orders.

"That's Tiny," Bubba said to Joel.

"Oh yes, I met Tiny earlier today. He was with Gunther when he picked me up from the airport," Joel replied.

"He loves to go for truck rides. Portia was kind enough to adopt Tiny after Captain Kyle's passing," Bubba explained.

"That was nice of her," Joel said as he watched Portia wait on customers. "Hey Bubba, what happened to Katerina? Where is she now?"

"She's gone, man. She's just gone. It's like she vanished. One day she was here, and the next, she was gone. We've lost too many people this year, Joel. Too many," Bubba sadly responded.

"I know. I'm sorry. I know what that's like," Joel said.

Nick sat down on the other side of Bubba, and a cute brunette skipped up to him, kissing him like crazy.

"That's one way of saying hello!" Gunther exclaimed.

"I got off work late," the brunette said as she snuggled up to Nick.

"Hey, Polly! This is Joel, one of our new greenhorns this year. Joel, this is Polly, Nick's fiancée," Bubba explained.

"Nice to meet you," Joel said as he stood and extended his hand to shake Polly's.

"Thanks, you too," Polly replied. Then she looked at Nick and grinned like a giddy schoolgirl, and a big dopy grin spread across his face. They couldn't contain their fondness for each other and proceeded with another round of lip wrestling for all the world to see.

"Will you two please get a room, so we don't have to watch?" Gunther joked.

Meanwhile, Joel watched Portia strut back to the cash register and computer, where she entered orders. He sat down and laid his Navy hat upside down on the bar top. Tiny looked at Joel and affectionately squeaked, alerting Portia that the crew was sitting behind her, so she spun around on the heels of her thigh-high leather boots. "Well boys, can I get you some drinks or something to eat? Or the usual?"

"So, guys, you want the usual?" Bubba asked the crew, and everyone nodded in agreement. "Let's go with the local ale. Joel, this is the best beer you will ever have!"

"Sounds good to me," Joel agreed.

"Oh, and Portia, could I please order a basket of truffle fries?" Bubba added.

Portia entered the order into the computer and then served the guys their ale, fresh from the tap. She promptly poured herself a beer mug full of brandy, not a tumbler like a normal person.

Kirk and Hank felt the need to grace everyone with their presence, so they sat down on the other side of Polly.

"Great show tonight, Portia," Kirk said in an I'm-going-to-charm-the-pants-off-you voice.

Portia cracked a fake smile at Kirk but didn't say anything in return. Instead, she took a sip of brandy and scratched Tiny on the head.

Bubba picked up his beer mug. "Folks, I would like to make a toast. To Joel Layton, a newly retired Navy Captain of the USS Roland, a guided-missile destroyer, thank you for joining the crew of the Alexandria. We look forward to working with you this season. Thanks for your service to our country. Hip hip hooray!"

"Thank you," Joel replied, feeling honored and embarrassed at the same time as he clinked beer mugs with Bubba, Gunther, Nick, and Polly. Kirk and Hank refused to participate. However, the one who got to Joel was Portia. She stepped closer to the bar, looked Joel in the eyes, and clinked mugs with him, making him smile from ear to ear.

Suddenly, Gert appeared from the kitchen and served Bubba his fry basket. "Hey boys! How are you this evening? Hey Joel!"

Gunther spat beer on the bar top. "What are you doing?"

"Working! What does it look like? I need to earn my way in the world," Gert retorted as she threw her hands on her hips and glared at him.

"Well, if you were still at home with me and not cohabitating with that blonde trollop, you wouldn't have to work, now would you?" Gunther countered, then sadly sighed. "Come home with me tonight and let me wash your hair. I love you," he lamented as he leaned forward and propped his head in his hand.

"You're not touching my hair! Shovel your dung somewhere else, Gunther! You disgust me! I would rather dig a ditch with a spoon than go back to you. You stinky drunk punk!" Gert yelled, then stomped off to the other side of the bar.

"Why did you hire her?" Gunther angrily asked Portia.

"Why wouldn't I?" Portia answered his question with a question, not the least bit sorry for giving Gert a job and not the least bit intimidated by Gunther's lousy disposition.

Gunther replied with a loud, cough-inducing growl, precipitating a spumy, chest-rattling bark. Joel did his best not to shiver and choked back a heave himself.

"Joel, I don't know why, but I love that infuriating woman. I always have. I need to make her love me again," Gunther wailed before pounding his ale. "Portia, get me another one!"

She looked at Gunther and scrunched up her face.

"Now!" Gunther shouted.

"Oh, all right!" Portia exclaimed as she irately took the mug and refilled it, slamming it down in front of him, so ale spilled all over the bar and splashed on his rumpled shirt.

"So Portia, could you give us a little pole dance?" Kirk asked as he elbowed Hank in the ribs, and the two buffoons laughed.

"I dance when I want to. Not when someone tells me to," Portia tersely answered.

At any moment, Joel expected Gunther to haul off and bust Kirk in the mouth, but instead, Gunther said nothing. His attention was on Gert while he drank his beer much faster than was necessary.

Suddenly, Tiny happily squeaked and then jumped onto the bar, landing by Bubba's fry basket. Bubba and Tiny played tug of war with the last fry, and Bubba let Tiny win. "Those fries were great, Portia. Uh oh, I popped my tie wrap!"

Gunther grunted until he coughed, pulled two more tie wraps out of his pocket, rudely leaned across Joel, and slapped Bubba with them. "Here! We don't call you Chubby Bubba for nothing. Good grief, man! Go see Old Al, and buy a belt!"

As the evening went on, the crew hung around the bar, while Gert, Portia, the keyboard player, and the bass player served customers, and the drummer stood by the front door like the head of security. Gert rushed in and out of the kitchen with trays while Portia filled drink orders. Gunther fixated on Gert and sadly shook his head every time she walked by, and Joel watched Portia rush around the bar, giving those thigh-high leather boots one heck of a workout as a 1980s rock song blared in the background.

"She's real pretty, huh?" Bubba asked, then loudly hiccupped.

Joel had only been in town for five minutes and didn't want to let on that he had the hots for the local bar girl. He grinned, acknowledging Bubba's comment. Then Joel took a sip of beer and watched Portia sexily move to the music. She trotted in front of them, lined up a row of shot glasses, grabbed two liquor bottles, and did a few tricks with them before filling them. Suddenly, she jumped up on the bar top, strutted from one end to the other, and slid down the pole next to Gunther. Meanwhile, Kirk and Hank catcalled and whistled. Portia ignored the two hoodlums, then reached across the bar and took the shot glasses to a group sitting at the high-topped tables.

"We were so glad her ex got run out of town," Bubba began.

"Yeah, good riddance," Nick agreed as he lifted his beer mug to clink it with Bubba's.

Bubba took a big gulp before continuing, "You see, Joel, Portia's ex-husband Chuck was on our crew. When you first met him, you swore he was a nice guy, but behind closed doors, he was abusive. We didn't know, but he grabbed Portia and cussed at her. What kind of man puts his hands on his wife like that? It's unconscionable. We didn't know this until after last October's red king crab season. The night we got back into port, Kirk found Chuck screwing Alyona Volkvo behind The Bairdi Saloon."

"Let's just say, when Chris, Hank, and I got done with him, Chuck's face was black and blue," Kirk began. "If we had known he was grabbing her and cursing her like that, we would've bashed his face in sooner."

"Chuck and Alyona left and went to Kodiak. They dare not set foot in Aleutia again," Hank added, then took a swig of ale and slammed his mug down on the bar.

"We don't always agree, but we're on the same page regarding Portia. I'm a nonviolent guy, you know. I don't believe violence is the answer, but what Kirk, Hank, and Chris did that night was necessary," Bubba said in the manliest voice he could muster up.

"That's right, Bob. I think we have had enough agreement for one night. If you don't mind, I'd like to get back to despising all of you. Anyway, have a great evening. See you tomorrow," Kirk said as he and Hank stood up, tossing money on the bar top before leaving.

Joel closely observed everyone's interactions. Kirk and Hank were jerks; however, they had no use for men who abused women. Joel couldn't imagine a man treating Portia that way, but he was thankful that the crew, all jerks included, ran her abusive, two-timing ex out of town.

"So Joel, would you like to come to liturgy with us tomorrow? Afterward, there is a Watermen's Memorial Ceremony in the gym at the Aleutia Community Center. Lunch is included," Bubba said.

"Yes, please join us tomorrow," Gunther insisted as he stared into his empty beer mug with one eye.

"That sounds nice. Thank you. I would love to come," Joel replied appreciatively.

Meanwhile, Tiny squeaked, letting everyone know he wasn't the center of attention. Now that he had finished sniffing around

Bubba's empty fry basket, the punk rocker yawned, crawled into Joel's Navy hat, curled up into a ball, and fell asleep. The crew and Polly paused to smile and enjoy watching the tiny creature settle into his newfound bed.

"How old is he?" Joel asked.

"Kyle got him about 10 years ago, so Tiny still has many good years ahead of him," Gunther said with a smile.

"Sweet," Joel responded, then took a sip of ale.

Nick started laughing and motioned for the rest of the crew members to look behind them. "Reverend Thomas is at it again."

The reverend was a balding, middle-aged man with a slender frame and a goatee. When Portia tried to take his order, he opened his Bible and showed her a verse instead.

"He disapproves of Portia's path in life. Serving alcohol, bar dancing, wearing those boots," Polly explained.

"That and he loves ordering the Reuben here. He's a good guy. Portia needs someone to talk some sense into her," Gunther said as he shook his head disapprovingly.

Joel watched Portia's interactions with the reverend. She kindly listened to what the man of God had to say. Then she took the Bible and showed him a verse too. Reverend Thomas read it and smiled at her. Portia patted him on the shoulder. "Shall I get you the usual?"

"Yes, please," he responded.

"What did I tell ya?" Gunther said with a chuckle. "The Reuben is really good here. I got to say."

"Well Joel, I think you need to know who is who around here," Bubba began. "Portia's band members all work here too. See them by the door right now? The big bald guy is Ted Denson. He's Portia's drummer and security guy. He's really sweet on Rhonda Jackson, who is Portia's keyboard player. Rhonda can also play the guitar. She's a waitress here too. The young bald guy talking to them right now is Leonard Smith; he's the bass player. He works in the kitchen sometimes. Over here, you see that real preppy-looking guy at the other end of the bar? That's Dr. Sampson. He's the best chiropractor in Aleutia. If you hurt your back, he's the one to see."

Dr. Sampson was 50 years old with snow-white hair. He had a professional, albeit preppy, appearance with a sweater tied around his neck, draped a little too perfectly over his long-sleeved dress shirt.

"The woman next to him is Lora Yazzie. She's the city manager," Bubba explained, giving Joel the low-down on the townsfolk. Lora was a nice-looking, slender woman in her mid-40s with short black hair and a pale face that made her look like a fairy godmother. "Rumor has it that she and the doc are doing it. Lora has been seen coming and going from his office at odd hours."

Nick chuckled. "You might wanna think twice about getting on his exam table."

"Yeah, well, you are young. Wait until you turn 40 and need a chiropractor," Bubba said with a laugh. "Your body hasn't started aching, cracking, and popping yet, my friend. You just wait."

"Looks like Denny and Alicia are hitting it off," Gunther said as he pointed toward a couple standing by the windows, enjoying the last few remaining sunset colors over Eagle Bay.

"That's Denny Benally and Alicia Garcia. Denny is the head of the visitors' bureau, and Alicia works at the post office," Bubba explained.

Denny was a tall, middle-aged man with a fit, semi-muscular frame wearing a black toupee because no man's hair was that perfect or that black. While on the other hand, Alicia's shoulder-length hair was hers but was dyed blonde with unnatural brown highlights. She was a little meaty but not who one could classify as fat.

From their cozy but not overly intimate interactions, Joel

surmised that this had to be a second or third date, for Denny had his hand on the small of Alicia's back and was pointing off into the distance, pontificating about the beauty of nature.

"Denny's wife left him for a millionaire who was vacationing at the Aleutian Resort. Alicia just moved here from the lower 48. Some people move here for the excitement of moving to Alaska. Then they experience the weather and secluded lifestyle here, and they leave. But I think Alicia might hang around," Nick said.

"You know, Nick, I think you're right. And there's a handful of people here tonight that I don't recognize. I guess the Port House has become a new tourist attraction," Bubba said as he grinned at Portia strutting by in those delicious leather boots.

"Well, ain't that lovely! All those dang come here's are coming here to see Portia strut around in her tiny little outfits when they could be out climbing a darn mountain!" Gunther bellowed as he slammed his hand down on the bar. Meanwhile, Gert scurried by him with another tray, and Gunther couldn't endure it any longer. "That's it! I'm leaving! I'll see you boys tomorrow!" He then frantically pulled some crinkled bills out of his pocket and threw them on the bar. Gunther slapped Joel, Bubba, and Nick each on the shoulder and kissed Polly before stomping out the door.

"Good! I thought he would never leave!" Gert shouted as she came back through with the empty tray.

"Speaking of leaving," Nick began as he wrapped his arms around Polly. "I think we are going to head out ourselves."

Bubba started laughing. "Must you be so obvious?"

"Must you be so jealous?" Nick replied.

Bubba jumped up like he had a special lady waiting for him at home, which wasn't true—at all. "Yeah, well, I got to go too. I got plans."

Joel stood up and shook hands with Bubba, Nick, and Polly. "It was nice meeting everyone. Thank you for your hospitality."

"Oh, Joel! It's so good to have you here!" Bubba exclaimed as he went in for a Chubby Bubba hug, but Joel gently patted Bubba's shoulder and promptly stepped to the side.

Bubba turned to Polly and Nick to give them a double bear hug, but they were smart and quickly got away. Bubba grinned and shrugged his shoulders. "See you tomorrow, Joel."

"Bye, Bubba," Joel replied with a laugh as he watched Bubba almost trip and fall on his way out the door.

Joel sat down, with no one beside him except for Tiny, still sleeping comfortably in the Navy hat. Even though it was getting late, and Joel was sleep deprived, he decided to stay at the Port House a little longer. Suddenly, his phone vibrated in his pocket, so he pulled it out and saw he had a message notification. After staring at the phone confusedly, he slid his finger across the notification and was excited when a message from Adoncia popped up asking how he was doing. Joel was getting ready to type a response but noticed the camera icon. He tapped it, and the camera popped up. Feeling techie, Joel snapped a picture of Tiny and sent it to Adoncia.

More people left for the night, and the Port House quieted down. Still, Joel wasn't ready to go, and frankly, how was he supposed to move that precious little monkey sleeping peacefully in his hat? Tiny was so adorable that Joel could hardly contain his admiration, so he slowly moved his hand toward him and rubbed Tiny's belly with his index finger. Tiny chortled and rolled over on his back, signaling for Joel to keep up the excellent work. A few minutes passed, and Joel heard Portia's naughty thigh-high leather boot heels sneaking up behind him. Then she slowly went behind the bar, trying not to disturb Tiny.

Portia looked at Joel and smiled in disbelief. She watched Tiny with adoration in her overly green eyes, and Joel could tell she dearly loved him. "He hasn't been like this with anyone since...

since… Oh, never mind," she said as she leaned across the bar, exposing her substantial cleavage line, and Joel did his best to notice. Portia smiled and gently stroked Tiny's cheeks and chest while Joel rubbed his belly.

"Yeah, he's pretty cool when he's not making evil shrieking sounds at me and squinting his eyes," Joel said with a chuckle.

Portia laughed. "Yeah, he does that sometimes."

Joel saw Gert peering from the kitchen doorway. Then she hurried into the room like she wasn't happily eavesdropping. "Okay, well, I'm out of here. You kids have fun. Please do something I wouldn't do. I am old, and I am going to bed. Anyway, I have to get up to make this handsome fellow some breakfast. My cooking is the best thing to happen to The Harbor Inn! Tanya couldn't even heat up frozen pancakes. I don't know how she stayed in business before I came along. I will see you both tomorrow," Gert said with a yawn.

"Good night, Momma Gert. See you at liturgy tomorrow," Portia replied.

"Thank you again for everything. Good night," Joel said. He smiled, noticing that he and Portia now had the Port House to themselves.

"You have a nice place here," Joel said.

Still leaning across the bar, Portia looked into Joel's eyes, making him tingle from head to toe. "Thank you. The Port House hasn't been open long, but business has taken off. I wanted to create a place where people can come to escape life, a home away from home, with good food, friends, and music. Somewhere, they can watch the sunset and the aurora borealis."

"It looks to me that you have exceeded your goal," Joel replied.

"Thank you," Portia said appreciatively. "I'd like to ask you a question. Do you like my music?"

Joel didn't answer right away. Instead, he paused, staring into Portia's abnormally green eyes as the bar lights reflected on her liquor-colored hair. One thing Joel never did was lie and blow sunshine up people's backsides. "Honestly?" he asked.

Portia pulled back slightly, folding her arms and propping them up on the bar. She crinkled her nose, unsure if she was ready for his response. "Yes. Honestly," she replied, looking at him discernibly.

"No," Joel said boldly.

Completely exasperated, Portia's mouth flew open, and she slapped her hands onto her hips. She obviously wasn't used to being told such things because everyone, other than Gunther, kissed her butt and applauded her performances. "And why not?"

"Honestly, your songs are dark and depressing," Joel began as Portia's mouth flew open again, shocked that anyone would dare criticize her. "Please, let me finish. Portia, I think you are the most talented singer I have ever seen, but you're hiding your true talent behind your pain and the jerk who caused you to write those lyrics. Think about what you can do if you didn't let him taint your God-given gifts?"

"You're sizing me up! You don't know anything about me! You don't know me at all!" Portia hurled back at him as she frantically cleared empty mugs off the bar and put them in the sink.

"Okay, so I am correct. Otherwise, you wouldn't be so defensive. And, another thing, your hair is dyed. I can tell. And no one's eyes are that shade of green! Where do you buy contacts like that anyway?" Joel brazenly continued.

"Maybe I needed a change!" Portia shot back at him. Glaring at Joel like he was the biggest jerk on the face of the planet, she stomped those decadent thigh-high leather boot heels and defensively threw her hands back onto her hips.

"So, you're saying you weren't good enough the way you were? Wasn't your hair good enough? Your eye color wasn't good enough? Black nail polish is better than pink or red?" Joel asked as he stared into her eyes, feeling a connection with her that he had never felt with another human being. "All right, I'll say it! You're the most beautiful woman I've ever seen, and I wish you felt comfortable being who God made you to be. I want to see you! The real you!"

Portia was so stunned by Joel's words that she was momentarily speechless. She looked at him like he was the first person to tell her this. Her eyes glistened slightly, but she shrugged it off. "Okay, sailor, it's my turn to size you up. What are you trying to prove by going out on the Bering Sea?"

"I'm not trying to prove anything," Joel replied. At this point, he figured it wouldn't be a good idea to mention that his Spanish-prostituta friend found this job on the Internet for him.

"Sure you are. You need to prove it to yourself. And right now, you are hiding behind that ridiculous uniform. Are you ready to trade that in for cold weather gear?" Portia rudely said as she folded her arms across her hefty chest.

"Ridiculous? You're darn right I am!" Joel exclaimed, becoming even more aggravated with her.

"Really? Well, Captain, I don't think you know who you are either. Who are you when you take off that uniform and dress like a civilian? Who is Joel Layton? Could you answer that question? Could you?" Portia interrogated him as she slapped her hands on the bar in front of him as if she were a courtroom judge.

"Touché," Joel reluctantly replied. This lady of the bar saw right through him, just like he saw right through her. Joel wanted to be mad at Portia, but how could he? He couldn't, and he knew it. She saw Joel Layton, not Captain Layton of the USS Roland, like he saw the real Portia, not the hair-dyed, green-eyed bar girl.

Neither said anything for a minute or two, retreating to their private thoughts after such a serious conversation. Joel smiled at

Tiny, who was still fast asleep in his Navy hat. He continued stroking Tiny's fuzzy stomach, smiling at the precious monkey and his all-too-beautiful mother. Joel looked up at Portia and stared deeply into her eyes like he was peering into her soul. "I meant what I said. You're the most beautiful woman and talented singer I've ever seen."

"Thank you," Portia graciously responded as she smiled and blushed. She leaned across the bar again and voluptuously grinned. "Well, your uniform isn't ridiculous at all. And honestly, you wear it a little too well," Portia began as she eyeballed him like an ice cream sundae on an August afternoon. "Captain Layton, I think you're ambitious and knew what you wanted and went after it. I also think you're brave for retiring and coming here to work on the Bering Sea."

"Oh stop, you're making me blush." Joel chuckled as he felt his cheeks become rosy for the first time in his life. No woman had ever made him get rosy cheeks. Over the past 20 years, hundreds of women had thrown themselves at Joel, and not one of them ever made him feel tingly inside and blush like a teenager—not even Adoncia.

Tiny squeaked and stuck his paws in the air, signaling for Joel to keep up the exceptional belly rub.

"Tiny knows he can trust you. He doesn't do this with just anyone," Portia said.

"I like him too when he's not throwing poop at me! You should've seen the splatter range he had on my jacket. Gert was so kind and washed it up for me. Those little monkey arms are much stronger than they look!"

Portia laughed. Then she stopped, like it would be wrong to be happy.

"It's okay to laugh. You have a beautiful smile. You shouldn't be so reluctant to share it with the world," Joel said as he stared adoringly into her eyes, completely enamored by this bar lady who was stealing his heart even more with each passing second.

"Easier said than done when, when… Oh, never mind," Portia whispered as a sad expression overtook her face.

Joel could tell that there was more to Portia's story than what Bubba had told him earlier. Joel didn't want to pry or pressure her. He just wanted to do everything in his power to see that gorgeous smile stay on her face, for those full red lips were too beautiful to frown. Joel felt bold, so he slowly moved his hand toward hers, but Portia pulled it back and changed the subject, not ready to talk about whatever it was she wasn't prepared to say.

"Can I get you another beer? This is the only one you've had tonight. It's got to be warm and flat by now," Portia offered as she downed the rest of the mug of brandy.

"No, thank you," he replied as his eyes bugged out. He would throw right the heck up if he downed that much liquor in one gulp, and he was a big tough man. "That's a lot of brandy right there." Joel chuckled with his ultra-sexy smile, and he wasn't even trying.

"I can hold my liquor." Portia reciprocated with a come-and-get-me grin. Even though she tried, Portia couldn't fight it. Her cheeks became rosy, and somehow, beneath the artificial green contact lenses, Joel saw stars twinkling in her eyes.

Joel felt the attraction, he felt the heat, and he felt the connection between their souls. And darn it to heck, Joel couldn't take the small talk any longer. He stood up from the bar stool, smiled that oh-so-sexy grin, and said, "Dance with me."

"What did you say?" Portia asked as her luscious red lips curved upward, revealing pearly white teeth.

"Dance with me," Joel repeated in the sexiest, most seductive tone of voice that he could articulate. He grinned, then walked over to the jukebox where he took his time selecting the perfect tune, which was the oldie song playing when he saw his parents dance together in the kitchen, for the last time, right before they died.

As the music began to play, Portia dimmed the lights, turned on the disco ball, and walked over to the dancefloor.

The song began slowly and quietly with a light guitar riff repeating beneath a man's eloquent voice. Joel walked toward Portia, and she placed her hand in his as the disco lights reflected on the gold buttons and medals on his well-decorated Navy jacket. He held her hand close to his heart while he gently wrapped his other arm around her tiny waist and pulled her close, feeling the warmness of her body and the softness of her porcelain skin, and indulging in the pleasant scent of her perfume. As they swayed with the music, they stared deeply into each other's eyes, and Joel felt his body tingle with delight, unlike anything he had ever experienced. Nothing else—no one else—ever felt this right. Joel had traveled the world, met hundreds of people, and seen places that most people only dream about, but holding Portia by far surpassed all those experiences—like he had been waiting for this moment all his life.

The vocals intensified as the melody picked up tempo, and an orchestra chimed in. Joel held Portia close while the Northern Lights splashed the star-filled sky with celestial beauty, and once again, God showed Joel that everything would be all right. "God is good," Joel whispered as he leaned his forehead against Portia's.

During an orchestral solo, Joel held onto Portia's hand, lifting it into the air while he gently spun her a few times before pulling her back to him, wrapping both arms around her, holding her close for their beating hearts to touch. The power of one protected them, and Joel knew that as long as Portia was in his arms, everything would be okay. The world around them melted away into oblivion while shooting stars sailed across the sky, and the aurora borealis swirled over Eagle Bay like a light show set to music.

Joel didn't know how he would let Portia go when the song was over. A mere three minutes wasn't enough, but the brevity made this moment so special. He continued holding her close, her body touching his, inhaling the scent of her perfume, and savoring every flutter of his beating heart. Then the song, music, and magic ended, returning them to the awkwardness of time.

Portia abruptly pulled away like she couldn't handle the affection or happiness any longer. The smile faded as she trotted across the room to turn the lights back on and turn off the disco ball. "Well, it's getting late. I should get to bed soon. Big day tomorrow. Are you coming to liturgy?"

"Yes," Joel replied, missing the smile that adorned her face while he held her in his arms.

"Wait. You don't have regular clothes, do you?" Portia asked as she pointed toward Joel's Navy jacket.

"Uh, no," he answered. Once again, the bar queen saw right through him. Joel hadn't even thought about going shopping for regular clothes.

PORTIA'S LEATHER BOOTS hammered the floor as she scurried to the back hallway, came out wearing a leather jacket, and had a set of keys in her hand. "Follow me across the road to Aleutian Apparel & Gear. Old Al will hook you up with clothes and crabbing gear."

"It's 11:30 at night!" Joel exclaimed. "He's got to be closed."

Portia ignored his response as she swayed her hips out the Port House door. Joel tossed beer money on the bar top and followed her out the door and over to their trucks. Along the way, he heard a loud banging sound in the dumpster. "What the heck was that?" Joel asked, slightly panicked.

"Oh, that's well, uh, never mind," Portia replied as she walked over to the pink truck and unlocked the door.

Joel grinned, completely amused by her. "Nice ride," he said.

"Thanks, sailor. Now, follow me across the street!" she

exclaimed as she climbed inside, slammed the door shut, and put the key in the ignition.

And good gracious, Joel couldn't believe the sound of her engine. That ridiculously pink power-machine had a dual exhaust system that purred, not like a kitten, but like a cougar on the prowl.

Joel went along with it, for he was already knee-deep in the Portia quicksand. He followed her across the street, and they parked outside Aleutian Apparel & Gear's front door. Portia promptly jumped out of the truck, rang the doorbell, and banged on the door, not once, not twice, but multiple times. Joel heard terrible sounds inside the store, like pots and pans falling, along with the barking of what sounded like a very terrifying dog.

"What are you doing?" Joel asked in a yelling whisper. "Maybe the man was asleep!"

"He owes me a favor!" Portia shot back at him, aggravated that Old Al hadn't answered the door yet.

"For what?" Joel hurled back at her in the same tone she threw at him.

"Look, I'm the bartender. Anyone with a problem comes into my bar and drops their load on me while I serve them booze. I know everyone's secrets, and nobody wants me talking because I know who is screwing who!"

"Oh, I see," Joel replied bewilderedly, knowing somehow that made sense in Portia's brain, but probably not anyone else's.

Wearing a flannel bathrobe, Old Al stumbled to the door and opened it. He was a 70-year-old man with a profound belly, an almost bald head, and a slight comb-over. A significantly overweight bulldog with a loud snarl and a huge drool drip stood next to him.

"Oh, it's you. Good grief, Portia! Just because you stay up half the night doesn't mean the rest of the world does. I was dreaming about making love to a blonde supermodel on a beach in Maui, and here you come banging on my door and interrupted my beautiful fantasy! What the heck do you want?" Old Al grunted as he grabbed the bulldog's collar to keep him from attacking Joel, and then Old Al looked at Joel and asked, "Who are you?"

"This is Joel Layton. He needs clothes," Portia said in a yelling whisper.

"Well, I can see that," Old Al agreed, looking Joel up and down as if he had an uncivilized appearance. "Come on in, bud. Please, call me Old Al," he said politely as he extended his hand to shake Joel's and once again grabbed the bulldog's collar as it lunged at Joel's legs.

"Well, my work is done here. Old Al will hook you up. I'm going to bed now," Portia rudely announced.

"That's it? You're leaving?" Joel questioned her.

"Uh huh!" Portia condescendingly replied.

"Well, somebody should make sure you get back to your apartment. It is dark outside, not to mention those terrible noises coming from the dumpster," Joel said.

Old Al laughed and then pretended to turn it into a cough.

"I'll be just fine," Portia assured as she pulled her leather jacket to the side, revealing a pistol holster clamped to the tight, tiny waistband of her leather mini skirt. Next, she flashed a naughty smile as she lifted her right hand and pointed her first two fingers at her eyes and pointed them back at Old Al and Joel, which translated, *I've got my eye on you two.* The scantily clad bar queen spun on the heels of her thigh-high leather boots and clinked them extra loudly as she walked to her truck. She started the engine and abruptly drove away.

"Is she always like this?" Joel inquired as he carefully stepped inside the store, trying to evade the snarling dog and his astronomical drool drip.

"No, usually she's much worse. Well, let's get you some clothes, my friend. Oh, don't mind my little buddy Rufus here. He's actually a big cuddle bug. Although, I don't recommend bending over. He might try to bite your butt!" Old Al warned as Rufus looked at Joel, growling and exposing his extra pointy teeth.

Joel looked at the overweight bulldog and grimaced. "We don't have to do this now. I can come back during regular business hours."

"Hey, it's no trouble at all. Thanks to Portia, we are both awake anyway, so why not? Let's get you some clothes, boy. What do you need? Sneakers, boots, regular clothes, church clothes, pajamas?"

"Uh, I need all that," Joel responded.

"I see, boy. Rufus and I will get you all fixed up," Old Al kindly said as he patted Joel on the shoulder.

Old Al promptly took Joel's measurements, grabbed a cart, and filled it with everything Joel needed—pajamas, jeans, casual shirts, sweatshirts, winter apparel, dress clothes, undershirts, boxers, socks, hiking boots, and sneakers. One thousand dollars later, Joel had a brand-new wardrobe for his new life in Alaska. And Joel managed to make it out of the store without Rufus biting his arse.

Joel returned to The Harbor Inn around 1 a.m., completely exhausted and ready for a good night's sleep. He put on his new pajamas. Then he crawled into bed, and Portia's face was the last image to dance across the inside of his eyelids before he fell asleep.

WHEN PORTIA RETURNED to the Port House, she finished closing the bar, scooped up Tiny, who was still sleeping in Joel's Navy hat, and carried him upstairs, where she had a posh, open-concept apartment. Her bed and sofa faced floor-to-ceiling windows overlooking Eagle Bay, where the Northern Lights still painted the sky with glory. She walked over to the bed and gently set Joel's hat on the pillow next to hers.

A large, long-haired, black and white tuxedo cat was stretched out in the middle of the bed. "Hey, Screech," Portia said as she scratched his head. Screech meowed and purred in return as he rolled onto his back, but Portia knew better than give him a belly rub because Screech was a typical cat. Even though he asked for a belly rub, he really didn't want one.

Portia picked up a remote and turned on a rock fireplace across from the sofa, before hitting another button to open a large closet full of seductive leather outfits. This chick had plenty of money and knew how to spend it.

She yawned as she unzipped her thigh-high leather boots, took off her leather vest and mini skirt, and swapped them out for a white silk nightgown. Portia sat down at her makeup vanity, custom-built into the closet's center.

As Portia looked at herself in the mirror, Joel's words echoed in her mind, "So, you're saying you weren't good enough the way you were? Wasn't your hair good enough? Your eye color wasn't good enough? Black nail polish is better than pink or red? All right, I'll say it! You're the most beautiful woman I've ever seen, and I wish you felt comfortable being who God made you to be. I want to see you! The real you!"

Portia stared at her reflection in horror. That wasn't her hair, and that wasn't her eye color. She never used to wear thick, black eyeliner or black nail polish. However, the sorrow of the last year was unbearable, and she thought if she changed her appearance, she would feel better. After hearing what Joel had said, Portia realized that her plan didn't work. She sighed, opened a drawer, and took out a joint and a flask. She fired up the doobie, smoked it until it was gone, and took several large gulps of tequila. Over the last several months, marijuana and alcohol were the only things that helped dull her pain, especially at night so she could sleep.

Portia stood up and used the remote to close the closet. Then she went to the bathroom to brush her teeth, wash away the 10 pounds of makeup on her face, take out her green contact lenses, and spray herself with perfume. She turned off the lights and climbed into bed, facing Tiny in Joel's Navy hat, and facing Eagle Bay as the Northern Lights caressed the sky.

Usually, when Portia closed her eyes, she saw terrible flashes from the past, but not tonight. Instead, she saw Joel, so handsome in his Navy captain's uniform, and she remembered how wonderful she felt as he held her in his arms. For the first time in nearly a year, Portia fell asleep with a smile on her face.

Chapter 6. *Sunday*

At The Harbor Inn, Joel was warm and toasty beneath a down comforter in a king-size bed. During his Navy years, he was used to sleeping in a small space on the USS Roland, so a full-size bed underneath a plush quilt was a welcomed transition.

Joel's Sunday-morning slumber was interrupted by a notification on his phone. He rubbed his eyes and reached for it, pleased to see a new message from Adoncia, replying to the picture of Tiny sleeping in the Navy hat. He read her message and responded.

Adoncia: Oh, muy lindo! Is this your first new friend in Alaska?
Joel: He sure is. I met a lot of people yesterday. Speaking of which, I got to shower and get out the door. I have somewhere to be this morning. I will write you soon, my dear friend.
Adoncia: Smooches. ttyl.
Joel: What does that mean?
Adoncia: Oh Joel. You're so funny. Talk to you later.
Joel: Haha. Okay. I see now. Bye.

Joel looked at the clock and saw it was 6:30, so he jumped out of bed and went into the bathroom to wash up. After a five-minute bath in that ridiculous tub, he put on a black suit, including a black tie and a white button-up dress shirt. Then he walked over to the mirror to comb his hair, and as he looked at his reflection, Portia's words from last night echoed in his mind, "Who are you when you take off that uniform and dress like a civilian? Who is Joel Layton? Could you answer that question? Could you?"

For the first time in 20 years, he saw Joel Layton, not United States Navy Captain Layton of the USS Roland. He saw the boy his parents had raised, the teenager who had matured in an orphanage, and the man falling in love with the Port House queen. Last night, Portia fit perfectly in his arms like Joel had held a piece of Heaven. "God is good," he whispered, remembering the smell of her perfume and her heart beating next to his.

Joel grabbed his phone and keys, then hurried out the door for breakfast. As he walked down the staircase, the pleasant aromas of coffee and bacon greeted him like a Sunday morning from his childhood, for his mother had always made bacon on the weekends for him and his father. When Joel entered the dining room, he was greeted by Gert and Tanya in their Sunday best as they finished setting the table. Gert arranged the coffee, cream, sugar, water, and orange juice while Tanya set out pancakes, maple syrup, butter, breakfast potatoes, and bacon.

"Good morning, sweet cheeks!" Gert exclaimed with a loving smile that only a mother could make.

"Sweet cheeks, indeed!" Tanya naughtily concurred as she inappropriately puckered her lips and stuck out her chest while Joel did his best not to grimace.

"I don't know what to say. This looks and smells wonderful. I haven't had a homemade meal like this in a very long time. Thank you," Joel said as he sat down.

"Oh, no need to say thank you, my dear. It's all part of The Harbor Inn experience. I'll say grace," Gert said as she reached her hands out to Tanya and Joel. While Joel was thankful and eager to thank the Lord for this meal, he dreaded holding hands with Tanya because he knew she wouldn't want to let go when the prayer was over.

"Dear Lord, thank you for this food, and please bless it to our bodies. Amen," Gert eloquently prayed.

"Amen," Joel and Tanya said simultaneously. Just as Joel had predicted, Tanya didn't let go of his hand like he was the last man on earth she wouldn't let get away.

"Tanya! Let the man eat!" Gert implored as she kicked her under the table.

"Hey! Ouch!" Tanya exclaimed as she finally released her clammy grasp on Joel's hand, then looked at him with a ditzy grin.

"Well, dig in! Don't let everything get cold," Gert insisted as she poured their coffee, fresh from a carafe.

Joel added a small amount of cream to the dark roast coffee and drank half the cup before filling his plate with pancakes, potatoes, and bacon. Everything was delicious and had that old-fashioned taste only found at home. The fluffy pancakes melted in his mouth. And the potatoes were the perfect complement to the bacon, which was hickory smoked to perfection, cooked somewhere between crispy and chewy, falling under the category of just right.

Gert grinned and watched Joel gobble down his food like a hungry schoolboy who had just run a marathon. And then there was Tanya, who stared at Joel like she wanted to be his pancake.

"I always did enjoy seeing the boys eat! Chris and Kyle would always come over for breakfast on the weekends, and boy could they pack it away," Gert said with a heavy sigh as she added sugar to her coffee.

"Homemade food was hard to come by in my previous line of work," Joel said as he took another scrumptious bite of bacon.

"What you need is a woman who will cook for you," Tanya said, then took a sloppy sip of coffee, looked at Joel, and inappropriately licked her lips.

"Who do you have in mind? You don't cook!" Gert retorted as she kicked Tanya again.

"Ouch!" Tanya exclaimed and then leaned on the table, propping her chin in her hand and staring longingly at Joel. "I want a boyfriend."

Gert wasn't in the mood for Tanya's shenanigans, so she immediately shifted the conversation. "So Joel, did you enjoy hanging out with Portia last night?" she asked as she nonchalantly buttered her pancake.

Tanya's mouth flew open as she returned the favor, kicking Gert under the table.

"Ouch!" Gert squeaked, then slapped Tanya's arm.

A dopey grin spread across Joel's face just from hearing Portia's name, and he momentarily lost his ability to speak, almost choking on his pancake. Then he straightened his face to no expression at all. "Yes I did, Miss Gert."

Gert was beyond amused and elated by this. She laughed, then patted Joel on the hand. "Joel, have you been bitten by the love bug?"

Joel made no eye contact with the prying ladies as he stared at his plate, and he didn't do a good job of concealing his admiration for Portia because he felt his face heat up, burning red with a rosiness that only comes from falling in love.

Tanya was highly displeased by this, for she made another inappropriate lip pucker and then let out a fed-up, overly obnoxious huff like a middle school girl who didn't make the cheerleading team. All the while, Gert couldn't stop herself from poking fun at Tanya, but she did offer an excellent solution to Tanya's dilemma. "I think you should go out with Bubba," Gert suggested.

"Uh! Oh, come on! His name is Jonathan Timber, but he goes by Bubba. What the heck is up with that? There is no way I'm going out with that jeans-sagging, overly emotional twerp. No, I'm not dating Bob!"

Joel couldn't contain his enthusiasm for this conversation. He wanted Tanya to fixate on any other male but him. "Bubba seems like a great guy who would treat you like a queen. You would make a beautiful couple."

"Both of you can bite me! Especially you, Joel," Tanya replied with a wink that she thought was becoming, but Joel found disgusting.

At this point, Gert and Joel gave up trying to convince Tanya that Jonathan Timber was the catch of the century. They finished breakfast, and Joel helped the ladies clean up the dishes.

WHEN JOEL STEPPED OUT of his truck at the Aleutian Russian Orthodox Cathedral, sunlight sliced through large puffy clouds scattered throughout the blue sky and shone down on the cathedral, giving a celestial glow. A revitalizing breeze blew through Joel's hair while he looked up at the domes and was delighted to see the two eagles sitting on the golden crosses and glowing in the Sunday-morning sunlight. As he walked toward the doors, he smiled at the regal creatures and thought of Portia.

When Joel entered the nave, he was awestruck by the Russian Orthodox faith's holy peacefulness and magnificent artistry. Painted in glorious colors from floor to ceiling, the nave's walls depicted the life of Jesus Christ and presented the icons with large golden halos. In addition to the divinely painted walls, beautifully framed paintings of specific icons adorned the nave, providing stations for the congregation to venerate the icons and light candles.

Upfront, the framed icon of Jesus Christ rested on a stand beneath a prominent golden chandelier hanging from a high ceiling. Beyond the icon of Jesus, a small set of steps led to the iconostasis, a divider wall separating the nave from the altar, which portrayed large paintings of Jesus and the icons.

As Joel stood in the center of the nave, he relished in the

iconography and the talent that created these works of art to praise and honor God Almighty. Suddenly, a robust holy scent permeated the air, and beams of sunlight shone from the clear glass windows, illuminating swirling plumes of incense. Inhaling the glorious aroma and feeling the presence of God, Joel was wholly mesmerized as he looked up into one of the cathedral domes and saw the painted face of Jesus Christ smiling at him. At that moment, beautiful acapella singing echoed throughout the nave.

The divine scent of incense complemented the morning prayers being chanted from the choir loft, welcoming people as they tiptoed in from the narthex. Most people entered the nave and venerated the framed icons by crossing themselves, bowing, and kissing the icons' hands a few times; they also lit candles in the sand in front of the icons. However, when venerating the icon of Jesus Christ under the giant golden chandelier, people kissed His feet instead of His hands. Joel was so moved by being in the presence of God, inhaling the glorious scent of incense, and listening to the holy chants that he walked up to the icon of Jesus Christ, crossed himself, bowed, and kissed the Son of God's feet.

Joel walked to the right side of the room to stand and retreat to his private prayers since the Russian Orthodox congregation stands for the lengthy service. Only a few chairs were around the room's edges for those who couldn't stand for long periods of time.

Joel looked up just in time to see Portia in her stunning, conservative attire as she gracefully entered the nave. Who knew that she was the painted-up broad from the bar last night? This woman was in a complete state of consistent contradiction, and nevertheless, from the bar to the cathedral, Portia intrigued Joel. She wore a black dress with a matching lace headscarf, as was customary for Russian Orthodox women to do, in addition to not wearing lipstick when kissing the icons. Portia's makeup was light and conservative without blush or black eyeliner, but she still wore those ridiculously green contact lenses, which perfectly complemented her dyed-hair color. Despite the heavy sadness on her face, she was still the most beautiful woman Joel had ever seen in his life. With a despairing expression and wearing a black dress, Portia looked like she was in mourning, and this broke Joel's heart.

Portia approached the icon of Jesus Christ, crossed herself, bowed, swept her right hand to the floor, and kissed His feet. She lit candles at the remaining icons and venerated them as the holy chants echoed throughout the room and incense swirled in the Sunday-morning sunlight.

As Portia left the final icon, she looked at Joel and smiled, making him tingle from head to toe. Then she went to the narthex, where she picked up a little booklet and brought it over to him, whispering, "This is the entire Divine Liturgy, word for word, line by line. We know the Divine Liturgy by heart because we have been attending for so long."

"Thank you. That was very thoughtful of you," Joel quietly replied as he stared at her lovely face. "You look beautiful this morning."

Portia looked at Joel and blushed with a sad smile. "Thank you, Joel."

He wanted to do something to make the smile stay on her face and make her forget about whatever it was that made her despondent. Joel flipped through the booklet, pretending to read it intently, while nonchalantly whispering, "It's nice to see your face without all that extra stuff on it."

Portia promptly covered her mouth to keep her laugh from escaping her lips and echoing throughout the nave. Joel's plan worked because Portia smiled and blushed as she shook her head amusedly at him.

Joel was on a roll, so he looked at her with his debonair grin and said, "But I still don't know what color your eyes *really* are."

Portia closed her eyes and squeezed them tight so that Joel couldn't inspect them further. "They are green!" she exclaimed in a loud whisper.

"You really shouldn't fib in here," Joel replied as he tapped her elbow with his.

"I'm not fibbing. They are green. Right now," Portia insisted as she shrugged her shoulders and cracked a grin before retreating to her private prayers, thoughts, or whatever it was that went on in her wild brain.

Joel looked at her and smiled, his heart racing, feeling like the luckiest man alive. "God is good," he whispered as he flipped through the booklet, trying to figure out what page he should be on to follow along with the prayers. After a minute or two, he gave up when he couldn't find the right page, so he looked around the room. And lo and behold, here came Gunther, who didn't look half bad in his Sunday attire. With a gray suit and tie, a freshly shaven face, and slicked-back hair, Gunther had transformed from the grungy grump he was yesterday.

Gunther walked up to the icon of Jesus Christ, where he paused and bowed his head to pray before venerating the icon and kissing the Lord's feet. As he turned to walk away, Gunther noticed Gert across the room, where she lit a candle and venerated the icon of the Virgin Mary. A sad expression overtook his withered face as he walked over and stood next to Portia and Joel. "Hey green eyes. Hey Joel."

"Good morning, Captain," Joel respectfully replied.

Meanwhile, Bubba waddled around the nave, venerating the icons, and bumping into people. It wouldn't have been so bad if he wasn't holding a lit candle. He turned around and walked right into Tanya, and the edges of her headscarf caught fire. And hallelujah, Bubba was quick on his feet; he grabbed the scarf and clapped the fire out with his hands. Tanya looked at Bubba like, *Really? Did you really catch me on fire?* But then something miraculous happened. Tanya smiled at Bubba like he was some incredible warrior who had saved her life in a heroic act of courage. A beaming smile spread across Bubba's face, and he blushed. Bubba looked at Joel across the nave and gave him a thumbs up.

Good for you, Bubba! Cultivate this relationship with Tanya, so she leaves me alone, Joel thought as he chuckled and reciprocated with a concurring thumbs up.

As he stood amid his new friends, Joel smiled while he looked around the holy room, filling with the fine folks of Aleutia, coming together to worship on this beautiful morning. Nearly everyone Joel met last night was there, along with several other people he didn't know, but who were well acquainted with Gunther and the rest of the Alexandria's crew. Kirk and Hank weren't in attendance, but Polly and Nick most certainly were as the lovebirds walked around the nave holding hands while stars twinkled in their eyes. And young love was blossoming all around, for Alicia and Denny were close together, taking turns venerating the icons and kissing their holy hands. Meanwhile, Lora attended the Divine Liturgy with her balding husband this fine Sunday morning as Dr. Sampson flew solo, watching Lora intently from where he stood in the narthex.

Reverend Thomas and the deacons led the beautiful and lengthy service. Joel did his best to follow along with the litanies, antiphons, lessons, hymns, and prayers as the glorious scent of incense wafted through the room and swirled in the sunlight. The choir sang in the choir loft, like angels singing in Heaven.

When the service was over, the congregation departed quietly, and Portia remained close to Joel's side as they exited the cathedral. She paused and stared at the cemetery solemnly before walking toward the parking lot. Joel knew she was sad, but didn't want to pry. They walked quietly to her truck.

Suddenly, Joel heard a loud screech high in the sky. He turned around, and his heart fluttered when he saw the two eagles still sitting on the golden crosses. Joel gently tapped his elbow to Portia's and pointed to the regal creatures on the Domes of Heaven.

A smile replaced the solemn expression on Portia's face as she looked at the eagles. "Oh, wow! I love eagles so much. They are so majestic and look so wise, like they know things that we don't. I've always only seen one sitting there, and now there are two," Portia said as she looked at Joel.

"And now there are two," Joel repeated her words as he stared into her fake green eyes.

Portia's smile didn't last long because sorrow overtook her face again. *Why is she so sad?* Joel wondered. Then he opened the door of Portia's obscenely pink truck and offered his hand to her as she climbed into the driver's seat.

"Thank you. Are you coming to the memorial ceremony? We'd like for you to be there," Portia inquired.

"Yes, thank you. Bubba told me about it last night," Joel replied, trying not to blush because Portia wanted him to go too.

"Good. You can follow me to the community center. I'll show you the way, sailor," Portia offered.

"Thank you. I will do that. And hey, have I told you that your smile is beautiful?" Joel charmingly asked. Portia smiled and blushed at Joel's flirtations, and he felt tingly inside as he stared into her overly green eyes. "I'll see you in a few, huh?" Joel said as he closed her door.

As he went to his truck, Joel looked at the cathedral domes to see the eagles once more, and Portia's words echoed in his mind, "I've always only seen one sitting there, and now there are two." And with that last sweet echoing phrase, the two eagles flew away into the sunlight, over the bay, and toward the majestic snowcapped mountains of crystalized beauty, glowing in the Sunday sunlight.

At that moment Joel remembered that his name was engraved between two eagles on the bracelet Adoncia had given him. With this realization, he smiled as he stared at the mountains, and he whispered, "God is good." God is good indeed.

Chapter 7. *Memorial*

J oel followed Portia's pink pickup to the Aleutia Community Center. He immediately rushed over to her truck to open the door. However, she had all the windows down and was blaring a 1980s power ballad as she took off her headscarf and put on some lipstick. Somewhat amused by this, Joel patiently waited until Portia finished, rolled up the windows, and turned off the engine. She smiled at him as she ran her fingers through her hair. Then Joel opened the door and offered his hand to help her out of the truck.

"Thank you. Aren't you cavalier?" Portia replied, slurring her words like she was under the influence of something. She had a wild-eyed look and reeked of an herb mixed with an overly potent perfume.

"Uh, Portia, that is quite an interesting scent you are wearing," Joel boldly stated as he tried not to wrinkle his nose.

"Oh, so first, you don't like my music, and now you don't like my perfume. I see how it is." Portia grinned. "Follow me, sailor. I'll show you the way."

Joel walked with Portia into the gymnasium, where jazz music played softly, and the pleasant scent of a generous buffet greeted them. A large projection screen was the focal point of the room, with beautiful floral arrangements beneath it. Many round tables were beautifully set, labeled by fishing vessels, local businesses, and special guests.

"There's the one for the Alexandria," Portia said as she pointed to a table toward the back. Then they walked over to it, and Portia hung her purse on a chair.

"Here, let me get that for you," Joel insisted as he pulled the chair out for her.

"Thank you," Portia responded. She sighed, and a numb expression overtook her face as she stared across the room at the flower arrangements.

Joel sat down next to her and then whispered in her ear, "Everything will be okay."

Portia looked at Joel appreciatively. This beautiful lady of the bar had Joel's heart in the palm of her hand. And Joel couldn't contain his feelings, so he reached for her hand and kissed it.

Gert and Tanya sat down at the table as well. Gert placed both hands over her heart and said, "Ohh," as she watched the sweet exchange between Portia and Joel. However, Tanya didn't share Gert's enthusiasm because she still wanted to be Joel's pancake.

Meanwhile, a familiar cough echoed throughout the room while the happy expression on Gert's face changed to disgust as Gunther slowly approached the table and sat down between Gert and Joel. Before his butt hit the chair, he had a coughing fit, frothy and spumy to the utmost of nastiness. Joel put his hand over his mouth as if he were holding back a heave, Portia's eyes bugged out, Tanya grimaced, and Gert looked at Gunther like she was getting ready to deck him.

"Do you mind?" Gert growled.

Gunther swallowed hard with a wounded-puppy look on his face. Then he looked at Gert affectionately. "Sorry. You look beautiful, my love."

"Just because you took a shower this morning, shaved your face, and put on a clean suit, doesn't detract from you being a hacking and gagging slob! You do know the drugstore has medicines that can help with that, don't you? Yet you refuse to quit smoking and drinking. You don't do a thing to help yourself! Nothing!" Gert angrily snapped.

"I don't know about those things at the drugstore. I need you for that," Gunther lamented as he tried to rest his arm around the back of Gert's chair. She promptly pushed his arm off, and Gunther looked at her again with the wounded-puppy look.

"Hello friends!" Bubba jovially interrupted as he claimed the chair next to Tanya.

"Hello, Mr. Timber," Tanya replied as she looked at him, stuck out her chest, and puckered her lips.

"Wow! This is a new development!" Gunther shockingly exclaimed.

"Hey, Gunther, check this out," Bubba said as he opened his jacket slightly and pointed to a large, shiny belt buckle, showing Gunther that he was wearing a belt and wouldn't be needing any tie wraps. Gunther was amused; he gave Bubba two thumbs up.

The gymnasium grew louder as more people arrived. Joel looked around the room and then turned to Portia and smiled. But she was lost in her thoughts with that numb expression and still reeked of that herb-perfume concoction. *What the heck is that?* Joel wondered as he crinkled his nose.

Polly and Nick arrived and sat by Bubba. Gert, Tanya, and even Gunther smiled at them. However, there's always one or two people who bring drama and discord with them everywhere they go, and for the Alexandria's crew, this category certainly belonged to Kirk and Hank. Watching the two of them arrogantly swagger to the table pretty much said it all.

Both jerks cleaned up well and wore a suit and tie. Kirk looked pretty darn good, capitalizing on his dark and mysterious appearance, but still was nothing more than a tall, good-looking jerk. Honestly, any woman in the room would acknowledge his handsomeness, but Joel was still much better looking.

Kirk swaggered up to Portia, kissed her cheek, and sat beside her, while Hank sat on his other side by Polly. Gert and Gunther glared at Kirk, and Gunther stood up like he was going to take a swat at him. Gert patted Gunther's hand, and he sat back down, completely overwhelmed and overly hopeful because she had touched him. Then Gert realized what she had done was merely a reflex, and she looked at her hand like he had contaminated it. She frantically took hand sanitizer out of her purse and gave herself a generous squirt.

Kirk leaned over to Portia. "Joel doesn't look as impressive without his squid suit on."

"Kirk! You take that back right now!" Portia exclaimed.

Anger started in Joel's toes and burned up to his head. He wanted to tell Kirk to buzz off. However, he certainly wasn't going to retaliate by stooping to Kirk's level, and a memorial ceremony certainly wasn't the place for a brawl. Once again, Joel turned his cheek and looked the other way.

"Come on Kirk. Let's go grab an expresso from the coffee bar," Hank insisted as he stood up, taking the initiative to get Kirk away from the table for a bit.

"Yes, I guess that's going to be the strongest beverage they will have here," Kirk agreed and stood up too.

"He's just a miserable human being," Bubba began after they walked away. "Kirk was a Marine who went out on Other Than Honorable discharge. No one knows what happened. He won't talk about it. My guess is he was fighting because he doesn't get along with anybody. Even he and Hank get into it sometimes. Kirk's jealous of your accomplishments, Joel."

Joel nodded his head because everything now made sense about Kirk. "The Marine Corps supports the Navy. One can't exist without the other. We transported a lot of Marines on the USS Roland. I never saw a need for interservice rivalry. We will protect each other against the enemy. We joined to serve, not to belittle each other," Joel replied.

"Well said, Captain Layton!" Bubba concurred.

"Thank you, but it's just Joel now," he quietly replied.

The sweetest response of all came from Portia. She smiled and whispered in Joel's ear, "Yes, you should be very proud of your accomplishments. Are you not used to being called by your first name, Joel?"

That was like music to Joel's ears; hearing Portia say his name made him feel so lucky. "No, I'm not used to hearing my first name," Joel whispered back as he stared into her fake green eyes.

"You will get used to it, Joel. I promise," Portia said, then smiled.

A BELL RINGING quieted down the noisy room, signaling for the townsfolk to take their seats. Kirk and Hank returned with expressos, and Kirk smiled and winked at Portia as he sat down. Joel did his best to conceal his disdain, which he would have to do since Kirk was relief captain and they would be spending weeks together at sea.

The event began as Denny walked up front to the podium microphone while Alicia smiled at him from the front table. "On behalf of the Port of Aleutia Visitors' Bureau, thank you for attending our Watermen's Memorial Ceremony. But first, we must eat. As you can see, we have a delicious buffet prepared for you, so please help yourselves and enjoy this time together. After we eat, City Manager Lora Yazzie will begin the ceremony. God bless you all."

The meal went as expected. Bubba followed Tanya around like a puppy, and he piled food a foot high on his plate to the point that he would need a few extra tie wraps to assist his belt in holding up his extra-large, pleated dress pants. And it was no surprise that Polly and Nick spent more time staring at each other than eating, unlike the Alexanders. Gunther stared at his redheaded wife while she did her best to ignore him, except for cringing when he coughed. Meanwhile, Kirk and Hank told obnoxious jokes that no one wanted to hear, making everyone despise them a little bit more. And then there was Portia, who ate like a bird with a solemn expression on her face.

After 45 minutes, the bell rang again, and Lora began the ceremony. "Thank you for joining us today. In a few short weeks, the red king crab season begins, and after the holidays, you will head back out to catch those snow crabs. God bless all of you for braving the Bering Sea and putting food on our tables, and God bless your families for holding down the fort while you're away. Before our fleet departs for the red king crab season, please join us on October 15th for the Blessing of the Fleet, where we come together to pray for our brothers and sisters. After this past year, we experienced, all too well, the risks involved in this line of work," Lora said as she changed the slide on the presentation screen.

She continued, "Last year, five million pounds of red king crabs were caught, significantly less than the previous year of 16 million pounds. Our sailors were determined to make up for it during the January opilio season, and they most certainly did so by catching 15 million pounds of snow crabs, despite the arctic storm. While the catch was plentiful, it was wrought with tragedy as we lost five beautiful people from the Port of Aleutia. Earlier this year, their names were added to the Watermen's Memorial at the cathedral, but we also wanted to have a ceremony for us to come together once again, honor them, and let all of you know that we are here for you. We put together a biography for each person we lost this year. We also had a bronze plaque made for each family. If we stick together, we will heal together. We love you, and our loved ones will live on in our hearts forever."

Lora's words pierced Joel's heart like an arrow. Having grown up in a watermen's community along the Chesapeake Bay, Joel knew the dangers watermen face daily. He remembered the day his uncle died when a patent tong capsized his boat, the day his neighbor drowned after falling overboard, and then that terrible day when his parents died.

Lora began the biographies with Billy Gorman, an engineer on the Windswept Belle. Billy had been good friends with Gunther and Kyle since high school, and the three of them were known as the Prankster Triplets since the day they let 100 bairdi crabs loose in the high school as a senior prank. Over the years, Billy was active in the church and enjoyed volunteering at the community center. His wife became a widow, and his three daughters became fatherless when an acetylene tank caused an explosion when the Windswept Belle was 200 miles offshore. Billy was friends with Gordon Skenandore, a deckhand on the Aleutian Hero. Like Billy, Gordon also volunteered his time at the community center and was passionate about working with children. Also, like Billy, Gordon left behind his wife and two small boys after he fell overboard, and his body washed away, lost forever.

The city of Aleutia was also devastated to lose Georgia Boon, the fifth woman in Aleutia to work on a deep-sea fishing vessel. Georgia was a relief captain and engineer on the Bering Sea Lady, where she fell overboard and died of hypothermia in rough seas. Georgia left behind her husband and teenage daughter, who courageously planned to follow in her mother's footsteps and work on the Bering Sea Lady after high school.

Joel's heart sank as he heard the heart-wrenching accounts, reminding him of being an 11-year-old boy in an orphanage, crying himself to sleep for the first three months he was there. He knew how Billy, Gordon, and Georgia's families felt. Joel's pain never disappeared, but time helped it become more manageable.

He thought of Gunther, who hadn't only lost his brother and his son, but who also lost his close friends Billy and Gordon as well. The Aleutian community was so close-knit that they lost a family member when someone died. Once again, Joel's heart sank as he looked around the Alexandria's table, where everyone was so sad, knowing what was coming next; Lora was getting ready to talk about Kyle and Chris.

"On the first voyage for the Alexandria, we lost Kyle and Chris Alexander in an unspeakable tragedy," Lora began.

These words hit the Alexandria's crew like a lightning strike. It was as if a black thundercloud had appeared over the table, bringing back the pain and terror of that horrific day. Tanya and Gunther put their arms around Gert. Numb to the point of paleness, Portia leaned back in her chair and sighed as she shook her head from side to side, like she wouldn't let the words enter her ears.

Lora changed the slide on the screen to the same photo printed with the newspaper article hanging at the Port House. The Alexandria's crew was with Gert, Chris's wife and son, and Katerina. Lora paused and stared at the picture before continuing, "Kyle was the owner and captain of the Alexandria, and he dearly loved working with his brother Gunther and nephew Chris, who was a deckhand. Chris loved his family more than life itself. During the summer, he and his cousin Katerina would take a boat out to Orlov Bay and watch grizzly bears fishing along the shoreline. Chris was also a licensed pilot who gave aerial tours of Aleutia when he wasn't at sea. Chris's greatest joy was his family, his wife Lizzie, and their son Elijah, who moved away shortly after his passing. Gunther and Gert, please come forward and accept this plaque as a memory of your son and know that we love you and are here for you."

Tears streamed down Gert's grieving mother's face as she and Gunther stood up. Gunther walked with his arm around Gert as if he were keeping her from falling. Lora hugged them both, and then Denny handed Gert the plaque. The room was silent as they walked back to the table and sat down. Gunther attempted to put his arm around Gert again, but she shrugged it off and slapped it away. Even through her grief, she was still mad at him.

Lora continued, "Along with his brothers Gunther and Ralph, Kyle began Alexander Enterprises in Washington State. Kyle enjoyed working on the Bering Sea with Gunther and his nephew Chris. Kyle was a bit of a daredevil and enjoyed skydiving from Chris's airplane during aerial tours, which sometimes scared the tourists. He also liked to push the limits, going farther into Satan's Expanse than all the other fishing vessels. Kyle's greatest joy was his daughter Katerina, with whom he spent hours watching the Northern Lights when they weren't playing in their family band with Gunther, Gert, and Chris. Kyle always had a love for sharing music with his family. Kyle left behind Katerina, to whom he left ownership of the Alexandria. Katerina, will you please come forward."

Joel was immediately intrigued. *Katerina is here? Gert and Gunther's niece is here? Why isn't she sitting at the table with us? Where is she?* he wondered as he looked around the room for her. Then the sound of Portia pushing her chair back caught Joel's attention.

Completely expressionless, Portia painstakingly stood, and the room grew eerily silent as she slowly walked up front. Paralyzed, Joel watched her as the puzzle pieces fell into place. The brunette, who wore green contact lenses, thick eyeliner, and skimpy leather outfits with thigh-high boots, was really a blue-eyed blonde. Portia of Portia's Port House was Katerina Alexander, owner of the Alexandria and a shareholder in Alexander Enterprises.

As Portia approached Lora and Denny, Joel's heart burst with empathy and bled for her. *How much devastation is one person supposed to endure in such a short period of time? My God, she is brave,* Joel thought as he watched Portia gracefully stand in front of the entire town.

"Katerina, your father is dearly missed. Please know that we love you and are here for you," Lora said, then hugged her.

Denny handed Portia the plaque. She stared at it briefly before clutching it to her chest. Portia nodded appreciatively at Lora and Denny, then turned and slowly walked back to the table. Joel pushed her chair to the side for her to sit. Instead, Portia reached for her purse, and quickly left the room.

Like an anchor was strapped to Joel's heart, it sank to the floor and went kerplunk. He and Gunther stood simultaneously, both with the intent of going after Portia. Gunther made eye contact with Joel and nodded, letting Joel know that it was okay for him to go.

WHEN JOEL ENTERED THE LOBBY, he saw Portia sitting on the left side of a sofa in front of a window with a spectacular view. With the same numb expression, she continued clutching the plaque as she took a long sip from a silver flask, which Joel knew had to be full of brandy.

He quietly sat down on the opposite end from Portia. Trying to be clever and make her smile, Joel stared at her until she looked at him, and then he quickly shifted his eyes in the other direction, like *No, I wasn't looking at you.* Portia looked at him, like *What the heck?* Then she gazed out the window. Joel moved down the sofa a few inches, stared at her until she looked at him, and looked away again. He scooted closer, then pretended to accidentally sit on her. "Oh, I'm so sorry," he said as he sat beside her, dropped his arm around her shoulders, and whispered, "You look like you need a hug."

Joel's plan had the desired effect because Portia turned toward him and chuckled.

"There's that beautiful smile," Joel began. "So, I'm guessing your eyes are blue, and your hair is blonde."

She nodded as the smile left her face, and she took another long sip from the flask, then offered it to Joel.

Oh, why not? he thought as he took the flask and took a quick sip of brandy, immediately regretting this decision because the liquor scalded his throat and burned its way down to his stomach. Joel handed the flask back to her and then pulled her close. "You know what?"

Portia didn't say anything and continued clutching the plaque. Joel reached for her hand and whispered in her ear, "I think you are incredibly brave."

Portia's face twitched, and she shook her head as she disagreed with him while fighting back the tears.

"You don't have to be rough and tough all the time, you know?" Joel sweetly said as he pressed his cheek against hers.

"You don't have to be so blunt!" Portia shot back at him with a whole lot of attitude.

Joel saw through her charade and knew this was merely a defense mechanism to detract from her true feelings. He took a deep breath as he continued holding Portia close. She needed to know that he truly understood what she was going through—the devastation of losing a parent tragically at sea. Joel squeezed her hand and whispered again with his lips touching her ear, "My father was a waterman on the Chesapeake Bay. My mother went oystering with him one day, and a nor'easter blew in. They were dredging, and the boat capsized. A social worker picked me up from school and told me my parents were dead. I was 11 years old and was sent to an orphanage in Baltimore until I was 18. After that, I had nowhere to go, so I joined the Navy. I understand what you are feeling. Believe me. You are incredibly brave, Katerina Alexander."

Portia turned, so she and Joel were face to face. She squeezed his hand as she stared into his eyes. "Joel, I think you are brave too," she whispered as her eyes glistened.

Joel took a deep breath and gazed into her fake green eyes and at her beautiful face, once again feeling a connection with her that he had never felt with any other person.

But Portia's grief was still fresh and got the best of her. She reached for the flask and got ready to take another swig of brandy. This time, Joel gently touched her hand, then took the flask. "That won't help anything, you know?"

"It's numbing. It works just fine," Portia snapped.

Before Joel could respond, the gym doors opened, and the townsfolk began leaving the ceremony. And Gunther was the first person to check on Portia. He walked over to the sofa, where she and Joel were snuggled up close. Portia's green eyes lit up when she saw her uncle, and she stood up to greet him, still clutching the plaque close to her heart. She finally released her grasp on the plaque and held it so both Gunther and Joel could see it. Bronze etchings of Kyle and Chris's faces were next to the words, *In Loving Memory of Kyle Alexander and Chris Alexander.* A sad smile spread across Portia's face as she looked down at the exquisite artwork commemorating her father and cousin.

Gunther swallowed hard. "Are you going to hang it at the Port House?"

"Yes," Portia softly replied.

Gunther smiled at his niece, then ran his hand down the back of her head as he kissed her forehead. "I love you, kid."

"Kid?" Portia exclaimed as she shook her head and laughed. "Yeah, well, I love you too, and so does Aunt Gert. She won't admit it," Portia said as she waved at Gert and Tanya as they exited the gym. "You should go talk to her."

Gunther nodded at Portia like this was a great idea, then walked over to his wife. Instead of giving him a warm reception, Gert glared at him; then she blew a kiss to Portia and winked at Joel. After that, Tanya put her arm around Gert condescendingly, and they walked away.

Gunther flung his hands in the air and bellowed, "I need some ganja," before succumbing to another hacking and gagging fit from straining his voice too much. He whipped out the vape pen, took a few hits, and then took out a cigarette and a lighter as he stomped out the door.

Once again, Joel was in disbelief. Yesterday, he had monkey dung on his jacket, and today, his new captain just announced that he needed ganja. What was next? Someone extraordinary was next, and he was standing right beside her. Joel looked at his watch and saw it was nearly 3 p.m., and he pondered for a minute or two, thinking of something clever that would make Portia want to spend the rest of the day with him. He looked into her eyes and began, "So, would you like to…"

However, Portia had already concocted a plan of her own, for she rudely cut him off before he could ask her out to dinner. "I have a place I would like to show you today. Would you like to go?"

Joel felt tingly inside, and his cheeks blushed. "Okay. What do you have in mind?" he asked with a suave smile.

By this point, Portia was back to being her pushy, semi-rude, overly spontaneous self. "You will have to wait and see. Change into clothes and shoes that can get dirty and meet me at the Port House in an hour."

Joel was immediately intrigued. "Well, okay then. Sounds like a plan."

"Good!" Portia exclaimed. Without saying goodbye, scram, buzz off, or go to hell, she spun on her high heels and disappeared into the crowd exiting the gym, which for Joel, triggered the memory of Adoncia disappearing into the sea of bustling Gypsy Market shoppers.

Chapter 8. *Spithead*

Joel promptly returned to The Harbor Inn and changed his clothes. Then he stopped by the Aleutian Grocery Store, where he bought a picnic basket, filling it with a small party platter, a bottle of wine, a bottle opener, and two wine glasses.

As he pulled into the Port House parking lot, he chuckled as he parked next to Portia's pink truck. With the picnic basket in his hand, Joel opened his door and got out. Then a foul stench punched him in the face. "What the heck is that?" he exclaimed with a gag, then put his hand over his mouth.

Then Portia flowed down the apartment steps like a model on a runway. She wore a tight black turtleneck that hugged her chest perfectly and complemented her skin-tight jeans, showcasing her firmly lifted derriere. Waterproof-camouflage hiking boots adorned her feet.

Portia flashed Joel an alluring smile. "Get in my truck. I'm driving."

If Joel hadn't found her so intriguing and beautiful, he would've been offended by her rudeness. Instead, he laughed and asked, "What's on the agenda?" All the while, he wondered if he should inquire about the foul stench outside her restaurant.

"Spithead!" Portia exclaimed, throwing her hands onto her hips.

"I beg your pardon! That was abrupt!" Joel scoffed, thinking that she had called him an uncouth name and that maybe Bubba was right—that Katerina was gone, and Portia was crazy.

She laughed as she sexily flipped her hair around, and Joel immediately went weak in the knees.

"We are going to Spithead," Portia said.

Joel looked at her confusedly. He didn't understand, and Portia, being her pain-in-the-butt self, didn't feel the need to explain.

Suddenly, Joel heard the loud banging sound in the dumpster again. "Did you hear that? You have the loudest dumpster I have ever seen or heard."

"Oh, that's nothing." Portia chuckled as she shrugged it off. "Get in my truck. I'll drive."

"I could drive, you know," Joel retorted. He wanted to be the one driving on their date; at least, that's how he envisioned it.

"Okay, fine! Have it your way," Portia said as she opened the driver's side door of her absurdly pink truck, shimmied herself in, and slid over to the passenger side. "Fine, you drive! No problem."

"No, I meant my truck," Joel said as the foul stench intensified the closer he got to her pickup. Once again, he placed his hand over his mouth.

Portia grinned, trying to contain her amusement. Joel looked at her and raised one eyebrow as he climbed into the driver's seat of the pink dream machine and set the picnic basket on the backseat. As soon as he closed the door, Portia tossed him the keys, and he laughed.

"Do I amuse you?" Portia asked with her all-too-sexy grin that made Joel melt into a puddle of mush.

"You intrigue me," Joel replied as he started the engine. While his truck engine roared, her diesel engine purred like a sleek panther on the prowl. Joel certainly appreciated the fact that Portia enjoyed a nice ride, but her hot pink color choice, not so much.

As Joel put the truck in reverse, Portia turned on the radio, and a familiar oldie song came on, providing the perfect background music to begin their excursion to wherever they were going. Thanks to Portia, Joel had no clue. But she was hot, so he didn't care.

"Pull out of here and turn right. Then follow the road to the end, about four miles. Feel free to drive like a maniac. Get reckless!" Portia instructed, then blew a string of hair out of her face.

With a big-fat smile, Joel drove slowly and responsibly down Port Road because the road was in terrible shape. He also enjoyed taking his time, going slowly to enjoy looking out the window, and making his time with Portia last even longer.

She sang along to the oldie song, then laughed like Joel did something hilarious. "What are you doing?" Portia rudely asked as she ran her fingers through her hair.

"Uh, driving," Joel sarcastically replied.

Suddenly, Portia unfastened her seatbelt, slid down the seat next to him, and whispered in his ear, "Seriously, Joel, you drive like a turtle crawls."

Joel grinned and leaned his face against hers, feeling her skin's warmth and inhaling the pleasant scent of perfume. He gently rubbed his cheek against hers. "What's your hurry? What is going on at the spit place? Are we going to be late for something?"

"Spithead," Portia corrected him.

"Oh, whatever!" Joel scoffed, then laughed.

"You will have to wait and see!" Portia responded as she slid back to the passenger seat and buckled up.

Despite Portia's insistence, Joel continued driving at a turtle's pace. He enjoyed driving slowly on the Alaskan backroads, appreciating the mountains on the left and the fishing vessels anchored along the shoreline on the right, where the Bering Sea Lady, Aleutian Hero, and Windswept Belle gleamed in the Sunday-afternoon sunshine. Meanwhile, Portia sang along to the radio, switching between country and Rock & Roll stations like she couldn't make up her mind. But again, she was hot, so Joel didn't care.

"We are coming up on the Port of Aleutia Wharf," Portia began as she turned down the music as they passed a few buildings, a crane, and stacks of cargo-shipping containers. "A cargo vessel comes from Seattle every Friday, bringing everything you could imagine, vehicles, boats, food, fishing supplies, and so forth. When I was little, my dad brought me down here to watch the crane unload the cargo."

"That sounds like great memories with your dad. He seemed well loved by the community," Joel said.

"Yes, he was," Portia sadly replied.

Joel looked at Portia and smiled. The truck hit a pothole and jolted him, so he quickly gripped the wheel with both hands and kept his eyes straight ahead as they drove by a ferry service, refueling stations, floating docks, barges, and repair shops along the water's edge. Fuel tanks, propane tanks, tractors, excavators, tractor trailers, flatbeds, metal scraps, concrete barricades, huge rocks, and endless crab pots cluttered both sides of the road, like Captain's Way.

The clutter diminished as Port Road veered away from the large mountain on the left and turned into a narrow, dirt road on a cape, extending into Eagle Bay. Joel was in a waterman's paradise, for the sun shone so intensely that the bay looked like a sea of melting gold. On the other side of the bay, large and majestic clouds floated effortlessly above snow-capped mountains.

"It's all so very beautiful, isn't it?" Portia asked. Then she flashed Joel that oh-so-sexy, make-a-man-go-weak-in-the-knees smile.

"Yes, you are," he wittily replied.

"Thank you, but I was referring to the scenery," Portia said as she blushed.

"So was I," Joel answered with a chuckle.

THEY ENTERED AN EMPTY PARKING LOT next to an extensive marina, and Joel parked next to a small shack with an old wooden sign that read, "Spithead Dock." Other than the marina, the shack, and a trashcan, there wasn't anything else at the spit place.

"I hope you're ready!" Portia exclaimed as she abruptly jumped out of the truck and slammed the door shut.

"I've never been more ready for anything," Joel whispered as he got out of the truck. And lo and behold, the foul odor punched him again. *I thought we had left that behind at the Port House. What the heck does she have in the truck bed?* Joel wondered as he coughed and almost retched.

To Joel's surprise, Portia seemed unaffected by the stench, like she didn't even notice it. "Welcome to the Spithead Cape of Unalaska, Alaska!" she said.

Immediately, Joel saw personality similarities between Portia and Gunther; however, Joel feared he would duplicate Gunther's hacking and gagging if he stayed near the reeking odor any longer.

To hold back a heave, Joel walked away from the truck, trying to escape the vile scent. "Spithead is beautiful. Thank you for bringing me here," he replied as he took a deep breath of clean air.

Besides the pleasant sound of water slapping the shore and the gentle whirring of a brisk breeze, the Spithead Cape was peacefully silent and was a perfect place to spend a Sunday afternoon.

"What are we going to do at this spit place?" Joel asked in hopes of getting farther away from Portia's stinky pickup truck.

"Spithead," Portia responded with a grin.

Suddenly, a bird screeched in the distance, and a giant smile spread across Portia's puffy lips as she looked up to the sky with stars gleaming in her artificially green eyes. "It's time."

"Time for what?" Joel inquired.

She winked at him and then opened the rear passenger door of her malodorous truck.

What in the world is she doing? Joel wondered as he watched Portia put on a thick pair of navy-blue coveralls, a welding helmet, and insulated electrician's gloves, which were made of thick rubber and extended up to her biceps. Joel couldn't contain his curiosity between the foul odor coming from the truck and Portia's weird outfit. "Going to do some welding? Or perhaps perform a high-voltage shutdown? What's getting ready to happen here at this spit place? I mean Spithead!" Joel asked as he walked over to the truck, and the rotten stench whacked him in the face again.

"Get your camera ready but keep a safe distance. Don't follow me. I don't care how much you want to follow me. Don't do it!" Portia instructed as she went to the back of the truck, put the tailgate down, took out a large plastic container with a lid, and set it on the ground. She looked at Joel and winked before pulling the welding helmet down over her face and bending over to pick up the heavy container.

Joel couldn't stand by and let a woman lift something heavy in his presence. "Do you need help with that?" he asked as he rushed over to retrieve the container from Portia's grasp, almost hurling up his lunch, realizing that the container was the source of the effluvium.

"I got this! Stay back! Get your camera ready!" Portia's muffled voice instructed beneath the welding helmet as she struggled to lift the container and then lumbered her way over to the shoreline, where she all but dropped the container as she set it down.

By now, the high-pitched screeching came closer as each successive screech became louder than the last. Portia turned around to face Joel, gave him two thumbs up, took the lid off the container, and tossed it to the side. Then suddenly, the unexpected happened. Joel couldn't have predicted this one if he had tried. Five magnificent bald eagles swooped and dive-bombed Portia's head. *No wonder she is wearing a welding helmet,* Joel thought.

Not too shabby for a non-techie cell phone user, he brought up the camera in record time and took pictures and videos as more eagles descended, flying in from across Eagle Bay and down the nearby mountain. After about five minutes, Joel counted 25 eagles of various sizes and colors. Some eagles had white plumage on their heads, while others had blackish-brown feathers. The majestic monsters fought vigorously over the container, grabbing stinky fish with their talons and tearing into them with their hooked beaks. Screaming at each other and stealing each other's supper, the giant birds knocked each other off the sides of the container.

Joel had traveled the world, seeing places that most people only dream about, but nothing compared to this incredible moment. He could hardly fathom being on an Alaskan cape, watching over two dozen bald eagles eating together.

Portia slowly walked backward, trying not to disturb the eating frenzy, and ensuring that none of the eagles followed her. Once she reached a safe enough distance, she turned around, took off the welding helmet and gloves, and threw them into the back of the truck, which thankfully no longer smelled. Meanwhile, Joel watched Portia's every move in amazement.

"Aren't the eagles magnificent?" she asked while the sun shimmered on her hair, illuminating reddish-purple undertones.

"They aren't the only ones," Joel flirtatiously replied as he grinned at her.

Portia smiled as she watched the eagles. "People around here either love the eagles or hate them. I absolutely adore them! The eagles build nests in the trees in town and get defensive over them. They even attack people, but it's all about protecting their babies. I'd be envious to have a momma bird like that," Portia said as the smile left her face.

Joel paused from watching the hungry eagles and turned toward Portia, realizing she had never spoken of her mother until now. "You didn't have a momma bird like that?" he asked.

"No, I did not. She left us when I was five," Portia said as she stared at the hungry eagles, still vying for the last few bites of fish.

Joel's heart dropped when he heard this. *How could anybody leave Portia? How could a parent abandon a child? Portia is everything ridiculous and beautiful, all rolled into one. She is so deserving of love,* Joel thought. He had had a wonderful mother and couldn't comprehend another mother not being as wonderful and as loving as his mother was to him.

Portia turned toward Joel, so they were face to face, and she blushed when she looked at him, which made him blush as well. She jumped up on the tailgate, and Joel promptly sat next to her.

Neither of them said anything for a few minutes as they watched clouds roll in over the mountains and drop down into the bay with the rising fog. Joel breathed in the sweet and salty Alaskan air as he looked over at Portia while she brushed her hair behind her ear to keep the wind from blowing it into her face.

By now, the eagles had eaten nearly all the fish, and Portia and Joel watched the regal creatures fly away, a few at a time, until two eagles remained together along the shoreline as their white feathers glistened beneath the Sunday-afternoon sun.

"They love fish, so I buy a tub of bait a few times a week, come down here, and feed them," Portia said.

She made Joel's heart feel like it could burst forth with a tsunami of diamonds. He leaned closer to her, and her rosy cheek warmed his face. Joel grinned and looked at Portia, smiling at the two eagles. "You're so amazing and thoughtful, spending time and money to give these eagles a meal a few times a week. Thanks for bringing me here. I've never seen anything like it. I'm used to only seeing one or two bald eagles occasionally. Seeing this many at one time is simply breathtaking."

Portia smiled, happy that he shared her appreciation for these magnificent birds. "Most of the US's bald eagle population is here in Alaska. Did you notice the different sizes and colors? The female is larger than the male. The brownish-black ones are immature eagles and don't reach maturity until they are five. That's when they get their white feathers, and their beaks turn yellow. Their talons are very sharp for killing their prey; that's why I wear thick gloves and a welding helmet. They also have a hook on the end of their beaks for ripping open their fish, rabbit, or whatever they catch to eat. They are fierce and majestic, and I love them. Usually, one eagle remains here when all the others fly away, but now there are two, just like the eagles on the crosses."

"And now there are two," Joel repeated as he leaned into Portia, gently pressing his shoulder against hers.

One of the eagles happily screeched, and Portia and Joel watched the eagle couple bask in the sunshine along the rocky shoreline. Both eagles had white plumage on their heads and bright yellow beaks, indicating that they were mature. They also didn't fight over the last few fish like the rest of the flock did during the eating frenzy. These two were different. The smaller eagle held a piece of fish in his talons and lifted it toward his majestic lady's beak. She eloquently tore into the fish, took a dainty bite, and then let out a loud, happy screech again. After that, the male took a bite and reciprocated with a similar screech.

"They mate for life," Portia said as she turned her face toward Joel's, making his heart pound, and his skin tingle.

Joel moved closer to Portia and cupped her face in his hands, feeling the warmth and softness of her porcelain cheeks as he stared into her eyes. With his left hand on her cheek, he gently slid his right hand up the back of her head before running his fingers through her luscious locks of brunette hair. He gently caressed her cheek with the back of his hand before cupping her face again as he slowly moved closer. A radical explosion of warmth permeated Joel's body as his lips touched Portia's, filling him with more passion than he had ever felt in his life. A gentle Alaskan breeze swirled around them, the water slapped the shore, and the two eagles preened each other's plumage.

The world came briefly to a stop as Joel's kisses extended beyond Portia's lips, passionately landing all over her face. She adored this sweet act of affection because her hands made their way up Joel's neck and into his hair as she kissed his face before her lips found their way back to his.

Unfortunately, this heated moment only went so far since they were sitting on a tailgate, and the truck bed didn't have a mattress. After a few minutes, Portia and Joel came up for air, utterly drunk on their desire for each other.

"You know what we could do next?" Joel asked as he leaned his forehead against Portia's, knowing her answer would be yes.

Chapter 9. *Mount Ballyhoo*

Portia and Joel were breathless to the point of speechlessness. She blushed, and he felt the heat as well. Joel had to inhale and exhale several times before he was able to articulate his next witty proposition.

"May I interest you in a picnic? I brought a basket full of treats along with a bottle of wine," he asked, then jumped off the tailgate. Dizzy and lightheaded from their passionate kiss, Joel stumbled as he retrieved the basket from the backseat.

Portia was also lightheaded, which was completely evident when she hopped off the tailgate and almost faceplanted onto the parking lot. But Joel was there to catch her, just as he always would be.

He grinned as he held her hands. "So, what do you say? A picnic here at Spithead?"

Portia was on board with the suggestion; however, she had another location in mind. "That would be great, but let's go somewhere else. I know the perfect place. Let's go!" she exclaimed, then brusquely slammed the tailgate back into place.

"I would've done that," Joel began. "Where do you have in mind for this picnic?"

"Mount Ballyhoo," Portia responded as she turned and pointed to the mountain next to Port Road. "There's something up there I want to show you, and it's the perfect place for a picnic," she said as the wind blew hair into her face.

Joel gently brushed her hair behind her ear. Then he turned around and looked at the beautiful mountain. "Mount Ballyhoo looks like the perfect place for a picnic," he said, then smiled.

Portia took off the coveralls, and then Joel cavalierly opened the truck door for her, offering his hand as she climbed inside. He swaggered his way over to the driver's side of Portia's muscle truck. Somehow, he felt if he grunted and walked with a swag, it would make the pickup not look so screaming pink. However, nothing could un-pink that truck.

Joel started the engine while Portia fiddled with the radio. With her finger stuck in place in front of the preset buttons, she flipped her hair around and stared at the radio like she was making a life-or-death decision.

While Joel buckled his seatbelt, he kept his eyes on Portia. After longer than necessary, Portia still hadn't chosen a station. She kept staring at the buttons with her finger stuck in place in front of them, unsure of which one to push.

"Hey, this isn't a red or blue wire situation here. Just pick a station. I'm sure it will be fine," Joel said.

Portia turned toward him and laughed. "Hmm, do I want country or Rock & Roll? Sometimes, I want both at the same time, ya know?" she exclaimed as she finally gave in and selected the button on the right, just in time for a classic Rock & Roll song to begin.

Now that the music selection had finally concluded, Joel put the pink truck in drive and gently hit the gas, fully intending to drive slowly and leisurely out of the cape. Of course, Portia wasn't having this nonsense. She sexily tossed her hair over her shoulder, sang loudly to the music, and mocked Joel's slow driving. This stirred something deep within Joel's psyche. The hot girl by his side and the blaring music with thundering guitars and drums inspired him to get wild. And boy, did he ever. The retired Navy captain hit that pink gas pedal and drove like the reckless maniac Portia wanted to see, hitting every pothole, bump, nook, and cranny.

"Woohoo! Okay, now you're driving like a rock star!" Portia shouted above the thundering music.

"Or a cowboy," Joel cleverly replied.

"A cowboy rock star! That's what you are, Joel! My cowboy rock star," Portia said.

"Well then, that makes you my cowgirl rock star, now doesn't it?" Joel responded, his cheeks burning red with passion as he hit the gas pedal, hitting a pothole and splashing mud and grit all over the hood and windshield.

"Woohoo! Now we're talking!" Portia exclaimed.

Joel's heart pounded excitedly as his skin heated up from this sensuous woman's allure. He couldn't believe Portia's effect on him as he drove that intensely pink truck like it was on fire. Joel had always been a little uptight, and he felt good to let loose for the first time.

As the song ended, Portia turned down the volume so that she could give Joel directions. "Make a right turn onto Ulakta Drive to go up the mountain. Dag gone! I should be a tour guide."

Joel chuckled, remembering what Gunther had said yesterday about being a tour guide. *Yep, these two are definitely related,* he thought. Then Joel flipped on the blinker as he made a sharp turn for the road on the right.

"What's that sound?" Portia asked.

"Uh, the blinker," Joel sarcastically replied.

"Um," she began as she looked behind them, insinuating that there was no need to use the blinker because they were in the middle of nowhere and no one was behind them. "We don't use those here. Blinkers that is. We don't use them in Aleutia."

Joel knew this was hogwash. "You mean *you* don't use blinkers."

"Oh, heck no! I do as I please. I see no need to warn anybody about anything I do." Portia huffed.

Joel laughed and shook his head.

Portia changed the radio station. This time, a country song began playing softly, providing the perfect accompaniment for a leisurely drive up the bumpy-mountain road with a spectacular view of Eagle Bay on the right.

They passed piles of rotting wood on the left side of the road.

"That's what is left of Fort Denson. It was an Army base built in World War II to protect the Aleutia Naval Base," Portia explained.

"Wow, that's so neat. We must explore both places sometime," Joel said, immediately intrigued.

Meanwhile, Portia sang along to the country song as they drove by the remnants of Fort Denson's bunkers, barracks, ammunition-storage facilities, command posts, and tunnels.

Beyond this was one of the most spectacular views Joel had ever seen, despite his worldly travels. *My God, this is beautiful!* Joel thought as they approached a massive concrete circle with grass in the middle. It was right on the edge of the mountaintop, overlooking the inlet where Eagle Bay met the Bering Sea.

"That's a Panama mount for a 155mm cannon! And that must be the Bering Sea. Oh, this is beautiful!" Joel exclaimed.

"A perfect place for a picnic," Portia said, then looked at Joel seductively.

He promptly parked the truck and looked at her. By this point, the picnic was the last thing on his mind.

THEY UNBUCKLED THEIR SEATBELTS at the same time. Portia kept her eyes on Joel as she slowly slid closer to him. This time, she took the initiative and gently caressed Joel's cheek before sliding her hand up the back of his head. Then Joel cupped her face in his hands and kissed her passionately. She certainly knew how to set his soul on fire.

After a few minutes of intense kissing, Joel leaned his forehead against Portia's, pausing to savor the moment. "Well, I guess we better go have that picnic now," he eventually whispered.

Breathless, Portia made a pouty face, and Joel melted. The gorgeous bar queen made the sexy expression a little too well with those flawlessly puffy lips. And even though Joel was sitting, he was weak in the knees from it.

He took a deep breath and then reached for the picnic basket on the backseat. "Shall we go have that picnic, my cowgirl rock star?"

Portia nodded her head. Then they got out of the truck and went to the Panama mount, where they sat down, facing the inlet.

Giant sunrays pierced through large puffy clouds, turning the Bering Sea into ripples of shimmering glitter. And once again, Joel felt the presence of God, showing him that everything would be all right. And it most certainly was!

"Would you like a glass of wine?" Joel asked, then kissed Portia on the cheek.

"That sounds wonderful. Thank you," Portia whispered before giving his ear a goose-bump-inducing nibble.

Joel had to take a deep breath, close his eyes, and get his wits about him before proceeding. He slowly opened the wine bottle and poured two glasses of cabernet sauvignon. Meanwhile, Portia took out her phone, turned on an oldies mix of timeless music, and set it next to them, playing softly along with the whispering wind blowing gently around them.

Joel smiled as he handed Portia a glass. "This calls for a toast. To the future of…" he paused before continuing and stared deeply into her overly green eyes.

"Of what?" Portia asked with a suspenseful smile, knowing where Joel was heading.

"Us," he boldly replied as he caressed her cheek.

Portia's eyes lit up like the Fourth of July as her ruby-red lips formed a perfect smile. Her expression told Joel everything he needed to know. He kept his eyes locked onto hers, and Portia lifted her glass to clink his. They both took a sip, never breaking eye contact until an eagle screeching in the distance pulled their attention to the far-off mountain across Eagle Bay.

"Do you think that is where the two eagles went?" Joel asked.

Portia nodded her head as she took another sip of wine. Then she pointed toward the mountain. "That's Mount Sokolov, which is by two coves on the left, Vasiliev Cove and…" Portia paused and gave Joel a naughty grin before continuing, "Humpy Cove. And that's Orlov Bay," she explained, then pointed into the distance.

Joel cackled like a seagull. "Humpy Cove, huh? Well, we may have to check that one out."

Portia laughed as she downed her glass of wine while Joel was still two sips in on his.

"I go to Orlov Bay all the time in my purse seiner," Portia said with a wink as she looked into her empty glass, just like Gunther had done with his empty beer mug last night.

Joel took the hint, reached for the wine bottle, and refilled Portia's glass. She leaned forward, whispered "thank you" in his ear, and kissed him with her wine-saturated lips.

"You have a purse seiner?" Joel rhetorically asked as he leaned his forehead against hers. *Hmm, she has her own boat. That's incredibly sexy!* he thought.

"I have a few boats in addition to the Alexandria. I have a 1968, 117-foot purse seiner that Dad used for cod fishing back in the day. In 2000, he retired it from fishing, and we began using it for fun. That's when we removed the rigging and deck gear and added the jet ski. Several years ago, he made me a deal. He would give me the boat if I got my captain's license. She's in the shop right now having some work done and a fresh coat of bright red paint," Portia proudly replied.

To say that Joel was elated wouldn't do his feelings justice. He reached for Portia's hand, pulled it to his lips, and gently kissed it.

"When she's out of the shop, we could disappear into the sea."

However, Portia didn't share Joel's fantasy for disappearing into the Bering Sea. The smile left her cheerful face. "I never lose sight of the shoreline, Joel. I can't be far from land, especially after last season. If you're close to the shore, then you are close to getting help if something goes wrong."

Joel's heart went kerplunk. It's no wonder Portia felt that way after receiving the worst news of her life—that her father and cousin had died over 150 miles out. "I understand completely," he compassionately replied as he squeezed her hand.

Portia smiled lightly, then changed the subject. "This is my favorite place in Aleutia. Dad and I used to come up here to watch the Northern Lights. And, when the guys were on their way home from their crabbing trips, I would come up here and wait to see them coming into port. Then I would jump in my truck and fly down the mountain to meet them at the dock. I also come here with my guitar and notepad and write music sometimes."

"I envy your talent," Joel said before finishing his first glass of wine. He poured himself another and refilled Portia's glass for the third time.

"Music runs, well, it ran in my family. I kinda didn't have a choice about it. It chose me," Portia explained.

"Was your dad a musician too?" Joel inquired.

"He taught me how to play guitar. Music was the center of our family. When Dad and Uncle Gunther were at sea during my childhood, I stayed with Aunt Gert. I played guitar, and she played the piano while we sang together. When everyone was in port, Dad, Aunt Gert, Uncle Gunther, Chris, and I had our own band. It was so wonderful! When the guys were home, we used to play together at Bairdi's every Friday, Saturday, and Sunday night, sometimes more. Uncle Gunther has an incredible rock star voice, and he plays bass. Chris played the drums, and Dad and I played lead guitar.

We all sang. But since the accident, I've been the only one who kept singing and playing. Uncle Gunther started smoking and drinking, and he and Aunt Gert started fighting. Now, nobody has the heart to sing or play music anymore. I kept singing and writing, but my music is different now."

"You didn't always write anger music about your ex?"

"No…" Portia began. "The boys ran him out of town a few months before the accident, and well, I haven't written about losing Dad and Chris."

"Perhaps getting it out through music would help you instead of focusing your songs on your ex," Joel suggested.

Portia scrunched up her face. "That would probably end up being anger music as well, except worse."

"Why do you say that?" Joel asked as he squeezed her hand.

"Because I am angry that they are gone! I am angry because my father loved the sea more than me!" Portia irritably exclaimed.

Portia's response reminded Joel of what Adoncia had said all those years ago, "Every time you go to sea, you would desert me, even if you kept coming back. All you sailors are the same. You love the ocean first. You love your woman last." And Joel, a sailor himself, knew that this was true. He had always loved the ocean first because he never had a reason not to—until now.

Joel wasn't sure what to say, so he scooted closer to Portia and put his arm around her.

"Don't pity me!" Portia huffed like she was going to shrug off Joel's arm, but then she leaned into him.

"I don't pity you. I think you are the bravest person I have ever met! Getting up every morning after facing a tragedy takes a lot of guts. But you do it with your head held high. I'm here to listen if you want to talk. If not, we can just sit together and say nothing. Whatever you need," Joel said, then kissed her on the cheek.

"Last year, the red king crab season was awful, so Dad was

determined to catch the opilio crabs in January. I begged him not to go farther northwest into Satan's Expanse. I told him not to do it. The weather predictions were that it would be one of the harshest winters on record, but he didn't care. He didn't listen. He chose the sea over me and almost took everyone down with him. I hate him for that! And growing up, I spent most of my time with Aunt Gert because Dad was always working. I love her very much, but I hate him because he was always gone!" Portia fumed.

"You don't hate him. You know that," Joel whispered as he gently rubbed her shoulder.

"I don't know anything anymore," Portia sadly replied as she glared at the inlet.

Joel pulled her closer, and she leaned into him until they were cheek to cheek. "I think you should write about it. Find a way to translate those feelings. You can't stay in this state of mind. You need to transition out of it. Your father and Chris wouldn't want you this way, pretending to be someone else. They wouldn't want Gunther and Gert to be separated, either. Your father and Chris wouldn't want you not to sing and play music together anymore. Hey, pick up your guitar and a sheet of paper, and try it. See if you can write it out; maybe you will inspire everyone else to do the same. Seeing you write and sing about this may be what they need to help them heal from it too."

"The writing happens only when it wants to. I can't force it. If I am moved by something I witness or something somebody says to me, it strikes me, and I write. Sometimes, I will create something in my mind. I'll create characters and write about them. Overall, the best songs happen to me quickly. I write my best work in 15 minutes or less. When it's right, it's right. It's meant to be. I will start writing other songs and finish days, weeks, months, or even years later. Every song is special and different. My dad always said, 'You truly know you hear a good song when the first time you hear it, you think to yourself, *I could swear I've heard this before because the song is just that darn good.'* That's what I always strive for in my music."

"I understand completely," Joel whispered and wrapped his arms around her tighter. He adored everything about Portia and enjoyed learning about this inspiring woman. She had shared her passion with him, and he felt deeply honored that she had shared her most profound and private thoughts. He understood her love of music and how it made her feel closer to her family. "Music keeps everyone connected, even after they are gone. I remember the songs my parents always listened to when I was growing up. When I hear those songs, they take me back to those moments when we were together. Music is always there. Now, with technology, you never have to be without it. It's on your phone and there when you need it. There is a song out there for every situation. I couldn't imagine my life without music. That's how I got through the plane ride here. The music was there to calm me and make things seem less tense. I think of my parents, and I think of music. The last time I saw them, they were dancing in the kitchen before I went to school. That's my last memory of them, and that's the song I chose for our dance last night."

Portia looked deeply into his eyes and then kissed him on the cheek. "That was the perfect song choice."

"I thought so too," Joel began, then returned the kiss. "That's my favorite memory of them. What's your favorite memory of you and your dad?"

"Hmm, well, we used to watch the Northern Lights together. Sometimes, we would come up here and watch them from where we are sitting, and sometimes, we would watch them from the Alexandria," Portia softly replied as she brushed her hair behind her ear. "But, my last memory of him wasn't happy. I was very angry with him when they left for the opilio season last January.

We were on the docks before they left. I told him he left me too much as a child. I told him he loved the sea more than me. I told him that he shouldn't go to Satan's Expanse. I begged him not to go."

"And what did he say to you?" Joel inquired.

"He said, 'Sweet Katerina, don't be angry. I love you, and I'll be home soon.' Well, he lied! He lied to me!" Portia exclaimed with a quivering lip.

Joel pulled her closer and whispered in her ear, "He didn't lie about loving you. I'm here for you."

"I don't need anyone!" Portia huffed as she crossed her arms, and an angry expression overtook her face.

"Oh really? Well, I can tell you one thing, Katerina Alexander. You certainly didn't need the alcohol you had earlier at the ceremony. That won't help, you know? Drinking won't dull the pain," Joel boldly said.

The anger left Portia's face as Joel stared into her beautiful fake green eyes.

"Don't go down the same road as Gunther. I mean it when I say I am here for you," Joel reiterated as he caressed her cheek.

Portia smiled slightly and then placed her hand over Joel's hand as it rested on her cheek. Then she hugged him and whispered, "Thank you."

Joel held her, feeling her heartbeat, smelling the scent of her perfume, and feeling the warmth of her cheek. "Write about your dad and Chris. Give it a try. Maybe it will help. And hey, if you don't want to show me, if you don't want to show anyone. Fine. No problem. But maybe singing about it will help everyone else too. Maybe it will encourage Gert and Gunther to go back to their music, and maybe each other."

"I never thought of it that way," Portia responded, then rubbed her cheek against Joel's.

"I hope you do write about it. I would love to hear it, though, when you do," he whispered as his lips gently brushed against her ear.

"Thank you," she said, clinging to him even more.

Joel resisted saying, "You're welcome," because he felt that she was giving him more than he was giving her, even though that wasn't the case. They were giving each other so much joy, and they had only known each other for 24 hours.

There was still so much to learn about this intriguing woman, so Joel kept the questions coming. "So, what genre do you consider yourself?" he asked as he ran his fingers through her hair.

Portia pulled back slightly, so her forearms rested on Joel's shoulders as she stared into his eyes, making his heart flutter. He couldn't stop the smile from spreading across his face or the stars from dancing in his emerald eyes as he looked back at her.

"Well, I love country music, but I also love the power of a hardcore rock song. So, I am kind of torn, you know? Sometimes, I want to hear the lyrics of an old-fashioned country song with loud electric guitars jamming like a 1980s rock song. Some days, I sing country and rock it out on the electric guitar," Portia explained.

"You could be famous, you know?" Joel said with a grin.

"I'm in my late 30s. I'm too old to get a record deal. Thank you, but that ship has sailed, sailor!" Portia cackled as she reached for her wine glass.

"You are never too old to live your dreams. Don't be afraid to be *you*, Katerina," Joel said as he rubbed a few strands of her hair between his fingers, insinuating that her dyed hair was unnecessary. "And hey, blue eyes are sexy too. I would love to see them sometime."

"I like my new hair and eyes," Portia contended.

"It's great, but it's not you," Joel whispered as he pulled her in for yet another deep, passionate kiss.

PORTIA ADORED THE WAY Joel's lips felt against hers. She loved the tender way he caressed her cheek, making her feel valued and wanted. Such a simple, delicate act of affection meant more than money could ever buy. And here she was, sitting on top of Mount Ballyhoo with a man who saw beyond the dyed hair and green contact lenses; he saw right through the charade and was falling for Katerina Alexander, not Portia of Portia's Port House.

She hadn't felt comfortable talking to anyone about losing her father, but she knew she could trust Joel. She shared her deepest, most private thoughts about how angry she was with Kyle. Portia hadn't told that to anyone, not even Gert and Gunther. With no husband to lean on, she stood tall on her own two feet and faced this unspeakable tragedy all on her own—until God sent Joel her way. Joel took one look at Portia and saw her strength, and as he held her in his arms, Portia felt like she could be Katerina again.

Portia's heart pounded as she reached her hands up to Joel's face and placed them on his cheeks, kissing him more passionately than she had yet. She could've stayed on that mountaintop, kissing the Navy man for the rest of her life. Portia leaned her forehead against Joel's as she took a deep breath, inhaling the brisk mountain air swirling around them as an oldie song played, and eagles screeched in the distance, probably at Humpy Cove.

"How about we quit talking about me and talk about you," Portia insisted as she grinned at Joel, draping her forearms over his shoulders again, so she could see his handsome face.

"What do you want to know?" Joel asked, then smiled.

"Any ex-wives?" Portia inquired.

"No," he answered.

"Excellent. Any girlfriends?"

Joel looked at her skeptically for a moment and then laughed before he shook his head and said, "No, not really."

"Not really, huh? Interesting. I can deal with that! So, tell me about Joel Layton," Portia said as she gave him a swift kiss.

Joel shrugged his shoulders but didn't say anything in return. Portia sensed his hesitancy in replying to this question, so she answered it for him. "You have spent the last 20 years as a Navy man, always wearing an impressive uniform with shiny buttons and medals. You don't know how to be who you are, either. You remember being Joel Layton, who grew up fishing on the Chesapeake Bay with your parents, and now since you retired from the Navy, you are trying to find your way back to him. Right now, you only know that you love the water and always will."

Joel didn't reply right away. Instead, he reached his hands up to Portia's face and kissed her, making her feel like no man ever had.

"So, did I describe you perfectly?" Portia inquired.

"Yes. I love the water, and I can't escape it. I knew that I wanted to be a captain like my dad. Except, I wanted to be a Navy captain. There is nothing like sailing out into the unknown, feeling the vessel move up and down with the waves, smelling the salt air, and thanking God that you are floating on an ocean that He created, not bound by the rules of the land. At sea, I feel free, like anything is possible. My father always taught me that the water is powerful and deserves respect," Joel responded as he looked into the distance where the sunrays kissed the inlet, where Eagle Bay met the Bering Sea.

Portia knew this type of man all too well. Just as Joel was programmed to love the ocean, Portia was programmed to love everything about a sailor. She reached for his hand and gave it a gentle squeeze. "You don't fear. You enjoy the rush of the unknown, knowing anything could happen. When you are at sea, you are one with the water. It's like the ocean waves pulse with the blood that pumps through your heart, veins, and entire body. You feel off course when you're on land because you aren't flowing with the tide."

"Exactly. But, you know what else I do love? I love coming into the port of a foreign country and then exploring the city for a few days. I walked on cobblestone streets, explored ruins, attended cathedrals, ate delicious food, listened to unique music, and talked with interesting people. It was wonderful. Then I was back on board out on the ocean where I belonged. I had no home to go to when I was on leave, so I just traveled and explored. I haven't had a home since I was 11 years old. I have no family," he replied.

"Sounds exciting and lonely at the same time," Portia observed.

"It was, until now," Joel said as he stared into her eyes, making Portia's heart flutter.

As they drank wine and snacked on cheese and crackers, Joel talked about his years as a Navy captain, elaborating on his exciting travels. Portia eagerly listened to his stories as if every word was a symphony to her soul. She visualized him aboard the USS Roland and saw him strutting through the cobblestone streets of Europe, while wearing that stimulating white uniform with gold buttons and medals, turning the head of every woman he passed.

And as much as Portia hated to admit it, she understood a sailor's love for the water, which led her to realize that what she had said to her father was unfair. She knew it was wrong that she had told him that he loved the sea more than her, but she also knew that he didn't take it to heart. He didn't leave on his last voyage angry with her; he left loving her with every fiber of his being. And thanks to Joel, Portia was able to see that now.

As Portia looked at Joel, she smiled, knowing that she couldn't change a man like this, and if he changed, his spirit would break. Her father, Chris, and Gunther loved the sea more than life itself, and if they stopped their livelihood, it would've been like their oxygen supply had been cut off, just like Portia would die if she never sang or played guitar again.

Music was her sea. Just as the rhythm of the waves pulsed

throughout Joel's bloodstream, music notes beat to the rhythm of Portia's heart. For the first time in her life, Portia had met someone who truly understood her, and she had met a man she truly understood as well.

PORTIA'S PHONE DIED from playing music, leaving her and Joel with the beautiful sounds of nature. With the Alaskan breeze swirling around them, carrying eagle songs from a distance, no other music was necessary other than the gorgeous melody of nature arranged by God Almighty, the creator of life, love, and music.

For quite some time, Joel sat with his arm interlocked with Portia's in completely comfortable silence as they watched God paint the sky with glory. Not one moment felt awkward from the lack of conversation, making Joel feel extremely grateful that this beautiful woman had come into his life.

The gentle breeze carried the scent of Portia's perfume, and gracefully kissed her brunette locks as the setting sunrays made them glow, creating the illusion that her hair was shimmering with divine light. Joel kissed her and then leaned his cheek against hers as they enjoyed the view of Eagle Bay and watched two eagles gliding with the breeze toward the setting sun. This sunset would most definitely be one to remember. Joel reached for his phone and snapped photos of God's spectacular display of light, splashing the fading blue sky with pinks, oranges, and yellows, illuminating puffy clouds along with rising fog and mist.

Is this really happening, or am I having the best dream of my life? Joel wondered, realizing that God was again showing him everything would be okay. Every moment he had had until now was a moment that brought him closer to this very moment in time. Every roadblock, every heartache, every laugh, every tear, and one influential prostituta brought him to this blessed moment.

Joel was so thankful that he felt like his heart could burst, and he needed to hold Portia in his arms and feel her body close to his. He scooted back and moved behind her, wrapping his arms around her waist. He rested his chin on her shoulder, so they were cheek to cheek as they watched the sun drop lower in the sky as if it were falling into Eagle Bay.

Portia yawned from the encroaching darkness. And Joel yawned as well and then glanced down at his phone, not realizing how late it was. "Sunset is at 9:30? Wow."

Portia rubbed her cheek against his, making him tingle from head to toe. "You are in Alaska now, Joel. The sun sets this late here. Isn't it marvelous?"

"It certainly is, my dear. It certainly is," Joel replied as he held her closer while they watched the pageantry of the clouds, everchanging with beauty and vibrancy. He held Portia close to his heart as they sat on the Panama mount until the colors faded from the tantalizing sky.

"Let's get you home. You had a long day," Joel whispered in Portia's ear.

He packed up the picnic basket and walked with his arm around her as they returned to the truck. Joel helped her into the passenger side, and she snuggled close in the middle seat as he slowly drove down the mountain. When he parked the truck at the Port House, he kissed Portia on the cheek to awaken her. "You're home," he said, then smiled as she yawned and rubbed her eyes.

"Thank you for a wonderful day and for being there for me," she whispered as she gently touched Joel's cheeks, initiating a passionate goodnight kiss.

"No, thank you," Joel replied, then kissed her in return. "Let's get you inside."

They both got out, and Joel handed Portia the keys. They walked up the staircase to her apartment door on the right. The thought of sleeping without Portia in his arms tonight was just unbearable. All night, he wanted to kiss and hold her in his arms beneath the sheets. But as Portia unlocked the door and turned the doorknob, Joel flashed back to that night in Rota and couldn't—and wouldn't—enter the door on the right. He respected Portia too much to stay.

Chapter 10. *More Than Me*

Joel rested his hand on Portia's shoulder, then gently slid it up her neck until he cupped her cheek, sending a tingling sensation throughout her entire body and making her skin burn with passion. He reached his other hand up to her vacant cheek and then passionately kissed her lips. Her heart pounded as she reciprocated this hypnotizing lip lock. *Dang, he's a good kisser!* Portia thought as she reached her hands up to his face, never wanting to let go.

Their foreheads touched; then Joel brushed his lips against Portia's ear and breathlessly whispered, "Goodnight." He stared deeply into her eyes and gently caressed her cheek with the back of his hand. As he turned to leave, Joel tripped, almost falling down the staircase.

"Careful there, cowboy." Portia chuckled as she blushed.

"See the effect you have on me, rock star? Go on inside. I want to know you're safe before I leave," Joel insisted as he stood at the bottom of the steps.

Portia's heart fluttered like a butterfly sipping nectar on the first spring flower. She had a man who not only walked her to her door but who also wanted to know she was inside safe and sound before he left. She smiled, nodded, and kissed Joel before she entered her apartment and closed the door.

Joel hadn't even started the truck yet, and she missed him. And Portia had to be a pain in the butt about it. She couldn't just accept the happiness and go with the flow. The smile left her face. *Darn you, Joel Layton!* she angrily thought, realizing she was falling hard and fast for him. He made her heart flutter and skin burn with passion and was so magnificent that she immediately began missing him, even before he left the parking lot. Emotion overfilled her, and Portia longed for numbness in which she felt nothing.

It's no wonder she felt this way. Portia was terrified of becoming attached to another man because three of the most influential men in her life had gone away. Her marriage ended. Then a few months later, Portia faced more loss when Satan's Expanse claimed her father and cousin.

Then Joel strutted into her life like a fallen-down storm cloud. To say that Portia was terrified of becoming attached to him, trusting him, and losing him, would be an understatement deeper than the Bering Sea. Considering this, Portia's position on life and love was completely understandable. While on the other hand, her desire to cope with it all by becoming the Port House queen was debatable. She was hot and could wear provocative leather outfits, so why not?

A hangry cat and a pissed-off monkey greeted Portia as she entered the apartment. They weren't dummies when it came to satisfying their needs. They were hungry and wanted fresh food, so they turned on the charm. A chorus of melodious monkey squeaking along with cat purring, chortling, and meowing serenaded Portia as she took off her jacket and turned on the lights. "Okay, okay," she patronizingly said as the leaping monkey and prancing tomcat followed her into the kitchen.

Tiny climbed up Portia's leg, jumped onto the counter, and puffed up his white crest as he impatiently waited for his supper.

"Don't you even think about throwing caca at me, Mr. Tiny," she admonished as she opened the refrigerator and took out a small bowl of precut fruit. Tiny let out a loud, appreciative squeak as she set the bowl in front of him, and he promptly retrieved a fruit slice.

Meanwhile, Screech frantically rubbed against Portia's legs and vibrated his tail like a firehose getting ready to burst forth with a deluge. "Dude, no happy peeing. I mean it." She chuckled as she gave him canned food and set it on the floor beside his water bowl. The fluffy lad wasted no time gobbling down his supper, taking great care to knock food chunks around the bowl's perimeter, so Portia would have to clean it up later.

Portia promptly took a steamy shower, feeling the rush of hot water caressing her tired muscles, instantly feeling tension melt away and coziness take over. She dried off with a luxurious towel and wrapped it around her body, tucking it around her perky bosoms. After that, Portia brushed her teeth and took out her overly green contact lenses. Looking at herself in the mirror, she saw a brunette with blue eyes looking at her discernably.

While applying her anti-wrinkle cream, Portia envisioned herself with blonde hair again. *I could dye it back*, she thought. Excellent idea, but she wasn't ready to climb that mountain yet. Portia wasn't prepared to face Katerina because that would mean facing the anguish her ex-husband caused, reliving the pain of losing her father and cousin, and forgiving Kyle for going to Satan's Expanse and dying. And doggonit, Katerina Alexander might as well have been killed at sea along with Kyle and Chris, so the hair dying would wait until another day. Until then, Portia of Portia's Port House would prevail, thigh-high leather boots included.

Portia quickly brushed her hair and gave herself a generous squirt of perfume before shimmying into a knee-length, red silk nightgown with a matching robe. Then she topped off her bedtime attire with a pair of fluffy white slippers. She yawned, acknowledging that she was exhausted but not tired enough to sleep; she was anxious over the day's events. For the umpteenth time in the last nine months, Portia had to publicly face the death of Kyle and Chris. This was emotionally draining, and the pain of her divorce was still fresh. Whenever someone mentioned her ex-husband or the accident that killed her father and cousin, it immediately triggered a painful lump in her throat. A particular song played on the radio, or someone said something that triggered a memory; then the pain came flooding back.

Despite the heartache and sadness of the last year, happiness re-entered Portia's life when Joel strutted into the Port House. Now, she faced the dichotomy of joy and sorrow. One thing was for sure; she needed to work on her response to both.

FEELING A LITTLE CHILLY, Portia tied the belt on her robe as she walked across the living room and turned on the fireplace. The flames roared as they reflected on the windows. Then Portia was immediately stunned by the majestic, swirling colors of the Northern Lights dancing over Eagle Bay, which prompted memories of her father, as they always did. She closed her eyes, took a deep breath, and swallowed hard, trying to push the lump out of her throat and keep it from reaching her eyes. Then she remembered what Joel had said, "I think you should write about it. Find a way to translate those feelings. You can't stay in this state of mind. You need to transition out of it. Your father and Chris wouldn't want you this way, pretending to be someone else. They wouldn't want Gunther and Gert to be separated, either. Your father and Chris wouldn't want you not to sing and play music together anymore. Hey, pick up your guitar and a sheet of paper, and try it. See if you can write it out; maybe you will inspire everyone else to do the same. Seeing you write and sing about this may be what they need to help them heal from it too."

"Okay," Portia replied as if Joel were there. She took a deep, refreshing breath like she was getting ready to climb a giant mountain. She grabbed a notepad and her electric guitar, then sat on the sofa where she had a front row seat to the aurora borealis. The power of a divine presence manipulating energy, magnetic fields, plasma, and gas to create swirling and twisting colors that danced across the star-filled sky was more than evident. Only the hand of God Almighty could make such a spectacular display of artistry, give Portia love as she had for her father and cousin, and bring happiness back into her life.

With her eyes fixed on the luminous night sky, Portia returned to happy memories of watching the Northern Lights with her father. One memory led to another, and her frantic mind ran away with a life of its own, beyond her control, like she was watching a movie. She visualized sitting on Mount Ballyhoo's Panama mount with her father when she was a child. The image kept replacing itself with scenes of Katerina and Kyle, increasing in age. Those cherished years flew by as the colors hastily transformed within the Northern Lights.

The flashbacks ended with Katerina and Kyle's last visit to Mount Ballyhoo, a week before Kyle's final journey to the Bering Sea. This recollection pierced Portia to the core, causing a lump in her throat. With grief, one trigger leads to another, and it was only natural that her mind inevitably replayed the last conversation she had had with him.

As they stood on the dock before the Alexandria departed for the opilio season last January, Kyle reached out to hug Katerina goodbye. Instead of reciprocating like she usually did, Katerina stood with her arms folded across her chest. She had sternly told him, "You wait until it's the coldest season on record, and this is when you choose to go farther northwest to Satan's Expanse. There is a huge chance that there will be an arctic storm, yet you're going anyway. It's going to be a war zone out there. I hate you for leaving me so much as a child and for leaving me right now."

"My sweet Katerina, don't be angry. I love you, and I will be home soon," Kyle compassionately said, then kissed her on the cheek and gave her an unreciprocated hug before stepping aboard the Alexandria for the final time.

As she sat on the sofa reminiscing, the intense lump in Portia's throat shifted to pain. She did her best to swallow, to choke back the agony, but this time, she couldn't do it. She had to confront the tragedy head-on. Insufferable tears filled Portia's eyes like a dam getting ready to break as she replayed this scene multiple times. And with each replay, she saw that Kyle was undeterred by her harsh words. He forgave her before their exchange ended, and now, Portia needed to forgive him for leaving her so much as a child and going to Satan's Expanse last January.

Anger set in as the pain in her throat intensified, leading to the one thing she loathed more than anything in the world. Over the past nine months, she refused to let the tears flow. However, tonight, she was unsuccessful in this endeavor. The dam broke as the tears scorched her face as she watched the swirling colors of the Northern Lights over Eagle Bay. She intensely gripped the guitar until her hands cramped and squeezed her eyes shut to the point they ached, thinking that if she closed them hard enough and long enough, the emotion would come to a halt.

Portia took several long, deep breaths while she steadied her emotions and got into the zone of creativity. She strummed a chord and slowly opened her eyes, face to face with the Northern Lights and symbolically face to face with her father.

In the first verse, Portia sang to Kyle like he was there, watching the Northern Lights, just as they did so many times throughout her life. She sang about his decision to go farther north and how an arctic storm turned the Bering Sea into a war zone, just as she had predicted. With a quivering lip, she sang about the waves claiming his life, verbalizing that he was gone.

Then the Northern Lights splashed across the night sky, making a shimmering reflection, illuminating Eagle Bay's rippling waters. Her feelings were like the aurora borealis; the everchanging colors mirrored her emotions, sad one minute and angry the next.

In the chorus, Portia sang about how her world was full of light when her father was alive. Now that he was gone, she was in complete darkness, except for the Northern Lights, which once symbolized happiness but became a reminder of her father and his untimely death. She concluded the chorus by rebuking Kyle for loving the sea more than her.

In the second verse, Portia wrote about how she now had to sing alone without her father, her one true hero who instilled a love and passion for music in her. Like the ever-changing colors of the Northern Lights, she shifted this emotion to anger. Once again, insufferable tears scalded her cheeks as she emotionally sang about hating and loving Kyle simultaneously. Then she repeated the chorus, infusing every note, every tear, and every chord with the most powerful vibrato her voice had yet to achieve.

In the final section, Portia put everything on the line. She courageously examined the faults in her grieving process and admitted that she used alcohol and marijuana, attempting to dull the pain. Then, like the vacillating hues of the aurora borealis, she returned to anger and confronted Kyle for dying, ending with the possibility that she might forgive him someday. When the songwriting concluded, the Northern Lights dissipated.

After Portia wrote a new song, she always spent a few hours playing it over and over, perfecting every note and strum of the guitar. She stayed up into the wee hours of the morning, singing her heart out as if Kyle was sitting there with her. Eventually, the night sky faded as the sun rose in the east, and Portia smiled at the new day dawning. However, the smile turned into a yawn, and she realized she better get some shuteye since she planned on debuting the new song that night at the Port House.

A STRANGE RINGTONE blasted Joel's eardrums, waking him from a deep sleep. Squinting and yawning, he turned on a lamp and reached for the phone, and a huge smile overtook his face because he had a video call from Adoncia. He answered the call, happy to see her.

"Oh wow, there you are! This is cool. However, some people are trying to sleep, you know?" Joel said with a chuckle, not the least bit annoyed that she had awakened him.

"¡Lo siento mucho! Oh, you're in bed." Adoncia paused before continuing in a whisper, "Are you alone?"

Joel gently slapped his cheek and smiled, pretending to be appalled by her inquiry. "Yes, I'm alone. I've only been here for two days," he amusedly scoffed. "Oh, sweet Adoncia, still living up to your name, you are as beautiful as ever."

"¡Gracias cariño! ¿Cómo estás? And how is that adorable monkey? ¿Está él ahí?"

Joel grinned at her alluring Spanish accent and the red dress that perfectly clung to her well-rounded chest. "No, Tiny the monkey belongs to…"

"Joel! You met a woman!" Adoncia interrupted him.

His cheeks burned red with uncontrollable blushing that even Adoncia could see through a cell phone screen halfway across the world.

"Joel, dios mío. I can see you blushing from here," she said.

"She owns the Alexandria," Joel began. "Her family has such a sad story. Her father was the original captain, and he died last January during an arctic storm while trying to save his nephew. So now, Gunther is the Alexandria's new captain. Tiny was her father's monkey and would go out on the Bering Sea with them. But now, he stays with her at the Port House."

"What's her name?" Adoncia asked.

"Portia," Joel replied as a giddy grin paralyzed his face.

"Interesante. Tell me más," Adoncia insisted as she leaned forward, exposing her all-too-plump chest.

Meanwhile, Joel tried not to be distracted by her sexiness. "Portia isn't her real name; it's a cover. She just opened a bar called Portia's Port House, where she tends bar, dances, and writes and sings her own music. She is beautiful and talented, but she has been through a lot in the last year; she has tried to change everything about herself. Her real name is Katerina Alexander. When her father and cousin died, she changed her hair from blonde to brunette and her name to Portia."

"Oh, Joel. You're the persono perfecto to show her that being herself, that being Katerina is muy buena. I have a sense about these things, and I know she is the one for you," Adoncia replied.

"Are you psychic?" Joel asked.

"Only when it comes to you. Eres precioso para mi," Adoncia said as she placed her hand over her heart, which was distracting since her cleavage line was so substantial. "Promesa, you'll invite me to the wedding."

Joel chuckled. "Wedding? I think you're getting ahead of yourself. But yes, if there is one, yes, of course. Enough about me. How are you? How is business? My favorite lady of the night," he asked while reminiscing about their many lip locks over the years, vividly remembering the sound of the wind chimes on her front porch, the ocean slapping the shoreline, and the smell of marzipan escaping the cottage windows.

"Business is va fuerte. I had a line 30 men long outside my puerta anoche. After the first 25, I had to send the last five away. A prostituta can only take so much!"

"Oh, Adoncia, I hope that you find a new livelihood. You deserve so much love," Joel said.

"Well, I couldn't wait around for you, ahora podria? Anyway, I'm old enough to be your mother! Well, from a teenage pregnancy, that is. But, there is no denying that I'll always miss tus besos and..." She stopped herself with a smile.

"We have such wonderful memories together. I miss you too," Joel said bittersweetly as he looked at the time. "Adoncia, I should go. I need to get ready for breakfast. Let's do this video chat again soon. It's so wonderful to see you. I'll send you some pictures. And please send me a picture of yourself, so I can add that to your info on my phone."

"¡Cosa segura! I'm so glad you are finally using your phone. I'll send you a Spanish selfie y fotografias de Rota. Te amo, Joel," Adoncia said.

"Te amo, Adoncia," Joel responded before ending the call. Then he promptly scrolled through his album and texted her pictures from last night.

Joel: Portia took me to a place called Spithead to feed bald eagles. This is where we kissed for the first time. The sunset was taken from Mount Ballyhoo.
Adoncia: ¡Magnifico!

Within a minute, Adoncia sent Joel a cleavage selfie with a series of heart emojis, and a massive grin spread across his face. *She looks smoking hot,* he thought, feeling techier than ever and replying to her with a smiley face emoji. *Wow, there are faces and poop signs on here too,* Joel thought with a laugh as he swiped through the many options. He promptly saved the selfie and added it to Adoncia's contact information.

AFTER A QUICK SHOWER AND SHAVE, Joel went downstairs and into the dining room, but it was empty.

Gert hollered from the kitchen across the hall, "Breakfast is in here, darling!"

Joel hesitantly entered the kitchen. Luckily, only Gert was there, and Tanya was nowhere to be seen. He breathed an enormous sigh of relief on that one. Meanwhile, Gert set an omelet, coffee fixings, and a glass of juice on the table just for him. The freshly brewed coffee, and the smell of cheese sizzling with green peppers, onions, and ham alongside freshly buttered, toasted rye bread kicked Joel's hunger into overdrive, making his stomach growl like a grizzly bear.

"Thank you. This smells incredible," Joel gratefully said.

With a reminiscent smile, Gert sat next to Joel as she sipped coffee and watched him eat, and he was immediately reminded of breakfasts when he was a little boy. His mother always made a western omelet and sat with him while he ate. His father had been out the door two hours earlier to work on the boat, so Joel always loved that time with his mom.

After a few minutes, Gert's reminiscence turned to curiosity. "So, you got the hots for my niece?"

Joel almost choked to death on his omelet to the point he accidentally spat a piece of egg across the table. Now twice embarrassed, he promptly took a sip of juice and then a gulp of coffee.

Gert couldn't contain her laughter. That made her day, and Joel laughed too. And frankly, he had nothing to be embarrassed about at all. He was an honest, good-looking man who always spoke the truth and would most definitely be straightforward about his feelings for Portia.

"Why yes, ma'am, I do. She's the most gorgeous woman I have ever seen, and I am completely intrigued by her. She's an angel trapped inside a dark cloud, struggling to find her way out. I wish she knew it's okay to be Katerina," Joel replied.

"Boy, you got it bad!" Gert exclaimed as she patted his hand. "That pretty much sums her up."

"Yeah," Joel responded with a sigh, knowing that Gert was hurting as much as Portia, and he wished he could help.

"She's hurting bad. We all are," Gert softly said as the jovialness left her face.

She stood up and went to the counter where she had set out a mixer, measuring cups, bowls, and baking ingredients, with the most noticeable item being a bag of chocolate chips. And Joel immediately knew what she was doing, getting ready to make chocolate chip cookies, something else his mother often did. More memories from his childhood came flooding back, and a reminiscent smile spread across Joel's face as he finished his last few bites of breakfast and watched Gert measure the flour, sugar, salt, baking soda, and vanilla. Then she creamed the butter before slowly adding the sugar, eggs, vanilla, and dry ingredients. Once satisfied with the dough's consistency, she slowly mixed in the hefty bag of chocolate chips. "Woohoo!" Gert exclaimed as she put the dough in the refrigerator and preheated the oven. After that, she took the beaters off the mixer, keeping one for herself and handing the other to Joel, just like his mother had done.

"Thank you," he replied with a smile, then promptly took the first bite of chocolate chip cookie dough that he had had in nearly 30 years, and it tasted just like home. Joel savored every bite, slowly lapping up the tasty morsels until the beater was almost pristine. Then he carried his dishes to the sink, rinsed them, and put them in the dishwasher.

As a child, Joel had often helped his mother bake cookies, and for the first time in nearly 30 years, he finally had the opportunity to do that again. He didn't want this moment to pass him by, so he walked over to Gert and asked, "May I help?"

"Oh yes, darling! I would love that!" Gert exclaimed as she removed the dough from the refrigerator. "Here, get two tablespoons of dough and then drop it onto the ungreased cookie sheet. You can get about 12 on each sheet."

Joel promptly washed his hands and then happily filled the

baking sheets while Gert finished the dishes. With Joel's attention to detail, each cookie was in perfect proportion to the others and was evenly and perfectly spaced.

"Good job, darling!" Gert smiled at the excellent work and patted Joel on the shoulder. Then she carefully put the pans in the oven.

Joel eagerly waited for the delicious scent to fill the house, and once again, he remembered making cookies with his mother and impatiently waiting for them to bake. It wasn't long at all, but it felt like an eternity to a little boy. And here he was, now 38 years old, knowing that the cookies would be ready before he knew it.

"When I was little, I used to help my mom bake cookies. She always turned the oven light on, and I would sit in front of the oven door and watch them bake. I know it was only 10 minutes, but it felt like forever waiting for them," Joel reminisced as he sat down at the table, never once taking his eyes off the oven door. At that moment, the glorious cookie scent filled the room, and he slowly and deeply inhaled. "I love this smell so much," he quietly said, remembering his mother sitting with him while the cookies were in the oven.

"Oh yes, my dear. And it's so wonderful being a mother and watching your little ones enjoy it. My little Chris and Katerina did the same thing. They would sit side by side on a beanbag chair in front of the oven, and every minute, my little Chris would ask if they were done yet," Gert said as her eyes glistened. She paused and then sadly sighed, staring at the floor as she envisioned little Katerina and Chris sitting on their beanbag chair. "Anyway, I am so glad you are here!" She hugged Joel, and for the first time in 27 years, he received a mother's hug, which brought a sparkle to his eye.

"Okay, it's time!" Gert hurried to the oven, put on a pair of oven mitts, and opened the door. "Ouch! Tanya needs to spring for some new oven mitts, so I don't burn my pretty little fingers! She's more worried about her lip injections. That's where she is this morning. Good gracious!" Gert exclaimed as she quickly set the cookie sheets on the stove and rushed to the sink to run cold water over her hands.

"Is there anything I can do?" Joel asked as he jumped up to help.

"Oh no, darling! You sit back down. We're gonna have some warm cookies and milk!" Gert said as she reached for a hand towel. Then she promptly filled two glasses with milk, set them on the table, and filled two plates with generous servings of warm chocolate chip cookies. Joel's mouth began watering when she put the cookie plate in front of him. The anticipation of that first dreamy bite of a warm cookie was almost too much to bear.

"Thank you so much," Joel said as he smiled at Gert and then looked at the decadent cookie plate.

"No, Joel. Thank you!" Gert replied as she patted his hand. "Now, don't let those cookies get cold. Dig in!"

"Well, if you insist!" Joel said as he picked one up, feeling the warmth on his hands as melted chocolate oozed down his finger. He took the first bite, and the cookie melted in his mouth. The delicious buttery cookie had a hint of saltiness balanced with the perfect amount of chocolate morsels. Gert's cookies were spot on, no doubt from years of perfecting the recipe. She was an exceptional cook and undoubtedly an exceptional mother, which made Joel so thankful that God had brought her into his life.

WITH A STOMACH FULL OF CHOCOLATE CHIP COOKIES, Joel was ready to get on with his day. He had no immediate plans, which he wasn't used to because he always had a full schedule in the Navy for the last 20 years. Free time like this was a new phenomenon. He thought about calling or texting Portia to say, "Good morning," then realized they never exchanged numbers.

Whenever the USS Roland was in a foreign port, and Joel didn't know what to do with himself, he sat on the dock and admired the massive vessel. But now, the guided-missile destroyer was a memory of the past, so he did the next best thing. He went to the Alexandria's dock, which was conveniently beside the Port House.

When Joel entered Port Road, he saw that the Port House parking lot was empty, except for a couple of cars and Portia's pink truck, still in the same place he had parked it last night. He smiled and continued toward the Alexandria, looking as stately as ever in the Monday-morning sunlight. Joel smiled at the iron lady, then backed his pickup into a parking spot along the dock. Then he rolled down the windows, turned an oldies station on high, got out of the truck, and put down the tailgate.

Joel was a little anxious and didn't feel like sitting just yet, so he paced up and down the dock. At that moment, one of his favorite songs started playing, reminding him of singing it with his father on the workboat. Suddenly, he shuffled his feet, snapping his fingers, singing along like he was 11 years old, and fishing up a pot full of blue crabs. As the timeless tune transcended time, Joel was simultaneously in Unalaska, Alaska, and on the Chesapeake Bay.

PORTIA WAS SOUND ASLEEP until Tiny abruptly landed on her pillow, and Screech jumped on her stomach. They were hungry, their breakfast was late, and they wanted it ASAP.

"Oh, you two! All right, I'll get up and feed you! After that, I'm going back to sleep," Portia grumbled as she stumbled out of bed and into the kitchen. She gave Tiny a fresh food bowl and Screech a can of food, so he could lick off the gravy, make a terrible mess, and not eat it all.

Portia went to the window, looked toward the dock, and couldn't believe her eyes. "Joel?" she rhetorically asked as she reached for a pair of binoculars to spy more effectively. "What in the world? What are you doing? Having a private dance party?" She put her hand over her mouth like she was trying to contain her laughter. Then she looked through the binoculars again and giddily smiled.

Suddenly, two bald eagles swooped down on the Alexandria, one landing on the bow and the other on the wheelhouse roof. Portia's heart fluttered as she watched Joel sit down on the tailgate to admire the regal creatures and take pictures of them. She reached up to the window glass as if she were touching him.

Meanwhile, a wave of fatigue hit her like an avalanche. The smile succumbed to a yawn since she had stayed up all night. With Gert and Rhonda opening the bar for lunch, Portia went back to bed, so she would be well rested for the new song's debut that night. She took one more gander at Joel through the binoculars, blew him a kiss, climbed back into bed, and immediately fell asleep with a smile on her face.

LATE IN THE AFTERNOON, Portia was awakened by a screaming monkey, a hissing cat, screeching eagles outside her door, and banging sounds in the dumpster. She rubbed her eyes and opened them only to see Tiny's scrunched-up face staring at her. Portia scratched his head and petted Screech's back. Both critters chortled in return, knowing that their human loved them and that the prospect of dinner was in the not-so-distant future.

Portia looked at the clock on her nightstand and was shocked to see how late it was. The Port House was already full of the old folks, finishing their 4:30 p.m. dinner, and would soon be filling with the night crowd, which included the Alexandria's crew.

"Ahh! I've got to get ready for the show!" Portia jumped out of bed.

Portia quickly fed the critters, had some coffee, and took a hot and steamy shower as she mentally prepared to do something she had never done before, perform an original song about losing the two people she loved most. As the bar queen saw her reflection in the mirror, she looked deep into her blue eyes and remembered something her father had always told her, "Your eyes are bluer than the sea, my dear Katerina."

Portia took a deep breath and replied to Kyle as if he were there. "Yes, but you loved the sea, more than me." Suddenly, a wave of grief filled her blue eyes, and she gripped the counter and leaned over the sink as she tried to swallow away the painful lump in her throat.

All the while, Joel's words from yesterday echoed in her mind, "And hey, blue eyes are sexy too. I would love to see them sometime." A small laugh escaped her lips, and she smiled as she threw away the green contact lenses. From this point forward, she would be a brunette with blue eyes.

With her head held high, Portia teased her hair until it exemplified the perfect amount of sass and put on her makeup, which included black eyeliner and red lipstick. She trotted over to her closet full of costumes. "What to wear? What to wear?" Portia muttered as she frantically sorted through her overly decadent attire that always left her spectators wanting more.

As her hands grazed over an extensive selection of leather and sparkly garb, Portia paused when she found a black and gold fringe dress. "That's the one!" she exclaimed as she removed it from the hanger and shimmied into the foxy ensemble. The tight, two-inch-wide shoulder straps assisted the built-in brassiere in exceptionally puckering her heaving chest like she was a saloon hooker from the gold rush era. Meanwhile, the dress provocatively hugged her curvaceous hips, providing a symmetrical contrast to her heavy chest, drawing even more attention to her tiny waistline, which made other women so envious they choked on their hush puppies. And to put the icing on that honey bunny, the dress length was beyond delicious and wouldn't leave anyone unsatisfied. The dress barely covered her tight rear while the fringes extended halfway down her thighs, leaving the perfect amount of space between the fringes and the tops of her thigh-high leather boots.

Portia took a long, deep breath, then looked at her reflection in the full-length mirror, and once again, Kyle's words echoed in her mind, "Your eyes are bluer than the sea, my dear Katerina."

And once again, she responded to him like he was there, "That's great, but tonight, I'm still Portia." She just wasn't ready to let go of the rest of her new persona. Her sassily teased, liquor-colored hair, black eyeliner, red lips, boobs up to her chin, tight fringe dress barely covering her backside, and thigh-high leather boots would stay.

Now that she was ready, it was showtime! Portia sent her band members a group text message.

Portia: New song alert! I'll be downstairs in five minutes. Please get the stage and lights ready. Back me up as you see fit.
Ted: Woohoo! Roger that!

Usually, Portia sent the band new music ahead of time, and then they practiced before the Port House opened. But other times, like this one, Portia announced a new song, and the band members improvised on the spot.

Portia's heart pounded with anticipation now that the band was getting in position. She paused to take a deep breath, tried to steady her nerves, and prepared herself to sing about her father's death. She was going to do this, not just for herself, but for Gert, Gunther, and the rest of the crew, for they needed it just as much as she did. She took one more deep breath, then left her apartment.

Portia waited in the upstairs hallway until she heard the gong, which signaled to the crowd that the bar queen was getting ready to perform and for her to start clinking her heels down the stairs, so everyone could hear her coming.

Time dragged on ever so slowly that Portia could almost hear her heart pounding as if each heartbeat sent thunder and lightning throughout her entire body, starting in her chest, radiating through her high heels, and shooting out sparks along the way. Once again, she heard Kyle's voice talking about her blue eyes, and a lump tried to form in her throat. She swallowed hard and pushed it away as she remembered Joel telling her that blue eyes were sexy too.

Once Portia reached the bottom of the stairs, she paused. She took another deep, electrifying breath and sashayed her hips, with nothing but the sound of high-heel-leather-boot clinking filling the low-lit room. The bar queen sauntered onto the stage, picked up the sparkling silver electric guitar, and took her position in front of the microphone. Then the stage lights blasted on, illuminating Portia in her black and gold fringe dress with boobs up to her chin and blue eyes twinkling like sapphires.

At that moment, Joel's emerald eyes locked onto Portia's sapphires for the first time, and she could tell he was happy to see her blue gems. A large smile spread across his face, making her heart feel like it wanted to leap from her heavy chest, but with that dress holding her bosoms so tight, that would be pretty difficult.

Everyone was there, just like always, including the Alexandria's crew, along with Gert, Polly, and Tanya, whose lips looked extra plump. Kirk and Hank were catcalling jerks, prompting Gunther to grunt with disgust. Gert stood as far away from Gunther as she could. While on the other hand, Tanya stood oddly close to Bubba, who yanked up his britches, desperately in need of a tie wrap. He was on sensory overload; he looked at Portia, then at Tanya, then back to Portia, and then to Tanya.

The townsfolk cheered, expressing their eagerness for Portia's performance to begin. She didn't usually take this long to start a song, but this would be the first time she sang about Kyle. Once again, a lump formed in her throat, and her eyes glistened slightly. Her hands froze, unable to strum the first chord, but when Joel nodded his head to her, Portia found the strength to begin.

Portia swallowed the lump away and smiled at Joel. She lightly strummed the electric guitar while she softly sang, hitting full vibrato by the second line; then she pounded the guitar strings with equal forcefulness. Meanwhile, the bass and drums kicked in, adding thunder beneath her voice. They maintained this power for the rest of the first verse.

You said
It's what you needed to do
You went farther north
It was a war zone
It was an arctic storm
The waves they claimed you
Yeah, they claimed you

Ted pounded the drums right before the chorus began, revving up the engine for Portia to sing her heart out as she powerfully strummed the guitar.

You took away the sun
You took away the light
I'm living in the dark
Like every day is night
The Northern Lights
No longer make me smile
Something I haven't done
In quite a while
Coz you loved the sea

More than you loved me
Yeah, you loved the sea
More than me

And this was just Portia's style, tender lyrics with a kick-butt, Rock & Roll motor. As she pounded the guitar strings during the transition from the chorus to the second verse, she could've sworn that she saw Kyle and Chris in the crowd, cheering her on, but deep down, she knew that wasn't possible. Portia closed her eyes and swallowed, pushing the lump back down her throat again. When she opened her eyes, Joel compassionately smiled and nodded his head, signaling for her to keep going.

And once again, this fueled Portia's fire, giving her the strength she needed for the second verse. As she sang, she became more interactive with the crowd, making eye contact with Gert and the Alexandria's crew.

I'm here
Without you singing with me
You were my hero
And I've been so mad
Better than being sad
Sometimes I hate you
But, I love you

As she sang the last line, Portia's voice cracked. It was much easier being angry with Kyle for dying than accepting that he was gone and acknowledging how much she loved and missed him. Meanwhile, Gert struggled to keep it together while Gunther stood motionless, not wanting to show any emotion. And then there was Bubba, who blubbered like a baby, using his hanky with one hand and holding his britches up with the other.

Portia kept her eyes on Joel as she sang the chorus again, knowing it would be better to focus on him than look at Gert or Gunther. They shared in this heartache, and she wanted to make it through the remainder of the song before a rogue wave of grief struck.

She stoically held it together as she flipped her hair around and rocked out an impressive guitar solo before singing the last section, where she put everything on the line—her sorrows, her regrets, and her addictions.

I can't take it
So I drink
And I smoke
Don't wanna think
Maybe I'll forgive you
For going away
Maybe I'll forgive you
Someday

Typically, Portia would've sung the chorus once or twice more before concluding the song, but this time was different. She had just divulged her deepest secrets, admitting that she was drinking and smoking pot to dull the pain and that she wasn't ready to forgive her father for leaving her and dying. A waterfall of tears streamed down Portia's cheeks as the crowd applauded, and even though love surrounded her, she wasn't up for any discussions. With her eyes still locked onto Joel's, Portia whispered, "Thank you," into the microphone. Then she set down the guitar and left the room. She went to her apartment with no intention of returning to the bar.

WHEN PORTIA ENTERED HER APARTMENT, her legs became weak, and she dropped to her knees. At that moment, she heard footsteps behind her, and the apartment door closed. Joel gently ran his hand down her head and back. He carried her to the sofa, gently setting her down, so his arm was around her; her thigh-high leather boots were draped over his lap. After they got situated, he reached his hand up to her face and softly caressed her cheeks.

"The song was beautiful. You are so brave. I'm proud of you," Joel said and then kissed her forehead before continuing to caress her face.

"Thank you," Portia whispered as she closed her eyes and savored his sweet and gentle touch. She opened her eyes and then reached her hand up to his as it rested against her cheek. "I was afraid you wouldn't want me after you heard the last part," she said as she pushed his hand harder against her face.

"On the contrary, putting yourself out there like that took a lot of guts. But drinking and smoking will make the sadness more intense. You know what? You have the most beautiful blue eyes that I have ever seen. Thank you for letting me see them."

"Better than the green?" Portia asked as her eyes spilled over once again.

"Better than the green," Joel repeated as he caressed her face and kissed her forehead again. "It's okay."

Joel made Portia feel safe and like everything would be okay, and she couldn't contain the building adoration she felt for him at that tender moment. She stared deeply into his eyes, reached her hands up to his face, and passionately kissed his lips, feeling her entire body tingle with happy goosebumps.

Joel felt the same way, for he leaned Portia back against a pillow and kissed her passionately while caressing her cheek, neck, and partially down her chest, stopping in a respectable place. The kiss was so electrifying that Portia felt the weight of the world fade away as she imagined Joel's muscular physique against her body. But doggonit, Portia and Joel were interrupted when Screech chortled and Tiny squeaked from where they were sitting on Portia's bed. Tiny popped his fluffy head up from Joel's hat while Screech stood up and stretched his back.

"That's an enormous cat! Is he a Maine Coon?" Joel inquired.

"No clue. He was once a scruffy, scrawny little kitten that Dad found at Spithead two years ago, and now look at him. Isn't he magnificent?"

"He sure is, but he kinda looks like he wants to eat me," Joel said as Screech laid down like the Egyptian Sphinx with his paws stretched out in front of him. The regal feline fervently twitched his tail and whiskers, putting his ears back and motioning a silent meow as he glared at Joel. "It's okay, buddy. We can be friends," Joel nervously said as he stared at the agitated cat.

"The best thing to do with him is to ignore him until he comes to you. And he will," Portia explained.

Now that Tiny figured out that the visitor was Joel, he jumped off the bed and across the room before springing onto Joel's leg and lovingly squeaking at him.

"He hasn't made those sounds since he was with my dad," Portia explained as she gently scratched Tiny's crest.

"Then I am honored," Joel responded as he rubbed Tiny's belly.

Portia was awestruck by the affection between Tiny and Joel. Animals are excellent judges of character, and the fact that Tiny had chosen Joel showed what a kindhearted soul Joel Layton truly was. Portia watched the faint wrinkles form along Joel's forehead, eyes, and cheeks as he smiled lovingly at Tiny. Joel's aging facial features were heart-fluttering, and Portia fell for him more with each passing second.

"You can take your hat back," Portia said.

"No, Tiny will get more use out of it now than I will," he replied as his attention shifted back to Portia, making her heart flutter again. "You're beautiful, Katerina Alexander. You and your blue eyes are beautiful. I'm falling for you—fast like a waterfall," Joel whispered as he gently glided his fingertips along her collarbones and then up the side of her neck until the back of his hand caressed her cheek.

She closed her eyes and smiled, adoring his tantalizing touch that left her wanting more. "I adore waterfalls," Portia breathlessly said and then leaned forward and kissed him.

Suddenly, her stomach growled, making it known that she hadn't eaten all day. "Oh, I haven't eaten since last night," she explained, slapping one hand over her mouth and the other over her stomach like that was going to shield the sound.

"That's pretty cute, you know? And you know what else? Eating is a good thing," Joel said as he took this opportunity to give her an admonishing kiss.

Portia closed her eyes and gently placed her hands on Joel's cheeks as she reciprocated this darling kiss, interrupted by another stomach growl. She pulled back slightly and laughed. "Are you hungry too?"

"Yeah, now that you mention it, I am," Joel replied with a chuckle.

"Do you like Reubens?" Portia asked.

"My favorite." Joel grinned.

"Mine too. That's the only sandwich my dad knew how to make. We ate it a lot when I was growing up. Well, I'll text downstairs and have two sent up. The perks of owning a restaurant," Portia said.

"Sounds wonderful," Joel replied.

Portia's phone was on the nightstand, so she got it and sat on the coffee table in front of Joel while she texted the order. Then she looked at him and couldn't contain her flirtations. "Well, if I have any hopes of eating, I must slip into something a little more comfortable. This isn't the type of dress one can wear and expect to eat," Portia sultrily said as she reached down and began slowly unzipping one of her boots. And, of course, Joel was all too willing to offer his assistance in this matter.

He placed his hands over hers and then took over, unzipping both thigh-high leather boots and slowly removing them. He caressed and massaged her silky legs, making Portia's heart flutter like an eagle taking flight. The sweetness continued as he slowly caressed her arms the same way he did her legs. Except this time, Joel's lips kissed her forearms, then down to her fingertips. Portia immediately felt flushed and tingly as she felt the rage of passion burning throughout her body.

She moved to the sofa next to Joel, scooting to the side, so her back was to him. She looked at him over her shoulder while seductively whispering, "Could you please help me with my back zipper? It's a little stiff."

Joel was delighted to help. He promptly took her hair in his hands, ran his fingers through it, and gently set it over her left shoulder. His lips glided across her neck and shoulder as he carefully and slowly unzipped the back of her fringe dress, tracing her spine with his fingers as he pulled down the zipper.

"Thank you," Portia breathlessly replied as she leaned her head back and rubbed her cheek against his. She slowly stood up, holding the dress in place, so her ladies wouldn't pop out now that the tight fringe dress wasn't restraining them. Taking extra care to sway her hips, Portia slowly walked to her closet to retrieve the perfect dinner outfit—a long, spaghetti-strap, leopard-print dress with a dramatic slit up to her hip. With every move, she felt Joel's eyes feasting on her scantily clad figure, which was okay with her.

As Portia was heading to the bathroom to deck out in leopard, someone knocked on the door. Joel jumped up to answer it, and Gert charged in unexpectedly.

"This tray is heavy and hot!" she exclaimed as she set it on the kitchen counter before noticing Portia, half-dressed and holding her dress over her chest to keep the girls inbounds. Always on point, Gert wittily asked, "Honey, aren't you cold?" Then beaming like a flower beneath a sunray, Gert held her hands over her heart while smiling and looking back and forth between Portia and Joel. "Oh, you two!"

"Thank you, Momma Gert," Portia imperatively replied, signaling with her hand that a hasty exit was in order.

"Well, I guess my presence isn't necessary anymore. Enjoy your dinner," Gert began as she turned toward Joel. "And I guess I won't see you at breakfast tomorrow morning," she said and then mischievously winked.

"Love you, Aunt Gert. Bye!" Portia exclaimed as she continued holding the dress over her chest.

"Have a great evening, you two!" Gert responded, then laughed her way out the door.

Portia looked at Joel and chuckled before slipping into the bathroom to put on the leopard dress. It clung daringly to her chest and fit snuggly around her tiny waist; and that long, dreamy slit up to her hip showcased her tightly toned legs. When Portia opened the bathroom door, she seductively posed in the doorway.

"Hey there, kitty cat," Joel said.

Then Portia sauntered up to him.

However, Screech thought that greeting was for him, so he ran up to Joel and promptly sharpened his claws on Joel's new shoes.

"Screech, no!" Portia admonished as she rushed into the kitchen to open a can of cat food so that he would leave Joel alone. She knew that a river of cat pee was the next card this feline would play if he wasn't distracted. Meanwhile, Tiny squeaked and shrieked, protesting for equal attention and demanding his fruit cup, so Portia promptly fed him as well.

Portia and Joel finally sat at the table and devoured their tasty sandwiches, fries, and root beer. However, dessert wasn't necessary because they already had what they needed. Portia and Joel turned to each other, neither holding anything back, as the Northern Lights danced over Eagle Bay.

Chapter 11. *Country Rock & Roll*

J oel wrapped his arms around her tightly toned body as she gently nibbled on his ear, sending chills up and down his spine. Her skin was soft, and her hair smelled like a mixture of mango sangria and salty ocean air. The allure of this sensuous woman with her heart beating against his was a lot for Joel to bear.

As the ocean breeze swirled around them and the moon reflected on the waves, Joel's lips pressed against Adoncia's before she led him into the cottage and alluringly paused by the bedroom on the right. Suddenly, alarm bells sounded inside Joel's brain, booming like a gong, vibrating throughout his body, and causing him to toss and turn. Then he abruptly sat straight up in bed. Awaking from a dream, he exclaimed, "Don't enter the bedroom on the right!"

Joel's heart pounded like he had just run a marathon. He rubbed his eyes, took a deep breath, looked next to him, and saw Portia peacefully sleeping. Joel smiled as he carefully laid back next to her, thankful that his outburst didn't awaken her. Watching the dazzling bar queen sleep, he thought of Adoncia and that fateful day so many years ago when he didn't enter the bedroom on the right. What a blessed moment in time, for it led him to this moment in Unalaska, Alaska, with Portia sleeping by his side.

To Joel's amazement, Portia was still wearing the leopard dress. Meanwhile, he was still wearing his shirt and jeans from yesterday as well. Hence, the bar queen and the Navy man only got so frisky last night. With a big inhale, and an even bigger exhale, Joel released a pleasant sigh of relief, knowing that he and Portia hadn't entered the metaphoric bedroom on the right because they were still fully clothed. However, this realization didn't stop Joel's eyes from watching Portia's heaving chest as she breathed, leaving him to wonder, *Hey, maybe she is cold,* so the thoughtful hunk reached for a throw blanket on the bottom of the bed then gently draped it over Portia as she slept. *We were so tired that we just passed out,* Joel recalled as he carefully tucked the blanket around her shoulders before gently caressing her cheek.

And that was the truth. Last night, there was some smooching, hand wandering, and an abundance of passion. More importantly, however, there was also the relaxation of being in the arms of a woman who knew his deepest thoughts and feelings and with whom he felt content enough to fall asleep in a peaceful, unawkward silence, which Joel had yet to experience, until now.

Yesterday, Portia and Joel had a rather eventful day, so falling asleep early was to be expected. Portia had been awake the night before, writing "More Than Me," while Joel spent the day with Bubba, who had invited him to a bingo tournament at the Aleutia Community Center. Joel spent the day (yes, the entire day) playing bingo with Bubba and the 80-plus crowd, and he had a great time. Joel had always enjoyed talking with the elderly because they were so wise and experienced. He sat next to a man named Henry who told Joel his life story, most notably about his service in World War II. And while Joel enjoyed his day with Bubba, Henry, and the bingo tournament, which Bubba won, it was mentally exhausting.

In addition, Joel still had jet lag and recalled yawning as he and Portia had finished dinner last night; then they had indulged in a generous serving of each other. Joel remembered kicking off his shoes, pulling Portia close, and wrapping his arms around her. Decadent smooches followed as he slowly and passionately kissed her, which quickly morphed into their sweetest, most sultry kisses to date. That's when Portia gave Joel *the look.* The titillating bar dancer slowly walked backward toward her bed as she held onto his hands. Then Joel gently laid her down and continued holding her and kissing her face, neck, and shoulders until they fell asleep in each other's arms while stars shimmered in the night sky, comets shot across the universe, and the Northern Lights danced over Eagle Bay.

Suddenly, Joel's recollections were interrupted by Screech and Tiny abruptly jumping onto the bed and executing an altercation between the pillows. *Well, this is a new experience,* Joel thought as he watched the little twerps duke it out like they were the final contestants in a boxing championship. Screech loudly hissed and showed off his pointy, vampiric teeth as he threatened Tiny with air swats, not making contact, but coming close enough. Tiny threw himself against Joel's head, clinging on for dear life like he had transformed species from a monkey to an octopus.

"Hey, hey, guys! What's going on?" Joel exclaimed as he placed his hand over Tiny to comfort him.

Screech ramped up the intimidation factor by growling as he continued swatting at Tiny, motivating Joel to close his eyes to prevent a claw from piercing his retinas. The drama ripped Portia from her peaceful slumber, and it was a good thing she had quick reflexes. She quickly sprang into action by grabbing Screech and pulling him into her arms, restraining him from whacking the monkey and subsequently Joel, which would've been a double victory for the fluffy jerk.

However, this had the opposite effect. Screech wasn't in the mood to calm down and snuggle. Instead, he growled, hissed, and threw himself out of the bed and across the room, chattering and grumbling along the way, most likely intending to piss on something that somebody liked.

Portia and Joel laughed, amused by the interspecies spectacle. Then Portia shrugged her shoulders and laid back down to face

Joel, who still had the monkey clinging to his head. Now that Screech had stomped off, Tiny loosened his hefty grip and chortled the sweetest little chirps as he slid down Joel's face and snuggled close to his neck. All the while, Joel kept his hand on him, gently petting his silky fur.

"How did you sleep, my beautiful rock star?" Joel asked.

"Well, let's see, sailor," Portia began as she scooted closer to him. "I fell asleep in your arms with you kissing my face. I don't think I have ever slept as well as I did last night."

Tiny jumped up on the headboard. Meanwhile, Joel pulled Portia closer, caressing her cheeks, hair, neck, and shoulders.

"How did you sleep, sailor?" Portia asked.

Joel was so enamored by her that he could hardly speak for the gigantic smile plastered on his face. "Best night of sleep in my life too," he whispered.

"Good," Portia replied, then kissed him. "I slept so well that I feel very refreshed and revitalized like I want to write another song. You have inspired me, Joel Layton," she said as she reached for his hand, then slowly kissed each finger.

Joel grinned and felt his heart flutter as he savored each kiss that fell from her sexy lips. "Will you write me a song today?"

Portia blushed. "I can certainly try."

"I'd like it if you did," Joel responded as he leaned closer, their cheeks touching.

"Okay, I'll see what I can do," Portia answered as she rubbed her cheek against his before nibbling his ear, sending ticklish chills up and down every inch of Joel's body. He needed to leave, so they didn't enter the metaphoric bedroom on the right. Portia was the real deal; he respected her too much to move too fast.

JOEL HADN'T BEEN GONE 15 MINUTES, and Portia missed him. She was still clinging to the high of waking up to his smiling face, which triggered a wild surge of creativity, spinning like a whirlwind within her body. To Portia, there was nothing like the spontaneity and wild bursting of ideas when the muse struck. However, this rush wouldn't last long, so she acted fast. She hurried into the kitchen, fed the critters, and brewed a pot of coffee.

Portia occasionally fired up a joint to heighten the writing experience, but this time was different; she woke up high on life, and that was enough. The bar queen got right to it; she promptly grabbed her electric guitar and sat on the sofa overlooking Eagle Bay. When she held the pick next to the strings, scenes from the other day flashed before her eyes, and the topic of the new song revealed itself. When she and Joel drove to Mount Ballyhoo, Portia recalled her finger being stuck in front of the preset radio buttons and her indecision of choosing a country or rock station. The rock station became her choice, and they thoroughly enjoyed the thundering guitars, bass, and drums as they drove through the Alaskan countryside.

Next, Portia chuckled as she recalled Joel driving leisurely until that reckless moment when he got wild, let it all loose, and hit that pink gas pedal as she had shouted, "Okay, now you're driving like a rock star!" And Joel had so wittingly replied, "Or a cowboy." Then Portia dubbed him the "cowboy rock star."

After that, Portia replayed the conversation she and Joel had on Mount Ballyhoo when he had asked her what genre her music was, and she had replied, "Well, I love country music, but I also love the power of a hardcore rock song. So, I am kind of torn, you know? Sometimes, I want to hear the lyrics of an old-fashioned country song with loud electric guitars jamming like a 1980s rock song. Some days, I sing country and rock it out on the electric guitar."

"That's it! Country Rock & Roll!" Portia shouted as she slammed the pick against the guitar strings, announcing the title of her next masterpiece. Then she envisioned a plow with a powerful blade that tilled pavement into a fine powder when the average plow just turned up dirt—a metaphor exemplifying country music with a Rock & Roll motor. The metaphors continued as Portia envisioned rolling country music and Rock & Roll together into a joint, smoking it, and getting high.

After 45 minutes of writing about her radio, truck, cowboy rock star, a pavement-breaking plow, and a musical joint roll, Portia had written her most outlandish masterpiece yet. The song deserved an equally incredible performance, and that's when Portia had her next epiphany. After closing that night, the bar queen would host an intimate cabaret for Joel by debuting her new song with a foggy chair dance beneath the spinning disco ball.

There was much to do to pull this off on short notice. For the choreography, Portia was a talented dancer and would improvise her moves on the dancefloor. However, the background music needed to be written and recorded via a software program. Time was of the essence, so Portia promptly poured another cup of coffee and set up her laptop and keyboard. Another bang-up Port House performance was in the works.

THE CLOCK STRUCK 4 P.M., alerting Portia that she needed to shower, style her hair, put on something seductive, and get downstairs to work the bar. She had been practicing and recording her new song all day. Still wearing the leopard dress, Portia had added her bathrobe and fluffy slippers to the ensemble and was on her third pot of coffee.

Just as Portia stood up from the sofa, she received a text message from Kirk checking in, which he often did since he was the handyman for the Port House as he was for many businesses and homeowners around Aleutia. He had a knack for fixing things (and womanizing lonely housewives). Since the Port House opened, Portia needed help with maintenance, and Kirk offered his services.

After the Port House's grand opening, the Port of Aleutia had a rather substantial earthquake, which loosened the dancing poles on each side of the bar, and Kirk all too willingly tightened those babies back up. Being the thorough and self-ingratiating handyman that he was, Kirk checked in to see how the poles were doing, always creating an opportunity to flirt with Portia, even if she didn't reciprocate.

Kirk: How are those poles holding up? With all your dancing, I wouldn't be surprised if you've shaken them loose. :)
Portia: Thx for your concern, but they're holding up to the challenge.
Kirk: Glad to hear. Is there anything else you might need my services for? Leaky faucet, squeaky door… back massage? ;)
Portia: Haha. Well now that you mention it…
Kirk: Go on.
Portia: I do need the memorial plaque hung by the door, and there is a light in the back hallway that just went out.
Kirk: You got it hot stuff. I'll see you at 5:30 to take care of those.

Portia shook her head and laughed at Kirk's persistence. After he, Bubba, and Chris ran Chuck out of town, Portia went on a few dates with him. Kirk was kind to her through her divorce and when her father and Chris died, but there was no hiding the fact that he was a good-looking, self-consumed, arrogant, cat-calling jerk. She kindly told him that she wasn't ready to date and wanted to be just friends. Ouch.

Portia looked at the clock again, realizing she needed to get herself in gear. As she turned to walk toward the bathroom, Screech suddenly humped up his back, sprinted across the room, and jumped into the litter box, where he proceeded to take a big poop and celebrate his victory by slinging litter everywhere. Meanwhile,

Tiny excitedly squeaked and jumped up and down. Unfortunately, from previous experiences, Portia knew what Tiny wanted, and she had to beat him to it. She rushed across the room and grabbed the pooper scooper. Just as she put the scooper in the litter box and collected Screech's stinky gift, Tiny leapt into the box, landed in the scooper, grabbed a turd, and ran away with it.

"Tiny, no! No!" Portia exclaimed as she frantically chased the thief around the apartment four times before catching him and wrangling the turd with her bare hands. However, Tiny clung to a small handful, and the little jerk shrieked as he threw it at Portia's forehead.

"I don't believe you just did that!" Portia shouted. After disposing of the scat, she thoroughly washed her hands and face. Then she put Tiny in the bathroom sink and gave him a warm bath, which he loved. Meanwhile, Screech indignantly sat on the coffee table where he sprawled out on his back with his fluffy tummy fur sticking straight up and proceeded with a bath, licking his paws and cleaning behind his ears.

"I certainly hope that you are impressed with yourself, sir!" Portia said to him as she carried Tiny in her arms and gently towel dried him, which he enjoyed even more than the bath.

Once Tiny was dry, Portia kissed him on the head and set him down on the floor. He promptly ran across the room, jumped on the coffee table, and bit Screech's rump. King alpha cat wasn't having any of that. He chased Tiny around the apartment six times before the monkey jumped on the counter and on top of the fridge. Screech was too big and fat to make it onto the counter, and the little punk rocker knew it.

"Oh, good grief, you two! I got to get to work!" Portia yelled, then went to take a shower. She sassily styled her hair and applied makeup in record time, red lipstick and kitty cat eyes included.

The voluptuous bar queen decked out in a skin-tight, black

leather suit that covered her entire body except for a giant oval exposing her chest and cleavage. Portia topped off this delicious attire with a pair of designer, closed-toe, come-and-get-me black leather pumps. Smoke may as well have filled the room because this spicy lady was on fire. She stood in front of the full-length mirror, putting the finishing touches on her hair and makeup. Tiny jumped up on the boudoir, looked Portia up and down, and let out the pretty lady whistle, a little trick Kyle had taught him.

"Why thank you, kind sir," Portia said.

PORTIA CLUNG TO THE MEMORIAL PLAQUE as she walked downstairs to the bar. Somehow, holding it close to her heart made her feel closer to her father and cousin, but it also triggered a mini tsunami of grief in her throat, which she did her best to swallow away, something she was all too used to doing these days.

The older townsfolk enjoyed the Port House's happy hour specials before the rowdy 40-year-olds arrived. Surprisingly, Lora was there with her balding husband, which was a rarity. Tucked in the far corner by the jukebox, Rhonda and Ted played checkers and nibbled on appetizers. Meanwhile, Reverend Thomas enjoyed his Reuben sandwich and the splendid view of Eagle Bay.

"Well, look at you, babe! You look great!" Kirk exclaimed as he swaggered in through the Port House door.

Gert glared at him as she carried a tray of food over to Lora and her balding husband's table. As soon as she turned around, Kirk hugged Portia, who cringed because his jacket smelled smokey and his breath reeked of whiskey.

At that moment, Joel entered the Port House. Kirk's back was to the door, so he had no idea that the Navy man had arrived.

"Hi, Joel!" Gert loudly said, alerting Kirk to Joel's presence.

Portia clutched the plaque and pulled away from Kirk. Then Joel slipped his arm around her waist, pulling her close.

Kirk couldn't keep his big mouth shut. "Portia, let me know if you want a real man and get sick of this limp squid," he asininely said.

Portia looked at Joel and could tell Kirk had pushed his button a little too hard this time. She was right because Joel promptly grabbed Kirk by his stinky smoke-saturated jacket and slammed him against the wall.

Ted placed his hand on Joel's shoulder. "I'll take it from here," Ted insisted as he grabbed Kirk, dragged him out the door, and pushed him out into the parking lot, where he fell, creating a cloud of dust when his tight buttocks hit the ground. Like nothing out of the ordinary had just happened, Ted returned inside, and he and Rhonda continued their checkers game.

JOEL TOOK A RICKETY BREATH as he walked over to the door and watched Kirk erratically drive away. Once Kirk's truck was out of sight, Joel turned around, and his heart sank when he saw Portia still clutching the plaque. He walked over to her and gently caressed her cheek.

"Joel, I like your style," Gert said as she walked up to Portia. "You all right, honey?"

"Just fine," Portia whispered, still clinging to the plaque.

"May I hang it for you? Where would you like it?" Joel asked.

Portia's cheeks blushed red as she nodded, and Joel couldn't hold back the intense feeling of admiration that overtook him, leaving him feeling warm and fuzzy inside, so he gently rubbed her shoulder.

"Over there by the door, please. I want people to see it when they first walk in," she softly replied.

"I'll grab the stuff," Gert said as she hurried over to the bar and returned with an old red toolbox.

"Thank you," Joel said as he took out a nail and hammer.

The bar grew eerily quiet as Joel worked, and the hammer banging echoed throughout the room. Once the nail was in place, Joel turned around and looked deep into Portia's blue eyes, signaling that it was time to let the plaque go. She pulled it close to her heart like she was hugging it goodbye and sighed as she handed it to him. And it was then that Joel first saw the oval of flesh across Portia's chest, and he did his best not to choke on his own spit and not show any facial expressions whatsoever. *Where does she buy these leather outfits? Does Aleutia have a red-light district?* Joel wondered.

And Joel wasn't the only one shocked to see the oval of flesh. Gunther entered the Port House, and when he saw it, he almost had a psychotic episode. "Good grief, kid! Put on a shirt!" He looked around, suddenly realizing what Joel was doing and why the room was so quiet. With a hack that preceded a nasty cough, Gunther stood next to Gert, who cringed.

After Gunther's throat convulsion subsided, Joel looked at Portia and nodded his head, and she nodded hers in return. Joel slowly turned around and carefully hung the plaque on the wall adjacent to Eagle Bay. Then he looked out the window just in time to see a golden sunray with an orange hue piercing the clouds, shining down on the bay and shimmering the ripples with a million sparkles. Once again, Joel felt God's mighty and remarkable presence.

"Thank you," Portia whispered as she walked up to Joel.

"Of course," Joel replied with an adoring smile.

Meanwhile, Gunther stepped closer to Gert. He couldn't resist the temptation to wrap his arms around her, so he moved in slowly and tried to slip his arm around her waist.

"You smell. Don't touch me! You stinky old coot!" Gert snapped as she hastily stepped away from him, crossing her arms and snarling like a pissed-off momma grizzly bear.

Gunther let out a long, ragged sigh before he reached into his pocket, took out a postmarked envelope, and handed it to Gert. "This came in the mail today from Lizzie. I thought you would want it. These are pictures from Elijah's birthday last week," Gunther solemnly explained.

Once Gunther's words sunk in, the color drained from Gert's face, and her hands trembled as she opened the envelope and looked at the pictures of their grandson. Gunther stepped closer to Gert and gently placed his hand on her shoulder. "Please come home. I need you. We need each other. Please, I'm begging you, Gertrude. Nothing is the same without you. I've lost Chris, I've lost my brother, and now I feel like I'm losing you too. I've got nothing without you. Please come home to me. Please," Gunther pleaded as his voice cracked.

Gert's eyes filled as she stared at the pictures and then looked at him. "Leave me alone," she whispered before carefully putting the photos back in the envelope, taking off her apron, and storming out the door.

The look on Gunther's withered, wrinkled, and stubbly face was beyond devastation. But Gunther wasn't without his theatrics; he flagrantly threw his arms in the air and shrugged his shoulders while he looked at Portia and Joel with a confused expression.

"I love you, Uncle. She just needs more time. I know Aunt Gert. She won't stay away forever. She will come home eventually," Portia reassured, then hugged him.

"I love you too, kid," Gunther whispered in her ear, then kissed her pale cheek. When he pulled back from the hug, Gunther was face to face with the oval of flesh and freaked out all over again, even putting his hands up to shield his eyes like the oval was going to blind him forever. "What in tarnation are you wearing? What's wrong with normal clothes and blonde hair, huh? Put on a sweater and some baggy pants! And sneakers!" Gunther shrieked, then violently coughed.

Portia flipped her hair over her shoulder and sarcastically pretended to consider Gunther's request. Then she shot back at him like a rebellious teenager. "Uh, no!" she exclaimed before pouncing on Joel's muscular chest and giving him a quick peck on the lips. "I'll get you both a beer," Portia said, trotting behind the bar.

And that's when Gunther gave Joel a look from the fiery depths of hell. He walked a few steps closer, crossed his arms, and locked his eyes onto Joel like he was getting ready to fire a Tarantula Boss Cannon in his direction. "Okay, Navy boy. You and me need to have a little chat!" Gunther implored as he pointed toward the bar, and he and Joel walked over and sat down in time for Portia to set out the frosted beer mugs.

"Well, holler if you two need anything. I need to help out in the kitchen since I'm down a waitress tonight," Portia said as she blew Joel and Gunther each a kiss before leaving the room.

Joel had never felt so uncomfortable in his life. His heart pounded, and sweat beads formed above his brow. His leg developed a nervous twitch, and he was one belch away from needing an antacid. He had survived boot camp and 20 years in the Navy, but none of those experiences had prepared him for this vexatious moment.

Gunther fiendishly enjoyed the uncomfortable silence as he took a long sip of beer. Then he exploded into an unprecedented outburst of laughter, which induced one of his infamous cough-hack-gag fits. After six coughs, at least four hacks, and one overly repugnant gag, Gunther finally proceeded with his admonishment. "Katerina is difficult, but she is easy to love. You hurt her and…"

"You'll kill me?" Joel filled in the blanks as he nervously gripped the mug handle until his hand cramped.

"Why so dramatic?" Gunther began with a chuckle that provoked another throat-clearing hack. "I was thinking castration. Let you live but suffer forever."

"I would never hurt her. But if I do, feel free to use me as crab bait because I wouldn't want to live anyway," Joel nervously replied as he wiped sweat from his brow.

Gunther looked at him and laughed as he slammed his beer mug on the bar top, making Joel almost leap off the stool.

"You know, boy, I keep trying not to like you, but you're making it very, very difficult! You seem up to the challenge for putting up with Katerina's shenanigans. She's not laid back or easygoing like my fine self. She did get my good looks, though. Her dad and I could've been twins," Gunther proudly spouted as he retrieved his beer mug, chugged it empty, and stared into it with one eye.

The nervous tension melted away, and Joel thought he was also trying not to like Gunther as well. Honestly, the bedraggled old coot made it nearly impossible not to like him, and would so even more, as time would soon tell.

Dr. Sampson conceitedly strutted into the Port House, expecting to find Lora alone. However, his balloon abruptly popped when his eyes met Lora's over the top of her balding husband's head, which had an uncanny resemblance to said balloon. Hence the preppy doctor retreated to his usual seat on the left side of the bar, where he had a direct view of Lora and the sun's glow reflecting on her husband's skull top.

Gunther shook his head. "If only her moron husband knew."

"The whole town knows, but he doesn't?" Joel inquired.

"He's dumb as a block, Joel. And then some!" Gunther swore.

"What's her husband's name?"

"Ya know, I've never cared enough to remember," Gunther amusedly replied as his throat convulsed from a deep, frothy crackle, which made Joel shiver to the point he could've tossed his cookies.

Gunther wasn't the only one having trouble with routine bodily functions. Bubba waddled up to the bar as he gasped and puffed like a beached salmon. "Hey, yall!" he managed to choke out as he took the seat on the other side of Joel.

As if Bubba wasn't already having enough issues breathing, his respiratory troubles magnified when Portia flounced up to the bar. "What can I get for you, Bubba?"

And that's when Bubba first saw the oval of flesh, beaming like a lighthouse in the night. A big dopy smile spread across his face before his mouth flew open. Despite his wide-open mouth, he still couldn't get enough air in, and he proceeded to pant and huff like he was getting ready to hyperventilate. All the while, he stared at the fleshy oval like a middle schooler reading a dirty magazine for the first time.

"Knock it off, Bubba! Or you're no longer deck boss! I mean it!" Gunther bellowed as he reached by Joel and walloped Bubba upside his podgy head.

The impact must've knocked some sense into Bubba because he promptly closed his mouth some, then breathlessly responded, "I'll take a light beer, please, Portia."

"You got it!" Portia replied, then quickly retrieved the beer.

Meanwhile, Bubba proceeded to huff and wheeze to the point Joel became increasingly concerned and patted him on the back.

While on the other hand, Gunther, who wasn't elegant in his discourse, couldn't keep his thoughts to himself any longer. "Are you having an asthma attack? What's the matter with you, boy?"

"Thank you, Portia," Bubba said as he took a big, sloppy sip of beer, promptly belched, and then wiped his mouth on his sleeve before continuing, "No, no asthma attack, Gunther. I'm just a little winded. That's all. Joel and I hiked to the top of Mount Ballyhoo this morning. I've decided that I need to exercise more, and like a good friend, Joel suggested we go hiking today. Thanks, Joel!" Bubba proudly explained as he leaned over without warning and gave Joel a great big Bubba hug, hanging on longer than was necessary.

"If you hiked this morning, why are you gasping for air now?" Gunther interrogated.

"We hiked for four hours. That's a very long time. I even forgot to pack a snack," Bubba said as he patted his overly substantial stomach.

"That was hours ago!" Gunther pontificated before cackling like a seagull that had just splattered upon an innocent bystander's shirt. Then he patted Bubba on the shoulder. "I'm just joshing you. Glad you and Joel had a good day. Try to catch your breath, bud."

Portia reluctantly gave Gunther another beer while Joel was halfway through his first one. The ravishing dame leaned across the bar, and all the boys certainly took notice of the beaming oval that heaved with every inhale.

"Where's Tiny tonight?" Bubba asked as he stared at the bar top, trying not to make eye contact with the symmetrical shape.

"The little cat turd thief is grounded! He was a bad monkey earlier and will be staying upstairs this evening," Portia explained as she looked at Joel and shrugged her shoulders.

"Now that is something you don't hear every day," Joel replied with a chuckle.

Portia's explanation was only to be matched by Nick's announcement as he, Leonard, and Old Al joined the boys at the bar.

"Hey, Portia. I was at Spithead today, and the eagles said to give you a message. They would like some herring delivered at your earliest convenience," Nick said with a grin.

"You tell my precious babies I will see them soon," Portia replied.

"Precious babies, my wrinkled backside! They crap all over my vessel!" Gunther retorted as he promptly finished his second beer and did his one-eyed stare into the bottom of the empty mug.

"Hey, I own the Alexandria, and the eagles can paint her however they please," Portia shot back at him.

"Oh, whatever!" Gunther teasingly responded, then whispered in Joel's ear, "See what I mean about her?"

The happy babbling continued as the 40-year-old crowd continued arriving, and the reverend and the older folks made a hasty exit. Thankfully, Kirk and Hank didn't appear after the incident earlier, and Joel relaxed and observed the interactions among the townsfolk. He enjoyed watching Portia intermingle with the locals and noticed how everyone with whom Portia talked was smiling, and Joel grew more infatuated with her with each passing second.

After making rounds from table to table, Portia came back around, looked at Joel with stars in her blue eyes, and leaned across the bar top in front of him. Ever so slowly, she leaned closer to him, while he leaned closer to her, and the enticing bar lady whispered in his ear, "I have a surprise for you tonight after the bar closes. Let's just say, I will perform my new song, just for you."

Portia's seductive words sent provocative shivers up and down Joel's spine as he slowly leaned a little bit closer and brushed his lips against her ear before he whispered back, "That sounds like a plan. I can't wait, pretty lady."

The fireworks show began. Portia took Joel's face in her hands and kissed him passionately. The room quieted down to the point that they heard Bubba's stomach growling. Then cheers echoed throughout the Port House.

"Oh, Portia's got herself a man!" Nick exclaimed as he patted Joel on the back.

"Yes, she does. A very good man," Bubba concurred as he teared up.

At a most inopportune moment, Joel's phone vibrated in his

pocket. With Portia standing across the bar in front of him, Joel discreetly pulled out his phone and saw that Adoncia had texted him a cleavage selfie in front of the Gypsy Market sign. Joel glanced at the picture and smiled before quickly closing out the screen and putting the phone back into his pocket. After that, he smiled at Portia, knowing she saw him swiftly check his phone. He needed to find the perfect time to tell her all about his prostituta friend and how this beautiful woman was the reason Joel came to Unalaska and met Portia. But when is the perfect time to tell your girlfriend about your busty prostituta friend who sends cleavage selfies? Is there really a good time for that?

"Hey, Portia, can I get a beer?" Old Al asked, diverting Portia's attention from Joel's phone and leaving Joel with an immediate sense of relief. Bullet dodged, for now.

The townsfolk spent the evening drinking beer and solving the world's problems as more people came and went. Everyone took notice of the growing affections between Alicia and Denny, which were grandstanded by another infamous make-out session between Nick and Polly as she gently stroked his hairless head. And speaking of bald heads, Dr. Sampson became increasingly fed up with the view of Lora's husband's shiny cranium, so the doc had three scotches and stomped out the door, knowing he wouldn't be getting lucky tonight. On the other hand, Gunther bantered with Old Al while Joel had the pleasure of talking with Bubba, who cried three times during their conversation because he wanted a girlfriend.

Joel had to admit that Bubba's emotional sensitivities made him uncomfortable. He was always concerned that a Chubby Bubba hug could come flying his way at any given moment. However, as a good friend, Joel did his best to cheer up his buddy and put a pep in his step. "Why don't you ask Tanya out?" Joel suggested.

Bubba's eyes perked up. "You really think she'll go out with me?" he asked with a sniffle before wiping his drippy nose on his shirt sleeve.

"You won't know until you ask," Joel said.

"Thank you, Joel. I think you and I could be soul brothers. You know just what to say," Bubba said as a large smile overtook his chunky face. The smile quickly turned into a yawn because he was tired from the Mount Ballyhoo hike. "I gotta go," Bubba said as he stood up to leave.

And Bubba wasn't the only one to bug out early. By 10 p.m., the bar was empty; the townsfolk must've been extra sleepy or amorous this evening, for everyone was out the door in record time. Wantonness was most certainly in the air, and Joel eagerly awaited the solo performance that Portia had promised. *What will Portia sing? How will she perform it?* Joel wondered as he reminisced about their first dance together beneath the disco lights, and a huge smile spread across his face.

The Port House was dead silent, except for the alluring sound of Portia's high heels hammering the floor as she left the kitchen and returned to the bar. "What are you smiling about, Captain Layton?" she seductively asked as she locked the doors.

"You. I'm smiling about you," he flirtatiously replied. Joel watched the sensuous lady sway her curvaceous hips from side to side as she dragged two chairs to the middle of the dancefloor, facing each other, a few feet apart.

Portia matched Joel's smile as she flashed him her dazzling pearly whites framed by those bodacious red lips. "Please wait here. I'll be back in 15 minutes," she said as she motioned for Joel to sit in one of the chairs. Then the starlit beauty hurried out of the room and up to her apartment.

PORTIA'S HEART POUNDED with blissful suspense. The anticipation of the private cabaret was so overwhelming that she had great difficulty peeling off the skin-tight leather outfit that clung so firmly and provocatively to her thin yet curvaceous frame. Then the starlet decked out in her seductive burlesque garb. With a mid-drift black leather vest pushing up the ladies, matching high-waisted shorts hugging her tiny stomach, and thigh-high boots adorning her luxurious legs, Portia was one hot tamale.

She couldn't just go trotting into the bar like this and open the buffet all at once. Accouterments as delicious as this leather decadence deserved a striptease appetizer. "What else to wear? A shirt, a shawl, or a dress?" Portia muttered as she searched her closet for something to cover up her torso until she was ready to rip it all off.

Meanwhile, Tiny woke up from his nap in Joel's hat, and when he looked at his hot momma, he let out the pretty lady whistle, which prompted Screech to puff up his fur with his black tuxedo jacket, perfectly framing his fluffy white chest.

Portia turned around and stared in astonishment at her furry little friends. "You two are brilliant!" she exclaimed as she took a white button-down shirt from the closet and gently removed Tiny from Joel's hat.

Thanks to her two little partners in crime, Portia had just hit the dinger on the sexy meter. With the Navy hat adorning her head and the white shirt buttoned just above her cleavage, Portia was ready to rock Joel's world. He may have spent the last 20 years traveling this beautiful earth, but Portia would soon take him places he had never been.

Before exiting her penthouse, she put on a wireless headset mic and grabbed the sound system remote control. The spicy starlit diva tiptoed down the staircase, taking great care not to hammer the floor with the spiky heels of those luscious leather boots, so Joel wouldn't hear her coming. Portia wanted every element of this steamy vaudeville to surprise him, especially the bang-up opening.

Immediately upon entering the bar, she simultaneously turned off the Port House lights, except for a few, flipped on the switches for the disco ball and fog machine, and pushed the play button on the sound system remote. Spinning lights encompassed the Port House while illuminating the rising fog. The lights and fog complemented the slow electric guitar strumming as it blared from the speakers, providing an opening even more dramatic than the usual thunderous gong that typically preceded the lady of the bar.

A simple yet powerful four-chord melody accompanied Portia as she climbed onto the bar top and foxily swung around the dancing pole on the right, which was the pole closest to Joel. The fog rose higher around him, and a voluminous smile plastered across his flawlessly crafted face, sending shivers up and down Portia's spine while kicking her sass into overdrive. With one arm and leg wrapped around that shiny pole, Portia leaned forward as she sang the first line, "I love a fiddle; I love its sound," before swinging around the pole and back onto the bar. Next, the foxy lady squatted down and back up, shimmying her shoulders, hips, and legs while singing, "I love electric guitars too loud!" The electric guitar ramped up at that moment like thunder and lightning beneath her powerful vibrato.

Portia felt Joel's eyes glued to her tight posterior while she strutted the length of the bar top as she sang, "I love a violin's do-si-do." She spun on her spiky leather boot heel, following up with, "I love a bass real deep and low!" Next, the saucy lady plopped her rear on the bar top. With one hand holding the hat in place and the other steadying her balance, she leaned back, kicked her legs in the air a few times, and then jumped off the bar with her high heels slamming the floor.

Portia sauntered through the shimmering fog to the vacant chair across from Joel. She stared into his emerald-green eyes as she ripped open the white shirt, exposing the risqué leather vest, showcasing her bouncy, bodacious knockers. For a moment, Joel's mouth flew open. But the man got his wits about him, closed his mouth, and looked at Portia with such an adoring and wanton expression that she could've made love to him right then and there.

However, the promiscuous dame resisted the urge as she slowly lowered the white shirt down her arms and back before slipping it off and holding it stretched above her head, all while swaying her curvy hips from side to side. She voluptuously spun the shirt in a few circles and tossed it to the side. After that striptease act, she frolicked up to Joel as she sang the pre-chorus.

I'm sitting here in my pickup truck
I'm staring at the radio; my finger's stuck
Do I want some country or Rock & Roll
No, I want country and Rock & Roll

In preparation for the chorus, Portia inched closer to Joel until she straddled her handsome beau. She stared adoringly into his eyes as she swayed to the music while taking off the Navy hat and gently setting it on his head where it so rightfully belonged. Portia seductively ran her fingers through her hair, still moving her hips to the beat. The disco lights reflected on the gold embellishments on Joel's Navy hat and illuminated the twirling fog around them.

The passionate bond between Portia and Joel was impenetrable. The earth could've combusted into a fireball, and neither of them would've known it one way or another. Even nature celebrated in their wonderment, for the Northern Lights lit up the sky with swirling colors that shimmered on Eagle Bay.

Portia slinked backward toward her seat, where she provocatively did a chair dance while belting out the chorus. The leather-kissed diva sat down then promptly popped her legs open and closed, before spinning sideways on the chair, leaning back, and kicking her thigh-high leather boots all the way out, while singing, "I want a motor with a thunderbolt / A plow that breaks pavement with just one note." She stood up facing Joel and moved her hips from side to side, rubbing her hands up her cheeks, throughout her long hair, and down her sides as she stared into his eyes while singing about the whimsical joint roll.

> Roll the two together; let's light a smoke
> Together we'll get high on Country Rock & Roll
> On Country Rock & Roll

In preparation for the second verse, Portia lifted her toned leg in that oh-so-sexy leather boot and kicked her chair off to the side since she would be sharing Joel's chair from this point forward. In all her voluptuous grandeur, the bar queen sultrily danced toward the Navy man, promptly pushed his legs together, and straddled him, all while moving her hips in circles and running her hands through her hair and down her sides.

After this sensual display, Portia took Joel's face in her hands while singing, "I love a cowboy's tight dark blue jeans / I love a rock star's shiny stud seams!" Following this, Portia went in for the real deal. She sat down on his lap and got close to his face, draping her arms around his neck, staring intensely into his eyes, and singing, "I love a cowboy's snakeskin boots / I love a rock star's leather suit!" All the while, Joel's hands gently gripped her hips as the dainty superstar continued swaying to the rhythm and staring into Joel's eyes during the second pre-chorus.

> I'm sitting here in my pickup truck
> I'm staring at the radio; my finger's stuck
> Do I want a cowboy or a rock star
> I want a cowboy who's a rock star

In preparation for the chorus again, Portia stood up and backed up a few feet before dropping down to her knees, almost disappearing into the fog while leaning back until her head touched the floor. She began singing the chorus as she slowly shimmied herself back up to her knees, "I want a motor with a thunderbolt / A plow that breaks pavement with just one note!" Following that, Portia leaned forward on her hands and stuck her tight butt in the air, singing, "Roll the two together; let's light a smoke." As she sang the rest of the chorus, the dazzling diva rolled over on her side, propped herself up with her arm, and placed her head in her hand, "Together we'll get high on Country Rock & Roll / On Country Rock & Roll."

Next, the seductress took great care to shake her bum as she crawled across the floor to the stage, where she alluringly stood up and ran her hands up and down her sides, across her cheeks, and throughout her shimmering hair. She picked up the electric guitar and rocked out a solo while walking toward the middle of the foggy dancefloor, then seductively sang the next section.

> Take a big draw of that smoking, smoking
> Ooo, a chair dance, dazzling high
> Take a big draw of that handsome, handsome
> Cowboy rock star delight

After that, Portia took off the guitar and laid it carefully on the stage. When she turned around, Joel stood up from the chair. As he walked toward her with his hand out, Portia felt a million flutters in her heart, which amplified when she placed her hand in his. Joel pulled her close, and they glided to the music like two eagles floating on a breeze above a foggy bay. They held each other close and swayed to the beat as Portia sang the chorus for the final time.

Even though the song ended, their embrace continued as the

disco lights and fog danced around them and the Northern Lights reflected on Eagle Bay's shimmering ripples. Joel reached up to Portia's chin and caressed her cheek before passionately kissing her.

"Thank you. That was amazing. I've never had my own strip show before." Joel chuckled as he leaned his forehead against Portia's. "You're the sexiest woman alive."

"You are very welcome, Captain Layton," Portia replied as she straightened the Navy hat on his head. "This is where it belongs," she said, then kissed him again.

"I'm no longer Captain Layton," Joel whispered.

"Oh yes, you are. No one can take that away from you. I'll never forget seeing you all decked out in your Navy uniform for the first time. You took my breath away, Captain Layton. You're taking my breath away right now. You are a captain, and that hasn't changed even though you're no longer in the Navy. You're my captain now," Portia sweetly said as she wrapped her arms around him.

Chapter 12. *Comrades*

Gunther and Bubba invited Joel to lunch at The Bairdi Saloon to meet with some local fishermen. Joel had oldies on the radio, the window down, and the heat on high as he slowly cruised down the country road with Gunther's rat trap sputtering closely behind him.

An old, brown and white, hand-carved, wooden sign along the roadside made the saloon hard to miss. Joel flipped on the blinker and laughed as he recalled Portia making fun of him for using it before driving up to Mount Ballyhoo. But Joel followed the rules, used the blinker as he turned right into the lot, and parked next to Bubba, who eagerly waved like a little boy meeting his superhero for the first time. Meanwhile, Gunther's truck backfired and blew out an exorbitant amount of smoke as he parked it and turned off the engine.

In all its rustic splendor with dark log and white stucco exterior walls complemented by a colorful stone foundation, The Bairdi Saloon sat nestled along Aleutia Bay. An old, hand-carved *Established in 1895* sign greeted patrons as they entered through a dark green door with elk horn handles. Decades of foot traffic indented the original hardwood floors, providing a rustic complement to tacky green, gold, and white beer stein wallpaper. Black and white photos of antiquated fishing vessels and taxidermy mounts of bighorn sheep, elk, mule deer, cougar, and bear provided the perfect mix of maritime and mountain décor. And a moose-rack chandelier provided inadequate lighting next to a stone fireplace across from two pool tables. To add to the ambiance, the delicious scent of fried fish reminded Joel of his first dinner with Adoncia in Rota all those years ago, and Joel immediately knew what he would be ordering for lunch.

"Hey there, gentlemen! Ain't seen you for a while!" The husky voice of a bald, 60-year-old man exclaimed from behind the bar.

"Hey there!" Gunther reciprocated the manly gesture.

"Hey, Zac!" Bubba exclaimed as if he had seen his second favorite superhero of the day.

Gunther squinted at Bubba's jubilation before continuing, "Zac, I'd like you to meet one of the new greenhorns this year, Joel Layton. Joel, this is Zac Hamilton. His family has owned The Bairdi Saloon since its inception in 1895."

"Inception? Gunther, that's a good word! I'm going to use that later today." Bubba cackled as he elbowed Gunther in the ribs.

"Hey, I have my moments of intellectual serendipity." Gunther chuckled as he preppily fixed his wrinkled flannel shirt collar, which appeared to be much cleaner than his stinky, smoke-saturated jacket and paint-splattered boots.

Joel laughed before extending his hand toward Zac. "It's a pleasure to meet you."

"Joel is a real Navy captain!" Bubba added.

"Really? How cool is that?" Zac exclaimed, totally on board with Bubba's enthusiasm. "Thanks for serving our country, man."

Gunther was perplexed by the ever-jovial Bubba, but he couldn't disagree with Zac's response. "Yeah, we're lucky to have him. Anyway, enough of this sappy stuff!"

"What made you decide to come to Aleutia, Joel?" Zac asked.

Joel paused, for he had to choose his words carefully. Now wasn't the appropriate time to divulge that his presence in Aleutia was the result of a prostitute's persuasion. "It just kinda happened. Clicked on the right Internet link," he vaguely answered.

"Oh, well, that's great! Welcome to the Aleutian family," Zac began as he looked at Gunther. "Well, sit over at your usual table with the boys. They've been here since breakfast and just switched from coffee to beer! I'll be over shortly to take your orders."

"We only need one menu. The rest of us know what you serve. The menu hasn't changed in 50 years. When you have food this good, why change up?" Gunther said as he winked at Zac and patted Joel on the shoulder.

"No problem." Zac laughed as he handed Joel a one-page menu with minuscule print.

"Hey there, comrades!" Gunther bellowed as he sat down at the table full of day drinkers.

Joel immediately recognized all the men at the table since they were at the Watermen's Memorial this past Sunday.

"Gunther, how are ya?" a middle-aged man with red hair and a freckled face jovially replied as he reached to shake his hand.

"Other than being old and ugly, I'm doing all right," Gunther wittily responded. "Everyone, I'd like you to meet Joel Layton. Our newest greenhorn!"

"He's a retired Navy captain!" Bubba exclaimed.

The red-haired guy stood up and extended his hand to Joel before introducing everyone. "Hey, thanks for your service. I'm Captain Arnold Babanin of the Windswept Belle. This handsome dude next to me is my brother Donald; he's our deck boss. Across from me is Captain Winifred Karchagin of the Aleutian Hero and Captain Jack Smith of the Bering Sea Lady."

"Thank you. Nice to meet all of you," Joel responded as he shook everyone's hand, then sat down on an antique chair that loudly creaked. Meanwhile, he laid the menu on the table; it wasn't even worth trying to read it. They all ordered the saloon's signature fish and chips dish with a draft beer, which was okay with Joel.

"Looking forward to your first year as skipper?" Captain Babanin asked Gunther.

"Yes. Although, I wish I were still one of the relief captains and a deckhand. But, things change, and here I am," Gunther somberly replied.

"I hear that," Captain Babanin began. "It's gonna be tough without Billy this season. He was a good worker and an all-around good person. It's just not fair that he's gone."

"How's Millie and the girls?" Bubba asked, then told Joel, "Millie was Billy's wife."

Captain Babanin gulped beer and sighed. "It's been hard on them. Real hard. Millie and the girls moved in with Millie's parents. Thank goodness they had somewhere to go because she couldn't keep the house without Billy's income. Millie got hired at the community center, though, so that's a very good thing."

"She probably feels close to him there. Billy's volunteer work meant the world to him," Gunther sadly added.

"I can't believe we lost Gordon either. Best friends, dying within days of each other. It's hard to imagine this really happened. Billy, Gordon, Chris, Kyle, Georgia, all gone way too soon," Captain Karchagin lamented.

"And Georgia was my momma's best friend. Momma has Louis and Tasha over for dinner every week," Bubba emotionally explained.

Joel's heart sank as he listened to everyone talk about the people lost earlier in the year. Having spent seven years in an orphanage, Joel understood this life-altering devastation all too well. He felt the sorrow of his colleagues, and he understood and respected their devotion to the sea, despite the tragedies they all faced. And unfortunately, he knew what they all knew; more disaster would come in this line of work. It was inevitable.

Everyone was thankful for the distraction when Zac brought out two trays of beer and fish and chips. After setting down the trays, he promptly returned to the bar to answer the ringing phone. Tanya and her recently injected lips suddenly appeared and served the beer, followed by the fish and chips, triggering Gunther to have a psychotic episode.

"What do you think you're doing? Don't touch my food!" he roared.

"I've been working here for a while now, so deal with it!" Tanya snapped, not daunted by Gunther's words.

Joel nudged Bubba with his elbow, insinuating that Bubba should take this opportunity to strike up a conversation with Tanya.

"What do I say?" Bubba whispered in a panic.

"Start with hi," Joel suggested.

Tanya served Bubba his plate while she eyeballed Joel. Bubba coughed nervously, then wiped sweat off his forehead before mustering up the confidence to speak. "Hi, Tanya. Thank you, Tanya, for my plate. Your lips are looking extra plump today. Did you get a refill?"

"Why thank you, Bubba. I did, and nobody had said anything about it yet. You're the first person to notice," Tanya genuinely replied as she set the last plate on the table. "Can I get anything else for you fellas?"

"Leaving would be sufficient!" Gunther retorted. "Take your fake lips with you!"

Tanya shot Gunther an evil look, then looked at Bubba, puckered her refills, and stuck out her silicon chest before returning to the kitchen. The dazed expression on Bubba's face was equivalent to when he first saw the oval of flesh last night at the Port House.

You go, Bubba! Not what I would've said to a woman, but then again, Tanya sure did seem to like it, Joel thought as he picked up his knife and fork, getting ready to dig into the fish and chips.

"Joel, go see Old Al to get your gear for the cold temperatures,"

Captain Babanin began. "We don't want you getting hypothermia. The water will be 38 degrees and dropping. There could be 60-mile-per-hour winds and 40-foot seas."

"Just as long as we don't get any of those darn freak waves. You never know when one or two of those monsters will hit, especially in Satan's Expanse. I saw a 75-footer two years ago just as Paul pulled up a pot. Thank God he didn't get pulled overboard by it. He would've been a goner," Captain Karchagin said as he did a full-body shiver.

"Kyle and I saw a 95-footer in 1997 in Satan's Expanse. How we all survived is only by the grace of God. Then, of course, we all know what happened last year," Gunther added with a sad sigh.

"Joel, did you ever see a rogue wave when you were captain of the USS Roland?" Bubba inquired.

"Unfortunately," Joel responded quietly, deciding whether or not he really wanted to talk about it. Everyone stopped eating and stared at him, waiting for the Navy captain to share his story.

"Five years ago, this past August, a 120-footer knocked the destroyer on its side. We rapidly lost oil pressure, and the engines cut off. We lost five crew members that day. The USS Roland regained control pretty quickly, but we'll never get those sailors back," Joel solemnly shared as he tried not to relive the event.

"Wait a second. I remember seeing that on the news. That was you! You were interviewed and given a Navy Cross. Joel, you saved the crew," Captain Smith said.

Bubba patted Joel on the back, for he had met a true superhero, indeed. Gunther felt the same way since he looked at Joel with the utmost respect and approval. Everyone's reaction touched Joel's heart. He felt a tickle in his throat and swallowed it away before the lump started to form. This rogue wave was a defining moment in his life. Little did Joel know that another defining moment was in the not-so-distant future.

Joel had met the families of the USS Roland's lost sailors, and he saw the sorrow they would live with for the rest of their lives. After attending their memorial ceremony, he was devastated and considered leaving the Navy. However, he knew that wasn't the answer, that it wouldn't bring those sailors back—or bring his parents back. Storms and rogue waves were a reality that he and all sailors faced.

Captain Karchagin lifted his beer stein to give a toast. "To Captain Layton, a true hero. We are lucky to have him join us on the Bering Sea."

Each man lifted his stein, and they all clinked them together. Once again, Joel swallowed away the rising tickle in his throat. He appreciated the kindness of his new friends and colleagues. God was showering Joel with blessings as he embarked on this new journey in Alaska. *God is good,* Joel thought. God is good, indeed.

For a few minutes, no one said anything as the men chowed down on their fish and chips before Gunther struck up another conversation. "So, Babanin, did you get your IFQ?"

"Ya know, I was impressed. It's better than last year. I was glad to see that the TAC went up," he answered.

Joel had no idea what they were talking about whatsoever. He knew all his Navy terminology, but these acronyms were gibberish to him.

And he didn't contain his confusion well because Captain Babanin started laughing. "Got yourself a greenhorn, Gunther. Hey Joel, it's okay; we were all greenhorns in the beginning. This is your year of transformation."

Gunther laughed and gave Joel a friendly nudge. "Yeah, you'll be sorting crabs. We'll teach you how to do that too."

"We only keep the males. Females and juveniles get thrown back," Donald explained.

Bubba whispered in Joel's ear, "Don't worry. We'll give you a crash course when we get out to sea. I'll show you how to sort the crabs too. The IFQ is the individual fishing quota. Each owner gets a set number of pounds to catch. The TAC is the total allowable catch. So, for this season, the TAC is 10 million pounds for Bering Sea red king crabs."

"Makes sense. Thanks," Joel whispered in return.

"Hey, no problem. You'll *catch* on quickly," Bubba replied, elbowing him over the pun.

"I hope this upswing continues," Gunther began as he looked at Joel. "The amount we're allowed to catch has declined significantly since the 90s. Kyle and I caught a lot more crabs back then."

"Ain't that the truth, Gunther. Oh hey, remember little Tasha Bernard? She now has the Betty Sue out of Port Claus. This season, I'm leasing part of our quota to her. She's trying to get going in this business, following in her daddy's footsteps, so we thought we would help their family," Captain Karchagin said.

"Is that right? Good for her. She was always a good kid, and her father was a good man. You see, Joel, this is how most of us get going. We share our opportunities, and we help each other out," Gunther explained.

Joel smiled and politely nodded his head. "Yes, Captain."

Donald's phone loudly received a text message. He paused to read it, then announced, "Come on, Captain. We gotta go. Our delivery is at the docks."

"I hope it's right this time." Captain Babanin chuckled as he stood up and threw some money on the table. "Well, boys, we got to skedaddle. It was a great lunch. Good to see all of you. Nice to meet you, Joel. We are glad you are here! We'll see all of you at the Blessing of the Fleet."

AFTER LUNCH, everyone went separate ways. With little time left before shipping out to sea, Joel decided to purchase his gear. He had no idea what this entailed, so he went to see Old Al as Captain Babanin had suggested. This time, Joel would be shopping during regular business hours, not late at night with Portia trotting around Aleutia in her thigh-high leather boots and packing a pistol.

Snarling with his ever-present drool glob swinging from side to side, Rufus greeted Joel as he walked into Aleutian Apparel & Gear. *That is one ugly dog,* Joel thought as he stared at the agitated mutt and wondered if he should attempt to walk by him or wait for Old Al to come out from the back. However, Joel felt bold, so he crouched down, eye level with the wrinkly mongrel.

Rufus promptly showed Joel his sharp teeth, then sloppily licked up his slobber wad, which made Joel's mouth water as he choked back a heave. Then Rufus looked up at Joel with puppy eyes full of love. Joel slowly reached his hand toward the hound's nose, so Rufus could get a good sniff before Joel attempted an ear scratching, which Rufus loved. *Eh, he might be somewhat cute,* Joel thought.

"Hey there, Joel!" Old Al exclaimed as he walked up to him.

Joel stood up. "Good afternoon, sir."

"I see you and Rufus are now friends. You passed his test. The behind-the-ear scratch means you will have a friend for life," Old Al said as he gave a treat to the ugly doggie.

Rufus promptly took his treat over to his bed near the counter, where he proceeded to create a new drool drip as he chowed down.

"What can I do for you?" Old Al kindly asked.

Joel was hesitant to respond because he wasn't exactly sure what he needed to buy. "I need gear."

"Ah, yes. You need bib pants and a bunch of other stuff. I hope you like bright orange, and I hope you like suspenders," Old Al replied with a smile as he patted Joel on the shoulder.

"Suspenders?" Joel asked.

"Bright orange, boy. Don't worry. It comes with a matching

jacket. The key is, layer to keep warm. The foul weather out there will be unlike anything you have ever experienced," Old Al said as he walked over to a rack of orange waterproof pants with suspenders and matching jackets. He picked out everything Joel needed: wet gear, boots, warm clothing, a sleeping bag, and a pillow. In addition, Old Al threw in a bright orange apron along with wrist and arm covers. "Boy, this is your first season. I can almost guarantee that you will be filling bait bags. Take an apron. Trust me."

"Whatever you think I need, I'll get. Thank you," Joel responded as he walked over to the counter and watched Old Al ring everything up.

"Your total is $2,150.50. Warmth ain't cheap, son," Old Al said.

"No problem," Joel answered, handing him a credit card.

After he took the payment, Old Al didn't say anything while he bagged Joel's gear. He sighed before looking Joel in the eye. "Don't let Kirk get to you. He's just jealous of you, that's all."

Joel was pretty taken aback by this. Old Al was a nice, old guy who disapproved of Kirk's demeanor. It took a lot of guts and character for a man to say that about his son.

Joel paused and nodded at Old Al, unsure what to say but still showing respect and acknowledging his comment. "Thanks for all your help today. I appreciate it. Now I won't freeze to death."

"No problem, kiddo," Old Al replied.

Joel smiled as he carried several bags of gear out to his truck. Even Old Al called him kiddo, but this didn't bother Joel. He liked having Gunther and Old Al calling him son, boy, and kiddo, and having the older guys to admire.

With each passing day, Joel was blown away by the new colleagues and friends he made in Aleutia. He enjoyed getting to know the crew, exploring the town, hiking along the water, and, most of all, enjoying the leather-kissed evenings at the Port House.

Chapter 13. *Flying Boat*

The lady of the bar had outdone herself once again. Portia wore a cold-shoulder snakeskin dress that ended a couple of inches above the tops of matching thigh-high boots, and she had volumized her hair to perfection. Joel almost slapped himself in the face to ensure he wasn't envisioning a fantasy. Nope, no fantasy—just a bar queen doing her thing.

As the crowd died down for the evening, Portia leaned across the bar in front of Joel while the faithful little monkey sat between them, begging to be the center of attention.

"What is something that you don't like? Something, you absolutely despise," Portia inquired and then knocked back a tequila shot.

"Is this a trick question?" Joel asked with a chuckle, ever amused and always on his toes because there was no predicting what would come out of Portia's beautiful mouth.

"Hey, I'm the one asking questions," the seductive bar queen retorted with a sultry grin.

"Flying. I don't like flying," Joel admitted.

"Why?"

"Coz, I just don't like it," he replied. Joel had never thought about why he didn't like flying. He just knew he didn't care for it, and when the recycled air got stuffy, he felt like he would hurl. Beyond that, there was never a need for him to psychoanalyze it.

Portia leaned farther across the bar and stared so profoundly into Joel's eyes that he felt their souls connect. "You don't like flying because it's the opposite of what you love. You love the ocean."

Joel felt his heart do a somersault because Portia saw right through him. "Well, I never thought of it that way, but you're right. I'm meant to be floating on the waves and with the wind. But I must admit that I have always enjoyed amphibious aircraft. I'm just not a fan of commercial travel."

"Have you ever flown with anyone? For fun?" Portia queried.

"Well, no, just myself. I always found flying to be kind of lonely. Never felt that way at sea. I always knew everyone on board."

Portia nodded her head like all the pieces of the puzzle fell into place. "You've never had the fun of traveling somewhere with friends or…" she stopped herself before continuing.

"Or family," Joel finished the sentence for her, never breaking their impenetrable, soul-binding stare. He reminiscently sighed. "When I was a kid, we took a few road trips. We were poor, so flying wasn't an option. But those trips were so wonderful. Anyway, you've flown before, I take it?"

"Only in the great state of Alaska, not very high up, and always with land in sight. You can't live in Alaska and not have flown in a single-engine tin can." She laughed.

"Have you ever been anywhere else?" Joel asked.

"Nope, I've never left Alaska. I've been all over the state but have never left it. Nope," Portia yammered as she blew a stray strand of hair out of her face.

"Never? Ever?" Joel inquired. He couldn't imagine staying in one place his entire life, but then again, he had no family and no reason to stay in one place—until now.

"Nope, why would I want to leave? This place is so beautiful that I couldn't imagine being anywhere else," Portia replied.

Turning the tables and now reading the beautiful book of Portia, Joel responded, "Or maybe, you never had anyone you wanted to travel the world with. I remember you telling me that you're also afraid of the sea because of what it did to your family, and that's why you're afraid of being too far away from land."

Portia's eyes glistened as she continued staring deeply into Joel's eyes. She reached for his hands and squeezed them tight, sending tingling chills throughout his body.

Thank you, God, for bringing us together. I love this woman! Joel thought as he leaned across the bar and kissed Portia's puffy red lips, not caring if he got lipstick all over his face. He was never sure of much in his life, other than loving the ocean and wanting to be a Navy captain, but now at 38 years old, he knew he wanted to be covered in Portia's lipstick for the rest of his life.

And here they were—Joel, a world-traveling ocean lover—and Portia, the land-loving, Alaska-bound native—so many differences, yet so many likenesses. They had only known each other for a week now, but to Joel, he felt like he had known Portia forever. This past week had been the best in his life. Considering the magnificent places he had traveled during his time in the Navy, no other place compared to his fascination with the Port of Aleutia.

The next day, Joel would begin another week by attending the Divine Liturgy at the Aleutian Russian Orthodox Cathedral, where he and Portia would worship under those magnificent Domes of Heaven with two eagles sitting on the golden crosses while adoring the Sunday-morning sunlight. What a glorious start to yet another week celebrating the privilege of being alive on God's magnificent earth.

And with only three weeks left before the Alexandria would depart for the Bering Sea, Joel wanted to spend every waking moment he could with Portia before he left, so it was high time that he asked his lady out on a date.

"Hey, Portia, could you come back here for a minute?" Gert hollered from the kitchen with her salty twang.

"I'll be right back," Portia said, then leaned across the bar, kissed Joel, and kissed Tiny on his head before she spun on her high heels and sashayed her snakeskin hips all the way to the kitchen.

She looks good coming and going! God really went all out when He crafted this beautiful lady, Joel thought as a dopy grin splashed across his face, which must've been something because Tiny called Joel out on it. The monkey uttered a cackling shriek that prompted Joel to pull his face back into the appropriate position. "Oh, you're just jealous." Joel chuckled as he rubbed Tiny's chest and belly.

The monkey's distraction was short-lived because Joel's mind reverted back to Portia as he replayed their conversation, giving him the perfect idea for a date after liturgy. Feeling techie, Joel searched for *Unalaska seaplanes* on his cell phone and was pleased to see a link for *Unalaska Flying Boat Tours*, which had a picture of a Thompson J-45 Muscovy on the homepage. Joel smiled and was delighted with this finding, for he knew this airplane from his Navy training.

The Muscovy was an amphibious aircraft from the 1940s that was used on land and in the water, patrolling against attack submarines during World War II. This magnificent waterbird also had two engines, which met Joel's criteria perfectly. If an aircraft didn't have at least two engines, there was no way in heck that he was flying in it. The fact that this plane could float like a vessel and perform landings and takeoffs from the water was a bonus.

Meanwhile, Tiny wanted to help Joel make these plans, so the monkey clung to the back of Joel's hand and the phone.

"Yes, you can be my special helper," Joel said with a smile as he read the tour choices, which included Akutan Island, Bear Viewing, Sea Lion Viewing, and Northern Lights. Pleased with the options, Joel carefully removed Tiny's paws from the cell phone and then called to make a reservation.

A raspy male voice answered, "Hello. Pete Hanson with Unalaska Flying Boat Tours here."

"Hello. My name is Joel Layton. I want to book a flight

tomorrow, only for two people, and I want it to include all the tours together. Can you do that?"

"Well, no one else has booked anything tomorrow. It ain't going to be cheap, son. Never had anyone want to combine all the tours."

"I know that plane can stay in the air for at least 20 hours, and money isn't an issue," Joel responded, while keeping his eyes on the back hallway, so Portia wouldn't stumble upon the conversation.

"Oh, so you're a Navy seaplane buff, eh? Boy, I flew this plane in World War II. She kept me safe and served her country well. I'll see you tomorrow at 1 p.m. at the end of Muscovy Drive. We will depart from Nateekin Bay."

"Thank you, sir. Looking forward to it. Have a good night," Joel replied, then ended the call. *This guy tells great jokes. There's no way any pilot from World War II could still be piloting at that age,* Joel thought as he looked at Tiny and chuckled. Suddenly, Joel heard Portia's heels clonking the floor, so he cleared his cell phone screen and then laid the phone face down on the bar top.

"Why so secretive?" Portia asked as she walked up to the bar with a disconcerting expression and her arms folded across her chest.

"Oh, it was just one of the guys," Joel fibbed, and not very well because Portia looked at him skeptically, but luckily, she didn't spend too much time pondering it. Instead, she seductively leaned across the bar, and Joel stared into her blue eyes. He took her hand and gently caressed her arm. "So, may I take you out on a date tomorrow afternoon, right after the Divine Liturgy?"

A sultry smile spread across her face, which blushed with a rosy hue. "I would love that."

When Portia uttered that infamous little word, Joel was immediately stupefied, as if he were under the influence of a powerful drug. *Oh, love! Portia said 'love,'* Joel thought, while an immense, dazed grin overtook his face, and his entire body tingled.

Suddenly, his cell phone dinged and buzzed, and he knew who was chiming in at this most inopportune moment. *Adoncia, I know it's you,* Joel thought. No one else would text Joel this late other than his favorite lady of the night as he sat across from his favorite lady of the bar.

Joel ignored the notification. Meanwhile, Portia squinted her eyes slightly but said nothing as her squint quickly turned into a yawn. And Joel couldn't resist her sleepy face. He leaned closer to her, cupped her face in his hands, and kissed her.

Tiny squeaked loudly and covered his eyes with both paws, like he was getting ready to witness something obscene. Portia took Joel's hands, held them by her face, and gently rubbed her cheeks on them, before covering them with kisses, making Joel melt into a puddle of mush. Then Tiny let out a deafening, ear-piercing shriek, then pretended to fall over dead. Portia and Joel couldn't contain their laughter. Portia quickly scooped up Tiny and kissed him until he cooed; then he perched on her shoulder.

Joel wanted to take them both upstairs and spend all night with Portia in his arms. However, the man had strength and control. Joel wouldn't enter the bedroom on the right at Portia's Port House this evening. And as much as it pained him, and as hard as it was, he stood up from the bar stool. "Well, I better leave before I lose my strength."

Portia sighed and nodded her head in agreement. Joel picked up his phone and quickly glanced at it before putting it in his pocket. Just as he had suspected, he had received another text message from the beautiful *prostituta.*

Joel felt Portia's discerning eyes, but then she yawned again, which turned into another beautiful smile. "Good night, Joel Layton. I'll meet you at the cathedral in the morning," she said as she leaned across the bar for a good night kiss.

After another heart-fluttering lip lock, Joel slowly pulled away. "I'll see you in the morning," he said as he slowly walked backward, never taking his eyes off her snakeskin dress, and bumping into a few tables and chairs along the way.

ALWAYS AN EARLY RISER, Joel was up before the sun for a morning run. He needed to maintain his muscular Navy physique, which would be a challenge with the delicious meals he was having lately, especially with Gert's home cooking. Speaking of which, Joel enjoyed another one of her decadent breakfasts before he left for the cathedral.

When he got out of his truck, Joel was once again amazed by the brilliance of the sun's holy light as it magnified the cathedral's white walls, red roof, green domes, and golden Russian Orthodox crosses. He paused by the cemetery fence, took a picture of the shimmering cathedral, and then promptly texted it to Adoncia. But Portia walked up next to Joel as he sent the text, startling him to the point he jumped. However, the witty sailor quickly put his phone on silent and slid it into his pocket while looking at Portia, unable to stop the giant, ridiculous smile that spread across his face. The lady of his heart was beautiful, and he loved her simple, elegant attire on Sunday mornings. She was stunning in the full beauty of simplicity in a classy black dress with a matching lace headscarf.

Joel stared deeply into Portia's blue eyes as he put out his arm to escort her to the cathedral along the holy pathway through the rows of wooden and stone crosses. Suddenly, two eagles with their white feathers glowing in the Sunday-morning sunlight came gliding in on a breeze, each landing on one of the gleaming golden Russian Orthodox crosses on the stately Domes of Heaven.

Portia and Joel paused to admire the two eagles basking in the holy light, and Joel couldn't help but think that he and Portia were just like those eagles. After a couple of minutes, Portia and Joel continued walking toward the doors and entered the narthex. Even though he had seen the nave before, Joel was still captivated by the brilliance of the artwork portraying the icons.

Majestic sunrays burst through the Dome of Heaven as if they were shining through the hands of Christ, whose elegantly smiling face was painted in all His holy splendor. Then incense drifted through the air, and Joel deeply inhaled the heavenly scent as it invigorated every element of his being.

As the morning chants began, beautiful angelic voices echoed throughout the cathedral. Portia and Joel venerated the icons—crossing themselves, bowing before the beautiful artwork, and kissing the icons' hands. Joel adored lighting candles with Portia and then holding her hand as they approached the icon of Jesus Christ, where they took turns kissing His holy feet.

Never once had Joel felt so content and happy as he did when standing beneath the great golden chandelier, holding the hand of the woman he loved. He smiled at Portia as the morning sunlight glimmered on her brunette locks, and he couldn't resist the urge to lean over and kiss her cheek. This moment was interrupted by the clearing of a very raspy throat that could only belong to Gunther. Portia and Joel looked over their shoulders and smiled at him before walking to the right side of the room to retreat to their private prayers while Gunther approached the icon of Christ.

More of the townsfolk entered the nave and venerated the icons. Gunther joined Portia and Joel on the right side of the room while Gert stayed on the left side. Bubba mustered up the confidence to stand next to Tanya, who looked incredibly pleased to have him by her side. After all, he was the only one who noticed her lip refill.

The Divine Liturgy began as the choir sang like angels in the choir loft and incense swirled in the sunlight's celestial glimmer. Joel reached into his pocket for the booklet Portia had thoughtfully given him last Sunday, and he endeavored to follow along with the beautiful litanies, antiphons, lessons, hymns, and prayers.

When the lengthy service ended, Portia and Joel held hands as they exited the cathedral and walked along the path of wooden and stone crosses. They looked to see if the two eagles were still on the crosses on the Domes of Heaven. And the eagles were still there. The regal birds looked at Portia and Joel, then flew away together, disappearing into the clouds, which were sliced by brilliant golden sunrays, shining down and sparkling the bay waters while revealing the omnipresent devotion of the one and only Almighty God.

"WE DON'T HAVE MUCH TIME. Change your clothes. We will be leaving in T-minus 15 minutes," Joel wittingly instructed as he and Portia climbed the staircase to her apartment.

"Roger that, Captain Layton. Where are we going? How should I dress?" Portia asked as she unlocked the door.

"The location is a surprise. Dress comfortably for both indoors and outdoors. Even though I love them, I don't recommend high heels," Joel suggested.

"Oh, okay. I'll find something boring to wear on my feet then," Portia replied with a giggle.

Joel laughed, then went into the bathroom to change out of his dress clothes and into jeans and a long-sleeved, button-up, Navy blue shirt.

In under T-minus five minutes, Joel was ready to go. On the other hand, Portia needed the other 10, so Joel walked over to the sofa and sat down between Screech and Tiny, who both wanted his undivided attention. Joel did his best to pet Screech and Tiny equally, so neither would feel slighted. However, Screech was jealous that Joel had the audacity to pet the monkey as well. In cat logic, the only option was to remove the competition, so Screech hissed and growled as he swatted Tiny off the sofa.

"That wasn't nice!" Joel exclaimed in a yelling whisper as he leaned down to see if Tiny was okay.

But the little punk rocker rallied. Tiny looked at Joel like *I got this*; then he jumped on the sofa, shrieked loudly, defecated in his paws, and threw it at Screech, splattering the excrement across his fluffy white chest fur.

There was no time for laughter. Joel promptly retrieved wet paper towels from the kitchen and carefully cleaned Screech's chest while he purred until he drooled. *Cats drool when they purr? Who knew?* Joel thought as he scratched Screech's ear and even worked in a friendly chin scratching, which resulted in drool dripping all over Joel's hand. Joel looked down at his sopping-wet hand and decided it was time for a good handwashing. Then he sat back on the sofa and checked his messages on his phone as if nothing weird had just happened, like an agitated monkey throwing poop at the cat.

Joel smiled when he saw that Adoncia was online and that she had replied to the picture of the cathedral he had sent her earlier that morning. He responded to the message, and he and Adoncia had a quick exchange before the T-minus 15 minutes was up.

Adoncia: ¡Hermosa iglesia! How is your chica?
Joel: She's perfect. I'm going to tell her I love her today!
Adoncia: ¡Maravilloso! How and when are you going to tell her?
Joel: Today at some point.
Adoncia: You don't know cuando?
Joel: Well, not exactly. When the moment is right. I booked a flying boat tour for this afternoon and evening, so I'll tell her at some point.
Adoncia: Hmm. Bueno. My advice to you Captain Layton is don't be an idiot!
Joel: I beg your pardon? ;-)

Adoncia: Don't be an idiot and just blurt it out. Find the right, special moment. Que sea memorable para ella. Oh, I got to go! ¡Tengo un cliente para el dormitorio de la derecha! Ttyl

And just like that, Adoncia was offline, and Joel's heart sank as he envisioned her greeting some random man at the door of La Cabaña de la Prostituta and leading him into the bedroom on the right. He sadly sighed because Adoncia deserved so much more than that.

"Well, sailor. I am ready to go at T-minus 14 minutes," Portia said as she walked over to him.

"You look beautiful," Joel replied as his eyes feasted on her buffet of beauty.

Portia wore a gold sequin shirt that fell off one shoulder, with tight black jeans, and over-the-knee croc-leather boots with flat soles. She also teased her hair to the ultimate level of sexiness and dazzled her eyes with sparkly gold eyeshadow, black mascara, and black eyeliner. And to put the sprinkles on the cupcake, she had smothered her lips with a deep red, come-and-get-me lipstick that made Joel's entire body quiver.

Portia's shirt was as gaudy as the Port House sign that lit up the roof every night. However, it was pure Portia, and Joel loved it. A tingly feeling began in his toes and shot up to his head. He loved her so much that he almost told her then. As he got ready to open his mouth and blurt it out, Adoncia's words, "Don't be an idiot!" echoed in his mind, stopping him from proclaiming his undying love right then and there. And once again, Joel listened to the influential words of his favorite prostituta.

He threw his hand over his mouth to keep the three little words from escaping his lips and then promptly jumped up and stood at ease. "Well, we should get going," he said with a nod.

Portia looked at him like he had lost his mind; then she put on a black velvet jacket. Meanwhile, Screech and Tiny sat on the coffee table in a ray of sunshine like two little angels on their best behavior.

"Look at you two! My sweet babies. They didn't give you any trouble while I was changing, did they?" Portia asked.

"Um, nothing too out of the ordinary," Joel replied with a snicker as he and Portia left the apartment and went to his truck. He escorted her to the passenger side and opened and closed the door for her.

"Nice ride you got here!" Portia exclaimed. "You know I got a thing for big trucks," she said with a wink.

"Do you, now?" Joel grinned as he started the diesel engine. He put that power-machine in reverse, spun around, and turned right onto Port Road, then turned off again onto Muscovy Drive.

Portia didn't say anything for a few minutes until they saw a sign for *Seaplane Tours*. "Uh oh," she muttered as if something terrible had just happened.

"What's wrong? Did you forget something at your place? We can go back," Joel asked as he hit the brakes slightly.

"No, I didn't forget anything. Um, did you book a flight tour?" Portia apprehensively winced.

"Yeah, why?" Joel stuttered, growing concerned that she already hated the surprise.

"With Pete Hanson?" she inquired.

"Yeah, why?" Joel repeated.

"He's 100 years old but has a good reputation and is known for being a very good pilot. People still fly with him all the time," Portia explained.

"He said he flew the Muscovy in World War II, but I thought he was joking," Joel responded as he gripped the steering wheel until his fingers ached.

"No, he wasn't joking."

Joel's heart started pounding, and he swallowed hard, like choking back a heave after hearing one of Gunther's hack attacks. Then to make matters worse, Adoncia's words echoed in his mind about not being an idiot when he told Portia that he loved her.

Good grief! Hopefully, the pilot won't die of old age during the flight, Joel thought. Thankfully, he had taken some basic aviation training classes, so should he have to commandeer the plane, he could execute that task like a champ.

Joel gripped the steering wheel and sighed as he turned into the parking lot. Some of the tension was alleviated when he saw the gorgeous Thompson J-45 Muscovy sparkling in the sunlight, looking like a well-maintained aircraft. Pete was even on the parasol wing checking the oil.

Hmm. Well, this may not be so bad after all. The plane looks okay, and thank God it has two engines, Joel thought as the heart thumping subsided.

"I'm surprised he could get up there. He's a bit wobbly these days," Portia muttered with a cringe before she jumped out of the truck.

"Oh dear," Joel mumbled as the heart thumping kicked back up.

"Hey Pete!" Portia hollered.

"Oh hey, Portia!" Pete exclaimed as he put the dipstick back in place. He wobbled a little bit as he walked over to the ladder to climb down.

Portia wasn't kidding about him being wobbly, Joel thought as he steadied the ladder.

"Thank you, boy!" Pete said as he carefully stepped onto the tarmac. He was skinny and mostly bald, with just a few gray hairs. Despite his age and wrinkled appearance, Pete had the energy of a 60-year-old. "Isn't she magnificent?" he asked as he patted Joel on the shoulder.

"The Muscovy is magnificent, sir," Joel replied.

Pete burst out laughing and then almost fell over from the exertion. "No boy, I was talking about Portia!"

"Oh, Pete. You shouldn't tell him about us." Portia played right along with the game.

"The picnics down at Priest Rock, the long, long flights to Anchorage for dinner, and the private chair dances at the Port House..." Pete indulged his fantasy as he put his arm around Portia's shoulders.

Private chair dances at the Port House? Joel wondered as he furrowed his brow.

Pete saw Joel's reaction, and then he cackled like a seagull. "Oh, I'm just messing around with you kids. In fact, I stopped by for a beer late the other night and saw Portia giving you quite the chair dance. Joel, she must really like you! She must really like you a lot!"

Joel almost choked on his own spit. It was one bizarre thing after another. He had just cleaned monkey poop off the cat, and now, he was getting ready to go on a flight with a 100-year-old pilot who had seen his girlfriend giving him a chair dance.

"Pete, how much did you see?" Portia asked, horrified yet slightly amused.

"Enough that I feel like I need to give you the talk! You crazy kids!" Pete chuckled as he turned toward Joel with his arm still around Portia. "I've known her since she was a little girl. I grew up with her daddy's dad! Great men!"

"Yeah, they were," Portia began with a sad smile. "Hey Pete, Joel is a Navy man too. He just retired from being captain of a destroyer and moved here to work on the Alexandria."

"Boy, let me understand something here. You left your command as captain to come here to be a greenhorn and work with Gunther and Jonathan Timber? God bless you, son! I admire a fellow veteran. I love my water bird so much. I was so blessed to get her after the war," Pete proudly said.

"I've flown in one before; the Muscovy is quite the aircraft," Joel said.

"She only goes 110 knots, but she holds 1,750 gallons of fuel and can stay up for over 20 hours, as you know! That's what made the Muscovy so beneficial during the war. I patrolled for submarines during World War II; my job was to keep the Port of Aleutia safe. I loved it so much here I stayed. The Muscovy isn't used in combat anymore; now, it's mainly just for aerial firefighting. Mine is the only one in the world that does tours! I've been in business since before the Cold War began. My flight engineer died in 1980, so I've been flying solo since then. Come to think of it, it's been at least 20 years since you've been on this plane, Portia."

"Well, Joel and I are overcoming our fears today. I don't like being too far from land, and Joel doesn't like flying," Portia explained.

"I'm glad there are two engines," Joel said.

"They are authentic Flint & Henry 1200 horsepower engines. But, we only need one to fly, and using one reduces the amount of fuel. Eh, you know what they say; less is more," Pete said with an ornery chuckle.

Joel's eyes bugged out, and he looked at Portia. *What have I done?* he wondered. Portia sensed his uneasiness, so she grabbed his arm and clung closely to him.

Suddenly, Pete squinted his right eye and shook his head. "Oh no."

"What's wrong?" Portia asked.

"One of my contacts just flew right out of my eye. Since I had that cataract surgery, my eye keeps spitting it out. I should never have trusted that doctor and his stupid laser. Excuse me kids, let me find my extra lenses. I'll bring my drops for the flight, so this doesn't happen again at a high altitude. Oh yes, Joel, there is the matter of my fee," Pete said as he squinted harder while holding his hand in the opposite direction of where Joel was standing.

Too stunned to respond, Joel stared at Pete in disbelief. Portia pinched Joel's rear, and he promptly regained his senses. He shook his head as if Portia had abruptly awakened him from a deep sleep. Then he reached into his pocket and handed Pete a stack of cash.

"Thank you, son!" Pete said while still scrunching his right eye. He kissed the cash and hobbled to his office building.

"What just happened? Did I dream this? An extremely elderly man who had cataract surgery and whose contact lens keeps flinging out of his eye will fly us in a two-engine plane but only use one engine!" Joel began to sweat.

But Portia calmed him down. She stood in front of him and put both hands on his chest. "He's probably just joking. He jokes nonstop. It's what he does. Hey, it will be an adventure. Where are we going anyway?"

Joel felt the heat dissipate, and he returned to a normal temperature. "I booked all the tours in one."

"That must've cost a fortune," Portia said sweetly.

"You're worth it," Joel said as the tip of his nose found hers. They kissed, and the kiss made time fly because they were still in a lip lock when Pete returned.

"Hey, love birds. Turn down the sweat lodge. I can't have you steaming up the windows in the Muscovy. Come on. Let's go," Pete instructed.

Joel held Portia's hands and looked her in the eyes. "Well, what do you say?"

"Let's do this," Portia answered.

PETE POINTED TO THE BODY OF THE PLANE. "This part floats in the water. That's why we have high-mounted parasol wings. On the wingtips, there are floats to help keep the speed up when we're flying through the water. They retract after takeoff. Well, they used to. Broke a few months ago. I'll be sitting in that window in the pilot's compartment. The other set of windows below it was for a bomber, but luckily that's not used for that anymore. There is just a seat in there with a great view, but I thought you two would enjoy sitting in the gunner's compartment with that big set of windows toward the back of the plane. I had a nice bench seat put in back in the 60s." Pete paused and opened the side door for them. "Go ahead in and into the left. The Navy man can lead the way. I'm going to my seat. Make sure you're buckled. I'll talk to you on the radio. You can talk with the gunner's radio next to your seats."

Portia and Joel did as instructed. They went to the gunner's compartment and fastened their seatbelts, ready to begin this journey.

Five minutes passed before the engine started, and Pete's elderly voice came across the radio. "Don't get up at any time during this flight. If you need me, call me. We're ready for takeoff."

The Muscovy was about 20 feet from the water. Pete steered the plane toward the concrete ramp where the tarmac met the bay. The water bird immersed and moved at a slow pace until it reached a depth that was safe enough to retract the wheels and pick up speed. Then the flying boat plowed through the water.

"We have entered the Nateekin Bay, where I patrolled during the war. There's a small island straight out in front of us. It's called Hog Island, and a bunch of hogs live on it." Pete paused to laugh. "Just kidding, you will see for yourself in a minute or two."

The plane was loud, but that didn't bother Joel because he was on the water. Most importantly, he was on the water with the woman he loved. He put his arm around Portia's shoulders and kissed her on the cheek. She smiled and blushed.

The amphibious aircraft began to slow down. Portia and Joel leaned forward to look out the window as they approached Hog Island, which wasn't very big. A small patch of trees was in the center, and huge rocks surrounded the entire island. Pete steered around the opposite side of the island, where there was a sea lion haulout.

Joel couldn't believe his eyes. "There must be at least 300 of them!"

"Aren't they just darling?" Portia asked.

Pete slowed the water bird down and shut off the engine, so the plane wouldn't disturb the sunbathing critters. Their brown fur glowed in the sunlight as they laid in piles so thick that the top of the rocks wasn't even visible. Some weren't moving, just sleeping beneath the sunshine, snuggled close to their neighbors. Others sat straight up and tilted their heads back as if they were looking toward Heaven and thanking God for giving them life. Nearby, a rowdy crowd was flailing around and biting at each other's faces. Were they fighting, or were they playing? Neither Joel nor Portia knew, but what the two of them did know was that they were enjoying God's beauty together. Joel felt compelled to put his lips to Portia's ear as she stared out the window. However, Adoncia's words once again echoed in Joel's mind, so he listened to his favorite prostituta and not so patiently waited for the perfect moment to tell Portia that he loved her.

Pete restarted the engine and hit the gas, steering the Muscovy out to the middle of the bay. "Prepare for takeoff."

Joel took a ragged breath and leaned back, hoping he wouldn't get nauseated. Meanwhile, Portia reached for the radio and put in a request to Pete. "Can you fly over the Port of Aleutia, please?"

"Sure thing, pretty lady!" Pete responded.

Portia bounced in her seat like a little girl. Joel was so distracted by her enthusiasm that he overlooked the takeoff, and they were airborne before he knew it. He swallowed to relieve the pressure in his popping ears.

Pete did more than just a flyby of the Port of Aleutia; he flew all the way around Unalaska Island. The flyby included all the bays and harbors, providing excellent views of the Spithead Cape, Mount Ballyhoo, and Priest Rock, in addition to the king crab fishing vessels, including the Alexandria, Windswept Belle, and Mariah Leigh, docked near the Port House. Portia and Joel took photos and videos since seeing their home from the sky wasn't an everyday experience.

Suddenly, the Muscovy began losing altitude, which was saying something because it wasn't that high. "Prepare for landing," Pete said across the radio before smoothly landing the water bird. Joel was thankful they didn't end up as fish food, but the trip wasn't over yet.

"I'm taking you to Orlov Bay to see if my buddy is there. You'll see what I mean," Pete said. A few minutes went by, and the Muscovy approached land. Pete slowed down, then shut off the engine. "Now, look toward the center of the cove, and you will see a giant rock. I swear he knows the sound of my engine because I have seen him every time I have stopped here in the last 15 years. Keep your eyes peeled."

Portia and Joel looked toward the rocky shoreline and spotted the giant rock in the center, which sat beautifully in front of hundreds of mature black spruce trees. *Wow, this place is beautiful,* Joel thought. He had no idea what they were waiting for, but he went with it, hoping whatever creature it was would show itself soon. Five minutes passed, and Joel saw something moving in the tree line. It was brown and quite large; the mystery creature was an enormous bear.

"There he is," Pete began. "That's my buddy. I call him Brutus. He is an Alaskan brown bear. He is huge and probably weighs close to 1,000 pounds."

Joel couldn't believe his eyes. Alaska was revealing herself to him, and he was thankful that every view, plant, animal, and rock was a new adventure waiting for him to discover. Joel snapped a few photos on his phone and then was distracted by a sniffle from Portia. He wrapped his arm around her and whispered in her ear as they stared out the window. "What's the matter?" he asked as he held her tight, but she didn't respond. "Please tell me. You can trust me." Joel reached his hand up to her face, guiding her chin toward his, so they could look into each other's eyes.

"The last time I came here, I was with Chris, Lizzie, and Elijah. We always came here to watch for brown bears. Chris and I had come here since we were teenagers," Portia explained.

"Happy memories," Joel said with a smile.

Portia smiled and collected herself. "Sorry."

"No need to apologize," Joel replied as he caressed her cheeks, then gently kissed her lips.

Portia looked out the window. "Brutus is beautiful. I've seen him many times. Although, Chris always called him Joe."

"Joe?" Joel said with a laugh. "I think he kinda looks like an Apollo."

"I bet all the locals have special names for him," Portia responded.

Joel wrapped his arms around her, breathing in the scent of her perfume. Not only did she smell like an angel, but she also smelled like a lifetime of love.

Then Joel looked out the window, only to see Brutus/Joe/Apollo leaving his stately rock and returning to the black spruce tree forest.

A few seconds later, Pete restarted the engine and turned the plane around to head to their next destination. "Prepare for takeoff, again."

Joel scrunched up his face. *Oh boy, another takeoff, which meant another landing*, he thought. He still wasn't comfortable flying, but he knew he had to put his issues aside because they were now heading away from Portia's safety net of the shoreline. She patted his leg just as he pulled her closer. There was no better feeling in the world—none whatsoever.

"NEXT, KIDS, we will fly a few miles out over the Bering Sea. I want Joel to see what he has gotten himself into," Pete said.

"Oh dear," Portia muttered.

Joel was excited but contained his enthusiasm as he held Portia tighter, for she was leaving her comfort zone. "It's all good," he whispered.

Joel's soothing words must've helped Portia. She inhaled and exhaled a deep, calming breath while releasing the tension in her muscles, enjoying this time with him.

Because it was a Sunday, not too many vessels were out working. Joel viewed the Bering Sea in all its undisturbed beauty, with only seabirds and buoys dispersed throughout the brinish expanse. The water wasn't completely glassy, for delicate ripples added texture to the seaway surface. Joel smiled because the tranquil sea reminded him of a calm day on the Chesapeake Bay.

"It's almost slick cam out there," he said.

"What did you say?" Portia asked as if Joel had spoken in a foreign language.

He laughed, knowing that she had no idea what he meant. Finally, he got even with her for Spithead.

"Really. I don't get it," Portia reiterated, back to being her pushy, pain-in-the-butt self.

"Slick cam means the water is really calm. This is a common phrase where I come from on Maryland's Eastern Shore. Sometimes, the bays and rivers look like a solid sheet of glass, and that is referred to as slick cam. You haven't seen anything until you have experienced a slick cam sunrise from a workboat."

"I can assure you it will not be slick cam when you're fishing up pots 150 miles out." Portia huffed as her muscles tensed back up.

"Look out the window. Isn't it beautiful, though?" Joel asked as he rubbed her shoulders before caressing her hair. He loved feeling her dazzling brunette locks gliding between his fingers. "Other than you, the ocean is the most beautiful thing I have ever seen."

Instead of huffing again, Portia sighed, prompting Joel to hold her closer and kiss her cheek.

"I just hope the sea doesn't take you away from me too," Portia whispered.

"Don't worry about it. I'll be fine," Joel said, even though he knew there was no convincing her otherwise.

Suddenly, the plane began to turn, and then Pete said, "We will arrive on Akutan Island in five minutes."

Time passed quickly as Portia and Joel enjoyed each other's company and the gorgeous mountainous view. As the Muscovy approached land, two church domes caught Joel's eye in the distance, and his heart thumped with excitement. He adored the cathedral in Aleutia and couldn't wait to see Akutan's place of worship. He kept his eyes fixated on the Domes of Heaven during the descent until the Muscovy's hull contacted the water.

"We've arrived on Akutan Island," Pete began. "Stay seated until I pull up on the tarmac and shut off the engines. I mean engine. Haha."

"Have you been here before?" Joel asked Portia as he gently squeezed her hand.

"Yes," Portia began with a weak smile. "I can show you around."

"I'd love that," Joel replied.

As the seaplane approached the shoreline, Pete lowered the landing gear, drove the old plane out of the water, and parked it like a truck. After a few minutes, he opened the side door and yelled for them to come outside. "Well, you two behave yourselves. I'm going to head down to the dock store to see if Bessie has an antidiarrheal. My old bowels aren't what they used to be." Pete shared way too much information before the old dodger hobbled away, almost getting blown over by a gust of wind.

"Did he just say that?" Joel asked in disbelief.

Portia laughed and nodded.

"Well then, shall we go for a walk?" Joel inquired as he reached his hand out for Portia's.

"There's a wooden boardwalk that goes for about a mile or so, and we can see Akutan Bay the whole way," Portia said as she took Joel's hand, then pointed to the right side of the island in the direction of the cathedral.

"That sounds perfect to me," Joel agreed.

He looked at Akutan Bay, shimmering like a rippling blanket of crystals. Joel had seen the sun sparkle on oceans, seas, and bays all over the world. However, he had never seen any body of water shimmer like those in exquisite Alaska. There was something different about the water here, or maybe, it was just a reflection of the resplendent woman by his side.

For some reason, unbeknownst to Joel, Portia didn't have much to say. He was slightly concerned, but he figured she was still uneasy about the Bering Sea flight. Holding hands, they walked along the bayside boardwalk above a marsh and listened to the gulls and eagles singing in the distance.

Joel inhaled the fresh mountain air mixed with a pleasant salty spray, and he enjoyed the scenery of this small fishing town, which was remarkably like Aleutia. And Joel saw something he hadn't seen since childhood. Several small, antiquated workboats were deteriorating in the quagmire along the bay.

"They are left there to die," Joel quietly said. He paused to take a picture of the old vessels.

"Huh?" Portia asked.

"That's what the old watermen on the Chesapeake Bay say

about abandoned boats. To them, their boats are living souls that die. When I was nine years old, I remember my father taking me to my grandfather's boat, the Emmaline Mae, at her final resting place in the marsh at Crabber's Point. I totally forgot about that until right now. I haven't thought about that in so many years. That's been happening a lot lately. I'm being flooded with memories from my childhood," Joel admitted as he stared at the dying workboats.

Portia wrapped her arms around him and kissed him on the cheek. "Sweet memories. Your parents are smiling down on you and are so proud of you."

"Thank you, Portia. Shall we keep walking, pretty lady?" Joel asked as he held her close and leaned his forehead against hers.

Portia took Joel's hand and led the way farther down the boardwalk. A refreshing breeze swirled around them as sandpipers softly squeaked while scurrying along the shoreline where they hunted for tasty morsels. All the while, Joel savored every second of the scenery and the dazzling woman by his side. She made him feel more vibrant than he had ever felt in his life. The rush of being next to Portia by far surpassed the thrill of being at sea, and this is how Joel knew he was in love.

They continued walking along the boardwalk until it led them to the cathedral. The beauty of the sun shining on this glorious house of worship took Joel's breath away, just as it had on his first day in Aleutia when Gunther showed him the cathedral there.

"This is the St. Nicholas Russian Orthodox Cathedral," Portia explained as she looked toward the center of the cemetery.

A lovely white fence added the perfect charm to the grounds, and the cemetery was peaceful and quaint. It was like Aleutia's, with ornate wooden and stone markers.

"It's so incredibly beautiful!" Joel excitedly replied as his eyes took in the exquisiteness of the Byzantine structure. The Almighty One had certainly chosen an ideal location for yet another holy place of worship. With mountains on one side and shimmering water on the other, there was no better place for God's house.

Portia somberly walked ahead without saying a word and entered through the cemetery gate. Joel followed her through the rows of graves until she stopped at one with a large Russian Orthodox cross headstone with the surname of Alexander. Beneath that, the names Adalina, Penny, and Kyle were etched in stone. It was obvious to Joel that this was her father's grave, but who were Adalina and Penny? According to the dates, Penny died the same day and year Adalina was born. Joel was taken aback by this because he had assumed that Kyle's final resting place was in Aleutia.

For a moment, Portia stood motionless, staring at the headstone with a blank expression. Then she slowly walked up to it and ran her fingers over her father's name. Joel slowly walked up behind her, then wrapped his arms around her.

"I've been meaning to come back here. I haven't been here since the funeral," Portia whispered.

Joel held her close. He had had such high hopes for the day, and here he had brought Portia to two places that brought back painful memories for her. "I'm so sorry. Everywhere I have taken you today has upset you."

Portia spun around to face him. "No. Don't be sorry. I'm loving this day. And I've wanted to come back here. I didn't want to come alone, and I couldn't ask Uncle Gunther or Aunt Gert to come with me. Thank you for bringing me. It's just that the last time I was here was the funeral, and there were flowers everywhere. And now, this is how it looks on a normal day. It's so hard seeing his name in stone," Portia's said as her eyes filled and spilled down her face.

Joel couldn't endure seeing Portia in pain. He reached his hands up to her cheeks and wiped away her tears.

"I'm all right!" Portia angrily exclaimed as she tried hard to push him away, but there was no way Joel would ever let that happen.

"You don't have to be tough all the time. You get to grieve. You get to be angry and upset. But one thing you do need to do is forgive him. Your father never would've left you intentionally. He loved you. How could he not?"

Portia's eyes welled again, and Joel held her tightly. "I got you."

"I'm sorry," Portia said as her voice cracked.

"Will you stop apologizing for being human?" Joel pleaded as he gave her a handkerchief. He was an old-fashioned man. His father taught him to keep a hanky in his pocket because, even if he didn't need it, somebody else would. Joel handed his unused hanky off to someone else for the first time. But not just anyone—the one.

"Thank you," Portia said gratefully.

"Let's sit down," Joel said as he led her to a stone bench across from the headstone. "I thought your mother was alive."

"She is. I think. Actually, no clue where she is or if she's alive. Penny was Dad's true love. They were married about five years before I was born. Penny died during childbirth, and Adalina died later that night. Dad loved her. He never got over losing them. Penny was from Akutan, so Dad requested to be buried here. He married my mother a couple of years later, but she was from the mainland and couldn't stand being a sailor's wife. She couldn't stand me. She left us. Dad used to bring me here, and we would sit on this bench together. He told me stories about Penny. I feel like I knew her even though I never met her. Joel, I'm glad you brought me here. I've been meaning to come. So, thank you," Portia said, then kissed him. "Have you been back to your parents' graves?"

"Yes," Joel said softly. "They died when I was 11, so I went to the funeral and was sent to an orphanage in Baltimore right after."

"That must've been horrible. I couldn't imagine. I'm sorry you went through that so young."

Joel felt a lump build in his throat. He took a deep breath, trying to smooth it out. "It was hard to make friends. Everyone around me being adopted, but nobody wanted me."

"I want you," Portia said as she looked him in the eyes.

"I want you too," Joel said, then sadly smiled. "When I turned 18, I was out of there, and I joined the Navy because I didn't have any other options. I knew I wanted to be a captain just like my dad, except I wanted to be a Navy captain and see the world. I wanted to make my parents proud even though they weren't here to see me. I went back to the Eastern Shore after my first four years in the Navy. I was 22, and it had been 11 years since they had died and since I had been there. I went back to our old house, and it looked the same. But they weren't there. Everything looked the same—the buildings, the houses, the streets. I went to the cemetery and took my mom a bouquet of orange roses, her favorite. That was a pretty tough moment," Joel said as his voice cracked and his eyes glistened. He had never shared this story with anyone other than Portia. "We're orphans," he whispered.

"You're so brave. I wish I could've been there for you," Portia said.

"Yeah, well, I think you're brave too. We're here for each other, now," Joel said as he leaned his forehead against hers.

Portia moved closer, sat in Joel's lap, and wrapped her arms around his neck. They kissed each other's faces until their lips met, then they kissed intently. Joel felt like they had floated from the earth and glided through Heaven.

Suddenly, the screech of an eagle caught their attention, and Portia and Joel looked up toward the sky, just in time to see two eagles land on the cathedral domes, just like the eagles in Aleutia.

"Dad told stories about how he and Penny always saw two eagles together. Joel, since you came to town, I've started seeing two eagles. Do you know what this means?" Portia asked as she cupped his face in her hands.

"It means we are blessed," Joel replied, then passionately kissed her.

PORTIA AND JOEL had extra time before meeting Pete back at the Muscovy. They stayed in the cemetery until Portia was ready to say her goodbyes, and then they walked down to the water where they watched the two eagles take off from their perches on the cathedral domes.

Joel didn't realize that he was hungry until his stomach started burning. "Is there somewhere I can take you to dinner?"

"We can go to the Akutan Cafe. It's right next to the plane and has a great view of the bay."

"Sounds like a plan," Joel said.

They walked back down the boardwalk to the Akutan Cafe, a small metal building along the water's edge. The smell of good country cooking greeted them and made them feel at home as they sat at a table with a perfect view of the Muscovy and the bay. Joel perfectly played the part of a gentleman by taking Portia's jacket and pulling out her chair for her. Neither of them ordered any alcohol, just water with no ice. Joel was pleased to finally have found someone who shared his dislike for how much space ice took up in a glass. They took their time eating and enjoyed a lovely dinner of splitting a house salad, a BLT, and a slice of triple berry pie, which they ate while enjoying decaf cappuccinos.

The sun dropped down between snow-covered mountains and created a tremendous orange glow, making the mountains glisten. "Now that's a Sunday sunset," Joel said, complimenting nature in all her holy splendor. "Speaking of which, we should get back to the plane; I can see Pete pacing from here."

Joel paid the bill, and he and Portia left the cafe and walked back to the Muscovy.

Pete rubbed his belly and squinted as he leaned against the

plane. "Don't get old, kids. It's hell on the bowels."

"Are you able to fly us back, or do you need to rest?" Joel blurted out for both selfish and unselfish reasons.

"No, I am perfectly fine. Now, I have indigestion because I can't stay away from the cafe's pepper and sausage sub. The other issue has been resolved, so I can fly us back with no problem." Pete started walking, then paused. "Oh no," he said, feeling his vest pockets.

"What?" Joel asked.

"My contacts must've flung out of my eyes again because I don't feel them, and I don't have my extra lenses. I can't see spit!"

Here we go again, except worse, Joel thought.

"Pete, you took out your contacts before the flight and wore your glasses. They are in your shirt pocket," Portia said as she reached over and pulled them out for him.

"Oh, how about that? So, they are. Hey, I'm just messing with you kids," Pete lied as he put on the glasses.

They boarded the plane, and within 15 minutes, they were in the water and then in the air. The sun had vanished from the sky, and a full moon began to rise, creating a picturesque golden glow on the snow-covered mountains resting perfectly in the bay and extending into the Bering Sea. The Muscovy may as well have been entering the gates of Heaven.

Portia snuggled close to Joel, and he leaned his cheek against hers as they gazed out the window. Her face was warm, her hair smelled incredible, and Joel savored every millisecond as he held her close to his heart.

A pirouette of colors appeared above the mountains as swirling ribbons of pinks, blues, greens, and purples exalted the sky. Only one explanation for this natural phenomenon was relevant. Scientifically speaking, the aurora borealis resulted from the combination of energy, magnetic fields, plasma, and gas. However,

Joel knew better. Only the paintbrush in God's hand could create such undeniable beauty, and only God could create a love like Joel's love for Portia.

Joel slowly glided his lips across Portia's cheek, stopping when they reached her ear. "I love you, Katerina Alexander," he quietly said.

Portia turned so her lips were touching Joel's. "I love you too," she breathlessly whispered.

They wrapped their arms around each other and passionately kissed as the Muscovy flew through the swirling colors.

Chapter 14. *Sail On*

Once the Muscovy landed and they said their goodbyes to Pete, the clock struck 11. Portia didn't realize how tired she was until the short ride back to the Port House.

"Hey there, sleepy head," Joel said as he caressed her hair. The slightest, gentlest touch from him made Portia tingle from head to toe.

When they arrived at the Port House, Joel was the ever-charming don who opened the truck door for his lady. They held hands as they walked up the staircase to Portia's apartment.

As she unlocked the door, Joel whipped out his cell phone. "Now that you're my girlfriend and we love each other, may I please have your phone number?"

Portia was so drunk on love she was too breathless to speak. She looked at Joel with her tantalizing grin as she reached for his phone to enter her number. When she tapped on Contacts, she noticed Joel had Bubba's, Gunther's, and Nick's numbers in there, along with a few other she didn't recognize, especially the foreign name *Adoncia* at the top. Portia was so dazzled by him calling her his girlfriend and saying he loved her that she quickly entered her number and handed the phone back to him, without giving his contact list too much thought.

"Thank you. Now I can text you that I love you," Joel said before initiating a long passionate kiss.

Portia adored the way his lips felt against hers. Come to think of it, she loved everything about Joel, and every day with him kept getting better. *Should I ask him to come inside? Maybe to hang out for a bit. Yeah right. Hang out. Who just hangs out? No one,* Portia thought as she kept on with the raging lip lock because saying goodbye was too difficult. She just wanted this moment—this feeling—to last forever.

At the peak of this sensual kiss, with their breath mingled and foreheads touching as he cupped her face in his hands, Joel paused for a moment before saying, "I love you so much, Portia. So much. And that's why I should go. If I stay, I won't be able to not show you how I feel."

"I love you too," Portia replied as her eyes filled with happy tears.

"Are you okay?" Joel asked as he kissed her entire face, ending at her lips.

"Of course I'm okay," she insisted as she shrugged it off. "Well then, sailor, you better get out of here, and call me in the morning."

"Deal. Now go inside, so I don't worry. I can't drive away with you standing out here in the dark all by yourself," Joel insisted.

"Oh, okay," Portia said. She gave him a quick kiss and did as he asked, then locked the door behind her.

Meanwhile, the greeting committee was right on point. Squeaking and yowling, Tiny and Screech promptly ran up to Portia. "Don't you two act like you love me. You just want food," Portia said as she watched their display. Screech rubbed on her legs while swatting Tiny until the monkey frantically climbed up her leg and then up to her shoulder. "Okay, okay. I'll feed you!" She set out their food and put Tiny by his bowl on the counter, but neither wanted to eat. Instead, they followed her to the sofa, where she sat down to watch the Northern Lights over the shimmering bay. "You're not hungry?"

The little fluff balls weren't the least bit hungry. They missed their momma and wanted to give her some love, which made Portia smile. She scooped them both up and snuggled them close.

The lights swirled over Eagle Bay, illuminating the sky with wonder, and reminding Portia of the flight through the dancing colors when Joel told her he loved her. And Joel was undoubtedly thinking of her as well because Portia's phone buzzed for a text message.

Joel: Goodnight, Beautiful. I love you. Sweet dreams.
Portia: I love you too. Goodnight, Cowboy.

Then Portia began pondering. She randomly recalled Joel at the bar the previous night, being secretive with his phone after receiving a text message. Then she remembered seeing him take a picture at the cathedral and type like he was sending it to someone. For some reason, these moments suddenly stood out to her. However, the sky's colors and a meteor streaking over the bay interrupted her train of thought.

THE NEXT MORNING, the cat and monkey had an altercation on Portia's pillow, rudely awakening her. Tiny clung to the top of her head while Screech swatted at him; however, he missed hitting the punk rocker and slapped Portia in the middle of the forehead several times.

"What? Oh, will you two knock it off?" Portia shouted. Now that she was awake, Portia thought she had been dreaming about a fairy tale evening with a prince. She dreamt about flying through the swirling colors of the night, which could only come close to emulating the beauty of what Heaven could resemble.

Her phone dinged for a text message, proving she wasn't dreaming at all. She had really been with a drop-dead gorgeous hunk of a man who had just told her he loved her as they flew through the aurora borealis.

Joel: Are you awake, my princess?
Portia: Yes. The two little monsters just got into a fight over my face, haha. So, I'm awake.

Her phone rang, and of course, it was Joel. "I love you. I had to hear your voice," he said.

Portia felt gooey inside. "I love you too," she replied with a dopey smile.

"I'm going kayaking today with Bubba and Nick. May I come see you this morning? I gotta see you. I have something for you."

Portia utterly melted at his words. "Aww, I would love that. Thank you."

"I'll see you in 20 minutes then," Joel said.

"Okay. I love you."

"I love you too. See you in a few," Joel said before ending the call.

Portia quickly brushed her teeth and hair. Then she spritzed herself with perfume. There wasn't enough time for her to change her clothes and put on makeup, so Joel would have to deal with her silk nightgown, matching robe, and fluffy slippers.

She rushed to the kitchen, made a pot of coffee, and fed the critters. "Now we need some tunes," Portia said. She looked through her music collection, which included an eclectic selection of Russian Orthodox chants, country music, oldies, Rock & Roll, and family recordings. Portia chose the album she had written and recorded with Gert, Gunther, Chris, and her father. She hadn't listened to it since Chris and Kyle died. However, that morning, she found the strength to break it out and would share it with Joel.

Just as Portia pushed the play button and turned on the fireplace, Joel rang the doorbell. She opened the door and saw a vision of handsomeness in a dark green waterproof jacket and matching pants.

"Good morning," Joel said with the biggest smile Portia had seen yet. She knew she was the reason for his smile, and this made her smile too.

Joel reached his hands up to her face and kissed her on the lips. "You smell wonderful, and I like your pajamas."

"Thank you. Come on in. I'll get us some coffee," Portia said as she held his hands and led him toward the sofa.

"That sounds great. Thank you," Joel said as he sat down. Screech and Tiny were quick to join him.

After she brought over the coffee, Portia and Joel sat together, enjoying their morning brew and the beautiful view of Eagle Bay.

"Okay, now close your eyes and put out your hands," Joel insisted.

Portia did as he asked while tingling with happy suspense. In a matter of seconds, she felt something cold against her wrist.

"Okay, open your eyes," he said.

Portia saw a silver identification bracelet with Joel's name inscribed between two eagles, and a warm sensation overtook her body. "Oh, Joel."

"This is an antique bracelet from one of my favorite places in the world, the Gypsy Market in Rota, Spain. A wise older lady told me to give it to my true love one day, and that's what I am doing."

"It's so old-fashioned. I love it so much. It even has two eagles on it. It's so perfect. Thank you," Portia gratefully replied as she looked Joel in the eyes and smiled.

"You're welcome. It makes me very happy to see you wearing it. To know, it's where it was intended to be," Joel said.

"Did you buy it from a Spanish psychic?" Portia inquired, slightly amused.

"Not exactly," Joel responded hesitantly.

"I have one of these," Portia admitted as the sound of her father's voice filled the room.

"You have one that says Joel on it?" he asked jokingly.

"No, my father had one that Penny wore. And that is him singing. We recorded an album with Chris, Uncle Gunther, and Aunt Gert. All originals. This is the first time I've listened to it since…" she paused.

Joel nodded his head. "The music is excellent, and now you have a bracelet for each wrist," he said, then kissed her on the cheek and wrapped his arms around her.

They snuggled up on the sofa for about an hour, drinking coffee and listening to the Alexanders' music. Time passed quickly, as it always does in moments such as these. Once the sun grew higher in the sky, Joel stood up to leave since he had to meet Bubba and Nick. He and Portia spent 10 minutes kissing goodbye before Joel found the strength to go.

"I'll see you tonight downstairs," he said.

"See you then, sailor," Portia replied.

JOEL HAD A GREAT DAY kayaking with Bubba and Nick in Nateekin Bay. He wasn't only thankful for the company he was keeping these days; he was also grateful for the physical activities to maintain his toned physique, considering the decadent meals he had been having lately. Joel and Nick enjoyed the fresh air while Bubba huffed and puffed for the duration of the kayaking trip. Overall, Joel thoroughly enjoyed their adventure, which brought him in eyeshot of moose, albatrosses, bald eagles, seals, and turtles. Alaska continued upholding her part of the bargain, providing Joel with continuous beauty, none of which, however, compared with the unrivaled beauty of Portia, queen of the Port House.

After Joel, Bubba, and Nick returned the kayaks, they met at the Port House to grab dinner and shoot the breeze because that's what folks do in a small town. That evening, the three gents walked into the bar like they were male strippers entering a bachelorette party, knowing they looked good and were there to give the ladies a good time. Gunther was already there, watching Gert serve the reverend his Reuben. Meanwhile, Tanya and Polly were yacking it up with Portia and playing with Tiny. As always, Portia was decked out to the nines; her ensemble included black thigh-high velvet boots with a matching velvet tube top, bolero, and mini skirt, all outlined with rhinestones. She also wore her silver ID bracelets, adding the perfect charm to this stunning attire.

Portia, Tanya, and Polly watched their virile men making an entrance. Joel, Bubba, and Nick sat next to Gunther, and the three ladies greeted their menfolk. Joel and Nick received kisses, while Bubba received a coy hello.

"Well, hi there, Bubba," Tanya said shyly before making the pouty lip face that made Joel's skin crawl.

"You're looking really good today, Tanya," Bubba responded enthusiastically.

Gunther gave Tanya and Bubba a weird look. But maybe Gunther was jealous since he got nothing from Gert. She walked by, and he gently reached for her hand. He couldn't contain his feelings any longer and poured his withered heart out to her in front of everyone. "Look, I'm going to be leaving soon. I don't want to go away with you being angry with me. Please talk to me. I love you. Tell me you still love me. I know you do."

"You repulse me. You're dirty, you smell, and you haven't cut your hair since…" Gert paused. She tensed up, and a sorrowful expression overtook her face.

"Yeah, well, you've quit living too. Please come back to me," he pleaded.

"You've got a long way to go before that will ever happen," Gert shot back.

"You mean there's still a chance for us?"

"I never said that!" Gert snapped. "I've got work to do."

Gunther sadly sighed as he watched her walk away.

Portia whispered in Joel's ear. "We got to get them back together."

"I agree. Let's work on his appearance first," Joel suggested.

"Good plan. Then we'll trick Gert into having dinner with him one night this week. I'll shut the bar down and have the staff here just for them," Portia said.

"What are you two whispering about? Portia, will you please get me another beer?" Gunther asked.

Portia winked at Joel as she went behind the bar. Joel watched her closely as she served Gunther a root beer.

Gunther gratefully reached for the mug, thinking he was getting another ale. He took a big sip. "What the hell is this?"

"It's root beer. Do you want Aunt Gert back? Then quit drinking," Portia admonished.

"You're one to talk!" Gunther retorted.

"I'm cutting back some and stopped the weed," Portia replied.

"Wait a second. You had weed and weren't sharing? You got any left?" Gunther inquired.

"Uncle!"

"I was just kidding," Gunther fibbed as he pretended not to like the root beer. "Yeah, well, I guess this ain't half bad."

Portia continued making her point. "Joel and I will help you get her back, but you must listen to us. We will plan a dinner for you two here, and we will go shopping for new clothes. And you need a haircut."

"Well, it's been a while since you and I have had some family time, so all right," Gunther agreed.

"Perfect. Now, no more beer!" Portia reiterated.

"Now that I think about it, I'll have a root beer too," Joel said boldly, being the ultimate team player. He looked at Nick and Bubba. "Guys, what do you say? Root beer for all?"

"Sure thing!" Bubba exclaimed.

"Root beer does sound mighty fine," Nick concurred.

By then, the rest of the townsfolk had arrived to take advantage of not only happy hour but also the meatloaf and mashed potato special Portia ran on Monday nights as well. Zac, Pete, Captain Babanin, Donald, Captain Karchagin, Captain Smith, Old Al, Kirk, Hank, Leonard, Ted, Rhonda, Alicia, Denny, and even Lora and Dr. Sampson were there, in addition to a few others Joel didn't recognize. The evening went on as usual, and Joel watched Portia strut around in her velvet boots and rhinestones. Meanwhile, Gunther goggled over Gert while Polly and Nick flirted, and Tanya and Bubba got to know each other better. All was right with the world until Adoncia texted Joel.

Hey there, handsome, flashed across Joel's cell phone screen, causing him to look from side to side, hoping no one saw it. Luckily, Gunther was drowning his sorrows in his root beer, and Portia was waiting on customers. Joel had no one looking over his shoulder, so he replied, *Hi, pretty lady. I miss seeing the Atlantic. Please send me a photo.*

Then Adoncia promptly sent him a cleavage selfie of her standing along the water's edge. She was forever beautiful, and so was the Atlantic Ocean sparkling behind her. Then suddenly, Gert's tray of dirty dishes crashed to the floor, creating quite a disturbance.

As Portia returned to the bar with a basket of fries for Bubba, she smiled at Joel, who rushed over to help Gert clean up the mess. Gunther and Reverend Thomas also helped, so Portia stayed behind the bar. Meanwhile, a flashing light caught her eye on the bar top, and she reached for Joel's cell phone, which was receiving a video call from a gorgeous Spanish woman with big hair, a thin face, and boobs up to her chin. Portia stared at the phone in horror, thinking, *This woman's cleavage line should be illegal.* Then Portia saw the name *Adoncia* next to the woman's photo, remembered seeing the name on Joel's contact list, and recalled Joel being secretive with his phone a few times. Portia contemplated answering the call, but the call ended without a redial.

"I knew I shouldn't have trusted him," Portia muttered as her heart sank to the floor. She just knew that she was going to get hurt again.

After Joel, Gunther, and Reverend Thomas helped clean up the mess, Joel returned to his seat.

Portia looked him in the eye and held up the phone. "Who is Miss Boobs, and why is she video calling you?"

"She's just a friend," Joel responded calmly. He wasn't squirming, but he was uncomfortable.

"That's what they all say," Old Al interjected, shaking his head at Joel.

Meanwhile, Kirk and Hank glared at Joel from the far side of the bar, keeping their distance from the rest of the crew.

"This certainly explains the secret text messages," Portia shot back as she snooped around Joel's inbox. "What do we have here? A collection of selfies from Miss Boobs!" Portia looked intently at the selfie Adoncia had just sent; however, she didn't stop to read the entire conversation.

"Please give me the phone," Joel insisted as he put out his hand.

"You're a liar!" Portia yelled.

"No, you are being unreasonable and presumptuous," Joel retorted.

"Unreasonable? Presumptuous?" Portia dramatically repeated.

"Oh, here we go," Gunther muttered.

"Those are big words," Bubba whispered to Tanya.

"Joel, would she be on your contact list if she wasn't so chesty?" Portia asked.

"If you would let me explain…" Joel began.

Portia cut him off. "Explain what? That you're a liar?"

"I haven't lied about anything. And I don't think right here, right now, in the middle of the bar, is the right place to have this conversation. You're blowing this way out of proportion."

"This is the perfect place and time!" Portia shot back, feeling the rage form a lump in her throat.

"She lives in Spain; she's just a friend."

"The caption under the selfie she just sent you says, La Cabaña de la Prostituta. She is a prostitute! I know some Spanish, Joel!"

"Our relationship was strictly platonic!" Joel insisted.

"Moose pucky!" Portia shouted.

"I love you, Portia. Can we please go discuss this in private?" he pleaded.

"Screw you!" Portia stomped off and went upstairs for the evening.

JOEL RUBBED HIS TEMPLES like he was fighting off a migraine, and he regretted his decision to drink root beer because, at this point, bourbon and cigars were necessary. As he reached for the root beer and took a sip, he felt the eyes of the room on him, most notably Gunther, Gert, Old Al, and the reverend, intently glaring at him.

"Well, boy?" Gunther agitatedly asked.

"I should go talk to her," Joel replied.

"It's best to leave her alone before she starts f-bombing you," Gunther suggested.

"I have no doubt that Joel is telling the truth. I got your back, buddy," Bubba said proudly and loudly.

Joel was astounded by Bubba's loyalty. "Thank you, man. That means a lot."

"Let me buy you another root beer. I bet there's a great story here. Please share it with us," Bubba insisted.

Downright nosy, like most people in a small town, everyone in the room crowded around Joel like it was story time in preschool. Gert had a furrowed brow but was ready to hear Joel's side.

Now thoroughly annoyed, Joel took a ragged breath and began, "So, about 10 years ago…"

"We can't hear you back here," Lora yelled from over by the jukebox.

"Wait! I got an idea!" Ted grabbed a handheld microphone and flipped a few switches on the sound equipment. He came back and handed Joel the mic. "Spill the beans."

Joel thought this was overkill. But he was already knee-deep in moose turds, so he grudgingly went along with it. He continued, "About 10 years ago, the warship I was on was being serviced at the US Naval Station in Rota, Spain."

"Wait a minute," Tanya interrupted.

Since Ted had appointed himself the moderator for this event, he rushed over, took the mic from Joel, and handed it to Tanya. "Go ahead," Ted said.

"What is the boat's name?" Tanya nosily asked.

Ted took the mic back and handed it to Joel.

"It wasn't a boat; it was a guided-missile destroyer," Joel agitatedly explained.

Meanwhile, Pete couldn't resist. He wobbled his way over to grab the mic. "Never refer to a Navy man's ship as a boat. That's grounds for a brawl." Then he held the mic out for Joel to respond.

"Thank you," Joel said.

"Just looking out for you. Now, please tell us about your platonic relationship with the Spanish prostitute. I don't want to die of old age before you tell the ending," Pete said.

Joel reached for the mic, feeling even more annoyed. He continued, "While in Rota, I went downtown and stumbled on the Gypsy Market. I was enjoying some live guitar music when a beautiful woman approached me and gave me her business card. Then she vanished into the crowd. I was young and curious. Yes, she was a prostituta, and I went to the address on the card, which ended up being her house, a cottage right on the ocean.

"I knocked on her door and asked how much she charged. She was about to lead me inside, but something happened. I noticed the faint wrinkle lines on her face. She was about 15 years older than me. She was beautiful, but tired. She sold herself for her livelihood, and that got to me. I told her I wouldn't be buying her services but just wanted her time. She was intriguing, and I wanted to learn more about her. So, we drank a lot of wine, had dinner, and stayed up all night talking. We became good friends. That's it. I went to Rota's Naval Station once or twice a year for the past 10 years and went to see her while I was in port. We just hung out. Seriously. Just hung out.

"A few weeks ago, I saw her one last time. She asked me what I was going to do after I left the Navy, and I told her I would find a job on the water somewhere. So, she got on the internet and found me the job ad for the Alexandria. And that was the night I called Gunther. That was also the night she gave me an ID bracelet that I just gave to Portia. It has my name on it. Adoncia bought it at the Gypsy Market and made me promise to give it to the woman I love. Since I've been here, Adoncia and I have been texting and having occasional live video calls. I have no family. I see Adoncia as family. I told her about Portia and sent her pictures of Alaska. We're friends. That's all. Yes, she does send me selfies that are a tad revealing. But that's just Adoncia. That's the way she is. You are all welcome to check my messages, and you will see I have told her how much I love Portia."

"No, Joel. We don't need to do that. We all love Portia. The last year has been hard on her. You need to tell her what you have told us," Gert interjected.

Everyone in the room concurred, so Joel promptly went upstairs to Portia's apartment. He knocked a few times. "Portia, may I please come in, so we can talk? I love you. I love you so much. Please let me explain."

"Go away. I don't want to talk to you. And don't you camp out in the hallway either. I'll have you thrown out," Portia yelled from the other side of the door.

Her words hit Joel hard. He had never been in love and known rejection. His heart fell to the floor, and his eyes filled. A hand gently caressed his back, and he turned around to see Gert's compassionate face.

"Give her some time. Portia will come around," she said.

Joel kissed Gert on the cheek and then walked away, feeling like a mound of bear crap frozen to the side of a rock in February.

THE FOLLOWING DAY, Joel wasted no time. He returned to the Port House at 10 a.m., and to his astonishment, the parking lot was full. Typically, Portia didn't open the bar until 10:30, yet it looked like a Saturday at 9 p.m. Joel parked next to Portia's obscenely pink truck and then went to her apartment. He knocked on the door, but there was no answer. Instead, he went to the bar's front door, took a deep breath, and entered. The whole town was there, like some big event was getting ready to happen, and everyone knew about it except for Joel. The room grew quiet, and the townsfolk stared at him. Joel spotted Bubba, Gunther, and Nick at the bar, so he joined them.

Bubba noticed Joel's bewildered look. "Portia put up a social media post. She has a new song," Bubba explained.

"You're in for one hell of a ride," Gunther said as he patted Joel on the shoulder.

Gert walked by and glared at Gunther. "It's a genetic trait! Dag gone Alexanders!"

Gunther was furious at the women in his life. He flung his hands in the air and shook his head, which inevitably provoked his nasty smoker's cough, frothy and loud.

Joel couldn't help but concur with Gert; two generations of Alexanders meant two generations of stubborn pains in the butts. And to make matters worse, Joel knew about Portia's anger music, and now he was the target.

Suddenly, the bar lights went on and off a few times. Then the gong penetrated the room, plummeting Joel's heart to the floor. He went to the dancefloor but stayed toward the back. He didn't want or need a front row seat to this show.

TAKING SEVERAL DEEP BREATHS, Portia stood at the top of the stairs. She wore a tight, mid-drift, silver sequined vest with a matching mini skirt and black thigh-high leather boots. Her fiery red lips, naughtily teased hair, and black eyeliner made her look like a corrupt schoolgirl.

She took another deep breath and slowly walked down the steps while a second gong preceded her entrance. Portia took extra care to sway her hips and clonk her high heels as she entered the bar, walked up to the stage, picked up the sparkling silver acoustic guitar, and joined her band. Ted, Leonard, and Rhonda were there, her faithful posse who had been up with her since 7 a.m., rehearsing the song she wrote in 15 minutes of anger the previous night.

Portia stepped in front of the microphone, and her eyes locked onto Joel's. He appeared disheveled, but she didn't care. She sang and strummed the first verse.

You said you'd love me forever
That's when I gave you my heart
But you threw it in the harbor
And now we're drifting apart

The rest of the instruments kicked in as Portia began singing the chorus.

So, sail on, sail on, my sailor
Looking for fish in the sea
And when you don't catch one
Don't come crying to me

Joel was expressionless, slightly disappointing Portia, but she knew the rest of the lyrics would get under his skin nicely. She sang the second verse, and then she sang the extended version of the chorus.

You are no longer my captain
I'll no longer be your mate
Sailor please chart a new course
Coz I'm not biting the bait

So, sail on, sail on, my sailor
Looking for fish in the sea
And when you don't catch one
Don't come crying to me
So, sail on, sail on, my sailor
Sail across the earth
Well, it's too bad the earth ain't flat
Then you wouldn't be a'coming back
Yeah, you'd be falling off the map

At this point, Joel crossed his arms, and his face turned an angry red. Bubba patted him on the shoulder. Gunther stood there with one hand covering his face, peering between his fingers.

Portia was pleased with the reaction, so she sang the third verse.

Now you're drifting out the harbor
Headed to the sea of tears
Oh yeah soon you will be drowning
Lonely and drinking some beers

Suddenly, Joel plowed through the crowd and over to the sound equipment. He turned off the speakers, and Portia signaled for the band to stop playing. She put the guitar on its stand, just as Joel entered the stage. Without saying anything, he motioned his right index finger toward her, then pointed toward the back hallway.

Portia winked at the audience, then sashayed her hips down the hallway and up the steps, with Joel following closely behind. She walked into the apartment first, and Joel came in behind her without closing the door.

"You are an infuriating pain in the butt! You know that?" Joel yelled.

"Yeah, well, you're a liar!" Portia retorted.

"I haven't lied about anything! If you would stop ranting and raving and let me tell my side of the story, you would see that Adoncia is just an old friend and that she is the reason I came here. She is the reason I met you. I never slept with her! We are just friends. That's it! I saw her only when the USS Roland was being serviced at Naval Station Rota in Spain. I saw her one last time before I retired, and you know what she did? She found me the Alexandria's job ad. She gave me the ID bracelet and told me to give it to my true love one day. And that's what I did! I gave it to you, Portia! I gave it to you!"

"You gave me a bracelet from a prostitute who sends you chesty selfies, and that's supposed to give me a warm fuzzy feeling?" Portia asked, bamboozled.

Joel handed her his cell phone. "Here, look at my text messages. Read through them all. They are all about me telling her all about you! How I love you and want to tell you that I love you."

Suddenly, Tiny climbed up Joel's leg and sat on his shoulder. Portia glared at the monkey because he rarely showed this type of affection to others. And at this moment, Tiny chose Joel's side.

Portia sighed, then did as Joel asked and read through his text messages with Adoncia.

"What do you see?" Joel queried.

"A lot of chesty selfies."

"Ignore the chesty selfies. Come on, the point is, yeah, she has chosen an unfortunate career, and her photos are provocative. That's just how she is. I only have eyes for you, even after your ridiculous display last night and this morning. I'm sorry I didn't tell you about her. I was going to at some point. I'm sorry. Okay?"

Portia looked at his phone, read the messages, and saw that he was right, even though she didn't care for the cleavage selfies. With a bewildered look, she handed the phone back to him.

"I won't let you find ways to sabotage us because you're too afraid to be happy. I won't let you do it. I can't stand this! I can't stand the thought of not having you in my life. Can we please kiss and make up? You get to be happy and enjoy life, Portia. But you gotta be an active participant, or it ain't gonna work."

"I'm sorry," Portia said as she sat on the sofa. "I wish that you had told me about her."

"Yes, I should've," Joel agreed. He sat down next to her and caressed her cheek, and the touch of his hand made Portia's entire body tingle. "Be happy. With me. Please. I love you," he said adoringly.

Portia couldn't fight it anymore. She loved him dearly, and she also couldn't imagine her life without him in it. "I love you too," she whispered.

They kissed and then hugged for quite some time, holding each other as tight as they could until their hearts beat in unison.

"Now, can we please go back downstairs and let everyone know we've made up," Joel asked.

"Okay," Portia said as she stood up.

As they walked out the apartment door, they were shocked to see the Alexandria's crew, Gert, Tanya, Old Al, Ted, Leonard, and Rhonda, huddled in the hallway eavesdropping, which was easy to do, considering that Joel had left the door ajar. Kirk glared at Joel intently, aggravated that he and Portia had mended fences.

Meanwhile, Pete hobbled his way up the stairs.

"Oh, here's where everyone is. You two made up, didn't you?" Pete inquired.

"Yes," Portia chirped.

Pete looked at Joel. "Dang, you're quick!"

"Don't be a dirty old man, Pete. Come on. I'll get you a bowl of soup," Gert said as she put her arm around him and helped him down the stairs.

Everyone else followed Portia and Joel back down to the bar, and then Portia went to the stage and took the microphone. "Well, everyone, Joel and I have made up. It was all just a big, huge misunderstanding. Thank you for coming. Lunch is on the house. We have a huge pot of homemade vegetable soup simmering. And we also have Aunt Gert's famous cornbread, so please stay and enjoy an early lunch today."

And that is just what they did. After a half hour of socializing, Gert, Portia, Joel, Rhonda, Ted, and Leonard served everyone root beer, vegetable soup, and cornbread. Portia knew there would be a mess to clean up, but the fine folks of Aleutia were her family; they were worth it. Time was short, for the red king crab fishing season would begin in under three weeks, and Portia wanted to savor every moment with the people she loved.

Chapter 15. *Crazy Sailor*

The crews prepared their vessels for the next few weeks preceding the red king crab season by stocking freezers and cabinets with food, loading crab pots, and filling fuel tanks. Joel spent his days aboard the Alexandria with Gunther, gleaning the older man's knowledge and preparing his heart and mind for the happy misery of being not just a deckhand, but a greenhorn—the lowest rank of all.

Joel spent his evenings at the Port House. He couldn't just show up at the bar every night and watch Portia work, so he helped by carrying heavy trays and serving customers. Every moment spent with Portia was a blessing, even if it involved serving the reverend his Reuben or Gunther his root beer, which became his drink of choice as he turned away from alcohol, all with hopes of winning back Gert.

As promised, Portia and Joel took Gunther to get a haircut and shopping for new clothes in preparation for a surprise dinner with Gert. And Gunther wasn't without his challenges. To begin with, they went to see Larry the Barber. While sounding like a routine trip to most, it was quite an event for the fine folks of Aleutia since the barber shop was next to a bald eagle nesting ground. Once Joel parked his truck, they covered their heads and ran like hell until they reached the shop door because an extremely protective momma eagle took offense to anyone near her humble abode. Gunther later had one of his infamous coughing fits while Larry was shaving him, and Larry told him never to return.

Following the haircut incident, Portia and Joel took Gunther to

Old Al's for some new duds. Rufus met them at the door with his dangling drool drip.

"Good grief, Portia! Can't we go somewhere else? I despise that drooling mutt. He bit my bum last time I was here," Gunther lamented.

"I told you not to bend over. I'm sorry about that, Gunther. Rufus can't help himself sometimes. You also had a french fry smashed to your arse," Old Al said as he extended his hand for a hello and an apology.

"Oh, all right, I forgive you. Just keep your ugly dog away from me. He also pissed on my boots," Gunther replied.

Rufus snarled at Gunther and then licked his chops, making the drool glob swing from side to side. Gunther grimaced.

"Speaking of boots, he needs a new pair that isn't paint and piss splattered. He also needs button-up dress shirts, jeans, blazers, undershirts, socks, and dress shoes," Portia explained to Old Al. "Probably needs some new flannel boxers too," she whispered.

"He can speak for himself!" Gunther declared as he threw his hands on his hips.

Portia tossed her head back and laughed, then turned on some 1980s rock music to get Gunther pumped. Meanwhile, Old Al picked out several outfits, and Portia made Gunther try them on—and model them. Gunther swaggered like he was on a runway, dancing and singing like a front man for an 80s rock band. As the pup's drool drip swung like a pendulum, Rufus inquisitively moved his head from side to side, watching Gunther strut his stuff.

Joel enjoyed this time with Old Al, Gunther, and Portia, and he sat down and kicked back to watch the show. Unexpectedly, Rufus jumped on his lap, and luckily, the drool drip stayed firmly suspended to the podgy pup's fat lip. Joel leaned back in the chair as far as he could, hoping the drool blob wouldn't fling in his direction. Other than that, Rufus was pretty darn cute. All the while, Joel smiled as he watched Portia in amusement, admiring her tenacious spirit as she went round and round with Gunther until he finally found clothes that met his approval.

When Gunther walked out in a black wool blazer, a white dress shirt, dark blue jeans, a leather belt, and dark leather work boots, Portia's mouth flung open.

"Yeah, I know. I clean up well," Gunther proudly announced.

"I don't want to see those other clothes again!" Portia admonished as she walked into the dressing room, grabbed his old clothes, and threw them into the trashcan, prompting a happy bark from Rufus.

"See, he will like you now that you look better," Old Al said.

Gunther squinted and gave Old Al a grumpy look.

"You look handsome, Uncle," Portia said genuinely. Suddenly, her phone dinged for a text message, and she paused to read it. "Okay, the bar has been closed and set up for you and Aunt Gert. I will text her and tell her I need her to work this evening. Once she's inside, Joel and I will lock all the doors, so she can't get out. Then Ted and Leonard will barricade the parking lot, so no one can get in and interrupt you."

"This is really gonna piss her off." Gunther laughed.

OVERALL, the plan worked perfectly. Portia, Joel, and Gunther went to the Port House and got in position. Gunther waited inside by a beautifully set table while Portia and Joel dressed in black and hid in the bushes next to the front door. Like clockwork, Gert arrived and casually entered the Port House.

"Portia? You said this place was busy. The parking lot is empty. Where the heck is everyone? And why did you tell me to wear my green velvet dress?" Gert shouted as she took a few steps, then stopped.

Portia and Joel acted quickly. They locked the door from the outside and pointed for Gert to walk farther into the room. Completely bewildered, Gert did as they asked; she walked several steps then stopped when she saw Gunther, handsome as ever, all decked out in his new duds with fresh cut hair and clean-shaven, standing in front of a perfectly set table as he held a red rose in his hands. However, Gert wasn't awestruck by Gunther's new look; she spun on her heel, promptly stomped back to the door, and shook the handle all while yelling, "Let me out of here! Let me out of here!"

"I wonder how it will go," Joel said as they made a quick getaway and hurried up the staircase to Portia's apartment.

"Why wonder when we can watch through my security cam? I have my laptop hooked up to the TV and a bowl of popcorn on the table! We won't have to miss a thing!" Portia said as she and Joel frantically opened the door, ran into the apartment, and jumped on the sofa.

"You're brilliant!" Joel exclaimed, then kissed her on the cheek.

"Look! Gunther's getting ready to make his first move," Portia said as she pointed at the screen.

Looking somewhere between sad and amused, Gunther watched Gert's display. After a minute or two, she finally realized she wasn't going anywhere, let out a loud sigh, crossed her arms, and turned around to face him.

Gunther hesitated for a moment. Then he walked over to her and reached out his hand. "Will you please join me for a drink?"

"What the heck happened to you?" she sputtered as she threw her hands behind her back.

"You don't like how I look?" Gunther sadly asked. He sniffed the rose, then handed it to her.

"Honestly, I forgot what you really look like," Gert replied as she snatched the rose and clutched it close to her heart.

"Oh, so you're insinuating that I look pretty good?"

"You look better than you've looked in the last year." Gert almost choked on her words as the last few syllables trailed off.

"Please go on a date with me. Let's go over to the table, have some root beer, and talk. No strings attached," Gunther suggested.

Gert looked at him skeptically.

"It's not like you can leave anyway," he pointed out.

She let out another overly dramatic sigh before walking over to the table where Gunther was the ultimate gentleman; he pulled out her chair for her and then placed the napkin on her lap.

Gunther's smile was the size of the Grand Canyon as he sat down across from Gert, whose expression grew more perplexed with each passing second.

Rhonda suddenly appeared. "Good evening. Don't you both look ravishing!"

"Oh great, you're in on it too," Gert sarcastically replied.

"I sure am. Some appetizers will be out in a few minutes. If you need anything in the meantime, just holler," Rhonda said as she gave Gunther a high five before returning to the kitchen.

Gunther stared at Gert, entirely and utterly mesmerized by the very sight of her. "Do you remember our first date?" he asked.

"How could I forget? You picked me up on your dirt bike."

"Yeah, and you loved it," Gunther reminded her.

"I don't think Principal Peterson felt the same way since I was in study hall inside the building when you picked me up."

"I popped some great wheelies in that hallway," Gunther fondly recollected.

Then something incredible happened. Gert and Gunther laughed simultaneously, and then their eyes locked onto each other's.

"There she is. I miss you, Gert. I'm sorry I haven't been who I should've been recently," Gunther said as he continued staring adoringly into her green eyes.

"You don't ever want to talk about losing Chris. We may as well have lost Lizzy and Elijah too. You just crawled inside the beer and liquor bottles and cigarette cartons. And heck Gunther, you might as well have died along with them. Go ahead and say it!"

"Say what?" Gunther sadly asked.

"That our son is dead!" Gert shouted as her voice cracked.

Gunther slid his chair next to hers; then he took a deep breath and uttered the words she implored him to say. "Chris is dead. I know he's dead. Me talking about it won't bring him or Kyle back and won't bring Lizzy or Elijah back either. But I promise you I'm changing. I quit drinking."

"Since when?" Gert skeptically asked.

"Two days ago."

"Oh, I'll hang my hat on that post!" she cynically exclaimed.

"I mean it. I won't have another drink as long as I live if it means I get you back," he said.

"And the cigarettes? You sound like a walrus with a chest cold," Gert said spitefully.

"I'll quit when crabbing season is over. I can't be shaky at sea," Gunther promised.

Gert looked at him incredulously.

"Please let me love you. Please let me take care of you. I need you in my life. It ain't worth living without you in it," he pleaded.

"You won't even take care of yourself!" Gert rebutted.

"I love you, Gert. I'm sorry our boy is gone. But we are still here, and Portia needs us. And that new kid Joel ain't a bad guy," Gunther said.

"He looks just like Chris. I thought I had seen a ghost when I first saw him," Gert admitted.

Gunther stood up and reached for Gert's hand. Meanwhile, Rhonda set appetizers on the table. Gunther looked at Rhonda and nodded his head, and she knew what to do. She went to the stage and flipped a few switches before exiting the room. Then an old recording of an acoustic guitar began playing, and the music made Gert smile. She placed her hand in Gunther's and walked with him to the dancefloor. Gunther slid his arm around her waist and held her other hand close to his heart.

"Do you remember this song?" he asked.

"How could I forget? I got up on stage and surprised you with it at our senior prom."

Gunther pulled her closer. "This is my favorite song you ever wrote for me."

"How did you find this?" she inquired.

"I may have pulled a few strings and got ahold of the old recordings from 1984 at the high school. Portia pulled the audio and burned a CD. I'll never forget you getting on stage in your yellow cape-collared dress with daisy garland in your hair—strumming your granddaddy's guitar and singing to me," Gunther reminisced, just as Gert's beautiful 18-year-old voice filled the Port House.

I never knew love before you
I never looked into another's eyes
I never kissed before you
You got my heart till the end of time
And we rode on your dirt bike
Through the trails of Ballyhoo
And I sang into your ear
You love me, and I love you
You stole my heart, you crazy sailor
I got something to tell you now
You're gonna be a daddy
When next year rolls around
And I can't wait to see your face
When our angel comes to town

The song ended with light strumming, and then the melodious clamor of cheering and applause from the audience at the 1984 Aleutian High School prom filled the Port House like Gert and Gunther had flashed back in time. The recording ended; then a slow love song from the 1980s played as Gert moved closer to Gunther, pressing her cheek against his.

"I really should've finished that song," she said.

"I think it's perfect the way it is. You knew I wouldn't have heard anything else after you sang, 'You're gonna be a daddy.'"

"And then you came up on stage, took the microphone, and got down on one knee," Gert happily recollected.

"I got you a pretty nice ring after that, once I saved enough money," Gunther said as he looked at her left hand, smiling because she was still wearing her engagement ring and wedding ring. "Couldn't take them off, could you?"

Gert smiled. "Then nine months later, our sweet little Chris arrived."

"He was perfect, wasn't he?" Gunther asked as he pulled Gert closer, then kissed her. "Come on. Let's have some appetizers and dinner. Then maybe you'll come home with me tonight, and we can watch the video recording of my proposal."

"Uh, have you cleaned since I left?"

"Not a darn thing!" Gunther admitted, not the least bit ashamed.

"Maybe we'll go back to the inn tonight instead until the house is cleaned."

"Eh, probably a good idea. Oh, how I love you!" Gunther said with a smile.

"I love you too," Gert replied.

THE NEXT MORNING, Gert, Gunther, Portia, Joel, Tanya, and Bubba had breakfast together in the kitchen at The Harbor Inn. Gert and Tanya set pancakes, toast, eggs, bacon, sausage, coffee, and juice on the table. The meal was informal; they reached for pancakes and toast with their hands as they loudly talked over each other while the television blared the local news in the background.

Joel didn't reach for food right away like the others. Instead, he sat back and enjoyed the moment. *This is what having a family must be like*, he thought.

"You want some coffee?" Portia asked, pulling him from his sentimental thoughts.

"Yes, thank you," Joel said before kissing her.

"Well, you better grab some grub while you can. I know how fast these carnivores devour their food," Portia insisted, then poured their coffees, reached for a pancake, and slapped a few pieces of bacon on top of it.

"Oh, speak for yourself, Miss Bacon on Your Pancakes with Maple Syrup!" Gunther teased.

Portia laughed and promptly reached for the syrup to douse her plate in sweetness as Joel reached his arm around her waist, pulling her close.

Jovial chatter filled the room until the weather report began. Gunther shushed everyone as he reached for the remote and turned up the volume.

The weatherman said, "I'm sure all of us remember last January's arctic storm, causing the deaths of 15 watermen and creating gusts up to 150 miles per hour on the islands of Unalaska and Akutan. Let's keep our fingers crossed that we don't have a repeat storm, or should I say storms? Due to the recent weather patterns, it's safe to say this could be a possibility. Also, there's been an increase in glacier calving, creating more icebergs than usual. The icebergs sit low in the sea waters and are hard to see, which can cause a lot of damage to fishing vessels. Many captains have upgraded to the W1100-GU4 unit from Dartha, which provides state-of-the-art iceberg detection, the best we've had in years."

Gert abruptly turned off the television as worry replaced her cheerful expression.

Gunther shrugged it off. "We got that unit. We should be fine if Bubba did a good job with the installation."

"I'm sure Bubba did a bang-up job!" Tanya exclaimed before puckering her lips and blatantly sticking out her chest.

"Why thank you, muffins," Bubba said, then gave her a bunny nose rub.

"I'm going to throw up!" Gunther choked back a fake heave.

Gert gave him a disapproving look, and Gunther relented. He obnoxiously sighed. "Oh heck, you two crazy kids. I'm happy for you."

Gunther's change of heart must've meant one thing. He got lucky last night.

Chapter 16. *Ice*

With the Alexandria's departure date approaching, Joel spent every moment he could with Portia. And they weren't the only ones with a budding romance, for Gert and Gunther's love burgeoned so much that even Gunther helped at the Port House in the evenings.

"Look at us lovesick pups," Gunther said as he and Joel sat at the bar before closing one night. "We love our women so much we're cleaning tables and serving customers."

"Speaking of which, I have something to ask you. Something I would like to have your blessing on…" Joel began without hesitation because he was never surer of anything in his life.

Gunther rolled his head in a circle, then squinted at Joel. "Boy, are you telling me that you have only known Portia for a few weeks, and you want to pop the question?"

Joel immediately began to sweat; however, he held his ground. "Yes, Captain."

"Yeah, okay, sure," Gunther said. Then he took a sip of root beer and laughed. "I'm just messing with you, kid. Hey, when you know, you know. If you want to marry my niece, you have my blessing. I've watched you. I've seen how you are with her."

"I appreciate that more than you know. Thank you. I love her so much, and I promise to always take care of her," Joel assured.

JOEL DIDN'T BUY an engagement ring because he had a family heirloom that he knew Portia would cherish. Besides a family photo album, his mother's engagement ring was one of the only tangible objects he had from his childhood.

As he sat on his bed at the inn, Joel reached into his duffel bag and took out a small, blue velvet box that had held his mother's ring for the last 27 years. He hadn't opened the box in at least 15 years because seeing it always stirred his emotions, but this was the perfect time to reconnect with this family treasure.

Joel slowly opened the box and saw the vintage, oval-cut diamond, still sparkling after all these years, just as it had sparkled the last time he saw it on his mother's finger. He took a deep breath as his eyes glistened, realizing how happy he was to have found a woman worthy of wearing his mother's ring.

Joel walked over to the window to look deeper into the diamond beneath the sunray that filled the room. The diamond's shimmer was handiwork of the Creator. "Beauty for beauty," Joel whispered as he stared in awe at the dazzling gemstone, then smiled as he envisioned his mother's ring twinkling on Portia's finger.

He carefully closed the ring box and reached for the expensive new laptop he had recently bought. He needed to plan a memorable proposal—something for the history books—something that included light. Suddenly, he recalled an article he had read recently about the Kaluga Ice Cave in Juneau and how its vaulted dome of ice reflected a heavenly blue light. Joel knew this would be the perfect place to get down on one knee and ask for Portia's hand in marriage.

JOEL ASKED PORTIA to clear her schedule for October 12th-14th and to pack a suitcase. Early on the morning of the 12th, they departed the Port of Aleutia Airport for a 10-hour trip to Juneau. Joel found it hard to believe that traveling to another city in the same state they lived in would take so surprisingly long. Nonetheless, it was time well spent with Portia by his side. Joel was impressed with how well she did with the flight as they were high in the sky and over water with no land in sight. And Portia wasn't the only one to do well, for she must've had a calming influence on Joel because he didn't experience any nausea or uneasiness about the flight either. He and Portia were together, and that was all that mattered. Joel enjoyed feeling her head on his shoulder for the duration of the flight and holding her hand as they walked through the airport.

In Juneau, Joel had reserved an elegant hotel room overlooking the Gastineau Channel, which had exceptional views of towering mountains, dressed in all their Alaskan beauty. He had also arranged for room service, and they had a fresh green salad, roasted potatoes, filet mignons, and red wine as the sun dropped lower in the sky.

After dinner, Joel poured champagne and lit candles around their private hot tub, which had a gorgeous view of the skyline. He and Portia climbed into the tub together and wrapped their arms around each other, thoroughly enjoying their uninhibited embrace of skin on skin. In this delicate moment, words weren't necessary, for their lips and hands did the work for them. Joel loved how Portia's body felt against his, knowing he needed this embrace for the rest of his life. He needed this gentle love every single night. Joel continued holding her closer than he had held her yet, running his fingers through her gorgeous locks as they drew closer—and closer—becoming one. Neither let go of the other, simply holding and caressing each other until the midnight hour.

The next morning, they woke up in each other's arms with their legs entwined after an unforgettable night of passion. A knock at the door announced the arrival of their 6 a.m. room-service breakfast, so Joel promptly leapt out of bed, grabbed his robe, and brought in a breakfast cart for him and Portia to enjoy coffee and cinnamon rolls in bed.

Thoroughly enjoying the view of Portia wrapped up in a sheet,

Joel sat down next to her. "We need to leave at 0800 hours."

"And what is on the agenda today?" she asked before taking a huge bite of a cinnamon roll.

Joel stared at her, unable to respond as he watched her slowly, and sexily, chew and swallow her food. He set down his coffee cup and rolled over on top of her, holding her head in his hands and covering her face in kisses until his lips found their way down the side of her neck and other lovely places. At 7 a.m., his cell phone alarm sounded, alerting them to pry their sticky paws off each other and get a move on it. Joel sighed and frowned. "We got to get dressed and get downstairs. Our taxi leaves at eight."

"What surprises are in store today?" she asked again.

"Wouldn't you like to know," he said, then kissed her on the nose, jumped out of bed, and walked backward toward the bathroom while motioning with his finger for her to follow him into the shower.

THEY RUSHED DOWNSTAIRS to meet the taxi.

"Please take us to Petrov's Hangar," Joel kindly requested as he and Portia climbed into a dingy cab. After a bumpy, 15-minute ride, they arrived at a hangar outside the airport.

"We are going on a helicopter tour," Portia happily surmised.

"How does the Kaluga Ice Cave sound?" Joel whispered.

"It sounds perfect! I've never been to an ice cave before!" she exclaimed. Then Portia thoroughly thanked him with a wild and passionate kiss.

The lip lock continued long after the cab was put in park, so the driver pretended to sneeze to interrupt them.

"Oh!" Joel laughed as he reached into his pocket for a credit card. "Sorry, man."

Joel and Portia held hands as they walked over to a silver and green helicopter where a tall, middle-aged man wearing a blue and red cold-weather suit stepped out from the cockpit to greet them with a thick Russian accent.

"Hello. My name is Viktor Petrov. I'll be your tour guide and escort you to the Kaluga Ice Cave. If you are not a believer now, you will be when we leave," he said as he shook their hands and gave Joel a clipboard and a pen. "Please sign. It says glaciers are continually moving, and Petrov's Tours is in no way responsible for your injury or untimely death should you be a dummy and fall. For example, if you were to fall into a crevasse, or if you die if the cave collapses on us. Either way, not Petrov's fault. The cave is assessed daily, so it shouldn't calve or kill us today. But if it does, then I cannot be sued."

"But, if you're there, you'll die too," Portia interjected.

"Ah, but I know the sights and sounds of stress marks in the ice. And I know how to make a quick getaway. Don't worry. I'll give you a warning," Viktor said as he licked his lips and looked Portia up and down.

Joel gave Viktor a disapproving look. Then he grudgingly signed the paperwork and handed it to Portia to sign too.

"I'm in!" she exclaimed, then signed without hesitation. "Let's do this!"

Joel appreciated Portia's eagerness to see the ice cave. Like him, she also craved the hidden danger, the suspense of knowing that something huge could happen at any moment. That is what made it so enthralling—to know that they would get to see something that was so beautiful, yet so fleeting, that would soon be gone, a tiny ice paradise created by the one and only Almighty God.

The helicopter flight was brief but wasn't without its grandeur, showcasing Alaska's majestic design—beauty so surreal and flawless that Joel thought they were entering the gates of Heaven. The aerial views of the National Forest and Kaluga Lake were splendiferous, only to be trumped by the pristinely bright glare of the Kaluga Ice Field, a gigantic glacier housing the Kaluga Ice Cave beneath it.

As they approached the ice field, Viktor began, "Lucky you, fine lady, your thoughtful man reserved a helicopter ride, unlike the folks who kayak from the visitors' center. Right now, we are flying over Kaluga Lake. To the right, you see Kaluga Falls, and straight ahead, unless you are a blind bat, you see the Kaluga Glacier, also known as the Kaluga Ice Field. The ice cave entrance is right down there where the glacier meets the lake because the lake ran through the bottom of the glacier—and bada bing! We have the Kaluga Ice Cave. I will land the helicopter in the ice field, and then we will make our way down."

"Oh, so we are going to hike across the glacier!" Portia exclaimed as she squeezed Joel's hand.

"Well, something like that," Joel replied, pleased with her response. He couldn't help but laugh as he watched her face when they flew past the center of the ice field and closer to a valley in the mountain range on the right.

"That's going to be like a two-to-three-mile hike. One way," Portia observed as her blue eyes bugged out.

"Hey, you trust me, right?" Joel asked.

"Well, yes."

"Then look out the window now," he said as they approached a camp including a few tents and about 40 dog houses. Portia's mouth flew open, and Joel knew she would love glacier-dog sledding across the Kaluga Ice Field.

Viktor landed the helicopter, and a swirling cloud of snow surrounded it until the rotor blades finished spinning. Once the cloud died down, he shut off the engine. "Put your spikes on your feet now, so you don't fall and break your rear ends. First, we'll go to the tent to have a snack and use the potty!"

Joel squinted his eyes, wondering if this man's humor was real.

As they stepped out of the helicopter, a choir of howling huskies and malamutes provided a beautiful Alaskan greeting. Each dog had its own house and loved life. Some boisterous pups rolled in the snow while others indulged in the warm sunrays on the housetops. All were eagerly awaiting their next sledding adventure.

While Viktor prepared the dog sled, Portia and Joel enjoyed light refreshments in a nearby tent. After half an hour, Viktor entered the tent and led Portia and Joel to the opposite exit. As they stepped outside, the sun almost blinded them, and the darling sound of puppy howls directed their attention to a large pen of 15 adorable, fluffy malamute and husky pups, the future sled team of the Kaluga Ice Field. Joel smiled when Portia rushed over to the pen and crouched down to pet the puppies through the openings in the wire fence.

An older gentleman from the camp introduced himself. "You must be Portia and Joel. I am Peter Petrov, Viktor's older but much better-looking brother." He shook hands with Portia and Joel and then stood next to Joel, watching Portia interact with the pups.

All the puppies were playing with each other, except for a tiny malamute who took exception to Portia's gentle touch. His face was white with grayish-black markings on his forehead and around his crystal-blue eyes. He had small white patches of fur that looked like eyebrows pointed upward and a white streak in the middle of his forehead. His back was a light powdery gray that came down over his legs like he was wearing a tuxedo.

"He likes you. Go inside the pen and play with him," Peter insisted as he opened the gate for Portia; then he and Joel followed her.

"Thank you, Peter. He's so perfect," Portia said as she picked up the pup, and he immediately licked her face.

"This little guy's name is Ice. He's friendly to us all but has never shown affection like this to anyone before," Peter explained.

Joel watched Portia intently as she held the puppy and gently stroked his back. For a moment, he visualized Portia holding a baby, but not just any baby—their baby, and he couldn't help but think that Portia would make a wonderful mother. This vision was yet another telltale sign that Portia was meant for him because he had never had this visualization for any other woman he dated.

Portia set the puppy down and walked across the pen to see the others playing next to a bench. Ice followed her, staying close to her heels, and then jumped into her lap when she sat down.

Joel continued watching her and thought how wonderful it would be for Portia to have a dog while he was away. "Hey Peter, are these puppies up for adoption?" he asked in a low whisper. "The king crab season opens in two days, and I'll be leaving. Portia's father and cousin were killed during January's opilio season, so she's uneasy about me going."

Peter compassionately nodded his head. "I know a lot of folks lost their lives out there. We usually keep and train these pups, but this little guy has found who he wants to love. I'll get the pup ready and bring him to the helicopter for Portia right before your flight. How's that sound?"

"Perfect. Thank you so much. What do I owe you for the little guy?" Joel inquired.

"Nothing. Who am I to stand in the way of true love? I'm certainly not going to make money off that."

"I don't know how to thank you," Joel replied.

"Just hang onto your beautiful lady and spoil the heck out of her every chance you get. You two married?" Peter asked.

"I'm proposing in the ice cave today," Joel whispered with a smile.

"God bless you, son. Last summer, I lost my wife of 30 years. The days are now longer and quieter," Peter sadly explained.

Before Joel could respond, Peter patted him on the shoulder and walked over to finish preparing the sled.

Joel joined Portia on the bench and did his best to pet every puppy. All the while, Ice remained a fixture in Portia's arms, for neither of them wanted to let the other go. However, a few minutes later, Viktor motioned for them to follow him to the sled.

"Bye, little buddy," Portia said sadly with a smile as she set Ice down, then walked out of the pen. Ice followed her to the fence and whimpered, and she got down and petted him one more time.

Portia and Joel followed Viktor to the sled, where six huskies were lined up and harnessed, ready for their trek across the glacier.

"This is Balto, Aurora, Juneau, Kaluga, Gastineau, and Frosty," Peter said as he introduced the sled dogs. Portia and Joel petted them before climbing into the sled seat built for two. When Viktor stepped onto the platform, the huskies jumped and howled in anticipation.

"Okay. We are off! Mush! Mush!" Viktor yelled as the canines took off like a steak dinner was waiting for them on the glacier.

The sun's glare on the glacier was intense but beautiful. The ice field shimmered and sparkled white, surrounding Portia and Joel with perfection, and it most certainly was perfect because God Almighty created this exceptionally stunning terrain. As they cruised along, Joel felt the brisk wind on his cheeks and inhaled the invigorating mountain air, all while feeling revitalized in a way he had never experienced, for he would soon be proposing to the love of his life.

For the first few minutes of the ride, they heard the remaining camp dogs howling in the distance, but not long after, the sound of the sled rails and Viktor yelling, "Mush," repeatedly was the soundtrack for the journey down a well-defined sled trail. On both sides of the path, undisturbed ripples in the snow resembled tiny mountains, a frosty canvas painted by the Almighty. Puffy, fast-moving clouds decorated a glorious crystal-blue sky, the perfect contrast to the shimmering white ice field below it. The extreme vastness of the glacier gave the illusion that the clouds and glacier touched in the distance, merging Heaven and earth.

Joel kept his arm around Portia throughout the ride as they enjoyed the remarkably incomparable experience. Then the Lord may as well had reached down from Heaven and pushed the clouds away, for they blew through as fast as they came. When the sled approached the edge of the glacier by Kaluga Lake, the sun came out full force, radiating down from a clear blue sky at the perfect time.

"Wahoo! Mush! Mush! I said mush! The sun is out! It's going to be beautiful in the ice cave. The bright sun makes it so much better!" Viktor shouted in his thick accent.

Once again, Joel was mesmerized by God's artistry in the sky, which made everything perfect for the proposal. "God is good," Joel whispered. God is good, indeed.

VIKTOR STOPPED THE SLED and firmly secured it, so the dogs couldn't run away with it. "Okay. You need to use your specialty equipment here. You got your spiky shoes on already, and here are your walking sticks. Now, you're ready for some glacier trekking!"

Portia and Joel got out of the sled. Suddenly, loud shrieks from the sky prompted the huskies to bark and howl at the top of their mighty lungs. Portia and Joel looked at the gloriously blue sky and were pleased to see two eagles flying side by side as if they were one. The regal creatures let the gentle breeze guide them as they drifted down to Kaluga Lake, until they found a tall black spruce tree to land in next to Kaluga Falls. Joel smiled and nodded, taking this as another sign from above. He reached his hand down into his pocket and clutched the ring box, knowing that his mother's ring would soon be on his future wife's finger.

"Okay. Enough with the silly eagles. They eat roadkill. Follow me," Viktor implored as he led them across a straightway of smooth ice before encountering some ripples with jagged ice chunks and canyons. "This area is full of ice vaults and crevasses. We got to watch out for seracs because they are unstable and very dangerous. You don't want to step on one for the sake of taking a selfie."

As they trekked across the glacier, occasionally pausing to snap a few photos, Portia and Joel thoroughly enjoyed looking down into the canyons and mini valleys of ice.

"If you want, I can give you ice axes, tie ropes around your waists, and let you climb down and up an ice wall," Viktor offered.

"You know, bud, if I was 10 years younger, then maybe," Joel replied with a chuckle.

"Yeah, I must agree," Portia said.

"Well, okay then. Probably a good choice. So, how about I show you some surprises? Follow me. Like you have a choice." Viktor cackled with a mischievous grin.

They continued stabbing the glacier with their spiky shoes for another 50 feet before they made their first major discovery, and what a discovery it was! Joel was elated to hear the stimulating sound of rushing water.

"A waterfall? How beautiful!" Portia exclaimed as she reached for Joel's hand, making him feel tingly from head to toe.

Joel grew more excited by the moment, for something even more beautiful than a waterfall was getting ready to happen. His heart thumped with excitement as he once again reached his hand into his pocket and gripped the ring box.

"There are lakes, pools, rivers, and waterfalls throughout the glacier. But there is something even more exciting," Viktor began as he motioned for them to follow him another 10 feet, where they looked down into a 15-foot-wide, blue icy abyss with swirling designs carved deep into the depths of the glacier. "That, my dear friends, is a moulin, which is created by a river of water."

"This is magnificent!" Joel exclaimed. Then he and Portia photographed the moulin and the neighboring waterfalls and crevasses.

"Thank you, Joel. This is so wonderful," Portia said gratefully, then kissed him.

Joel smiled and wrapped his arms around her. "This is wonderful, isn't it?"

"Okay. Let's go down to the ice cave. You think the moulin is beautiful; just wait!" Viktor insisted.

JOEL'S HEART FLUTTERED like a butterfly on steroids as they trekked down to the water's edge, near the ice cave's large entrance. Once again, he clutched the ring box, knowing his mother's ring would soon be on Portia's finger.

"Kaluga Lake carved out this ice cave, so a stream is still running throughout it. Don't go too far inside. Just in case, here are two flashlights. You two go exploring. I'll hang out near the entrance. Yell if you need me," Viktor said.

Joel felt the temperature drop as he and Portia entered the impressive blue dome, where the brisk, icy air kissed their faces, and the sound of rushing water blessed their ears as if they had entered holy ground. Joel walked in front of Portia, always the perfect gentleman, finding the safest path over the wet, icy rocks and around several waterfalls. They were strolling right along when suddenly, Portia loudly gasped.

Joel quickly turned around to see if she was all right. "What is it?"

With a smile, Portia pointed upward with her walking stick. Above them, a celestial blue glow emanated from the vaulted ceiling, illuminating nature's sanctuary. Joel felt God's presence in that blessed moment as the sun shone down through the glacier.

After spending a few minutes admiring the ice cave's ceiling, Portia and Joel continued exploring; however, Joel knew their time in the cave was fleeting because of how cold it was. He looped back around to the center of the ice cave next to the largest waterfall. Joel paused to enjoy the sound of the rushing water and to look up at the blue glow as the sun continued shining through the thick layers of ice and illuminating the waterfall with a cerulean hue. Then Joel felt his parents looking down on him with their blessing, and that is when he knew it was time for the moment that would change his life forever.

"Have you ever seen anything so beautiful?" Portia asked.

Joel smiled at her, reached for her walking sticks, and set them down. He took Portia's hands in his. "Portia, I've never seen anything or anyone as beautiful as you. I've traveled the entire world. I've walked the streets of Rome, seen the Great Wall of China, and walked beside the pyramids. All the glorious places I've seen in the past 20 years in the service were great, but nothing compares to my time in Alaska. It's not the sparkling waters of Eagle Bay or the Northern Lights that won me over. All that means nothing without you. I met you a few weeks ago, and I swear on my life Portia; these last few weeks have been the best in my life because of you. I've never been in love until you."

Joel reached into his pocket, carefully got down on one knee, and opened the old ring box. "I need you in my life—every day. I need to feel you sleeping in my arms every night for the rest of my life. I would be honored for you to be my wife. Will you marry me?"

"Yes!" Portia exclaimed without hesitation.

Ever so carefully, Joel removed his mother's ring from the box and gently slid it onto Portia's finger. He kissed the back of her hand as he stood up. Joel cupped her face in his hands and kissed her lovingly. As the kiss subsided, they paused, soaking in this precious moment as they wrapped their arms around each other.

"This was my mother's ring," Joel whispered. "I hope you like it. I thought this ring was so perfect for you."

"Thank you, Joel. I'm so honored to have it. I love that it was hers," Portia replied as she gazed into the diamond, which sparkled like a sapphire beneath the ice cave's azure glow.

Meanwhile, Viktor blew his nose so loudly it echoed throughout the cave. "That was so magnificent! I hope one day to find love," he confessed as he wiped his eyes with a scarf.

Joel ignored Viktor's emotional outburst and hoped Viktor would have the decency to give him and Portia some privacy. Joel continued holding her in his arms as they cherished this special moment. Angels may as well have been singing, and who is to say that angels' singing wasn't present in the rushing waters of the blue-tinted waterfall?

Portia would be his wife, Joel would be her husband, and they would be bound together for the rest of their lives. Soon, they would stand before God beneath the great golden chandelier and pledge their devotion to each other while the smiling face of Jesus watched them from the Dome of Heaven. A beautiful journey lay ahead, indeed.

Suddenly, Portia shivered because the ice cave was so cold.

"Okay, let's go back out to the glacier where it's warmer," Joel said with a chuckle.

They grabbed their walking sticks and returned to the entrance, where Viktor was still wiping his eyes. "I want to hug you both!"

Joel was quick to step to the side while Portia laughed and hugged Viktor. "You will find love one day, Viktor! Sooner rather than later. I got a feeling!" she assured.

"Then why did you say 'yes' to him?" Viktor scoffed.

Joel gave him another disapproving look. "Shall we go?"

"Don't get your knickers in a bunch, but yes, let's go. Follow me," Viktor amusedly retorted.

When they returned to the sled, the snow dogs howled and barked a joyful greeting, and Portia hugged and petted each happy Alaskan pooch. Then Viktor led them back to the camp on the same path in which they came. The ride was a little brisker this time, but it was all good because Portia and Joel had their love to keep them warm. They sat back and relished the beautiful ride, which included another flyby by the two eagles they had seen earlier. As they approached the dog camp, the choir of huskies and malamutes greeted them while Peter conveniently tended to the puppy pen.

After petting the sled dogs one last time, Portia and Joel followed Viktor to the helicopter, and he opened the door for them.

"Oh, here comes Peter," Portia observed.

Peter walked up to the helicopter with a bundled-up blanket in his arms. "Portia, we have a gift for you," he said as he pulled back the blanket to expose Ice's face before handing her the puppy.

Portia gasped and then promptly reached for the little guy. "Peter, are you sure?"

"He's all yours," Peter replied with a sparkle in his eye.

"Oh dear, I'm choking up!" Viktor cried, then loudly blew his nose.

"Oh, thank you! Thank you!" Portia exclaimed as she hugged Ice while he frantically licked her cheek. "I'll take good care of him. I promise."

"Yes, thank you Peter," Joel chimed in as he petted Ice on the head.

"You are most welcome. Just send me pictures of him from time to time. God bless you both," Peter said, then closed the helicopter door.

Viktor regained his composure, climbed into the cockpit, and turned on the engine.

"Thank you, Joel. This has been a wonderful day," Portia said before kissing him.

"It certainly has been. How do you think Screech and Tiny will get along with Ice?" Joel asked, realizing that maybe he didn't think this through completely.

Portia burst out laughing. "I guess we're getting ready to find out!"

Chapter 17. *Our Last Night*

J oel, Portia, and Ice spent the night in Juneau, took an early flight the next morning, and arrived late in the afternoon in the Port of Aleutia.

"Welcome home, buddy," Joel said as he and Portia watched Ice take in the sights, sounds, and smells of Aleutia as they walked to Joel's truck in the airport parking lot. Just a few short weeks ago, that was Joel when he landed in the Port of Aleutia, and now they had a sweet pup who did the same.

Before returning to the Port House for their last night together, Portia and Joel made a couple of stops. Joel needed to get his belongings from The Harbor Inn, and they had to pick up Tiny from Gert and Gunther's house. Rhonda fed Screech since he didn't require much care, just a once-a-day feeding and litter box cleaning. On the other hand, Tiny was exceptionally naughty and needy. Gert and Gunther were the only trusted people to care for Tiny in Portia's absence.

At the inn, Joel parked behind Tanya's and Bubba's trucks. He shook his head and laughed because he knew Tanya would still eyeball him like he was a steak searing on the barbie, and the same was true for Bubba's infatuation with Portia. Joel was thankful that the two awkward beings had found each other. Luckily for Tanya and Bubba, their relationship had entered the next level, which was most unfortunate for Portia and Joel, who found Tanya and Bubba having a late afternoon delight on the living room sofa.

"Call me by my full name!" Bubba roared in between several asthmatic-sounding breaths.

"Oh, Jonathan Harold Timber!" Tanya breathlessly exclaimed.

Joel slammed the front door shut, then loudly and unnecessarily coughed to interrupt them. And thank goodness it worked because Tanya promptly readjusted her skirt and jumped up while Bubba zipped up his fly and buckled his belt.

"Wow. You do know this is a B&B, and there are plenty of empty beds upstairs," Portia said disgustfully.

"We are just enjoying Bubba's last night in town," Tanya coquettishly explained as she puckered her lips, stuck out her chest in Bubba's direction, and then winked at her rotund fellow.

After witnessing such an explicit encounter, Joel immediately felt his lunch climbing his throat. "I'm just gonna grab my stuff, and we will be out of your way," he said before scurrying upstairs to retrieve his belongings from the bedroom on the right.

"Some things just can't be unseen, yall!" Portia shrieked as she covered her eyes with her left hand.

"Golly! Is that what I think it is? Are you two getting hitched?" Tanya inquired.

"You're engaged?" Bubba excitedly asked as he finished securing his belt.

Joel returned with his bags, having heard the conversation.

"I'm so pleased for you two! What a blessing!" Bubba gleefully exclaimed. He immediately hugged Joel, then hugged Portia too.

Tanya couldn't let the opportunity to embrace the Navy man pass her by, so she went for Joel, sparing no shame as she gave him a full-frontal hug, making his skin crawl.

"Uh, thank you," Joel replied appreciatively as he frantically pulled away from Tanya's silicone embrace.

"Well, you two, we will let you get back to your full name-calling. We have another stop to make," Portia said as she walked backward toward the door and motioned for Joel to follow her, and he was thankful for the quick getaway.

"I'LL DRIVE TO UNCLE GUNTHER AND AUNT GERT'S since you don't know the way," Portia firmly declared as she put her hand out.

"Well, okay then," Joel said as he flung her the keys.

Portia started Joel's truck. Joel held Ice during the ride, which was just as he had suspected. After turning right out of the driveway, the truck flew like a williwaw as Portia hit the gas for a mile straight before reaching a dead end, where a lovely house on stilts overlooked Captain's Bay.

"Oh yeah, one right turn. I would've gotten lost for sure," Joel said sarcastically as he firmly held Ice and considered getting the pup a helmet if he would be riding with Portia regularly.

"I just wanted to drive your truck," she retorted as she abruptly slammed on the brakes to give Joel a quick peck.

"You're something. You know that?"

"Don't you ever forget it," Portia responded as she drove slowly down the lane.

Gert and Gunther had no neighbors, just a view of God's gorgeous creation. They had a large barn and parking area, where Gert's SUV was parked beside a new pickup truck with a V8 engine.

"Gunther must've gotten rid of his rat trap and got a new truck. Aunt Gert hated that thing!" Portia said, then laughed as she parked near the house. She carried Ice as she and Joel walked up the steps and rang the doorbell.

Gunther opened the door and smiled. He was clean-shaven and was wearing a new flannel shirt and blue jeans, with a green tweed blazer with elbow patches. Tiny squeaked a happy greeting from where he sat on Gunther's shoulder.

"Hello there, you two! Come on in," Gunther exclaimed as he held the door open. Meanwhile, Tiny jumped onto Portia's shoulder, sniffed the puppy, and looked for bugs in his ears.

"Meet our newest family member. His name is Ice, and he's from the Kaluga Ice Camp," Portia explained as she snuggled him close.

"A puppy!" Gert shouted as she entered the hallway from the kitchen, where the tantalizing scents of olive oil and garlic followed her. "Please stay for dinner. I made lasagna, and it's almost ready! Joel, you do like lasagna, don't you?"

"It's one of my favorites," he gratefully replied and was so thankful she had asked them to stay because the meal smelled incredible.

"Excellent!" Gert said as she reached for Ice, kissed his head, and carried him into the kitchen.

"Uncle—new truck, new duds, clean house, new you!" Portia said as she hugged Gunther.

"Yeah, I've spent $65,000 in the last week. Don't ask how much it costs to clean this house! You know I didn't do it myself," Gunther replied with a chuckle.

"I could only imagine, but you got the job done," Portia said.

"I got her back," he responded.

"You never lost her, Uncle. Aunt Gert will love you forever."

"Well then, let's get some root beer and celebrate!" Gunther exclaimed as he walked toward the spacious dining room, which was decorated with antique furniture and oil paintings of antiquated fishing vessels. The room also had an exquisite waterfront view. Overall, the house was extremely welcoming, just like Gert and Gunther's personalities, making Joel feel right at home.

The decadent smell of Italian cuisine filled the room as Gert brought in Caesar salad, garlic bread, and lasagna, while Gunther filled tumblers with root beer. As they sat at the table, Ice insisted on sitting on his Aunt Gert's lap while Tiny jumped from Portia's shoulder to Joel's.

Portia picked up her fork and tapped the side of her glass several times. "Joel and I have an announcement to make."

"What is it, honey?" Gert asked.

Portia held up the back of her left hand to show them the engagement ring.

"I already knew!" Gunther admitted.

After she gasped, Gert slapped Gunther's arm and yelled with her salty twang, "Why didn't you tell me?"

"Coz I knew you'd get all gushy and wouldn't be able to contain yourself!" Gunther jovially retorted.

"Ahem!" Portia loudly replied.

"Oh, I'm so happy for you two! Welcome to the family, Joel!" Gert said with a contented smile that only a mother could make.

"Yes, indeed. Welcome Joel. We are so happy to have you," Gunther added.

"Yes we are," Portia chimed in, then kissed Joel on the cheek, continuing to make him feel like the luckiest man alive.

Between the comfort of the house, the homemade meal, and the excellent company, Joel's heart was full. The four of them enjoyed the decadent meal as they told stories from the past, laughing and joking, just having an all-around good time together.

After a couple hours had passed, Portia looked at her watch. "We should start heading out. Joel still has to unpack and then pack again."

"Yeah, do a load of laundry, would you?" Gunther teased as he pretended to sniff the air. "I'm just joking. Anyway, I'll go grab Tiny's baby bag from upstairs," he said as he stood up.

"I'll come with you," Portia responded.

PORTIA NEEDED A FEW MINUTES ALONE with her uncle before the Alexandria left for the red king crab season, especially since the following day would be so busy with the Blessing of the Fleet Ceremony before the crew would depart for the Bering Sea. She had many stirring feelings; the last time the crew was out, Kyle and

Chris didn't come back alive, and this would be the first time Gunther would be the captain of her daddy's vessel.

Portia and Gunther went upstairs and sat on a loveseat in front of a giant window with a spectacular bay view.

"Now listen to me, kid. Don't do what you do," Gunther admonished as he took Portia's hand.

"I don't know what you're talking about," Portia whispered as a small lump formed in her throat.

"Don't go off the deep end while we're gone. Don't hit the bottle too hard, and don't do dope without me! When in doubt, drink root beer. Stay close to your Aunt Gert. She needs you, and you need her," Gunther said.

"We need you. I hate the Bering Sea. She has taken so much from us," Portia quietly replied.

Gunther looked at her empathetically. "I miss your dad and my son every day. It's going to be hard, but…"

"But, I know you've got to go. I also know that you love the sea. And so does Joel," Portia said as she leaned closer and rested her head on Gunther's shoulder.

"You know you love the sea too. You're an Alexander. It's in your blood. I love you, kid," Gunther whispered.

"I love you too, Uncle. And yes, you're right," Portia responded as she pulled him closer and kissed his cheek.

MEANWHILE, Gert and Joel shared a similar conversation downstairs, while Gert held onto Ice, and Tiny sat on Joel's shoulder.

"I'm so happy for you and Portia. Joel, you are such a blessing to us in so many ways. We are so glad you are here," Gert began as she teared up. "You be careful out there. Please keep a close eye on Gunther. It's going to be hard on him, going back out there without Kyle and Chris."

Gert's words struck an emotional chord with Joel, for he had seen that same worried expression on his mother's face when he went oyster patent tonging with his father on a blustery winter day 25 years ago. Tonging for oysters was dangerous, and Joel's mother worried, as is a mother's job to do. All these years later, and nearly 6,000 miles away from Maryland's Eastern Shore, Joel sat in Unalaska, Alaska, once again receiving a mother's love. Gert filled an immense hole that had been in Joel's life for the last 27 years.

"I promise to stay close to Gunther. Thank you for everything you have done for me," Joel answered as he reached for Gert's hand.

"I haven't done a thing, darling," Gert said.

"Yes, you have. You're a mom, and you take care of everyone around you. You and Gunther have made me feel welcome. Thank you. And I promise I'll take good care of Portia. I promise you that," Joel replied.

"Well Gert, let these youngins get on their way," Gunther said as he walked in and set Tiny's baby bag on the table.

"Oh, okay," Gert sadly responded as she stood up and gave Ice to Portia.

They shared a group hug before Gert and Gunther stood at the door and watched Portia and Joel drive away.

THAT NIGHT WAS BITTERSWEET, for it was the last night for the Aleutian families to spend with their loved ones before they embarked on another dangerous journey. Some would live, and some would die—a reality they knew all too well.

Husbands and wives such as Gert and Gunther spent a quiet evening at home, while folks like Tanya, Bubba, Polly, and Nick engaged in activities that weren't exactly G-rated. While men like Hank were at the bar alone, broken families like Kirk and Old Al had dinner at The Bairdi Saloon, bonding quietly the best way they knew how. Nonetheless, everyone knew this was the last night to love, and that's what Portia and Joel did.

WITH TINY ZIPPED UP INSIDE HIS JACKET, Joel grabbed the luggage from the backseat while Portia carried Ice up the staircase to their apartment. Screech was stretched out in the middle of the bed, and he ignored Portia and Joel because he was mad that they had left.

Portia gave Ice to Joel, so she could pet Screech with the hopes of buttering him up before introducing the newest family member. Momentarily, the fat cat seemed pleased; he chortled, sat up, and purred for his momma. Then the unthinkable happened when Joel placed Ice and Tiny on the foot of the bed. Screech twitched his long whiskers as he regally looked back and forth between Tiny and Ice. He did this five times before lifting his fluffy paw to whack them with one giant swat.

Portia intervened by gently grabbing his paw and yelling, "No!"

Ice fearlessly scampered up to Screech and sniffed his nose before profusely sniffing his entire body. Screech handled it well until Ice licked his back fur in the wrong direction, prompting Screech to arch his back and hiss at the curious pup. Ice whimpered and scurried over to Portia, and Screech immediately bit the puppy on his backside. Then Ice howled and zoomed across the apartment. Screech wasn't about to miss the opportunity to chase the newcomer, so he tore across the room after him. The chase ended with Ice taking a gigantic poop on the rug by the back door, which made Tiny cackle like he was a laughing human.

Always the knight in shining armor, Joel quickly cleaned up Ice's intentional accident on the rug. Meanwhile, Portia scooped up the pup and carried him to the sofa to console him. Screech resentfully stomped across the room and jumped on the couch by Portia. Completely jealous over his new brother's affection, the tomcat threw himself down on his side and let out a loud huff.

After washing his hands, Joel walked over to the sofa, plugged in his cell phone charger, and set the phone on the coffee table to charge. All the while, Portia tried to get all three critters acquainted a little bit better, even though it was abundantly clear that they had a long way to go.

"Well, I do believe I need to take a shower to get the airport funk off me. Care to join me?" Joel enticingly asked.

"You know it!" Portia exclaimed as she promptly stood up, took off her shirt, and followed him into the bathroom.

I'm going to miss this at sea, Joel thought, while he watched his fiancée reveal her stunning, tightly toned body. Once they were both undressed, Joel turned on the shower to warm up the water, and steam filled the room as he stepped in first, then reached his hand out for Portia to join him. The hot water ran over their bodies as they delighted in their loving embrace. Not long after, their lips found each other. Eventually, they both washed away the 10 hours of travel they had endured earlier that day.

WHILE JOEL FINISHED his shaving repertoire, Portia walked out in a towel and then put on her silk bathrobe and fluffy slippers. She could get used to this, the feeling of contentment and knowing she had someone with whom to share her life. Sure, she had other people in her life before Joel strutted through the Port House doors. However, in the mornings, she didn't have someone to drink coffee with and watch weather reports with or enjoy those divine, lazy Sundays while bacon fried in the kitchen, smelling up the place. Even though Joel would be coming and going due to his life-long love of the open water, Portia knew she had a man who loved her.

She tied her bathrobe, then turned toward the bed. Shockingly, all three critters were sprawled out together. They were respectable distances from each other, but still, they were together. She petted all three of them, telling each little fluff ball how much she loved him. When suddenly, Joel's cell phone rang, breaking the solitude.

Should I answer it? Portia contemplated. She looked at the screen and saw that it wasn't a regular phone call. When Portia saw that it was a video call from Adoncia, she fiendishly grinned and answered it, only to be greeted by a closeup of the Spanish courtesan, which included her mile-long cleavage line.

"¡Hola! Joel? Are you there?" Adoncia asked as it took a moment for Portia's video to connect.

"Hi there. Joel's in the shower," Portia awkwardly greeted the prostituta her fiancée had visited for the last 10 years.

"¡Maravillosa! You must be Portia! Oh, I am so delighted to meet you! You are muy bonita!" Adoncia exclaimed with her thick Spanish accent.

"Hello, and thank you," Portia inelegantly replied.

"I was calling to wish Joel good luck. He leaves tomorrow, no?"

"Yes, in the morning," Portia stiffly responded as she heard the bathroom door open and there stood Joel, wearing only a towel as he exited the steamy room. For a moment, Portia forgot that she was on a video call with her fiancée's prostituta friend because the sight of her shirtless Navy man took her breath away. However, Joel's eyes bugged out when he realized what was happening. Once Portia collected herself and remembered she and Adoncia were talking, she burst out laughing. "Oh, here's Joel now," she said, switching the video view to Joel in a towel so Adoncia could see for herself.

"There he is, indeed! He looks like the cover of a romance novel. Hi Joel!" Adoncia exclaimed, not sorry for her verbal appreciation of Joel's hot bod.

"Hey, Adoncia," Joel responded as he gave Portia an unwieldy look.

"I wanted to wish you good luck tomorrow," Adoncia said as her eyes indulged in Joel's masculinity.

Joel firmly gripped his towel as he sat beside Portia on the sofa. Meanwhile, Portia changed the camera view so that Adoncia could see them both.

"Thank you, Adoncia. I appreciate it. Did Portia tell you the big news?" Joel asked.

"Big news?" Adoncia repeated.

"We're getting married!" Joel proudly announced as Tiny jumped on his shoulder.

"Oh, that's maravilloso! That makes me so happy! When's the wedding?" Adoncia exuberantly inquired.

"We haven't gotten that far yet," Portia replied.

"Well, I was thinking New Year's Eve. Then Portia can work on planning it while I'm gone," Joel said with a cheesy grin.

"I like that idea," Portia began as she smiled. "You must come to the wedding, Adoncia."

Joel certainly didn't see this one coming, which was evident when he looked at Portia with complete shock and surprise.

"Adoncia, thank you for finding Joel this job and sending him here. I would never have met him if it wasn't for you," Portia said graciously. And that was the truth. If not for the prostituta from Rota, Portia never would've met the Navy captain who stole her heart the first moment she saw him. "We will get you a plane ticket and a suite at The Harbor Inn. I can't wait to meet you," Portia insisted.

"Gracias," Adoncia replied, stunned by Portia's kind offer. "I can't wait either. I haven't left Rota in 15 years! It's time for a trip. I'm so looking forward to it!"

"Make sure you bring some cold weather clothes when you come. It's not as warm as it is at the Gypsy Market," Joel said.

"Bueno! I won't keep you two. It's your last night. Enjoy each other. Joel, please give Portia my number, so she can update me on how you're doing at sea," Adoncia requested.

"We will do that," Portia agreed.

"Thank you, Adoncia. Talk to you soon," Joel said.

"Bye, Adoncia," Portia said as she ended the call.

JOEL WAS STILL BUG-EYED but pleased that Adoncia and Portia were starting a friendship. This was a tiny bit awkward, but incredibly great.

He looked at Portia, shook his head, and laughed. "You're just full of surprises, aren't you?"

"You're one to talk," Portia retorted as she leaned closer to kiss him. "New Year's Eve?"

Joel reached up to her cheek and whispered, "Promise me something, please."

"Anything," Portia breathlessly replied.

"Promise me that you won't go back to that dark place. When you are in doubt, write for me. I know you're scared about us leaving. I get that," Joel said compassionately.

"And I know you got to go. And I know why. I'm your second love."

Portia's words stung like a bee and reminded Joel of what Adoncia had said all those years ago, "Every time you go to sea, you would desert me, even if you kept coming back. All you sailors are the same. You love the ocean first. You love your woman last." After hearing these words echo in his mind, Joel couldn't bear the thought of Portia feeling the same way that Adoncia did.

"Portia, you are definitely my first love. I won't go. I'll get a job somewhere on the island or on a boat during the day. I would do that for you."

"No. You love living at sea. You love being away from land for weeks on end. I won't kill your spirit or take that away from you," Portia insisted.

Joel leaned his face against hers, so their cheeks were touching.

"I love you. I'll come back to you. I promise," he ensured, knowing he could only do so much convincing. "Now is one of those times," he said as he pulled away and stood up.

"Huh? What are you talking about?" Portia asked with a perplexed tone.

Joel picked up the acoustic guitar and handed it to her. "When in doubt, write."

"What? Right now?" Portia took the guitar.

"Yes. Right now, and when I am gone. Right now, I want you to write a new song. Fifteen minutes, right?" Joel asked.

"You're kinda putting me on the spot right now," she nervously replied.

"I'm confident in your talent," Joel responded as he sat down on the opposite end of the sofa and turned, so he could watch the master songwriter work. Ice jumped on his lap, Tiny sat on his shoulder, and Screech threw himself down on the coffee table. "See, your audience awaits."

Portia sighed, indicating that she was giving in to Joel's request. "Please hand me my notepad."

Joel slid the notepad across the table to her. She looked at him nervously, reached for it, and jotted down some notes.

"Well, I did have a tiny tune pop into my head after we left Aunt Gert and Uncle Gunther's tonight," Portia admitted.

"Well, let's hear it," Joel requested, giving Ice a good back scratching.

Portia strummed a few chords, then sang, "It's our last night / Before you go away." She paused to write on the notepad, quietly humming for about three to four minutes. "Okay, how's this?" She sang as she strummed the guitar.

It's our last night
Before you go away

It's our last night
For you and I to stay
In each other's arms
Until the morning light
It's our last night
To love

Joel was blown away. The tune was beautiful, and Portia captured not just what they were feeling, but what all the crew members were feeling that night as well. Whether they're holding their husband or wife, fiancée, boyfriend or girlfriend, or having dinner with a parent, no matter how you looked at it, they had one last night to love. Portia had the talent to convey her feelings and those of everyone around her. She had a God-given gift, and Joel was pleased to watch it blossom before his eyes.

"It's perfect. I can't wait to hear the rest," he said.

"That was the chorus. Now to write the verses…" She hummed quietly again, tried out a few more chords, counted syllables on her fingertips, and wrote more down on the notepad. After about five minutes, she sang the first verse and pre-chorus as she stared into Joel's eyes.

Oh, here you are
Looking into my eyes
But tomorrow
You'll be out of sight
On your way
To your other love

Oh Bering Sea
Please bring him home to me

She sang the chorus again, and Joel's eyes glistened because of her extraordinary talent. The song had a beautiful melody and was undoubtedly one of those songs you could've sworn you had heard before because it was that good.

"I have to keep repeating what I've already written to keep writing. Not sure if that makes sense," Portia explained.

"It makes perfect sense. It's your writing process. It's beautiful, and I love it."

She smiled and then wrote on the notepad again. "Come down here closer. Look at my notes here. I already have the tune and syllables counted for the first verse, so I write out the number of syllables and then fill in the blanks with new words for the second verse. I also write the chord changes above the words."

Joel looked at the paper and saw what she meant. She made it look easy, like anybody could do it, but Joel knew better than that.

Portia repeated the first verse to get the tune down again, then wrote the second verse. After a few minutes, she performed the second verse and pre-chorus.

You said to write
That's what I'm doing now
Kinda strange
I'll do it anyhow
Coz I love you
To the moon and back

Oh Bering Sea
Please bring him home to me

Joel laughed at the first part. "I love it."

"Now, I'm ready to debut the full song."

"Let's hear it," Joel said as he pulled Ice close, and Tiny happily squeaked. Screech paid no attention as he frantically chewed the spaces between his furry toes.

Portia wasn't on stage under bright lights. She was wearing her silk bathrobe and fluffy slippers. Her hair was a mess, and she wasn't wearing any makeup. Still, she looked like a porcelain doll, pure and true, and there she sat with her sparkling silver acoustic guitar on the sofa, overlooking Eagle Bay, which glistened under the moonlight beneath a sky splashing with colors. Portia strummed a few chords and then sang the entire song, ending with the following section.

Wherever you are
My song
Will travel with the wind
Wherever you go
My love
Will follow all the way
Because I love you
To the moon and back

Oh Bering Sea
Please bring him home to me

"Please don't worry about me while I'm gone. I will be coming home to you. I promise. We have so much to live for. I can't wait to be your husband and for you to be my wife," Joel began, then gently kissed her lips. "The song was so beautiful. Thank you. It's my favorite one yet."

"There's plenty more where that came from. I'll write you more. I love you so much. I've never felt so loved before. I feel like I'm dreaming. That this isn't real."

"Oh, it's real," Joel said as he took the guitar and led her to the bed. He gently laid her down and undid her robe. With a quick tug of his hand, his towel came off, and he reached for a throw blanket. They loved each other, reaching new levels of ecstasy neither of them had ever known.

Then they just laid there, tangled up in each other's arms and legs, nodding off to dreamland. When suddenly, a whimper and a cold wet nose touched Joel's cheek. He laughed because Ice wanted to snuggle with his new dad. Joel reached for the pup, putting him beneath the covers since the fluffy lad was shaking like a leaf. Then Joel noticed that Tiny was asleep on his pillow, right next to his face, and Screech was sleeping at the foot of the bed, snoring and twitching his whiskers with every breath. Joel smiled, rolling over so he faced Portia. He was a happy man. He had three furry critters and a woman who loved him, and the following day, he would embark on his first voyage on the Bering Sea. What more could a sailor want?

Chapter 18. *Bittersweet*

The next morning, Joel woke up with his future wife in his arms. She looked like a sleeping angel with her porcelain face, perfectly plump lips, and lengthy eyelashes. Admiring her beauty inside and out, Joel watched Portia sleep for a little while, not wanting to awaken her. However, Ice had other plans; he walked up next to them and whimpered. Portia never slept through the whimpering of her fur babies, so she promptly opened her eyes and scratched the pup's chest. For a moment, she smiled, but the smile faded away as fast as it came.

"Oh, it's today already," she said as she looked into Joel's eyes.

He took a deep breath, for it was a bittersweet moment. Even though he was happy to work on the water again, this new voyage brought mixed emotions because this would be the first time he would say goodbye to someone he loved—someone who would anxiously await his return.

Joel kissed her. "I love you."

Portia smiled and took a moment to catch her breath before responding. Joel knew she was struggling with him leaving, but he also knew she was tough and would be okay.

"I love you too," she answered softly.

"You know what?" Joel asked as he caressed her cheek.

"What?"

"You will be my wife in 10 weeks, which means you've got a lot of planning to do," he said.

Portia smiled but didn't respond, so Joel knew he had to step up his game to reassure her. He rolled over on top of her and gently kissed her face. "I love you. I'm coming back for you."

"I love you too," she whispered.

Joel continued kissing her face and rubbing her cheeks. "Soon enough, you will be tripping over my shoes and complaining that I don't hang the towel up in the bathroom," he said with a laugh as he looked at the clock on the nightstand. "Speaking of which, it's six already. I need to get moving and take a shower."

Portia sighed. "Okay. I'll get breakfast together for us."

"Sounds nice. Thank you," Joel replied. He kissed her once more before going into the bathroom. He wasted no time performing his morning routine because he didn't want to miss one second with her.

Once Joel was dressed, the glorious scents of coffee, maple syrup, and waffles greeted him, and he immediately counted his blessings. "This smells so wonderful," he said as he sat at the table.

"Don't get too excited. The waffles were frozen, but they are homemade. Aunt Gert makes them once a month," Portia explained as she sat next to him.

"Gert is pretty amazing. She and I made cookies together once," Joel explained.

"Oh yes, her cookies are famous in this town."

Joel's satisfaction continued since he loved having breakfast conversations with his future wife. Then Screech slapped his leg, and Joel realized that he would also be acquiring three fur children who would make eating a challenge at every meal; however, he loved the furballs and wouldn't have it any other way.

When the clock struck eight, Portia put a leash on Ice. Then she and the pup walked with Joel to the dock to meet the crew.

OMINOUS CLOUDS WEAVED in between the mountains and hung low in the sky while an unforgiving mist splattered on Joel's face, and a brisk, damp wind cut right through his clothing, making him shiver, partly from the cold and partly from the suspense of the journey on which he was embarking. Then two eagles landed on the Alexandria's wheelhouse roof as he, Portia, and Ice approached the dock.

All the crew members were there, along with their loved ones. For a moment, Joel felt like he was in a time warp like everything around him was blurry. He had left port many times, too many times to count, but this time was different. Joel had a fiancée seeing him off, and he also had Gert, who so wonderfully reminded him of his mother.

"Take good care of my daddy's boat and catch some crabs!" Portia exclaimed. Then she hugged each crew member, including Kirk. That one made Joel bristle, but he knew Portia had a huge heart and wanted everyone to stay safe.

Joel looked at Gert, who he knew was struggling with saying goodbye to Gunther, so Joel hugged and kissed her on the cheek.

"Thank you, darling. You are like a son to me. I love you. Be careful out there," she said, then returned the kiss.

Gert's words went straight to Joel's heart, and he almost got choked up because it had been 27 years since his mother had said that to him. "I love you too," he replied.

"Hey Gunther, when's the new guy getting here?" Nick asked as his voice rose above the crowd.

"He should be here any minute," Gunther responded, then took a drag on a cigarette, prompting a slightly grotesque coughing fit.

Joel tried not to retch because Gunther's cough was disgusting and thick. But Joel laughed and thought back to their first phone call when he had called Gunther a "nicotine-saturated pain in the butt." Gunther was now his captain, and Joel was a greenhorn—a beginner, the lowest rank of all. However, he wouldn't share this station alone since there would be one more greenhorn on deck with him.

"I think the new guy is here now," Bubba announced as a taxi pulled up to the dock.

The crew members waited quietly, eager to meet the newest greenhorn. Perhaps they shouldn't have been so anxious for the newcomer's arrival, and maybe it would've been better if he hadn't shown up at all. Ironically, the term *greenhorn* was a fitting description since his appearance was completely unexpected as he crawled out of the taxi.

He was a skinny, pale 22-year-old, wearing all-black clothing except for the silver chain dangling against his pants. He had bright green hair spiked into a foot-long mohawk from the center of his forehead to the base of his skull. The sides of his head were completely bald, so this guy must've waxed regularly. And one couldn't pull off this look without having black-painted fingernails, multiple piercings, and a plethora of tattoos. But his jewelry was top-notch. The bull ring in his nose nicely matched the earrings on his lower earlobes and up the cartilages. To add to the mystique, his eyes were so big that he looked bug-eyed like he didn't even have eyelids.

Gunther couldn't take it, and Joel thought the captain would have a heart attack right then and there. It was too much for him to process this individual being his newest employee, so Gunther did what he did best in a stressful situation. He promptly lit two fresh ciggies, closed his eyes, breathed in the smoke, and exhaled the toxins. Then he walked up to the new guy, took another long drag, and blew a cloud in his face. "Are you Blade Renshaw?" Gunther asked.

"Yes, I am," the young man responded with a British accent.

Gunther took another drag on the cigarettes as he walked in a circle around Blade, who was so skinny he might have gotten mistaken for a piece of lint. Gunther stood in front of him, stuck the cigarettes in his mouth, and put his hands on his hips. With only his index finger, Gunther poked Blade on his shoulder to see if he would fall over. To Gunther's point, Blade stumbled backward but was quick enough to stop himself from falling. All the while, Blade remained bug-eyed as if he couldn't blink his gargantuan eyes.

In sheer disgust, Gunther said to Bubba, "Go take the insect below deck, so he can put his crap away."

Completely stupefied, Bubba's mouth hung open, and his feet didn't budge.

"I said now!" Gunther roared.

"Yes, Captain. Right now!" Bubba began, almost out of breath. He rushed over to pick up Blade's suitcase. "Come on, Blade. I'll show you to your new cocoon. I mean cubby," Bubba said as he motioned for Blade to follow him.

The rest of the crew members watched Bubba and the insectile man climb on deck. None dared to speak, knowing that Gunther was infuriated and that the newcomer would keep him pissed off at sea. Meanwhile, Gert burst out laughing like this was the funniest thing she had ever seen.

Gunther stood with his hands on his hips, staring at her. "Well, laugh it up, why don't you!"

"Oh come on, Gunther. You got to admit. That was funny!" Gert retorted, then continued laughing.

A huge smile spread across Gunther's face, and he laughed too.

"That skinny boy looks like a cockroach on meth!" Old Al declared.

Kirk was right on track with his old man. "Well, if we run out of bait…" he began.

"Nice thought, Kirk, but we don't want to kill the crabs," Gunther said as he dropped the cigarette butts and ground them into the dirt with his new work boot.

"Hey, that's not enough protein to catch one crab anyway!" Nick added.

"We will do our best not to smash the insect. All right, enough small talk. All aboard! Everyone, say your goodbyes. We got crabs to catch!" Gunther declared. Then he wrapped his arms around Gert and kissed her.

Meanwhile, Blade waited on deck while Bubba ran over to hug and sloppily kiss Tanya goodbye. Polly and Nick got their last few kisses in as well. Even Old Al and Kirk hugged. But Hank looked at the sky since no one was there to see him off.

Joel reached up to Portia's face and gently rubbed her cheek with the back of his hand. He cupped her face and passionately kissed her. "I love you, Katerina Alexander," he said as he hugged her one last time while savoring the scent of her perfume.

"I love you too," Portia replied.

Joel slowly and gently pulled away from her, holding onto her hands until he was too far away to reach them. He walked backward toward the dock, never losing eye contact with her, even while climbing onto the boat deck. By this point, the entire crew was on deck, and Gunther went to the wheelhouse.

Portia, Gert, Polly, Tanya, and Old Al interlocked their arms and stood together, waiting for the vessel to depart. Gunther started the engines, and the thundering roar gave Joel chills up and down his spine. He loved the sound of the Alexandria's engines like he had loved the roaring engines on the USS Roland. However, the two eagles weren't as keen; they took off from the wheelhouse roof and flew away, but not together. For the first time, Joel saw a pair of eagles fly off in separate directions, and that was the moment that he and Portia lost eye contact.

GUNTHER SOUNDED THE HORN as the Alexandria left the dock to join the Blessing of the Fleet lineup. And just like that, Joel was gone. The Alexandria hadn't even left the inlet yet, and Portia felt an emptiness in her heart. She picked up Ice and held him close, feeling his soft puppy fur against her cheek and neck. The pup knew what she needed, so he immediately gave her kisses. She held him closer because Ice was a gift from Joel and having him in her arms was a great comfort.

The women and Old Al drove to the Port of Aleutia Wharf for the Blessing of the Fleet Ceremony. The clouds remained portentous, and the mist thickened the heavy air as they walked to the center of the wharf. On the left side of the dock, there was a microphone and empty flag stands, and on the right side, a table displayed long-stemmed roses and carnations of various colors for the tradition of throwing flowers into the water.

Old Al and the women always attended the ceremony and picked out their flowers together; however, this year, they were missing Lizzie and Elijah, which was heavy on Portia's mind, and undoubtedly Gert's as well. The mere sight of the flowers gut-punched Portia because she tossed a flower into the bay last season for the Alexandria's crew. And not everyone made it home alive from that fateful voyage. Now, a year later, Portia's eyes filled as she selected two carnations in remembrance of her father and cousin, a yellow rose for the Alexandria's current crew, and a white rose—just for Joel.

Portia and Gert weren't the only ones with heavy hearts and mixed emotions. Billy Gorman's widow approached the flower table with her three daughters.

"Hey there, Millie," Gert said before hugging them. "Hello there, Krissy, Monica, and Little Jessie. It's so thoughtful of you to come today. I know how hard it is."

Millie reached for Gert's hands. "I know you understand. Thank you. Portia, I hear you are engaged to be married. Congratulations. May you be as happy as Billy and I were."

"Thank you," Portia replied as she hugged Millie and then her daughters. To say that she respected Millie would be an understatement because Millie's courage was so admirable. Her husband had died last season, and she and her children still stoically attended this event. Portia immediately felt guilty for her despair, knowing Millie had three children she had to care for and comfort. Since Kyle and Chris passed, Portia only had to look after herself.

After selecting their flowers, Portia, Gert, Polly, Tanya, and Old Al stood in the front row in front of the microphone. Crowds of people with umbrellas filled in around them, including Leonard, Ted, Rhonda, Pete, and Zac. Many people had their phones in position, ready to capture the beginning of the ceremony by picture or video. Portia strained her eyes as she scanned the bay for the Alexandria, but the iron lady wasn't in sight just yet, which meant the vessel was toward the end of the fleet lineup.

The opening ceremony began as the United States Coast Guardsmen carried the United States and the Alaska State flags and then set them in the stands. Then bagpipe players arrived and stood off to the side. Next, a choir from the elementary school sang hymns about the sea. The munchkins didn't need any music, for their tiny voices sounded like cherubs bursting from Heaven. Portia always loved hearing the little ones sing at the ceremony, but this year, their angelic voices tugged at her heartstrings, especially when she noticed Little Jessie in the front row.

After the children's performance ended, Reverend Thomas opened with a prayer. "Dear Heavenly Father, creator of Heaven and earth, creator of the Bering Sea, please bless this event today, dear Lord. The men and women going to the Bering Sea today know about the abundance you have given us in the earth's oceans, seas, bays, rivers, and lakes. They will bring it home to us to benefit our economy and put food on our tables. We all know the heart of a sailor is a beautiful thing, dear Lord, for you are the one who created it. The love of the sea is intrinsic and can never be taken away from them. Thank you, God, for these selfless souls and their journey to the Bering Sea. Thank you for their selflessness in bringing food back and working long hours without sleep in the harshest winter conditions, often in high seas, freezing rain, snow, sleet, and ice. Bless this fleet, Heavenly Father. Protect them from disaster and bring them home safely. Bless the families of the sailors as they wait here. It's extremely easy for us to feel uneasiness about their departure, so please, Almighty One, help us to stay strong and trust in you. Please let us remember this every day to receive your peace and honor it. Amen."

Lora took the microphone. Her balding husband was nowhere in sight; however, Dr. Sampson was in the front row, smiling from ear to ear and embracing any opportunity to be near his not-so-secret lover. The feeling was mutual; Lora grinned at him before opening her mouth to speak. "Thank you, Reverend Thomas. This morning, we gather to lift our fishermen and women in prayer and to recognize their selfless contributions to our economy, not just here in Alaska but all over the world. We would also like to thank the Coast Guard for their service. They serve and protect our fleet. Being an Alaskan waterman is one of the most dangerous jobs in the world. We are reminded of that every year, especially this past year, as we lost many iconic figures from our community. Thank you to those who serve us on the Bering Sea and all of you joining us today and wishing our fleet well."

The bagpipes played as Lora left the microphone, and the first few beautiful notes felt as if they flew right into Portia's heart. One cannot help but feel the emotion these powerful instruments evoke, especially at a time such as this, remembering loved ones who perished and saying goodbye to loved ones who may or may not return. The hymns the bagpipes played reinforced the realization that Joel and Gunther were gone. They were on the Alexandria on their way to sea, returning to where Kyle and Chris died less than a year ago. As the bagpipes played onward, Portia felt like she had lost her breath.

She wasn't the only one feeling this consternation. Gert slid her arm around Portia's waist and whispered, "Take a deep breath."

Portia did as Gert instructed, letting the salty air fill her lungs, and even though she wanted to curse the Bering Sea, she loved inhaling the salty mist because it smelled like home.

Next was the moment for which they had been waiting—when their loved ones would depart for the great unknown. As the bagpipes continued playing, Reverend Thomas walked back up to the microphone. By now, each vessel was in position and filled with anxious sailors eager to return to that dichotomous sea of wealth and destruction. With their engines roaring, the vessels were ready to cruise by the dock at their respective moments.

The first fishing vessel in the lineup was the Windswept Belle, and Reverend Thomas turned toward the bay as he gave the first blessing, "Dear Heavenly Father, please bless the crew of the Windswept Belle! May you watch over them and protect them from all harm. May the Bering Sea waters provide them with an abundance of king crabs. Amen."

Following the blessing, the bagpipes played louder as the Windswept Belle passed by the wharf while the crew members stood on deck and excitedly waved to the crowd. Next were the Aleutian Hero, the Bering Sea Lady, and several other vessels embarking on this journey. Portia's heart pounded with anticipation because she was eager to see Joel since this would be her last sighting of him. As she peered into the distance, Portia finally caught a glimpse of her daddy's vessel, and it was the last one in the lineup.

After several vessels went by, the Alexandria drew closer to the wharf, and the reverend gave the following blessing, "Dear Heavenly Father, please bless the crew of the Alexandria! May you give them hope and instill peace in them and their loved ones here in Aleutia. May they have a plentiful catch, dear Lord. Hallelujah and amen!"

The bagpipes played loudly for the Alexandria's crew as Nick and Bubba each threw a flower wreath overboard in remembrance of Kyle and Chris. Portia saw Joel walk up to the railing and start waving, and her heart pounded like thunder as she held her arm up high and waved the white rose through the air, wondering if he could see her amid the crowd of people.

With relentless intensity, a magnificent beam of sunlight blazed through the misty clouds and illuminated the Alexandria. Perhaps it was the good Lord offering a promise for a safe journey, or perhaps it was Kyle and Chris speaking to them from His kingdom. One thing was for sure; it was heavenly. The Alexandria quickly passed by the dock, and the infamous vessel was officially on its way to sea—beneath a ray of sunlight growing larger, following them out of the inlet and beyond the Spithead Cape.

Portia waved for as long as the crew was in sight. Then Gert put her arm around Portia's waist again. "They're gone now. Let them go," Gert insisted.

Portia took a ragged breath. "What if I can't?"

"You have to. You're going to be a sailor's wife," Gert replied.

Portia smiled and looked at her engagement ring, knowing that Joel had found a permanent harbor and that he must flow with the tide. She walked over to the dock railing with Gert, Tanya, Polly, and Old Al following closely behind her. In remembrance of Kyle and Chris, Portia slowly tossed the two carnations into the water and watched them float away before she threw in the yellow rose as she prayed for the Alexandria's crew to have a safe journey. Then she held onto the white rose and gently kissed the petals, before tossing it into the bay, while softly singing, "Oh Bering Sea / Please bring him home to me."

Even though it was brief, Joel was pleased to see Portia during the blessing as the Alexandria went by the wharf. Then the magnanimous sunray broke through the clouds and spotlighted the Alexandria, creating the illusion of rippling glitter on the water's surface around the mighty vessel.

The foggy mist that thickened the air turned a golden-orange hue as the sun burned hotter and brighter until the water droplets dissipated into oblivion. Joel looked upward, saw the clouds parting, and watched blue sky reclaim its rightful place. As the rest of the clouds drifted away, the sun shone with so much intensity that Joel could've sworn God was standing there on deck right next to him as he simultaneously felt overwhelming feelings of sadness and happiness.

Suddenly, a double rainbow appeared over the inlet as the vessel passed by the Spithead Cape. Once again, God revealed Himself to Joel through another spectacular display of artistry and provided light when he needed it. When the rainbows appeared, Joel's mixed emotions finally made sense. He was sad about leaving because he was leaving his home, something he hadn't had since he was 11 years old, and now, he was engaged to Portia and had a loving fiancée waiting for his return.

As he stood on the Alexandria on his way to the Bering Sea, Joel realized that God had revealed Himself during significant moments in his life. On the day his parents died, a glorious rainbow appeared after the deadly storm that took their lives. When Joel enlisted to join the Navy on his 18th birthday, he saw several beams of light break through thunderheads and illuminate the Inner Harbor in Baltimore. And who could forget the magnificent sunrise Joel saw in Rota, silhouetting palm trees against the morning sky on the day he met Adoncia at the Gypsy Market? She was the reason he came to Alaska, after all.

When he arrived in the Port of Aleutia, Joel was amazed when the sunlight burned through the clouds and mist, revealing snowcapped peaks of crystalized beauty and shimmering the surrounding bays. Then when Gunther took Joel to the cathedral, celestial light illuminated the Byzantine structure, and Joel saw two eagles together for the first time when they landed on the Russian Orthodox crosses adorning the Domes of Heaven. That night, Joel met Portia and saw the Northern Lights splash the sky with fantastical colors as they danced beneath a mirrored disco ball to his parents' favorite song. And now, beneath the most magnificent double rainbow he had ever seen, Joel stood on the Alexandria, drifting out to sea, leaving his first home in 27 years.

At that moment, a familiar oldie song from his childhood began playing through the Alexandria's sound system. Joel smiled with an overwhelming emotion because Gunther chose the same song that Joel's father had played when they crabbed in the Chesapeake Bay. Over the years, this song had stuck with Joel. And nearly three decades later, it provided the perfect accompaniment for his first voyage in the Bering Sea. Not only did this melody remind Joel of his childhood, but it also reminded him of Portia and the healing power of music.

As he swayed to the timeless tune, Joel took a deep breath, savoring the salt air, for it never smelled as good as it did at that moment. With the wind blowing through his hair and his hands gripping the railing, Joel leaned into the saltwater spray while a huge smile spread across his face, and tears filled his eyes. The oldie song mingled with the sea breeze, and Joel realized that he had everything he needed and everything he had always wanted. He had a great God, a good woman's love, a home, a family, a few friends, and a job at sea. His life was complete. He had it all.

Chapter 19. *I'd Rather Die*

J ust like she did when Portia was a little girl, and often when Kyle and Gunther were at sea, Gert invited Portia to stay at her house. Even though Portia appreciated the thoughtful offer, she declined this time because she just wanted to be alone. She didn't feel like painting fingernails and doing hair. Instead, she returned to her apartment to lounge in one of Joel's flannel shirts and watch movies with the critters. However, this changed when she walked into the silent apartment, only to find an indifferent cat, a sleeping puppy, and Tiny asleep in Joel's Navy hat on his pillow.

Meanwhile, the ticking of her father's antique clock on the bookshelf was the only sound filling the room. Each passing ticktock might as well have been a thunderbolt, for Portia felt like it pierced her eardrums and rattled her chest like fireworks. She raggedly sighed because she was sad, scared, and frustrated. Then Joel's words echoed in her mind, "When in doubt, write."

And Portia did as her sailor suggested. She promptly packed up her notepad, electric guitar, and travel amp since an acoustic ensemble wouldn't be sufficient to convey her feelings today. She needed the power and booming of the electric guitar; she required the plow that broke pavement with just one note because this would be another Country Rock & Roll song for sure.

Portia decided to get a little drunk to calm her nerves and assist her songwriting, so she grabbed a bottle of brandy and then opted for cigars over weed. She smiled as she walked by the refrigerator and threw a bottle of root beer into her bag as well. After three trips to her insanely pink truck, she started her monster engine and hit the gas like the bar-dancing, cowgirl rock star she was.

When Portia turned onto Ulakta Drive, she floored it and reminisced about the day Joel was driving, and he hit the gas as they drove out of the Spithead Cape. This time, however, she was riding through the countryside alone. With this realization, Portia slammed her foot down harder on the gas, flying by the World War II barracks, and held the pedal down firmly until she reached the Panama mount, where she abruptly slammed on the brakes before parking the truck.

Portia kept binoculars in the glove box, so she reached for them and got out of the truck to peer into the distance. Even though she knew it was an unrealistic expectation, she strained her eyes to see the Alexandria—or any vessel in the distance. When she realized no ships were in sight, she returned to the truck for the brandy and cigars.

Portia sat down on the Panama mount, and memories flooded her mind. She recalled the visits there with her father. Then she remembered being there with Joel, but now he was gone—in the same sea that killed her father and cousin. This realization was too much for her to face at one time. She lit a cigar and downed a lot of brandy as Portia, the Port House queen prevailed.

Now inebriated, Portia was terrified, feeling a new emotion she had never felt—loving a man so deeply she couldn't imagine living without him. That is how she loved Joel—to the deepest level of intimacy—to the point she wouldn't want to live without him if he didn't return.

Portia adored and loathed love simultaneously. She was elated to have Joel in her life, but she was mortified of losing him. Portia did what she knew best, drinking and smoking until the toxins got the best of her. With the brandy in one hand and a cigar in the other, Portia yelled into the wind, "Damn you, Bering Sea! Damn you, Kyle! Damn you, Chris! Damn you, Gunther! Damn all of you

Alexanders! Damn you, Joel Layton!" She choked on Joel's name, and her eyes flooded with tears.

Alone on the mountaintop, gazing at the dichotomous sea of destruction and blessings, Portia wept, not just for her fear of losing Joel but also for the pain of losing her father and Chris. She reached into her pocket, and there was Joel's handkerchief, right there when she needed it, right there when she needed him. Then again, his words echoed in her mind, "When in doubt, write."

Portia returned to the truck for the electric guitar, amp, and notepad. She sat down on the Panama mount and thought about Joel—how she loved him so dearly and was terrified of losing him. Her biggest fear became the subject of her next masterpiece, and her inebriety tremendously affected the lyrics and vocals.

Portia cranked the amp on high, then secured the electric guitar strap around her shoulder. The amp was connected to a wireless-headset microphone so that the master musician could give a five-star performance anywhere at any time.

Next, the foxy lady took a deep breath, letting the wind blow through her hair as she strummed the guitar. She sipped brandy and puffed on the cigar in between writing musical notations and singing. Within an hour and a half, the new song was complete. Angst, happiness, and fear were bound together in one dramatic composition.

Portia stood on the Panama mount and performed like this was the biggest show of her life—with the unrealistic, inebriated expectation that the Alexandria's crew could hear her. The lady of the bar held nothing back vocally or instrumentally, for the song was, no doubt, country meeting Rock & Roll in its finest fashion.

The first verse began slowly and softly as she recalled the night she and Joel met.

Ever since that night
In my crowded harbor bar
You came in like rolling thunder
From a fallen-down storm cloud

The beginning was an accurate summation because Joel was so dashing in his Navy full dress white uniform that thunder and lightning may as well have accompanied his entrance into the Port House; he certainly took Portia's breath away that fateful night. Next, she sang about how Joel read her like a book while she stood across the bar from him.

And I was drinking brandy
And you had a beer
You criticized my lyrics
You, criticized my fears

At this point, the tempo picked up power and momentum as Portia strummed harder and louder for a kick butt, ramped-up pre-chorus.

And ever since then
I've been trying to defend
My love for this Navy sailor man

The electric guitar exploded from the Panama mount as Portia strummed intensely, rocking it out and moving her body to the rhythm. As she sang the chorus, she performed with a new intensity, a higher level of talent she had yet to achieve, for her voice reached levels of power she had no idea existed. She did more than feel the lyrics; she was living them.

I'll give you a million reasons why
You know I'd rather die
Than live without your breath
Mingled in with mine
I know it's morbid
But it's true
The way that I need you
If love can't stand the test of time
I know I'd rather die

After the chorus, the tempo slowed for the second verse as she reminisced about her first kiss with Joel at Spithead.

Ever since the day
That we went to Spithead Dock
The eagles were flying crazy
And I told you to stay back
You wrapped your arms around me
Gently kissed my face
Oh you made my heart flutter
Oh, you made my heart race

The tempo picked up again; she sang the pre-chorus and chorus with even more intensity and hip action. With her exceptional powerhouse vocals, Portia concluded with an outro, driving home the notion that she was so intoxicated by Joel's love that she was losing her mind.

Oh, I need you by my side
Ooo, I'm losing my mind
To this fever that's called love
Oh, I'm so drunk

Oh, I'm so drunk on love
Ooo, whoa, ooo, whoa, ooo, whoa, ooo, whoa, ooo, whoa, whoa
I said ooo, whoa, ooo, whoa, ooo, whoa, ooo, whoa, ooo, whoa

When the song concluded, Portia got a bottle of root beer. "Time to sober up," she said, then took a swig and sat down on the Panama mount. She gazed into the distance, wondering where the Alexandria was, and hoping everyone was safe from harm. At that moment, an eagle cry mingled with the wind, and Portia frantically looked around, trying to see the distressed bird. She didn't have to look far because the majestic creature landed a few feet away from her on the Panama mount, and Portia couldn't believe her eyes.

She turned sideways so that she could see the eagle head-on. The eagle's eyes locked onto hers, and Portia felt a tingly feeling in her heart, radiating throughout her body, as she immediately felt a connection with the seraphic creature. Portia always had a special way with animals, but this was a different experience. And Portia knew that the creator of Heaven and earth was the only one who could make this happen.

Because of the eagle's large size, Portia knew it was a female. She continued staring into the exquisite bird's eyes. And the distressed shrieks quickly turned into a series of soft, gentle coos, so Portia, ever so carefully and slowly, slid closer to the eagle.

"I miss my man too," Portia whispered as she slowly reached her hand out and gently scratched the back of the eagle's head.

Time stood still as Portia and the lone eagle shared this priceless moment. The eagle's feathers were soft against her fingertips, and Portia continued caressing the regal bird while it cooed and stared into her eyes, letting Portia know that she wasn't the only one feeling this way. Then suddenly, the lone eagle flew away while continuing to call for its lover, and Portia longed to see two eagles together again.

Chapter 20. *Greenhorn*

A gentle pat on the shoulder pulled Joel away from his thoughts, and he turned around to see who had joined him on deck by the mountainous stacks of steel crab pots. He was greeted by Bubba's joyful face, smiling from ear to ear.

"You doing all right, buddy? You've been out here for a long time. I figured I would come check on you."

"Yes, just taking it all in," Joel replied with a shiver, not realizing how cold he was until now.

"Me too. Queasy from the high seas, but that will let up. Overall, I'm glad and sad at the same time, you know? Missing Tanya now. You got Portia. Good stuff, man. Good stuff!" Bubba said sentimentally.

"Hey cronies!" Gunther's voice suddenly exclaimed from the loudspeaker system. "First, I want to thank you for being a crew member. We had a tough time last January, and I am confident we will make Kyle and Chris proud. Nick, Bubba, and I wrote their names on each crab pot buoy so that they would be with us this season. They are our good luck charms. With that being said, let's catch some crabs and make them proud! The good news is that the water temperature is freezing, so we don't have to go quite as far west as I would normally suggest. We are going past Prince Edward's Basin; then we will drop three pots and do a little prospecting." Gunther paused to cough, which was extra disgusting through the speaker.

He continued, "As you have probably noticed, the seas are picking up, and the temperature is dropping fast. With projected record lows, it won't take long for ice to build up. For those of you who don't know, Kirk is the relief captain, and Bubba is the deck boss. Bubba will show the greenhorns where the cleaning supplies and the ice mallets are. Somebody's gonna be sledging the ice off the railings sooner rather than later. Speaking of greenhorns, I believe it's time to give them some cod and herring. Nick, get the cuisine ready. Joel and Blade, meet me by the coiler."

At first, Joel wasn't quite sure what Gunther meant. Then he put one and two together. The cod and herring were crab bait, and Nick went to prepare cuisine for the greenhorns. Long story short, Gunther expected Joel to put a raw and semi-rotten fish into his pristine mouth. To say he was apprehensive about this would be an understatement; however, he was a rugged man who would step up to the plate and slay into that fish for a home run. Joel took a deep breath, ignored his already queasy gut, pumped himself up, and walked with a manly swagger over to the coiler, with Bubba following closely behind him.

Gunther entered the deck with Kirk and Hank, who both had self-ingratiating expressions on their faces. The two jerks were all too ready to take pleasure in watching Joel's discomfort, and he wouldn't give those menacing brutes the satisfaction of seeing him struggle.

"Where is Blade?" Gunther asked in disgust.

"Last I saw, he was having tea and biscuits with jelly in the galley," Bubba tattled.

"Tea and biscuits with jelly?" Gunther repeated with as much sarcasm as he could inflict into the words. He took a deep breath and ran his fingers through his hair. After that, he lit a cigarette with a large-flamed cigar lighter. Then he stomped over to the gear room door, opened it, and grabbed a mic. "Blade, leave your tea and jellied biscuits and get your scrawny butt on deck now! If you don't, I'll get you and throw you overboard for the sharks to devour!" Gunther roared before stomping back to the coiler, muttering along the way, "Tea and biscuits with jelly? Really?"

Then Nick appeared, holding two plates filled with cod and herring and handed them to Gunther to begin the greenhorns' initiation. Wearing only a black t-shirt with a skull print on it and matching jeans that were as black as the night sky, Blade stumbled out of the gear room, and a giant wave crashed over from the opposite railing, splashing him from behind and soaking him to the point his mohawk drooped.

"You're gonna need some stronger hair gel!" Hank exclaimed while Kirk laughed and applauded.

Shaking like a chihuahua, Blade walked over and stood next to Joel. The crew stared at Blade because not only did his mohawk droop, but he also had streams of water flowing from his enormous eyes.

Gunther was aghast. "Boy, are you crying?" the captain asked in horror.

"No, sir. I have always had a saltwater sensitivity to the eyes," Blade replied with his heavy accent.

"Then why in the world do you want to be a fisherman? No, wait! Don't answer that. You're here. It doesn't matter now. Here!" Gunther bellowed as he forcefully handed him the herring plate. Then he turned toward Joel and gave him the cod plate. "Welcome to the Bering Sea family," he said with a smirk, laughing and patting Joel on the shoulder.

Oddly enough, Joel felt honored to receive the plate of bait. And even though the effluvium of decomposing fishiness made him want to keck, he maintained his gallant composure.

Gunther stood in front of Joel and Blade, and the rest of the crew gathered close. He looked at Blade and shook his head in disgust once more before proceeding with the instructions. "Now, you must bite the fish on the back of its head and neck, then chew it for half a minute before spitting it out. Nick, get your timer ready," Gunther commanded.

"Yes Captain! Timer's ready!" Nick eagerly replied.

The Alexandria was rocking and rolling from the increased seas, and a salty mist splattered across Joel's face as adrenaline pumped viciously throughout his veins. He took a deep breath to steady his excitement and promised himself he wouldn't puke until everyone walked away. Not that one could hold barf back, but today, Joel would learn how to perform that task. There was no way he would allow Kirk and Hank to see him spew.

"Ready, set, go! Bite into those fish, you greenhorns!" Gunther fiendishly yelled.

Joel tore into the back of the cod's neck, then promptly took another bite, and the fish was warm and slimy against his tongue and the walls of his mouth. *How deplorable and nasty, Nick must have heated the fish in the microwave*, Joel thought as fish scales jammed between his teeth, and his mouth watered like he was going to chuck it all up right there on his new work boots and everyone else's. Despite all this, Joel maintained his valiant composure. On the other hand, Blade quickly heaved up his jellied biscuits and herring, splattering the remnants against the coiler and all over the deck. The puking seemed contagious; Nick leaned over the railing to vomit as well.

"What was that? A sympathy puke?" Gunther laughed as he patted Nick on the back. "Y'all better find your sea legs fast. I don't want puke all over the Alexandria!"

Despite his yack attack, Nick was right on point. He spun back around and continued with a five-second countdown before Joel could spit out his mouthful of cod that he was intently chewing. "Five, four, three, two, one! Spit it out, Joel!" Nick shouted.

Joel immediately rushed to the railing and spat out the crab bait without succumbing to the gag reflex.

Gunther laughed until he almost threw up as well. "Great job, Joel! You have what it takes. Insect boy with the floppy mohawk, your capabilities remain to be seen. Anyway, welcome to the Bering Sea! Both of you! We have a long ride ahead of us. I have elected Joel and Bubba to make cheesesteak subs for dinner tonight," Gunther said with a laugh as he patted Joel on the shoulder, then headed back to the wheelhouse while Nick, Hank, and Kirk went to the engine room.

As soon as everyone but Bubba left, Joel leaned over the railing and threw up his toenails, never retching so hard in his life. Bubba never left Joel's side and handed him a napkin when he finished tossing his cod and breakfast waffles into the Bering Sea.

"Thanks, man. Oh, that was awful. That's the only time I have to do that, right?" Joel asked, then held the napkin over his mouth.

"Eh, sometimes a deckhand gets told to do it for good luck. Come on inside. I'll give you an anti-nausea med," Bubba insisted.

"That would be good," Joel said as another wave of nausea hit, and he violently heaved over the railing again. And then a few more times after that.

"Oh, maybe we should skip the pill version and just give you an injection in the butt!" Bubba suggested.

Joel leaned back up and gripped the railing. "Yeah, injection please," he responded as a wave crashed on deck, soaking him to the core as if he wasn't already miserable enough.

"Wait here," Bubba began as he and Joel entered the gear room. "I'll get the needle. Hang tight for a few minutes."

Joel nodded his head, took a deep breath, and swallowed hard. The rocking and rolling of the Alexandria from 60-mile-per-hour winds and 25-foot seas met Joel's nausea full force. He squeezed his eyes shut and leaned against the wall. This nausea was almost the worst he had ever experienced. Although, there was a night in Rio de Janeiro, during his young Navy days when Joel overindulged in sangria, among other things, and well, that's a story for another day.

AFTER A FEW MINUTES, Bubba returned with the needle. "Okay, show me some hip."

Joel gave Bubba a nasty look, then lowered his wet pants slightly, anything to get that puke feeling to go away. After the quick jab, Joel promptly pulled his jeans back up. "Thank you, man. I will put some dry clothes on and maybe hug the toilet until this kicks in. I'll meet you in the kitchen in a few."

"Why don't you lie down? I got dinner covered," Bubba selflessly suggested.

"No, I will be there. The captain told me to help cook dinner, and that's what I intend to do. Thank you for having my back," Joel answered.

"Of course! Hey, the meds work fast. You'll be feeling better in no time. Let me know if you need more. It's probably going to be a few days before you settle out," Bubba explained.

"A few days? This is from the cod."

"No, Joel. You're experiencing seasickness; the cod just brought it on quicker. The trick is to keep eating and drinking. If you can't eat anything, at least drink water. I can't get you home to Portia and then have you die of kidney failure. Odds are, you'll feel better in a day or two—or three," Bubba said with a wince.

"I haven't had seasickness since I joined the Navy," Joel admitted.

He went to the greenhorns' quarters, a super tiny room with a bunk bed that wasn't long enough for his legs. Blade had already claimed the top bunk where he was snoring like a lumberjack. Joel quickly reached into his duffel bag, grabbed some dry clothes, and went to the bathroom to change.

The bathroom was a hole in the wall so tiny Joel had to step into the shower to bend over to remove his shoes. By the time he changed his clothes and put away the wet ones, his gag reflex had settled down, so he ventured into the galley where Bubba was prepping for all the frying that was getting ready to ensue.

"What can I do?" Joel asked, stumbling into the kitchen as the Alexandria went over a giant wave.

"You can chop and sauté the onions and peppers. I set the pan out with oil already. I'm doing the meat on the griddle. And I set out a bottle of root beer for you to finish settling your stomach," Bubba thoughtfully replied.

"Thank you," Joel said before washing his hands. Then he opened the soda and took a few sips. Bubba was being so thoughtful, and such a good friend, the best Joel had ever had, and Joel knew he had to do something for Bubba in return. He would ask Bubba to be his best man at the wedding.

Joel began peeling and chopping the onions, which immediately made his eyes burn and water. Meanwhile, Bubba squirted oil on the griddle and threw on the meat.

"Hey man, I got something to ask you," Joel began.

"Sure buddy. What is it?" Bubba inquired as he turned toward him.

"Would you be my best man?" Joel asked.

Bubba was speechless. He smiled and immediately hugged Joel, whose eyes were gushing from the onions. Meanwhile, Blade, who had repaired his mohawk, walked into the galley as Bubba shouted, "Yes, Joel! Yes, I would love to!"

The burning sensation in Joel's watering eyes intensified, pouring like waterfalls. He wiped away the tears with his sleeve as Bubba continued giving him the biggest Chubby Bubba hug to date.

"I'm gobsmacked! You handsome gents!" Blade exclaimed before the Alexandria went over a huge wave, and the motion slammed him onto the galley floor like he was an anorexic flounder.

"I'm gonna be in Joel's wedding! He's marrying Gunther's niece," Bubba explained as he let go of Joel and flipped the meat on the griddle.

"Oh, brilliant!" Blade said as he stood up as if nothing had happened. "Can I help with dinner? I know my way around a kitchen pretty well."

"Oh no, that's all right. Joel and I got this. Just kick back," Bubba replied.

"Uh oh," Blade yelped as he grabbed his stomach before moaning and yacking in the galley trashcan. "I'm regretting all that ginger root I took," he said after the last not-so-dry heave.

With the sound of Blade's gags and the smell of sizzling onions, peppers, and processed meat, Joel almost proceeded with a sympathy puke. He reached for the root beer to abate the heave and felt the effervescences make their way down his angry digestive tract.

Bubba promptly grabbed another root beer and took some pills out of a first aid kit. "Take these meds and drink the soda. It will help," Bubba said as he handed them to Blade.

Joel continued drinking his root beer and was thankful that his nausea had momentarily passed. He stirred the onions and peppers, something he had never done in his life.

Once Bubba and Joel finished cooking the veggies and meat, Bubba made the subs by smearing the rolls with mayo before adding the meat, cheese, and veggies. He plated each sub, then grabbed the galley mic to announce, "Dinner's ready!"

Within a few minutes, everyone appeared except for Kirk, who was at the helm for Gunther. For that, Joel was thankful because he felt lousy and didn't feel like dealing with Kirk when he didn't have his game on. Now he could focus 100% on gagging down the gigantic sub when he would much rather have saltine crackers.

Each crew member got his sub and root beer and piled into the booth. Joel sat next to Nick and hoped for an end seat in case he needed a quick getaway to spew, but that didn't happen because Bubba promptly slid in next to him. Then Hank, Blade, and Gunther sat on the opposite side. As Gunther took the seat next to Blade, he couldn't contain his repugnance.

"I see your mohawk has revived itself," Gunther said sarcastically.

"Yes mate," Blade replied.

Everyone at the table gasped. How dare a greenhorn refer to the captain that way.

"What did you call me, boy?" Gunther asked as he squinted his eyes.

"It's an expression," Blade nervously twittered.

"Yes, that's a word used in England that means *friend* or *buddy*," Bubba explained.

Gunther gave Bubba a displeasing glare before looking at Blade. "Okay, I'm Captain Alexander to you. You got that, insect boy?"

"Yes, Captain," Blade responded.

Gunther shook his head and then took a huge bite of the sub. "Good job on the subs, boys! This is excellent," he said, then chowed down like he hadn't eaten in a week.

Joel channeled the same strength he had during the greenhorns' initiation as a macho expression overtook his face when he took a huge bite of his cheesesteak sub. Surprisingly, it tasted good, despite puking up Portia's beautiful breakfast and the rancid cod earlier. However, a heave quickly replaced the excellent taste, which Joel disguised as a sneeze, and thank goodness nothing came up. He mentally gave himself a pep talk for eating the sub in its entirety without yacking it up on the spot.

Gunther watched Joel intently as if he could read Joel's mind. He stared at Joel for a few moments, and then he grinned as he asked, "So, how are you all doing with the seasickness?"

Joel looked Gunther in the eye, then took another huge bite of the sub. He wouldn't appear weak; the crew didn't need to know that he barfed like everyone else.

"I'm doing all right," Bubba answered first.

"I've never had seasickness," Hank said boldly.

"You're lying!" Bubba said, then laughed.

"Blade, how are you doing with it? Since this is your first trip on the Bering Sea and all," Nick kindly asked.

"It's bloody awful. I've never chundered this much in my life," Blade responded, looking at his untouched plate.

Completely bewildered by Blade's lexicon, Gunther asked, "You've never what?"

"Oh, sorry. Chunder means *to vomit*," Blade explained, then held a napkin over his mouth.

"Eat your sub, boy! Gotta take it like a man if you're going to be out here. You're gonna eat. Then chunder. Chop bait. Chunder. Chop bait. And chunder again. Then chop more bait. It's going to be great!" Gunther declared before devouring the rest of his dinner.

Bubba couldn't deal with Gunther's insensitivities. "Blade, keep eating and drinking. Drink plenty of water. It will go away," Bubba said.

"Ha! Mine lasted my entire first season. I barfed the entire trip. Now, it is usually the first two days and usually once a day after that," Nick shared.

"You're not helping, Nick!" Bubba exclaimed.

Meanwhile, Joel struggled to swallow his next bite, for the conversation may as well have been in the toilet along with the recycled food. Talking about puking, while feeling like puking, while trying to gag down a sub after puking, Joel looked at his dinner and then broke out in a cold sweat.

After that not-so-delightful conversation, no one said much for the remainder of the meal. The crew members retreated to their respective bunks to rest up for the hard work that was to come. Joel spent his first night on the Bering Sea tossing and turning in the lower bunk and making numerous trips to the bathroom to hurl. His sea legs needed to show up and fast.

THE NEXT MORNING, much to his surprise, Joel woke up feeling better. He didn't know if this healthy feeling was permanent or short-lived, but he embraced it either way. Joel said a morning prayer, asking God for good health, a safe journey, and plentiful crabs, then of course, the best for last, thanking God for the love of a good woman. Portia was his new beginning, and he was so thankful for that.

After his morning prayers concluded, Joel reached for his cell phone to look at the pictures he had taken over the last few weeks. He smiled and felt a flutter in his heart as he enjoyed the memories of feeding the eagles, flying through the Northern Lights, and taking selfies on the glacier. Then there was the first photo of Portia and Ice. Joel smiled even more as a tear almost entered his eye.

Gunther's raspy, smoker's voice boomed from the speaker system, pulling Joel away from his private thoughts. "We should be at our location a little bit after lunchtime today. Everybody, get out of bed and have breakfast," Gunther said.

Joel promptly jumped out of bed and rushed to shower and get ready for his day. He decided to forgo shaving, thinking the extra stubble would help keep his face warm when working on deck.

The smells of bacon and coffee greeted Joel as he entered the galley. He sat down with Nick, Bubba, Blade, and Hank, then ate the bacon, egg, and cheese biscuit Nick had prepared. Joel forwent coffee in hopes that soda would continue to soothe his gut, keeping his fingers crossed for a nausea-free day.

Breakfast was as tasty as it smelled. As they ate, the crew

members didn't have much to say, which could've resulted from the poor company due to Blade's peculiarities and Hank's not-so-sunny disposition. Smartly, Joel had sat on the end to make a quick getaway. He finished eating first, so he got up to throw away his napkin and wash his plate. At that moment, Kirk entered the galley and poured a cup of coffee. He took a sip as the Alexandria went over a colossal wave, causing Joel to stumble and bump into Kirk's arm, splattering coffee all over Kirk's shirt.

"Watch it, squid legs!" Kirk barked at Joel. "How does Portia like being with a squid?"

That was the final straw. Joel had had enough of Kirk's asininity, and it was high time he ended it. The Navy man took a deep breath as an I'm-gonna-jack-you-up smile spread across his face.

"Uh oh, kerfuffle time!" Blade shouted as if he were getting ready to watch two heavyweight champions duke it out. Luckily for Blade, no one responded to him.

The rest of the crew members eagerly awaited Joel's reaction. And that's just what Joel did; he reacted. This time, Kirk mentioned Portia; he went too far. Joel grabbed him by the front of his coffee-stained shirt and slammed him against the galley wall. Kirk wiggled like the slimy worm he was, and Joel slammed him against the wall a second time.

"I got a lot to say to you, and you're gonna listen!" Joel yelled into Kirk's ear as he firmly gripped his shirt collar. "You don't join the service for the fame and money. You join to serve and protect your country. And you better have honor and respect for your fellow service members, regardless of their military branches. You went out on Other Than Honorable discharge because you have no honor for your fellow man, no honor for yourself, and certainly no honor for our country! Don't you ever refer to me as a squid again, and don't ever utter Portia's name to me again, either! I'm going to make you a deal. You stay out of my way, and I'll stay out of yours!" Joel roared. The admonishment ended with Joel slamming Kirk against the wall again, initiating Kirk's reluctant response: a grunt and a half-baked head nod.

"This is a brilliant argy-bargy!" Blade spectated.

Kirk and Joel agreed on one thing; they both looked at Blade and yelled, "Shut up!"

Joel relinquished his grip on Kirk and left the galley. He needed to regain his cool, so he went up on deck to get some fresh air. As he exited the gear room, Joel was slapped sharply in the face by a chilly sea breeze. Then suddenly, his stomach rumbled, and water filled his mouth. He rushed to the railing next to the wheelhouse and barfed over the side of the vessel. So much for breakfast. It was so good that Joel got to have it twice.

Gunther yelled out the side window. "Joel, when you finish chundering, get up here!"

After the sixth dry heave, Joel trusted that nothing else would come up, so he wiped his mouth on his sleeve, did as Gunther instructed, and went to the wheelhouse.

"So, you do throw up like the rest of us?" Gunther laughed.

Joel wasn't feeling the humor but managed to conjure up a weak laugh in return. "Yeah, I guess so."

"I got something to say to you, boy."

"Yes, Captain," Joel replied.

"I like how you conduct yourself. I like how you handled Kirk. And yes, I saw the whole thing. I have surveillance cameras all over," Gunther admitted.

Meanwhile, Joel broke out in a sweat. He wasn't sure if he was blushing or getting ready to yack again. Despite the woozy feeling, Joel was pleased to have Gunther's approval. "Thank you," Joel replied.

"Well, the hug fest is over. Move along," Gunther motioned with his hand for Joel to leave. "Get out of here before you puke again. I really mean it, Joel. You don't look so good!"

"Yes Captain," Joel said, then exited the wheelhouse just in time for the next round of heaving to commence.

JOEL WENT TO THE GREENHORNS' QUARTERS since he didn't feel like socializing. To pass the time, he napped in between beautiful thoughts of Portia. After a few hours, Bubba announced that lunch was ready. *Yippy skippy. More food to eat, and more food to chuck up again,* Joel thought. He was either puking or eating, or was it the other way around? It was all just a bunch of misery. Joel would be happy when the crabbing finally got going.

He joined the crew in the galley for lunch. Tuna salad with pickles and hot pepper flakes was on the menu, just what the seasick person desired. Joel hoped the mayonnaise was fresh and kept cold because he never ordered such a salad in restaurants since he didn't trust who prepared it. However, he would barf no matter what, so it really didn't matter this time anyway.

Everyone was there except for the captain. The crew members grabbed their grub and crammed into the booth. Once again, Joel opted for the end seat because he didn't like feeling trapped; he always had an exit plan. Meanwhile, Kirk glared at Joel but was wise enough not to open his ugly mouth. And then there was Blade, who thoroughly inspected his sandwich before taking a hesitant bite.

"Oh, will you just eat it!" Gunther's voice shouted from the speaker. After the outburst, he continued, "Well, boys and girl, we are here. Joel, I want you up in the wheelhouse with me. Blade, you're gonna clean up the kitchen and then the heads. Everyone else, get on deck and put out three pots to test the waters. Then we will wait 30-33 hours to see if we got any crabs. Let the fun begin!"

After they ate, the crew members left their lunch dishes since Blade was appointed custodian of the day. Nick, Bubba, and Hank went on deck, and Joel went to the wheelhouse.

"So boy, you done puking?" Gunther asked as he pointed to the co-captain's chair.

"For the moment," Joel replied as he sat down.

Gunther laughed so hard his laugh turned into a frothy cough. Then he cleared his throat three times before continuing, "I wanted you up here with me. You can see better up here how we put out the pots. You will be on deck chopping bait when we set up the string. Yeah, I know, every greenhorn's dream, but it's where we all started."

"I'm looking forward to it, Captain," Joel said sincerely.

"You're a good liar." Gunther laughed. He waited, intently watching the crew members on deck until everyone was in position, and Nick turned around to give Gunther a thumbs up. Gunther grabbed the microphone. "Let's do this!"

He explained the process to Joel. "Mr. Sensitivity, tie wrap boy, operates the crane. I don't know how a man with his skill set can be so emotionally delicate! I don't get it, but he is the best worker here. I just step to the side when he wants to hug me. Bubba operates the crane to bring the pot over from the stack, and the deckhands stabilize the pot as it goes onto a hydraulic lift, which is attached to the side rail by a hinge. Once secured, the trap door gets opened, and the bait is put in. Nick is doing that right now. That will be you and Blade when we set up the string. Now, Nick is closing the trap door. The lift is tilting and sliding the 800-pound pot into the sea. Hank throws in the shot; then Nick throws in the buoys. You see, Joel, there is a rope attached to the pot as it sinks; this rope is called the shot. Then there is another rope connected to two buoys attached to the shot. This lets us know where the pot is. They'll put two more pots out, so watch the process."

Joel watched as Bubba operated the crane and maneuvered the pot onto the hydraulic lift with the deckhands' help. Nick loaded the bait, Hank threw the shot, and Nick threw in the buoys. They did this one more time, and then they were done.

"Easy peasy. Now, we get to wait for 30 hours and get to bond and enjoy each other's company," Gunther said as he rolled his eyes and lit a cigarette. "Good job, boys," he said into the mic.

Joel remembered the first time he went oystering in the Chesapeake Bay with his father. His father explained how to use the hydraulic patent tong, operated by foot pedals. Little Joel was mesmerized by his father and knew he wanted to be just like him. That was a life-changing day in Joel's childhood, and nearly 30 years later, Joel recalled word for word what his father had said to him on that cold, sunny morning, "It's a dangerous job. But you know what? Somebody has to do it. And that somebody might as well be me. I ain't made for working in some stuffy office with a bunch of lemmings. I work in God's country, and in God's country, I will stay."

THE NEXT 33 HOURS went as follows. They ate, and some of them barfed. Then the process repeated. Joel did manage to yack up his tuna salad. He wanted to blame the wonky mayo for the gastrointestinal episode but chalked it up to the seasickness instead. Either way, it was deplorable and nasty. After that, though, Joel kept his dinner down that night and breakfast down the following morning. And surprisingly, his lunch stayed down after that too. Perhaps, time was all he needed for his sea legs to return. He was back in action.

The other crew members enjoyed the idle time because they knew hard work was ahead. But Joel didn't share in this enjoyment. Downtime was his enemy. He would rather work, so he went to the kitchen looking for dishes to clean, anything to keep busy. Instead, he found Bubba and Blade in the galley, having the audacity to consume jellied biscuits and tea.

"This is excellent. Is this currant jelly?" Bubba asked.

"Aye, mate. And tea from London," Blade responded. "Would you like some, Joel?"

"No thanks. I'm keeping on the soda to keep the ole stomach happy," Joel replied as he opened the fridge and grabbed a root beer.

"Very well," Blade said. He reached into a satchel, pulled out a sewing kit, and proceeded to darn his socks at the galley table.

Bubba looked at Joel, shrugged his shoulders, and laughed before taking another sip of tea and reaching for another jellied biscuit. Joel didn't doubt that the jellied biscuits and tea were delectable; however, this wasn't the time or place for dabbling in delicacies.

Suddenly, Gunther's raspy voice boomed from the speakers. "Everybody on deck, now!"

Adrenaline pumped with voracity through Joel's veins. The long, awaited moment had finally arrived. It was time to pull the first pot.

THE CREW MEMBERS put on their cold weather gear and reported on deck.

"Nick, show the greenhorns how to snag the shot!" Gunther instructed from the wheelhouse.

"Aye aye, Captain!" Nick eagerly responded since Gunther could hear everything on deck.

Bubba and Nick got into position while Kirk and Hank stood off to the side with their arms crossed.

Then Bubba explained the process to Joel and Blade. "This is a grappling hook, and a rope is attached to it. Nick will throw the hook between the two buoys to retrieve the pot, snagging the shot."

Nick threw the hook, pulled up the buoys, and handed Bubba the rope.

Bubba talked as he worked. "You see, next we run the rope through the mechanical winch, then hoist the pot out of the water."

The 800-pound pot full of king crabs swung hard against the railing. Then Nick and Hank moved quickly, securing the pot onto the lift.

"We have to be extra careful. If a wave crashes over, the pot can go swinging. The last pot we pulled is when we lost Kyle and Chris," Nick somberly recollected.

The crew said nothing as each man joined in an unplanned moment of silence for the fallen crew members.

"Keep moving boys," Gunther said compassionately, for he knew the pain of losing Kyle and Chris all too well, if not more than the others.

The men snapped back into action; Nick, Hank, and Kirk finished securing the fully loaded pot.

"Whoa!" Nick cheered exuberantly, which prompted cheers from the crew. He opened the trap door, and many giant burgundy crabs tumbled onto the sorting table.

Meanwhile, Blade was so overcome with excitement that he picked up a crab, which promptly bit him by grabbing onto both of his scrawny arms.

"You dummy! I gave you gloves before we came out. Why didn't you put them on?" Kirk yelled in disgust.

Blade was too busy screaming to hear any utterance other than his own lamentation. To make matters worse, a wave crashed over the side, knocking him onto the deck floor, subsequently drooping his mohawk. "Ahhhh! Mate, stop biting me!" Blade yelped as the crab clung tightly to his forearms.

"Bubba, pull Blade up and hold him steady," Joel exhorted. Because he wasn't a moron and already had his gloves on, Joel wrestled the crab off Blade's toothpick arms, then tossed the spiny, deep-sea beast back onto the sorting table where it belonged.

Gunther had been quiet for long enough. "What the heck? Sort the crabs and tell me how many there are, please! Maybe throw the insect on the sorting table, so the crabs can have a snack while they wait. Let's get on with this."

"Now that's a kerfuffle! An argy-bargy!" Kirk snidely exclaimed, prompting laughter from Hank, who only smiled or laughed when it was at someone else's expense.

Ignoring them, Bubba explained the sorting process. "Blade, go wait by the opposite railing and just watch," he said before shifting his attention to Joel. "We only save the males, and the shell width has to be at least seven inches long." Bubba reached for a crab and flipped it over on its back. "Now, this is a female. If you see a rounded abdominal flap like this, then it's a lady, and she goes back to the sea. The males have triangular flaps." After he threw the female crab overboard, he grabbed another crab and measured it with a crab gauge. "This male is exceptional. Its shell width is 11 inches long, and it has a six-foot leg span. I'd say it's almost 24 pounds in weight. Look at this beauty!" Bubba said enthusiastically as he safely handed the crab to Joel.

Joel carefully held the gargantuan crustacean. He knew that king crabs were big, but it wasn't until he held one that he realized how massive these creatures truly were.

"Joel, turn around, so I can take a picture," Gunther said from the wheelhouse.

Joel did as the captain asked while staring at the angry crab that would soon be on someone's dinner plate. "How long do they live?" he asked.

"Up to 20-plus years," Nick answered.

Joel stared into the crab's beady little eyes, tossed it onto the table, and pushed it into the holding tank.

Bubba handed Joel a crab gauge. "Let's get sorting!"

Joel joined Bubba, Nick, Hank, and Kirk to sort crabs while Blade stood off to the side, applying pressure to his crab bites. Joel's eyes burned from the salt spray while waves crashed over their heads as they sorted and counted the crabs. When they finished, Nick turned around and said, "70," while motioning the number with his hands to Gunther. Then using the crane, Bubba moved the crab pot back to the stack.

"Excellent job! Let's see what pots two and three have for us! Let's have some fun, ladies. See if the greenhorns can throw the hook! Blade, you go first!" Gunther insisted. He laughed, but it turned into a cough instead.

"This ought to be good," Hank muttered.

Reluctantly, Nick handed the hook to Blade. "Aim between the buoys."

Joel backed up and moved to the side because he didn't trust Blade with anything sharp.

Blade viewed this task seriously. He took a deep breath, licked his index finger to test the wind, and moved his arms back and forth while breathing in and out loudly like he was warming up for football practice.

"Oh, will you just throw the blasted hook? We ain't got all day!" Gunther shouted.

After his large eyes had an episode of involuntary bulging, Blade threw the hook, but instead of the hook going over the railing and into the sea like it should've, it flung toward him, getting stuck in his work boot.

"Really?" Gunther yelled in disbelief.

Blade howled and screamed, and everyone but Kirk helped. Bubba and Nick restrained Blade. Then Joel and Hank worked together to pull the hook out of Blade's boot.

"Did it pierce your foot?" Bubba asked.

Blade shook his head, then took a deep, whiny, and high-pitched breath.

"If it didn't puncture you, why are you screaming?" Hank asked.

"Because it scared him. He's a wimp!" Kirk sneeringly retorted.

"Is everything okay? Somebody give me a thumbs up," Gunther inquired.

Nick gave Gunther the sign he wanted.

"Good. Well then, get him off the deck now! Blade, you're not allowed on deck during operations unless otherwise appointed. You got that?" Gunther instructed.

Blade was visibly distraught. He stood up and stumbled into the gear room.

"Dang! Anyway, Joel, let's see what you got," Gunther said.

Failing wasn't an option. Joel had successfully held back vomit in front of the crew, so he could undoubtedly retrieve the shot without difficulty. With his eyes on the buoys, he threw the hook and successfully snagged the shot.

"Outstanding! Job well done!" Gunther cheered.

"Wow Joel!" Bubba shouted as he hugged him. "It usually takes multiple tries for a greenhorn! You're the man!"

"Step to the side, Joel!" Gunther snickered.

Bubba put the rope in the mechanical winch to bring up the pot. Nick, Hank, and Kirk secured the fully loaded pot onto the lift. The five of them jumped in and sorted their catch. Joel fit in as if he had always been there. Waves crashed over him, salt spray burned his eyes, and the cold air made his nose and lips numb. All the while, he felt tiny icicles forming in his eyelashes.

After they finished sorting, Bubba moved the pot over to the stack.

"Sixty-five!" Nick reported to Gunther.

"Yahoo, boys! Let's get pot number three. Joel, throw the hook again!" Gunther implored.

Adrenaline bubbled like a hot spring through Joel's veins. With his eyes on the buoys, he threw the hook and successfully retrieved the shot. He was on fire, and there was no stopping him now. Joel pulled up the buoys and handed Bubba the rope to fasten into the winch. Praise be to God; they caught 75 crabs in the third pot.

"Kyle and Chris are our good luck charms! This makes me very happy! Let's set up the string. It's gonna be a long night! Blade, you're cooking us a high-calorie, high-protein meal for dinner; I'm thinking bleu cheese bacon burgers. If any of you doesn't like bleu cheese, too bad! Joel, you're chopping bait. Everyone else, you know what to do! Let's do this!" Gunther said.

WITH 60-MILE-PER-HOUR WINDS, 30-foot seas, and freezing rain, the Bering Sea was ready to reveal her dark side to Joel, just in time for his first greenhorn task.

Nick called him to the bait station and demonstrated as he spoke. "Today's your lucky day. Not only are you a greenhorn, but you're our bait master too. It's just as glamorous as it sounds. Get blocks of cod and herring from the freezer; then load them into the top of the bait chopper. They are heavy as hell. Make sure you wear gloves and don't drop them on your feet. Once the machine grinds them up, you put about this much in a bait bag."

Nick waited for Bubba to operate the crane, lift a crab pot from the stack, and maneuver it toward the lift. Nick walked across the deck to help with the rest of the process. Once he and Hank secured the pot, Nick opened the trap door and put the bait bag inside before returning to Joel. "And that's pretty much it. Do this 249 times, and then you're done," he said like it was no big deal. Then Nick patted Joel on the shoulder and went to help Bubba and Hank.

"Get chopping, greenhorn! We can only work as fast as you do!" Kirk arrogantly said as he left the deck and went to the engine room.

"No pressure there," Joel muttered as he filled a bait bag.

Despite being frozen, the ground-up cod and herring bits smelled deplorable. Suddenly, Joel became hot and sweaty underneath his cold weather gear, and a tremendous gagging sensation formed in his throat. He paused because he knew what was coming next. Water filled his mouth, and he quickly barfed over the railing. Then he hurled again. And once more after that.

"Watch out!" Gunther yelled from the wheelhouse side window before following Joel's example and upchucking into the Bering Sea as well.

Joel finished chundering and quickly stepped back to avoid Gunther's splatter range.

After the final heave, Gunther chuckled, which turned into a coughing fit. "I hope you know that was a sympathy puke! We are men! Puke and back to it!" He laughed like a madman and then slammed the side window shut.

Joel felt too bad to laugh. Instead, he dragged himself back to the bait station, willed back the rest of the vomit, and proceeded to fill the bait bags and load the pots like the rugged man he was.

THE CREW WORKED for two hours straight as Bubba operated the crane, Hank and Nick secured the pots onto the lift, Joel put in the bait bags, Hank threw the shot, and Nick threw the buoys. With 60-mile-per-hour winds and waves crashing on deck, launching the pots took twice as long as it would've with calm seas. All the while, Joel felt ice building up on his clothing and face, and he knew he would soon be beating ice off the railings, another task not to be coveted. When Gunther announced that dinner was ready, Joel breathed a sigh of relief and looked forward to the brief break.

"Get your grubby butts down into the galley for some bleu cheese bacon burgers, compliments of insect boy," Gunther commanded through the loudspeaker.

Expecting to see ketchup and mustard bottles next to a greasy pile of bacon, Gunther, Joel, Bubba, Nick, and Hank entered the galley. Instead, the pleasant sound of classical music greeted them. Meanwhile, Blade wore a tuxedo as he stood in front of the table, which was oddly adorned with a red velvet cloth. All the dinner plates were set, waiting to be devoured by the hungry gents.

Gunther wasn't appreciative of Blade's extravagant labor. "What is this? What did you make?" he fumed.

Blade's eyes slightly bugged out, but he stood his ground as he answered the captain, "Puffed chicken pot pie with a light croissant topper."

"Puffed? Light croissant topper? These men are working, burning thousands of calories through hard physical labor, and you prepare a light croissant topper? They need protein, high carbs, and high calories! I told you to make bleu cheese bacon burgers!" Gunther pontificated.

"Hey Captain, it may be good. Let's try it," Bubba said as he eagerly slid his chunky bum into the booth.

Gunther gave Bubba a disapproving look, then sarcastically motioned for everyone else to sit down. This time, Joel didn't get an end seat. Instead, he got smashed between Bubba and Gunther, who got right up in Blade's face and bulged his eyes out at him before sitting down.

Meanwhile, Blade's eyes pulsed with nervous excitement as he awaited the crew's reaction to his decadent meal. The crew members looked at each other from side to side, almost afraid to taste what the insect had concocted. There was no denying that it smelled good, for the pleasant scent made Joel develop an appetite, despite the severe yacking he had endured just two hours earlier. He was extremely pleased to have chicken since it would set better on his agitated gut than a bleu cheese bacon burger. Joel was never into eating cheese that looked moldy anyway.

"Well, bon appétit!" Gunther sarcastically said, then took a bite.

The crew members tasted the food as well.

When the buttery croissant and decadent pot pie filling hit Joel's tongue, he remembered his excursions in England. He hadn't had a meal this delectable since the day he toured Cornwall.

"Blade, man, this is amazing," Nick said, then went in for another bite. "What do you think, Hank?"

"It's not bad," Hank answered reluctantly.

"I think it's out of this world. Joel, how about you?" Bubba asked.

Joel didn't want to piss off Gunther, but there was no denying how superb this meal was. "Blade, this is excellent. Thank you."

Everyone looked at Gunther, waiting for him to yell obscenities and insults at the young chap. To their shock and amazement, Gunther did neither. "Well done, Blade. I think you have found one of your jobs. You are the official chef for this season. Just always remember to give us as many calories as possible. Lose the tux, music, and tablecloth; it's overkill."

"Thank you, Captain. I'm chuffed!" Blade replied with a smile.

"You're what?" Hank inquired.

"I'm happy you feel that way. I am grateful," Blade explained.

"Oh well, shut up, sit down, and eat with us then!" Gunther insisted.

FOR THE FIRST TIME, Joel experienced working in terrible conditions in the darkness beneath the Alexandria's bright lights. She was sturdy and firm, providing the crew members with everything they needed. However, the relentless Bering Sea had the power to destroy her beyond repair, setting her on a path of no return, plummeting to the bottom of the sea floor where the king crabs scurried without a care in the world. The hidden danger that rippled within always kept Joel on his toes. Now he was part of a team again, even as a bait chopper; he had his job, and he would be the best darn bait master the Bering Sea had ever seen.

Joel, Bubba, Nick, and Hank worked well into the early morning hours, pushing forward without slowing until they completed the string. By the time they reached the last pot, Joel couldn't feel his face or fingers.

After the final pot made its much-anticipated entrance into the angry sea, Bubba helped Joel clean up the bait station. "Go get some sleep," Bubba said.

"I'm so pumped up; I don't think I can sleep," Joel replied as he reached out for a friendly handshake, trying to avoid a Chubby Bubba hug.

"Oh, I got something that can help you with that. Follow me," Bubba insisted as he headed toward the gear room door.

"It doesn't involve me dropping my britches again, does it?"

Bubba laughed. "No, it's just chamomile capsules."

Joel took the chamomile and then retreated to his lower bunk in the minuscule greenhorns' quarters, where only the point of Blade's bright green mohawk stuck out from the covers, like a shark's dorsal fin lurking ominously in shallow waters. Joel chuckled, then stripped down to his t-shirt and boxers and crawled into his bunk. He had to lie sideways and bend his legs to fit, but it was better than nothing. He had a job on one of the most elite fishing vessels on the Bering Sea, and a gorgeous fiancée waiting at home; he was beyond satisfied with his new life.

Before going to sleep, Joel enjoyed a few photos of Portia on his phone. Even when he wasn't home with her, he still wanted her to be the last image he saw before falling asleep. Angels come in all shapes and sizes, and his angel was a beautiful bar queen with thigh-high leather boots and an electric guitar.

"God is good," Joel whispered. God is good, indeed!

Chapter 21. *War Zone*

The following day, the crew members entered the galley at 10:30 a.m. when Blade announced that brunch was ready. Joel's back ached as he walked, and he couldn't figure out if his joints and muscles were hurting from working on deck or from sleeping on that sad excuse for a bed in the greenhorns' quarters. On a positive note, his stomach felt normal, so he enjoyed a glorious cup of coffee with steamed milk, compliments of insect boy whose mohawk was looking particularly sharp that morning, making him live up to his very odd first name.

"What's for breakfast, Blade? It sure does smell good in here!" Bubba jovially asked.

"Blood pudding with baked beans," Blade replied with a sinister grin.

"Where did you get the blood?" Hank disconcertedly inquired.

"It's pig's blood. You have an excellent selection of meat in the freezer, mates. And baked beans are another breakfast delicacy in England and Wales," Blade explained.

The crew paused and stared at Blade in disbelief. These were manly men, but not a darn one of them was willing to consume blood pudding, not even Bubba, who would eat just about anything.

"Um, dude, I don't think we can eat that," Bubba said nervously, taking one for the team.

"You guys! I'm just twitting you!" Blade exclaimed, then started laughing.

"Twitting? Can you please speak English?" Kirk asked.

"I don't speak English. I speak British. And I'm joking. Twitting means *teasing*. Of course, I didn't make you blood pudding and beans for breakfast. I don't have the proper equipment here to harvest the blood. I made soufflés that I added sausage and bacon to and then made toast with lots of butter," Blade said as he motioned for everyone to sit down at the table so that he could serve their plates.

"Blade, you are the man. I appreciate your buffoonery! That's the best prank that's happened on this vessel! This morning's breakfast sounds great. Lots of calories, carbs, and protein!" Gunther said from the wheelhouse.

Blade looked up at the galley cam and gave Gunther two thumbs up.

"Buffoonery? Big word," Bubba muttered as he slid his plump bum into the booth.

Joel and the rest of the crew thoroughly enjoyed Blade's greasy, protein-packed breakfast; however, Joel was concerned about the line that would soon form outside the head.

WITH TIME TO KILL AFTER BRUNCH, Joel didn't feel the need to chitchat in the galley with the others. Instead, he ventured to the wheelhouse to hang out with Gunther.

As he entered, Gunther was gabbing on the phone. "I've got someone who would like to talk to you, Joel," Gunther said as he handed the receiver to him and then promptly lit a ciggy.

Joel's heart skipped a beat. "Hello."

"Oh Bering Sea / Please bring him home to me," Portia projected the flawlessness of an angel as she sang to Joel once again.

"Hey, pretty lady," Joel replied, melting at his fiancée's acapella greeting, almost feeling misty at the sound of her voice.

"I love you, Joel Layton," Portia sweetly said.

Joel felt warm all over, for the cold Bering Sea winds were no match for the warmth of Portia's love. "I love you too," he responded.

Meanwhile, Gunther sat back in the captain's chair, pretending not to listen, but there was no way he couldn't.

"How are you, Ice, Screech, and Tiny doing?" Joel asked, wondering if he had forgotten any of the critters since the number kept growing.

"Screech only slaps Ice twice a day now instead of 10 times. Ice still isn't fully house-trained yet, so I am extremely hopeful of expediting that process. Aunt Gert and I have been working hard. Last night, Ted and Old Al got drunk while playing dominos, and Old Al hit on Rhonda. Of course, Ted took offense. Then Pete hit on Lora in front of Dr. Sampson. You know, a typical night in the Port of Aleutia. Also, Milena stopped by and is doing well. Hadn't seen him for a while."

"Who is Milena?" Joel asked.

"That's her dumpster moose," Gunther whispered.

"Oh, you haven't met him yet. Milena is the moose that likes to sniff around the dumpster. He comes right up to the back steps sometimes, and I'll feed him apple slices," Portia explained, like this was nothing out of the ordinary.

Relieved that Milena was the source of the peculiar dumpster noises, Joel smiled. He loved learning more about this woman he so hopelessly loved. "Maybe Milena will make an appearance when I get back," Joel said.

Gunther couldn't contain his laughter. "You crazy kids."

"Portia, you have avoided the question long enough. How are you doing? You didn't answer me," Joel asked again.

"I'm doing all right. Just worrying about all of you every second, doing my best to stay busy."

"You have a wedding to plan too," Joel said.

"Aunt Gert and I are working on that. I picked out my wedding dress this morning. I hope you like it," Portia replied.

Joel forgot Gunther was there listening to every word. "You know I will love it. You will be so beautiful."

Gunther jokingly made a sound like he was going to heave, loud enough that Portia heard it too.

"Tell Uncle Gunther he will have to wear a tux," Portia said with a laugh.

"I think I'll let you tell him that," Joel responded.

Suddenly, the phone signal cut in and out. "You there?" Portia's voice crackled.

"Yes, but the connection is bad. I love you and will talk to you soon," Joel said.

"I love you too, Joel Layton," Portia said before static covered her voice.

When the static changed to silence, Joel hung up the phone. Even though he was sad the call dropped, he was thankful he got to talk with her.

Gunther grinned and rolled his head around to look Joel in the eye. "You got it bad, boy!"

Unexpectedly, a fax came in, and the amiable conversation halted. Gunther promptly got up and read it. "Oh no," he said while staring intently at the paper, squinting his weary eyes and rubbing the back of his head. He grunted, sat down, and grabbed the microphone to address the crew. "There's an arctic storm brewing in the Pacific. It's moving slowly, so we should have time to pull the pots. Then let it pass before heading home. We can outsmart it. We've done this before, and we'll do it again. Our job is to bring home crabs, and that's what we're going to do. We will pull the pots a few hours early, then go toward Louis Ridge to let it blow over, staying the hell away from Satan's Expanse. Bubba, get me an ice report on deck. It's looking pretty thick out there." Gunther set the mic down, nervously ran his fingers through his hair, and sighed. "Welcome to the moody Bering Sea, Captain Alexander," he said to himself before turning toward Joel. "You ever been through an arctic storm, boy?"

"No, but plenty of hurricanes and monsoons."

"Well, you're in for a treat. Glad we got you on board. If anything happens to Kirk and me, you will bring us home. I am confident in that," Gunther said.

"Thank you. Let's hope it doesn't come to that, but I am always happy to fill in as needed. I know I need to work my way up to earn that right," Joel replied.

Gunther smiled and nodded. "You got what it takes—and then some." He reached for the mic again to talk to Bubba, who had just entered the deck to assess the ice. "What you got for me, Bubba?"

Joel looked out the wheelhouse window and was astonished by the icy buildup beginning on deck. The Alexandria looked like a thin layer of snow covered her; however, it wasn't snow. It was a thick layer of ice.

After a minute, Bubba responded from the mic in the gear room. "We need to get to work deicing now."

"10-4," Gunther responded. Then he addressed the crew, "Greenhorns, get your gear on and get on deck now. We got ice buildup. The ice report isn't as bad as I have seen, but it is still bad. Watch out for possible ice chunks falling from overhead."

"Let the fun begin!" Joel exclaimed as he walked to the door.

"Get out of here, you greenhorn!" Gunther shouted before laughing and coughing simultaneously.

AFTER DRESSING IN COLD WEATHER GEAR, Joel paused as he entered the deck. The bitter Alaskan air slapped him in the face, and he recalled the many times he had changed his route for hurricanes and monsoons when he was captain of the USS Roland, a 510-foot-long guided-missile destroyer. However, the current moment didn't give him a warm and fuzzy feeling because he had never experienced an arctic storm, let alone on a vessel such as the Alexandria, which was only 120 feet long. Joel felt an uneasiness because he wasn't the one in control. He had to trust and respect his captain, and that's just what Joel did.

He couldn't help but worry about Portia and Gert, knowing they would watch the weather reports. Joel shivered at the thought of Portia sitting alone in the bar and watching the arctic storm warnings because he would be out of his mind worrying about her if they're roles were reversed.

And there Joel was, in the middle of the Bering Sea, with a monstrous storm brewing in the distance, bringing him a danger unlike any other.

JOEL MET BUBBA AND BLADE by the coiler and was taken aback by Blade's next antic. Blade wore swimming goggles that surprisingly, yet sufficiently, covered his gargantuan eyes while further accentuating his insectile appearance. Bubba took one look at the newbie and lost it. "Blade, I don't think you will be able to see well enough with those on. Please remove them now! They aren't safe!"

"I think I'm going to honk!" Blade abruptly exclaimed, then put his hand over his mouth.

"You mean like a goose?" Bubba confusedly asked.

"No!" Blade shrieked like an alley cat as he sprinted and then upchucked his soufflé into the tumultuous Bering Sea.

"I am deducing that honk is another word for vomit," Joel surmised, feeling exceptionally pleased that he wasn't the one yacking this time.

"Agreed," Bubba concurred.

After five minutes of disgusting hacks, gags, and heaves, Blade wiped his mouth off on his sleeve and then rejoined Bubba and Joel as if he had never left the conversation.

"Yes. Vomit, honk, chunder, all the same thing," Blade replied as he reached his thumbs inside the goggles to wipe off the condensation since the exertion of heaving made his gigantic eyes sweat.

"You can't wear those! It's not safe," Bubba implored again as he reached into his pocket and took out a knife. He cut Blade's goggles strap, and one would've thought Bubba had amputated one of Blade's limbs. The green-haired greenhorn let out another one of his infamous shrieks, which prompted Gunther to laugh loudly into the microphone for the entire vessel to hear as he watched from the wheelhouse.

Bubba didn't see the humor. He proceeded with the deicing instructions as he handed Joel and Blade each a mallet. "Knock the ice off the railings and throw as much as you can overboard. I'll deice the coiler," Bubba instructed as he pulled a hammer from his pocket and got to work.

Blade swung at a chunk of ice on the railing, fell flat on his face, and screamed profusely. Once again, Joel assisted Blade with another predicament by helping the neophyte stand up and retrieving the mallet from his twig-like fingers.

Meanwhile, up in the wheelhouse, Gunther couldn't contain himself. "Just as I figured. Go back inside, Blade. Nick and Hank, get your butts on deck and help deice. Blade, clean my captain's quarters and all the shared heads. My bathroom needs a good scrubbing. Especially after that brunch. Keeping the Alexandria clean is just as important as deicing."

Now that Blade was safely inside, Joel could finally get to work. He used his well-sculpted bicep, pec, shoulder, and back muscles as he forcefully swung the mallet, too many times to count, and knocked the ice off the railings, making the Alexandria's stately blue paint visible once again. Despite the cold temperature, adrenaline flowed like lava throughout his body, causing the soreness in his muscles to dissipate. And to put the cherry on the sundae, his decadently greasy brunch stayed down; Joel had a chunder-free afternoon.

Wearing his cold weather gear and holding a mallet in his hand, Gunther joined the crew on deck. *He is a good man,* Joel thought as he momentarily stopped hitting the ice. And Joel wasn't the only one taken aback by this because Bubba and Nick also paused to greet their captain. On the other hand, Hank was his usual unappreciative self and continued working without any acknowledgment.

"What are you wackadoodles looking at? Let's get to this! Don't look at me like that. I was working out here with you last year. Oh, and Bubba, I'm temporary deck boss," Gunther commanded as he whacked a chunk of ice off the crane and threw it overboard.

Bubba laughed. "Yes, Captain!"

For 20 minutes, Gunther kept pace with the crew by beating ice off the railings, throwing the chunks overboard, and getting one heck of a workout. He moved slowly before suddenly breathing hard and dropping to his knees.

"Captain!" Bubba yelled as he and Joel rushed toward Gunther, with Nick and Hank following closely behind them.

"I'm all right. I'm just an old fart," Gunther stubbornly insisted as he stood up.

"Are you winded? How's your chest feel?" Joel asked.

Over the years, Joel had unfortunately witnessed several people have heart attacks on the USS Roland, and Gunther had the same gaunt and withered complexion that Joel had seen so many times.

"I'm fine. It's just asthma from the cigarettes. As I said, when I get home, I'll quit smoking," Gunther replied.

"I'm taking back over as deck boss, and this is not negotiable. We got this, Captain. Go back inside," Bubba asserted.

Suddenly, a rumble in the distance shifted the crew's attention to the metamorphosing sky as it ominously darkened.

"Must be a squall coming. I saw some on the radar," Gunther said as he sullenly gave into the crew's wishes and began walking toward the gear room.

A gust of wind blew through like a tornado, and a massive chunk of ice fell from the crane, hitting Nick's right shoulder, knocking him flat on the deck, and leaving him in pain.

"Let's get him to the galley and get his gear off," Gunther instructed.

"We got this, Captain," Joel said as he and Bubba carefully helped Nick stand. Joel was already worried about Gunther and didn't want him overdoing it.

Once they were in the galley, Gunther removed Nick's jacket. "Hang in there, buddy. I know it hurts."

Bubba took out his pocketknife and slowly cut Nick's shirt off in pieces. The crew members did their best not to gasp when they saw Nick's disfigured shoulder, where the bones were broken and shattered, not to mention the mangled muscles and tendons. Joel felt sick in the pit of his stomach, and his heart bled for Nick. He couldn't imagine how much pain their crew member was enduring.

Nick shook with agony as Gunther did his best to evaluate Nick's condition. "It's dislocated, or shattered, or all the above. Bubba, get him some pain meds; then put him in my bed, so he has room to get comfortable. Pack him in pillows the best you can. I will call the Coast Guard and see if we can get a helicopter to come. Joel, you're helping Bubba and Hank pull pots. Blade, stay inside and watch over Nick," Gunther commanded, no longer looking as gaunt and pale as he did earlier.

The conversation was interrupted by a loud rumble that preceded a clamorous bang, which caused the galley lights to flash on and off several times.

"What was that?" Gunther yelled as he ran to the wheelhouse.

Joel was worried about Gunther darting off like that, but he knew the captain had no choice. All hell was breaking loose, and Joel would've done the same.

"Come on, Nick. Let's get you comfortable, and I'll get you some meds," Bubba said.

Bubba and Joel helped Nick stand and got him situated in the captain's quarters. Joel carefully and slowly placed pillows around Nick, hoping not to cause further pain. However, Nick's discomfort grew more intolerable with each passing moment, so much so that he began crying hysterically, and Joel was worried that Nick would go into shock.

"What will Polly do without me?" Nick cried.

"You're not going to die. I know it may feel like it, but you aren't," Joel empathetically said as he squeezed Nick's hand and sat down next to him.

Bubba returned with the syringe and gave Nick an injection in the arm. "This should help in about 15 minutes."

Nick continued breathing hard as the lights flickered.

Bubba whispered to Joel, "This is bad. I hope the intercom still works."

"I'm gonna go up to the wheelhouse and see what's going on," Joel said.

WHEN JOEL ENTERED THE WHEELHOUSE, Gunther lit a cigarette while nervously shaking his leg. He acknowledged Joel, took a long drag, and blew out a cloud of smoke before he spoke. "Lightning hit us. We have no way to communicate and no way to track the storm. And no GPS. No way to call a chopper for Nick. And the EPIRB doesn't work. Maybe there was a faulty battery? Who the hell knows? The odds of having a faulty EPIRB are one in a billion. The good news is the engines still work, and we have power. But the only thing we have to guide us is my judgment, and if I screw up and unknowingly take us into Satan's Expanse, we're goners. That death trap has swallowed nearly 500 vessels over the years," Gunther said, then took another long draw on the cigarette. Almost blinded by the cloud of exhaled smoke, he opened the side window, like airing out the room would solve their problems.

"The captain's intuition is always best. You have been on these waters for decades. You know where to go, and you will bring us home safely. I have confidence in that," Joel said.

"I'm glad I have your vote," Gunther replied with a weak smile. "We have now fallen off the radar. Everyone will be worried. They will fear the worst—thinking that Satan's Expanse killed us like it did Chris and Kyle. This makes me sick to my stomach thinking of Portia, Gert, Polly, and Old Al. Everyone in town. We could very well get the worst! The storm could change paths and hit us while we think we are eluding it!" Gunther exclaimed as he pounded the counter and stared at the family photographs of himself, Gert, Katerina, Kyle, Chris, Lizzie, and Elijah, hanging on the wall.

"Are you changing your plan or sticking to it?" Joel asked.

"What would you do, Captain Layton?"

"I'd follow my gut," Joel answered, not exactly a textbook answer, but it was the best advice anyone could receive in a situation such as this.

"If we go home now for Nick, we will get hit head-on by the storm, according to that fax. My gut still says to pull pots now and head to Louis Ridge as planned, which is…" Gunther paused and extended his hand in front of him, moving it until he thought it faced the right way. "There, that way."

"I think that's a good decision," Joel said.

"The intercom system is down too. Please tell Bubba to get Hank on deck and pull pots as hard as possible. And Joel, make sure the insect stays inside."

"Will do, Captain," Joel responded.

WHEN JOEL ENTERED THE CAPTAIN'S QUARTERS, Bubba and Blade were sitting with Nick, who was woozy from the pain medication.

With no way to sugarcoat their current situation, Joel was forthright. "Lightning hit us. Everything is fried, including the intercom and navigation systems. The EPIRB is dead—no clue why. We have fallen off the radar and can't communicate."

Blade looked confused, but Bubba knew what this meant. "No way to issue a distress signal, call the Coast Guard for Nick, follow the storm, or find our way home," Bubba surmised.

"Correct. Captain Alexander wants us to pull pots now and then go to Louis Ridge as planned to wait out the arctic storm," Joel replied.

"Blade, you're in charge of meals and Nick. Bring us water bottles on deck. Then in two hours, please bring us sandwiches and more water bottles, so we don't lose time," Bubba instructed.

"It would be my privilege," Blade responded as he moved closer to Nick and stared at him intently with his ginormous eyes.

"Come on guys! First, my shoulder, now Le Freak?" Nick exclaimed as he slurred his words and rubbed his eyes.

"Hey, I'm British, not French," Blade retorted, then laughed. Luckily, he wasn't easily offended, which was an excellent attribute to have while trapped on a vessel with this bunch of brutes.

"Thank you, Blade. You're a real asset," Joel said.

"That's a Navy Captain telling you that, Blade," Bubba added.

Joel knew the look in Bubba's eyes and was concerned that he might have to step to the side. Meanwhile, Blade blushed and smiled.

"Blade, the meds could make Nick act weird. Just don't let him get out of bed. Joel, I'll get Hank from the engine room and meet you on deck. We got crabs to catch in 40-foot seas! Whoa, getting pumped!" Bubba exclaimed as he promptly hugged Joel, who didn't have enough time or space to step to the side.

"Hey skinny boy! Slide over here and kiss me," Nick professed as he reached out for Blade.

"Oh, tosh! That's a codswallop. I will not snog with you!" Blade vehemently replied.

Joel didn't know what it meant or what to think when he heard this. He was as flabbergasted as a moose that had gotten its antlers stuck in a dumpster.

STILL WEARING HIS COLD WEATHER GEAR, Joel was sweating like a fat man at a state fair in August, so he embraced the opportunity to get back on deck. Thunder growled like a grizzly bear as lightning streaked across the sky. The arctic storm was still a good distance away, so this squall was an unrelated precursor of more trepidation to come.

The portentous sky reminded Joel of being on the workboat with his father in the Chesapeake Bay right before a mid-September hurricane. His father had said, "Never lose respect for the water, Son. You never know what hand you will get dealt. Always fear the water, just as you fear and respect the Lord." Joel smiled, remembering that day like it was yesterday, and he recalled the choppiness in the Chesapeake Bay and how the sky looked as the outer bands of a category three hurricane approached them. And nearly 30 years later, reminiscing about that memorable day, Joel stood on the Bering Sea, with a squall approaching and an arctic storm brewing in the distance.

Even when the sky and sea were angry, Joel still found them beautiful. He pulled his phone out of his pocket and took pictures of waves crashing over the railing as sunrays pierced creepy black clouds above the vessel. Lightning crackled in the sky, and Joel could've sworn he heard Portia singing to him again, "Oh, Bering Sea / Please bring him home to me." She wasn't there, so it must've been a figment of his imagination. At least, that's what he thought.

Bubba and Hank interrupted Joel's thoughts when they joined him on deck.

"Joel, the three of us will take turns snagging the shot; otherwise, your shoulder will look like Nick's," Bubba said as he handed Joel the grappling hook.

Joel promptly threw the hook, but the wind blew it about five feet away from the buoys.

"It's all right. That happens. Throw it again, bud," Bubba said.

Joel pulled in the hook and snagged the shot on the second throw. Bubba promptly fastened the rope into the winch and brought up a fully loaded pot. Next, Joel and Hank secured it onto the hydraulic lift.

"Woohoo! Yeah! That's what I'm talking about! Not bad for the short amount of time they've been soaking!" Hank yelled.

Joel opened the trap door, and the spiny monsters tumbled onto the sorting table. The three of them worked quickly, sorting and counting the crabs before pushing them into the holding tank. Joel turned toward the wheelhouse windows, motioned 80 with his fingers, and then Gunther happily replied with a thumbs up and "Good job, boys."

"Only 249 pots left to pull. I hope you don't like sleeping!" Hank said with a laugh as he patted Joel on the shoulder.

What the heck? Joel wondered. Suddenly, Hank was Mr. Personality, but Joel didn't complain. Instead, he initiated a friendly handshake; then the burly men got back to the grind.

Countless times, waves crashed over the railing, knocking the deckhands down. Despite the high seas, they took turns throwing the grappling hook. Even with that, Joel's shoulder felt the strain, and he knew that Bubba and Hank must've been hurting too. But none complained. Joel was working at sea with a good team. And praise God; each pot was just as full of crabs as the last one.

After two hours, Blade delivered hot coffee and more water

bottles. Joel had to admit he enjoyed the steamed milk and the added toffee flavor. With the hot liquid running throughout his body, Joel embraced the warming sensation despite the icicles hanging from his eyebrows and eyelashes, not to mention the ones trying to form in his nose.

The crew worked through freezing, pelting rain. Strong gusts blew the pots, making it extremely difficult to secure them. Luckily, Joel and Hank had quick reflexes and the good sense to get the heck out of the way at the right moment, like stepping to the side for an impending Bubba hug. At one point, two 40-foot waves crashed over both sides of the vessel, washing all three of them across the deck. Praise be only to God that no one was injured. The Almighty One kept them safe from harm.

They continued working for hours, even though it felt like days. Several times, Blade came and went with food and beverage services, and the five-minute meal breaks were all the deckhands had. Sleep deprivation and intense physical labor in the most deplorable conditions one could imagine, deep sea red king crab fishing isn't for the weak.

"ONLY THREE POTS LEFT! We're almost done!" Bubba exclaimed as he got ready to throw the hook. Suddenly, there was a loud boom, and the entire vessel shook. "Oh, my Lord! Kirk! There's been an explosion in the engine room!" Bubba yelled as he dropped the hook and ran toward the gear room. Hank followed closely behind Bubba while Joel went to the wheelhouse.

"You read my mind," Gunther said as he painfully stood up from the captain's chair. He clutched his chest but moved quickly. "You're temporary relief captain at the moment. I'm going to the engine room. How many pots are left?"

"Three pots," Joel answered.

"Okay. We need to leave them. Stay straight. That will take us to

Louis Ridge—I think. I'll be back," Gunther said, then left the room.

Joel nodded, then sat down. As his butt hit the captain's chair, he saw a 45-foot wave directly in front of the vessel. He took a deep breath and clutched the jog stick before the monstrous wave broke over the bow. Then the stormy seas let up, at least for the moment.

AFTER AN HOUR, Gunther breathlessly entered the wheelhouse. "We got the fire out, and everything appears to be working okay. Well, enough for us to make it home. But Kirk is burned up badly on his left side, so we bandaged him up and got him in my room with Nick. Bubba gave him some pain meds and an antibiotic. Hank is taking over the engine room. It was really smoky down there," he said as he sat in the co-captain's seat, let out a heavy breath, and put his hand on his chest again.

Joel's heart sank as he grew increasingly concerned for Gunther. He couldn't bear the thought of anything happening to him.

"Captain, are you all right?" Bubba began as he entered the wheelhouse. "I got really worried about you down there."

Both Joel and Bubba looked at Gunther and waited for a response. Instead, Gunther tried to stand up but fell immediately to his knees.

"He's having a heart attack! Bubba, get a blood thinner and fast," Joel instructed, then gently grabbed Gunther from behind, holding him up.

Bubba opened a cabinet and pulled out the wheelhouse first aid kit. He put the pills in Gunther's mouth and poured some water in for him to swallow. "I'll get Hank and get him to help get Gunther downstairs and into a bunk. Hang tight," Bubba said before rushing out of the wheelhouse.

Meanwhile, Joel continued holding onto Gunther. "Stay with us, Captain," he whispered with a quivering lip, begging God not to take him.

"Get me a cigarette," Gunther muttered as he took a deep breath that almost turned into a cough, but he didn't have the strength to go through with it.

Joel was pleased that Gunther had a sense of humor during a moment like this; however, there was no way he would give the man a cigarette during a heart attack. "That's a negative, Captain," Joel replied.

A few minutes later, Bubba and Hank came in, carefully picked up Gunther, and took him to the crew's quarters. Joel's eyes glistened as he watched them leave the wheelhouse. His heart sank to his feet because he wanted to stay by Gunther's side, but he was now the captain responsible for bringing the crew home.

For an hour and a half, Joel simultaneously kept his eyes on the sea and the clock, eagerly awaiting an update on Gunther. The angst, fear, and worry ate Joel alive, for he had never been in a situation such as this. He had never been this worried about a family member or someone he loved. He prayed for Gunther to survive. The world most definitely needed Gunther Alexander in it.

Eventually, Bubba quietly entered the wheelhouse and sat in the co-captain's chair. Joel was used to seeing Bubba with a jovial expression on his chubby face, always happy and full of positivity, but this time was different. Bubba was visibly distraught, and Joel feared the worst for their esteemed captain.

"Blade is with Gunther. We had to shock him with the defibrillator. He's stable now, but Joel, we have got to get him to a hospital fast," Bubba said with a ragged breath.

Joel swallowed hard a couple of times and got his emotions in check. As relief captain, he faced a life-or-death decision. Nick had painful injuries, Kirk could get an infection that could kill him, and Gunther wouldn't survive waiting out the storm. "We should head for home. Gunther and Kirk don't have time to wait. This could put us in the direct path of the storm and possibly into Satan's Expanse, but we have got to try. Please have everyone wear their survival suits and ensure the holding tanks stay full, so we don't tip over. I don't want to take any chances."

"I agree with you, Captain," Bubba concurred.

At that moment, Joel slowly turned the vessel toward the rising sun. Without a functional navigation system, he followed his gut and stopped turning when he felt they were facing home. "Let's hope this is the right way," Joel replied, praying for God to bring him strength and keep them on the correct course. He looked at the pictures of Gunther, Gert, Katerina, Kyle, Chris, Lizzie, and Elijah that Kyle had hung on the wheelhouse wall just a year ago. Gunther was full of life and smiling as he stood proudly with his family. Joel's heart stirred with emotions because he had always longed to be in family pictures such as these, and he prayed that he and Portia would have many family portraits with Gert and Gunther for the years to come.

"Hey Bubba, I don't want Gunther alone for one minute," Joel said.

"He won't be. Between Blade and I, he will always have someone with him," Bubba answered as he stood up.

"Hey Bubba, can you please take over? I want to see him before the conditions deteriorate from the storm. Right now, it's calm seas," Joel said.

"Sure, Captain," Bubba replied as he patted Joel on the shoulder. "I got your back, buddy. It will do Gunther's heart good to see you."

"You're the best, Bubba," Joel responded as he felt a lump form in his throat. He swallowed hard several times and got his emotions in check before entering the crew's quarters, where Blade sat with Gunther.

"Hey Blade, may I have a minute with him?" Joel whispered.

"Of course. He has been sleeping on and off, but I know he will be happy to see you," Blade quietly replied as he stood up, then went to the captain's quarters with Hank, Kirk, and Nick.

When Joel knelt next to Gunther, his heart sank because Gunther looked so sick and pale as his chest violently heaved with each heavy breath he struggled to take. At first, Joel thought Gunther was sleeping, but then he opened his eyes and smiled.

"You got to do something for me, boy," Gunther said weakly.

"No, we're not having that conversation. You will be fine, and you are going home," Joel firmly replied.

"My heart isn't working well, Joel. Please, I beg you. Please promise me that you'll take care of Portia and Gert. I don't know how they will handle me dying too," Gunther pleaded.

"You're not going to die," Joel said firmly as his voice cracked, and the lump in his throat reappeared with a vengeance.

"I'm close to the gates, Joel," Gunther said as he blinked several times and grabbed his chest.

"They need you. They can't lose you. I need you. You're like a father to me. You're who I want to be when I grow up," Joel emotionally replied as tears streamed down his face.

Gunther put his hand on Joel's cheek, and Joel placed his hand against Gunther's. "Promise me. Please…" Gunther once again pleaded, this time, however, in a much weaker voice.

Joel let out a deep breath and gave in to Gunther's request, even though he didn't want to have this gut-wrenching conversation. He wasn't ready to let Gunther go, nor would he ever be prepared for that. But of course, he would do as Gunther requested because Joel was a man of honor, and that is why Gunther respected him so much.

"I promise," Joel whispered as he squeezed Gunther's hand.

"You are my son now," Gunther fraily said before closing his eyes and taking a long, deep, and ragged breath.

Chapter 22. *Strumming My Guitar*

After selecting the perfect wedding dress, Portia and Gert ended the day with a slumber party at Gert's house, along with Tiny, Screech, and Ice. Despite staying up late, drinking margaritas, and watching movies, they got up early the following day.

Gert met Portia at the bottom of the staircase and handed her a roll of paper towels and a spray bottle of cleaner. "Portia, I love you dearly, but you must teach your dog how to not relieve himself on my oriental rug!"

Portia laughed, took the spray bottle and paper towels, and cleaned up the mess. As she disinfected the area, the young pup watched with embarrassment, and Tiny popped his head out of Portia's robe pocket. Meanwhile, Screech judgmentally sat at the top of the stairs as he looked down on them all.

Portia went to the kitchen to wash her hands and was greeted by the glorious scent of Gert preparing their morning coffee.

"Have you seen the news?" Gert asked as she handed Portia a mug.

"Yes, I saw the arctic storm on the weather app. Gunther will probably go the opposite direction and wait it out at Louis Ridge," Portia replied.

"I haven't heard from Gunther. I usually hear from him twice a day. He didn't call last night. He always calls me before I go to bed," Gert said concernedly.

"I talked to Gunther and Joel mid-morning yesterday. Have you tried calling him?" Portia asked.

"I called multiple times. No answer. I'm so worried," Gert responded.

Unexpectedly, the doorbell rang, startling them to the point that Portia spilled her coffee. Ice went berserk while Tiny climbed out of Portia's pocket and sat on her shoulder.

"It's 5:15 a.m. What the heck?" Portia exclaimed as she and Gert went to the foyer.

When Gert opened the door, she and Portia were shocked to see a familiar man in a Coast Guard uniform.

"Are you Gert Alexander?" he asked.

"Yes, and this is my niece Katerina. She owns the Alexandria," Gert explained.

"I'm Captain Martin. The Alexandria has fallen off the radar. We haven't had any contact since yesterday afternoon. Have you heard from them?" the captain asked.

"I haven't talked to Gunther since yesterday morning," Gert replied as she fretfully placed her hand over her quivering mouth.

"What about the EPIRB? It was registered," Portia asked.

"There have been no signals transmitted to the satellite. Captain Babanin and Captain Smith were in contact with the Alexandria but hadn't heard anything since yesterday afternoon, so they called it in. The arctic storm has picked up speed, so we can't send out search and rescue units until conditions improve. The Windswept Belle and Mariah Leigh just came back into port. The Aleutian Hero and Diesel King are waiting it out," Captain Martin explained.

"So, are you saying you think the Alexandria sank?" Gert asked.

"It's the most likely outcome, especially if they were in Satan's Expanse. It's very rare for vessels to lose all radio contact and signal and return home. Typically, the Emergency Position Indicating Radio Beacon alerts us. But, as I said, we will send out the search and rescue air and sea teams when the storm passes and see what we can find. I can't give you false hope," the captain said.

"The last time I saw you, you came and told me my son and brother-in-law were dead," Gert said sadly.

Portia's heart dropped to a dark abyss beneath her feet. Everything around her warped. Her vision blurred, and she couldn't tell if her ears were ringing or if she heard static. She felt so utterly shattered and hopeless, and her heart stopped as if she couldn't breathe. Suddenly, Gert's voice interrupted Portia's thoughts and brought her back to the conversation.

"Thank you, Captain," Gert found the strength to say.

"I'm very sorry," he said before leaving.

"I don't believe they are gone. I won't believe it! I just lost my son! I will not lose my husband too! I will not lose the entire crew and your fiancée!" Gert exclaimed as she angrily slammed the door.

Portia's heart ached as she reached for Gert's hands. "I don't want to lose them either. But they are off the radar. I don't understand why there is no EPIRB signal," Portia choked.

"They are coming home! They have to! I won't accept anything else! I won't!" Gert yelled.

Portia's eyes filled so full she couldn't see, and hot tears scalded her cheeks. "I can't lose Joel! We just found each other. I can't lose Gunther and the crew. They are our family! This can't be happening again, Aunt Gert. It can't!"

"They are coming home," Gert whispered, then hugged Portia.

JOEL STARED AT GUNTHER'S PALE FACE as the ailing captain took another haggard breath, but his hand dropped from Joel's cheek this time.

"No!" Joel sobbed.

Suddenly, Gunther's eyes popped open, and color returned to his face. "Get ahold of yourself, boy! I ain't dead yet. Who's steering the boat?"

"Bubba," Joel muttered.

"Well, he's doing a terrible job!" Gunther said as loud as he could, breathless from the exertion. He took another deep breath before continuing, "You're the captain now. You heading to Louis Ridge or going home?"

"Going home. We need to get you, Kirk, and Nick to the hospital as soon as possible. We can't risk waiting."

"I trust your judgment," Gunther said as he raised his hand and patted Joel on the cheek again.

Joel smiled weakly while his heart burst with emotion.

"Get back to the helm, boy!" Gunther insisted, but he again got winded and couldn't speak for a moment. And Joel's heart sank once again. After a few deep breaths, Gunther found the energy to continue, "I love you, boy."

Gunther's words struck a chord deep within Joel's heart because this was something he hadn't had since his childhood. Joel's eyes glittered as he squeezed Gunther's hand. "I love you too, Captain."

"Okay, now that's over with. Get out of here and bring us home. And if I don't make it, you're a good kid; don't screw up!"

"Yes, Captain." Joel laughed as he stood up. He looked at Gunther, hoping this wasn't his last time seeing him alive.

When Joel entered the wheelhouse, he sniffled and didn't say anything. Bubba stood up and moved out of the captain's chair.

"Hey man, you look like you need a hug," Bubba said.

"Step to the side," Gunther's words echoed in Joel's mind, and he couldn't help but smile.

"Thanks, man. I'm all right. Please stay with Gunther. I don't want him to be alone. We are getting ready to go full throttle. We will outrun this storm, plow right into it, Satan's Expanse, or both. There's no telling," Joel replied.

Squinting from the rising sun, Joel put his hand out in front of him to double-check their course, just as Gunther had done earlier. The captain's intuition was a gift from God, and Joel knew if he always followed his gut, he would be doing the right thing.

Bubba patted Joel on the shoulder, then left the wheelhouse to go be with Gunther.

AFTER BREAKFAST, Portia and Gert went to the Port House to do anything they could to keep busy until they learned the fate of the Alexandria's crew. The bar's large-screen television played the local weather station for arctic-storm updates as they cleaned the floor-to-ceiling windows and mopped the floors. And to top off the cleaning frenzy, Gert polished the jukebox while Portia added extra shine to the brass poles that she twirled around way too frequently.

Eventually, Portia went upstairs to freshen up. Her outlandish wardrobe made her feel like a million bucks whenever she felt down. Since it was early in the day, she kept her attire somewhat lowkey, opting for a leather vest, blue jeans, and the flat, thigh-high leather boots that she wore the day she and Joel went to Akutan.

Portia teased her hair, put on some blush, applied red gloss to her puffy lips, and sprayed herself with perfume. She stared at herself in the mirror, trying not to succumb to a surge of emotion. There was no reason to believe the Alexandria had foundered just yet, so heads needed to be held high. After calming her feelings and being satisfied with her appearance, Portia cracked a slight smile, looked at her engagement ring, and pulled it close to her heart. She went downstairs to meet Gert in the kitchen, where cornbread and chili were in process, so Portia reached for her apron and got to work.

By 10:30 a.m., Portia retreated to the bar with Tiny on her shoulder. She unlocked the Port House door and was shocked to see a line of customers waiting patiently outside. She graciously greeted them because she knew they didn't come for the cornbread and chili; they came to support the Alexander family.

Pete entered first and hugged her. "They will be coming home,

Portia. You and I both know that equipment is unreliable and can fail. There's been many a lightning strike or ice buildup that has paralyzed communications. Gunther has been on these waters his entire life and knows his way home with his eyes closed. You remember that. Where's that gorgeous redhead?"

"Aunt Gert is putting the final touches on the chili. Make yourself at home, and we'll get you all fixed up. Thank you, Pete."

Portia's bandmates were next in line; she knew she could always count on them and that some healing music would be in their future. As they entered, Rhonda, Ted, and Leonard hugged her, knowing there wasn't anything they could say to fix the current situation, but they knew their presence was what she needed.

Rhonda sat next to Pete, and he promptly looked her up and down. "You're looking mighty fine today, Rhonda," he said flirtatiously.

She didn't miss a beat. "Shhh, Pete, we have to quit meeting like this."

"I'm gonna steal her away from you," Pete insisted as he elbowed Ted in the ribs. Then Pete burped, which prompted him to retrieve a bottle of liquid antacid from his pocket. He promptly took a swig like it was a flask of whiskey. "Bring on the chili!"

Ted chuckled and shook his head. "We do request that you keep the flatulence to a minimum."

"Hey, when you're my age, you never trust a…" Pete began.

"Okay, this conversation is in the crapper. I think we need a subject change," Leonard said with a laugh as he sat down.

Looking particularly out of sorts, Old Al walked in and hugged Portia. He came to the one place where he knew everyone would understand, for he also waited for an update on the Alexandria. Kirk was his son, and despite their estranged relationship, Old Al loved the miserable brute and wanted his boy to come home.

Old Al didn't need to say anything; Portia knew how he felt. She kissed him on the cheek and motioned for him to sit with the group. Tiny jumped to his shoulder and then jumped on the bar top, landing in Joel's Navy hat. Portia sadly smiled and then filled frosted mugs with root beer for everyone.

Old Al lifted his mug. "To the Alexandria's crew! May you find your way home safely."

They all clanged their mugs and took a sip of Gunther's newly preferred libation.

Gert appeared with a huge tray of cornbread and chili. Portia helped her steady the tray on a stand. Then she handed out napkins and utensils while Gert served the food.

"Please eat with us, Gert," Pete began. "I saved you a seat next to me!"

"Thank you, darling!" Gert appreciatively exclaimed.

The chatter was immediately reduced when the townsfolk diverted their attention to the TV for breaking news. "More now on the arctic storm churning up the Bering Sea. It's moving toward Unalaska and Akutan Islands. We are expecting 50- to 60-foot swells and 115-mile-per-hour winds. The Mariah Leigh and Windswept Belle have returned safely to the Port of Aleutia. The Bering Sea Lady and the Aleutian Hero have headed in the opposite direction and will be waiting out the storm. We haven't had any radio contact with the Alexandria in 24 hours. Conditions are deteriorating by the minute. At this point, no search and recovery teams can go out to see if they can locate a wreckage."

The newscaster's callous words shot through Portia's heart, and Gert dropped a bowl of chili, which shattered and splattered in a 10-foot diameter. Gert went down to her knees, and tears streamed down her face. Ted and Old Al rushed over to clean up the mess while Portia helped Gert stand and led her to the seat next to Pete.

"I'll finish serving the food. Portia, take a seat. We got this," Rhonda said as she jumped up to help.

"Thank you, everyone," Portia responded as she sat next to Gert and squeezed her hand. As their dear friends scurried about the bar to help, Portia looked out the window and saw a beautiful, yet sad, lone female eagle along the shoreline. She smiled and wondered if that was the same eagle she petted on Mount Ballyhoo when the Alexandria departed.

After a minute or two, the eagle took flight, dove down to the water, and caught a fish before flying up to the mountaintop to eat it.

As the day went on, Portia watched the kindness of her friends shine bright. They stayed until the evening hours as more townsfolk came and went, including Lora and her balding husband, Dr. Sampson, the reverend, and Zac.

"I know Gunther, and I know one thing for sure. An arctic storm will not take him down. He's been through them before and will be through them again. Keep your head up, kid. Your uncle and fiancée are coming home," Zac said before kissing Portia.

"Thank you, Zac. That means a lot," Portia replied as she held the door for him.

At half-past eight, after everyone left, Gert went upstairs to rest with the critters. Portia wasn't ready to veg out for the evening because customers could still linger in. She sat at the bar, picked up Joel's Navy hat, and put it on. Somehow, Joel's hat made her feel closer to him; it's no wonder Tiny found it so comforting.

Portia's phone dinged, making her heart skip a beat. *Is it Joel?* she hopelessly wondered. While the text wasn't from Joel, Portia did smile when she saw it was from Adoncia.

Adoncia: I saw the storm on the news. Is Joel okay?
Portia: The Alexandria is still out there. They fell off the radar over 24 hours ago.

Adoncia: ¡Lo siento mucho! I'll be praying. Please let me know when you hear something.
Portia: I will. Thank you, Adoncia. Xo

Portia set the phone down and fought back the ugly lump that tried to form in her throat. She looked at her father's ID bracelet on her wrist and recalled when he had said, "You truly know you hear a good song when the first time you hear it you think to yourself, *I could swear I've heard this before because the song is just that darn good.*" Then she looked at Joel's ID bracelet on her other wrist, and his words once again echoed in her mind as well, "When in doubt, write."

And that is what the lady of the bar did. Portia dimmed the lights and then turned on the disco ball, remembering her first dance with Joel as the Northern Lights filled the sky with splendor. She walked up to the stage, picked up the electric guitar, and sat on the stool. She sang and strummed the guitar, and the melody from her heart transcendentally intertwined with the wind and found its way to the ones she loved in turbulent waters.

THE DECISION TO PLOW directly into a monster arctic storm wasn't made lightly, for the Bering Sea conditions rapidly deteriorated with each passing second. With each cresting wave, Joel's stress level rose to new heights. He respected and feared the sea as he did the Lord, just as his father had taught him, but this experience would undoubtedly increase his reverence for mortality.

Pelting rain, snow, and ice intensified while 30-foot seas grew to 45 feet and rising. The Bering Sea could swallow up the Alexandria like she was merely a grain of sand, an infinitesimal nothingness. To the turbulent sea, 247 fully-secured, 800-pound metal crab pots may as well have been grains of sand as well, for Joel watched in horror as they slid across the deck, over the railing, and back into the sea—lost forever. At that moment, Joel saw his life flash before his eyes as images of his parents and Portia danced across the tempestuous waters in front of him.

Suddenly, a 60-foot wave crashed over the bow, briefly pushing the deck beneath the water's surface. While firmly clenching the jog stick, Joel crouched down low to the floor in case the windows broke, and he prayed that the impact didn't throw Gunther, Nick, and Kirk from their beds. And Joel thought that wave was terrible. He hadn't seen anything yet, for the lawless Bering Sea had yet to put him to the test.

Joel's mother had always said, "Don't worry. Things will get worse. Keep moving and keep your head held high." Her words echoed loudly in Joel's mind as another colossal wave hastened toward the vessel. He did the only thing a captain in his situation could do, something he learned from his father, right before a hurricane nearly decimated the Chesapeake Bay islands.

His father had said, "Son, you can't go around a wave. You can't go around a wall of water coming at you. So, what do you do? You pull back on the throttle and approach the wave at a 35-degree angle, praying to God you don't founder. If you weren't a believer when you left the dock, you will be when you return. And if you make it home, you better thank the Lord for another day. Thank him all day long, every day, for being alive, and go to church and thank him every Sunday!"

Thirty years later, that advice was still valid. Without hesitation, Joel steered the Alexandria at an angle to the monster wave as he prayed and cried out to God, "Please keep us safe, Father! Please protect us and bring us home to the ones we love!"

The ghastly wave, white caps, and foam sprayed over the bow, splashed past the wheelhouse, and crashed onto the deck. The remaining crab pots washed in all directions, and one violently crashed into the wheelhouse window, creating such a loud collision that Joel's entire body trembled. He promptly ducked low to the floor, braced for the impact, and waited for the glass to break and water to come rushing in.

"This is it!" he cried. But to Joel's amazement, the window remained intact, the water didn't rush in, and he didn't drown as he prayed. "Thank you, God! Thank you!" Joel exclaimed with a giant sigh of relief. The Alexandria had dodged another bullet; however, this certainly wouldn't be the last, for the arctic storm and the Bering Sea had yet to show their true vengeance.

Joel stood up and looked at the photos Kyle had hung in the wheelhouse, in perfect view from the captain's chair. Joel was mesmerized by the young, blonde Katerina before she became the brunette bar queen she was today. He stared at her picture and prayed—oh, did Joel Layton pray that he would make it home to hold Portia in his arms again.

Suddenly, Joel saw the most extensive wall of water he had seen yet on the Bering Sea, and he knew they had entered Satan's Expanse. With a crest of 90 feet and climbing, this savage swell would be redemption or death. Joel held on for dear life as he put the vessel into a 35-degree angle to the wicked wave, but the Alexandria fell to her side, slamming Joel into the window while a beautiful melody swirled around him.

SINGING AND STRUMMING HER ELECTRIC GUITAR, Portia sat in her bar with a front row seat to the Northern Lights dancing over Eagle Bay. Beyond the pirouetting silhouettes of fantastical colors, lightning crackled in the distance. Portia got a terrible feeling in her chest because she sensed that the Alexandria was in trouble. The anxious feeling was so intense that she gasped and coughed, but Joel's words echoed in her mind once again, "When it doubt, write." Portia knew he was in grave danger, and as farfetched as it was, she believed Joel would hear her song if she played loud enough. She cranked up the amp and strummed until the music vibrated the Port House walls.

The lyrics came quickly with an exceptionally catchy tune that would've made Kyle proud because it was that darn good. The song in Portia's heart mingled with the Northern Lights and became one with the wind. She prayed as she sang, hoping Joel could hear her, begging and pleading for him to come home, so she could kiss his face again.

The song began with a falsetto and light strumming.

The sea, yeah she'll take you away
But I won't beg you to
Stay away from the lady with your love

Next, the guitar strumming picked up power, and Portia sang louder.

Well, that's okay
I'll be waiting on the shore
Till you're coming back for more
I'll be your lady of the bar
Where I'll be strumming my guitar

Portia broke into a wild guitar solo before proceeding with the chorus, which was improvisation at its finest. It flowed naturally like rain from a cloud, transcendentally uniting her music with the sea and the wind. As Portia began to sing the chorus, Gert sat down at the keyboard and played for the first time since Chris and Kyle died. Like Portia, she didn't need a cheat sheet of musical notations since great musicians can play from their souls. Portia looked at her aunt and smiled, then powerfully sang the chorus.

Let the chords find the stars
Shining above the ocean tide
Know what it's like to love a man
Who hates his feet on the sand
So I'll strum my guitar
Till the chords kiss the stars
Reflecting on the ocean waves
Home to lost sailors' graves
My heart prays you'll be safe
Till I'll kiss your face
So I'll be strumming my guitar
So you won't seem so far
Away

Portia looked at Gert again, and her heart filled with love. She adored this woman who was a mother to her. And after so many months, Portia was incredibly grateful to finally play music with her again. They faced the same pain and reality, and unfortunately, they both knew the hurt and fear of loving a sailor all too well.

Portia continued strumming, and to her amazement, her bandmates came back and joined them on stage. Ted played the drums, Leonard played the bass, and Rhonda grabbed the acoustic guitar—adding the perfect accompaniment to the second verse.

You're lost, in a storm on the sea
I'm so worried 'bout you
Felt my heart stop I'm barely breathing at all
But I look up
To the dancing Northern Lights
Oh I'm singing all my might
I am your lady of the bar
Where I am strumming my guitar

Portia sang the chorus again, with the powerful bass and drums booming beneath her vibrato. After that, she improvised the next section, stretching her vocals further than they had ever been. Portia filled each note with intense love, fear, and anguish.

You got the stars
You got the moon
You'll be home soon
This I know
I know
You got the sun
You got the light
You'll put up one heck of a fight
And come home
Come home

Portia strummed a phenomenal guitar solo as her talent crested to new heights. She sang the chorus twice as her voice floated with the wind and out to sea.

Joel had survived a 120-foot wave in the USS Roland and was determined to survive the 90-foot savage swell that slammed him into the wheelhouse window when the Alexandria fell to her side. And all he could do was pray.

Searing pain shot out of his right shoulder, and he was sure he felt blood gushing from his right temple. Despite the physical pain, and even though the vessel was nearly capsizing, Joel saw a flash of light, like the night sky and sea waters were celestially illuminated. The bright light was accompanied by the sound of an angelic singing voice while the Bering Sea tumbled the Alexandria like she was a puny grain of sand in Satan's Expanse.

Suddenly, the Alexandria sat upright as if the hand of God had reached down from Heaven and repositioned the iron vessel back to safety. Joel knew that divine intervention was the only reason this had happened, and he knew to whom the angelic voice belonged. It was the voice of his beloved Portia, which had taken flight as if it were on eagles' wings like the melody became one with the wind and was carried out to sea, surrounding Joel with her love when he so desperately needed it.

Now sitting back in the captain's seat, blood gushing from his temple and pain running out of his shoulder and shooting down his arm, Joel looked ahead and saw a break in the clouds where the moon and the stars shone in all their ethereal grandeur. Suddenly, a flash of light preceded the majestic aurora borealis as bright yellow and golden hues fluoresced into a cross. The celestial phenomenon continued as the whirling golden shades swirled into the silhouettes of two eagles flying side by side into oblivion.

After the Northern Lights dissipated, a moonbeam shone down through the break in the clouds and illuminated the Alexandria. Joel clutched the jog stick and followed the light, for God was leading them home. And even though colossal waves crashed all around the vessel, the Alexandria remained unharmed as she traveled on a steady path through Satan's Expanse.

After several hours, the break in the clouds turned pink and yellow as the parting clouds became illuminated by the morning sun. Thanks be to God, and God alone, Joel was going home! He appreciatively peered into the distance as the Alexandria traveled through the arctic storm with God as her escort, protecting her and the crew—ultimately leading the two eagles back together again.

NOW THAT SEVERAL HOURS had passed since the Alexandria was on her way home, Joel grew increasingly worried about the crew because neither Bubba, Hank, nor Blade had come up to the wheelhouse. *Are they all doing okay? Was the impact of the wave too much?* Joel anxiously wondered as he gripped the jog stick.

After more time had passed and once the sun was high in the sky, Bubba came in and gave Joel a much-anticipated update. "Is everything all right? I thought we were goners, Joel! You're covered in blood. Are you okay?"

"Everything is all right. I've seen things I have never seen before, Bubba. I saw the hand of God, and I heard an angel singing. We are going home! We're not completely out of danger, but we are headed in the right direction. How's everyone? How's Gunther?"

Bubba took a deep breath and gazed down at the floor before answering. Once again, Joel feared the worst because Gunther was in such a volatile state when he saw him last.

JOEL'S HEART SANK because Bubba was always forthcoming and quick to respond.

Bubba took a deep breath and swallowed hard before he answered. "It's been touch and go, Joel. I am afraid we could lose Gunther at any moment. I don't think he will make the trip back, and we can't call for help." He choked on the last sentence.

"Bubba, I just saw God at work. He lifted the Alexandria back to safety, and I have no doubt that Gunther and the crew will make it back alive. Is everyone else all right?"

"Yes, Nick got thrown off the bed, but a pillow broke his fall. Hank is bruised up from the engine room but is okay. Kirk is fine. Blade's mohawk drooped, and he chundered three times," Bubba explained.

"Well, good," Joel began as he looked ahead and pointed at the sky. "Look, the break in the clouds is getting bigger and bigger. The waves are still large, but they are dying down to 20-foot seas. Maybe we will meet up with one of the other vessels, and once the winds calm more, the search and rescue chopper will begin looking for us. Bubba, please get the binoculars and keep watch. Get the flares and smoke signals ready in case you see another ship, plane, or helicopter fly over."

Bubba promptly did as the captain requested, and an hour later, the cheerful chap excitedly burst through the wheelhouse door. "There's a boat in the distance, Joel! I think it's another fishing vessel!" he exclaimed as he handed Joel the binoculars.

Joel opened the side window, peered into the distance, and confirmed that it was one of the Bering Sea fleet vessels. "Excellent. Please watch and set off flares and smoke signals once it gets closer to us. Thank God! They will call the Coast Guard, and everyone at home will know we are safe."

"Tanya, Portia, Polly, Gert, Old Al, and whoever loves Hank, they will know we are okay!" Bubba shouted, then stood at ease and saluted Joel before returning on deck.

Joel laughed and shook his head as he continued looking into the distance. He watched the other vessel slowly get closer and thought about Portia and Gert, who he knew were sick with worry. Soon they would know the Alexandria would be coming home, and Portia would be in his arms again.

After 20 minutes, Bubba enthusiastically waddled back into the wheelhouse to give Joel an update. "It's the Aleutian Hero! Winnifred is on his way! I'll start setting off the flares and smoke signals now."

"Perfect! Thanks Bubba!" Joel replied.

As they approached the Aleutian Hero, Joel could tell she was an older vessel from the late 1970s. With a brand new white and cyan paint job, this iron vessel most certainly resembled a vintage goddess as she sparkled in the sunlight and glided effortlessly in stormy seas. Captain Karchagin slowly and carefully maneuvered his boat until it was a few hundred feet away from the Alexandria.

Since the two vessels couldn't converse, Bubba set off multiple smoke signals and flares. A few minutes passed, and then the

Aleutian Hero's crew replied with a smoke signal, letting Bubba know they had called for help. After that, Captain Karchigan moved into position to lead the Alexandria home.

"Thank you, God!" Joel exclaimed as he increased the throttle to follow the Aleutian Hero. "I'm coming for you, Portia. We will be home soon," he whispered.

BOTH VESSELS PLOWED through 15- to 20-foot seas beneath a blue sky filled with puffy clouds pierced by beams of sunlight. Bubba was in the wheelhouse with Joel, keeping watch for the Coast Guard. After two hours, the deck crew on the Aleutian Hero set off a smoke signal, so Bubba grabbed the binoculars.

"Joel, I see the helicopter!" Bubba exclaimed.

At that moment, Hank entered the wheelhouse. "How's it going in here? Is everything all right?" he genuinely asked.

"The helicopter is on its way!" Bubba excitedly said.

"Hey Hank, would you please take over for me? I want to help move Gunther and the guys," Joel asked.

"You got it, Captain," Hank amicably replied.

Normally, Joel would've been stunned by Hank's sudden disposition change. Perhaps their near-death experience profoundly affected Hank, just as Joel's father had said all those years ago, "If you weren't a believer when you left the dock, you will be when you return."

With Hank at the helm, Joel and Bubba waited on deck as the rescue helicopter approached the Alexandria from the stern. As a Navy captain, Joel knew the helicopter-rescue process all too well. The odds were in their favor, and the wind was exactly right for a direct hoist on deck. Joel stood at ease, not letting the 80-mile-per-hour winds and the force from the rotor wash affect his professional military stance. The Coast Guard was there to serve, and Joel greeted them respectfully, just as he had for the last 20 years.

The helicopter thunderingly roared while hovering for the rescue basket to be lowered. Once the hoist cable was far enough down, Joel and Bubba positioned the basket on deck and helped a paramedic climb out of it.

"How many are injured?" the male paramedic asked.

"Three men. We believe our captain has had a heart attack. We also have a deckhand with a shattered shoulder, and one was severely burned in the engine room too," Joel explained as he and Bubba led the paramedic to Gunther's bunk.

Joel hadn't seen Gunther in several hours, and he was horrified when he saw Gunther's labored breathing and pale, gaunt, and motionless face. Blade immediately moved so that the paramedic could examine Gunther. As the paramedic took vitals, Gunther opened his eyes and feebly lifted his hand toward Joel. Joel's heart sank as he knelt beside him and took his hand.

"Good job, kid. We survived Satan's Expanse. That wave wasn't like the 120-footer you got the Navy Cross for, was it?" Gunther weakly asked.

"It was pretty close, Captain. This wave was at least a 90-footer," Joel said as he squeezed Gunther's hand.

Gunther was out of breath from speaking, but he found a little strength to smile at Joel before closing his eyes again.

"He's had a heart attack and is not stable; we need to move quickly. Where's the rest of the injured crew?" the paramedic asked as he stood up.

"They're in the captain's quarters. I'll show you," Blade said.

Meanwhile, Joel continued holding Gunther's hand, and Bubba knelt next to him.

Gunther slowly opened his eyes and weakly whispered, "I love you boys."

"We love you too Captain," Bubba replied as his eyes filled.

"Yes, we love you, and we will see you very soon, Captain.

You're going for a quick helicopter ride and will be at the hospital soon. You'll be feeling better in no time," Joel reassured.

Blade sat with Gunther while Joel, Bubba, and the paramedic helped Nick and Kirk walk to the rescue basket on deck. Then Joel and Bubba went to Gunther's bunk, and Joel carefully lifted Gunther and took him on deck as well. Gunther felt limp and weak as Joel carried him. And Joel was worried that hoisting up to the helicopter would be too much for Gunther to endure.

The paramedic climbed into the basket first, and Joel and Bubba carefully lifted Gunther into the paramedic's arms. Meanwhile, Blade wasn't helpful to anyone on deck because the rotor wash kept knocking him over.

Considering the high-stress level, Joel had no use for nonsense. "Go back inside. Didn't the captain tell you never to go on deck again?" Joel yelled.

The hoist cable began to retract, and Joel looked at Gunther, who opened his eyes to give Joel a thumbs up for yelling at the insect. Joel smiled and gave Gunther a thumbs up in return. Then Joel and Bubba stood at ease as they watched the basket get hoisted up toward the chopper. Once the basket was inside, Joel and Bubba continued the militant stance as they watched the rescue helicopter fly away with their ill captain and injured crew members.

Joel didn't succumb to the lump forming in his throat, unlike Bubba, who sniffled loudly and had to blow his nose. And Joel couldn't help but smile, remembering what Gunther had said, "I don't know how a man with that skill set can be so emotionally delicate. Step to the side. It's what I do."

This time though, Joel didn't step to the side. Instead of hugging the sniffling chub, he patted him on the back and asked, "Hey Bubba, would you please be co-captain for the ride home?"

Bubba smiled, and he gave Joel two thumbs up.

Chapter 23. *Two Eagles*

ortia and Gert played with the band into the early morning hours, and Gert stayed the night, which was common when the men were at sea. With the Alexandria dropping off the radar, Portia and Gert were incredible comforts to one another during this stressful time, and they appreciated the extra love from Ice, Tiny, and Screech. Since the ladies had a late night, they didn't get out of bed until mid-morning when Ice howled because Screech swatted him.

"Well, I'm awake," Portia said as Ice dove under her arm and trembled. Meanwhile, Screech lay on his back and exposed his fluffy belly fur as he licked his paws while the sleepy-eyed monkey yawned.

"Oh, look how gray the sky is, and look at those white caps in the bay," Gert said as she sat up from her cozy nest on the sofa.

"It's that darn arctic storm. I'll make coffee and turn on the news to see if there are any updates," Portia replied. She turned on the television and went to the kitchen with Screech in tow.

The anchor gave Portia and Gert the update they had been longing to hear. "The arctic storm moved farther to the northwest, missing the Port of Aleutia and Akutan. We had some heavy wind, high surf, and sleet overnight, but that should be moving out soon. We just received word that the Aleutian Hero found the deep-sea king crab fishing vessel the Alexandria. Our sources tell us that the Coast Guard search and rescue helicopter was deployed to retrieve injured crew members from the Alexandria. Since their navigation system is down, the Alexandria is following the Aleutian Hero, and both vessels are expected back into the Port of Aleutia by tomorrow morning."

"Oh, thank you, God! Our boys are coming home!" Gert emotionally exclaimed as she reached for some tissues.

Portia felt a massive wave of relief as she looked at her engagement ring and sighed. Her fiancée was on his way home! But was he one of the injured crew members? "Who is hurt?" she rhetorically asked as she went to the window and looked at the gloomy sky and the whitecaps in Eagle Bay. "I have a bad feeling, Aunt Gert."

At that moment, Gert's cell phone rang. She turned on the speakerphone when she answered. "Hello?"

"Hello Gert?" a familiar man's voice asked.

"Yes," she answered.

"This is Captain Martin. The Alexandria has been located, but Gunther is believed to have had a heart attack. He and two crew members with severe injuries are in a helicopter and are enroute to the hospital in Aleutia as we speak."

"Can you tell us who the injured crew members are?" Portia inquired.

"Nick Peterson and Kirk Henderson," he answered.

Portia knew what this meant. Joel was at the helm and was bringing the Alexandria home. She was so thankful that he was okay and that she would be in his arms tomorrow morning; however, she was concerned for Gunther, Nick, and Kirk.

"Thank you so much for calling, Captain. We will go straight to the hospital right now to meet them," Gert said appreciatively.

"The crew is in my thoughts and prayers," Captain Martin responded before hanging up the phone.

Portia and Gert made a mad dash to get ready. Portia threw on some jeans and a tight sweater. Being the sexy, bar-dancing queen she was, she didn't own any loose ones.

Both ladies jumped in Gert's SUV and went to the small but well-equipped local hospital. Gert parked next to the heliport, and they waited for 10 minutes before they heard the helicopter approaching. As soon as the chopper landed, they rushed up the staircase to the helipad. The wind from the rotor blades made it difficult to stand, but there wasn't anything in the world that would hold back these tenacious Alexander women.

Once the rotor blades stopped spinning and the engine shut down, Portia and Gert went up to the helicopter door along with the emergency room staff. The flight crew brought Gunther out on a stretcher, and they lifted him onto a gurney. Portia and Gert went immediately to his side, and Gert took Gunther's hand. Portia had never seen her uncle look so pale and ill, and she momentarily felt sick. Gunther had oxygen on, and Portia couldn't tell whether he was breathing or not.

"I love you, Gunther," Gert sobbed. "You're home now. They're going to get you all fixed up."

"I love you, Uncle. You will beat this," Portia said as her eyes filled. Her lower lip quivered because she couldn't bear to lose Gunther, especially after losing her father, and she knew Gert would never recover from another tremendous loss.

Portia and Gert walked with the hospital staff as they wheeled the bed toward the automatic doors.

"I'll meet up with you in a bit, Aunt Gert. I'm going to wait for Nick and Kirk," Portia said before walking back toward the helipad. After squeezing Nick and Kirk's hands and telling them everything would be okay, Portia walked with the hospital staff as they took the guys to the emergency room. Then she sent Adoncia a text message to tell her that Joel was okay.

TICKTOCK. IS ANY SOUND MORE ANNOYING? Portia wondered. She stared at her shoes, at the floor, at the walls, out the windows, and at her wonderful friends who sat with her and Gert in the waiting room. Tanya put her arm around Polly, who was having a tough time waiting for word on Nick. Old Al didn't say much, but the concern for his son was all over his face. So thoughtfully, Ted, Rhonda, and Leonard brought brunch even though Gert was stubborn and refused to eat. However, Portia never did turn down a cup of coffee.

After two hours, a doctor said that Nick had a shattered shoulder, and Polly went to sit with him while he waited for surgery. Meanwhile, Kirk was on an antibiotic drip after the doctors cleaned and dressed his burn wounds. An hour later, the moment for which Portia and Gert had been waiting finally came.

"Gert Alexander?" a doctor asked as he entered the waiting room.

"Yes," Gert replied as Portia and their friends gathered close.

"We performed several tests and found two blockages. Gunther's heart is not getting enough blood flow or oxygen. He needs double bypass surgery. The good news is Gunther is now stable, and we are preparing him for surgery this afternoon," the doctor said kindly. He reached his hand up to Gert's shoulder. "You may go sit with him until the OR is ready."

Gert was overcome with emotion and couldn't speak. She hugged Portia and followed the doctor to see Gunther in the Intensive Care Unit (ICU).

After another two hours of hearing ticktock, staring at her shoes, at the ceiling, out the windows, and at her friends, Portia agitatedly sighed. Her back ached because the waiting room seating was uncomfortable, and she squirmed, not so much from the pain but mainly because she loathed waiting for anything. She wanted Joel, and she wanted to know for sure that Gunther would be okay.

Portia threw her hands over her face and sighed again, which sounded more like a muffled scream. The agony of waiting was almost too much to bear. And the ticking and tocking of that pesky waiting room clock was three ticktocks away from Portia smashing it with a nearby lamp.

THE HOSPITAL HAD A SEPARATE, two-bedded waiting room that was unoccupied, so Portia and Gert laid down and got away from those awful chairs. As to be expected, neither of them could stay asleep for long. Then Gunther's surgery kept getting pushed back, and he didn't enter the OR until 2 a.m. At 6:30, Portia went to the cafeteria and got coffee for herself and Gert. They sat in the waiting room, enjoying sunrise over Eagle Bay.

At half-past nine, Gunther's surgeon sat down with them. "The surgery was a complete success. With a proper diet and exercise regimen, we expect a full recovery. He's in the ICU, and Gert may visit with him briefly."

"Thank you so much for saving my uncle's life. Aunt Gert, I'll be waiting here," Portia said.

"Okay, sweetie," Gert replied before promptly going to the ICU.

Thank you, God, Portia thought, then stared out the window for a while, relishing her last sips of coffee from her third cup. She stood up and walked to the trashcan to throw it away. Then Portia glanced out the window; a flying bird caught her eye, so she walked closer to the window just in time to see a beautiful lone eagle land along the shoreline. Its mate flew up to it a few seconds later, and they touched beaks like two kissing humans. At that moment, Portia saw a reflection in the glass of someone walking up behind her. Happy tears immediately filled her eyes because she knew to whom the masculine reflection belonged.

Portia turned around, directly into the arms of the man she loved. She and Joel embraced, their hearts beating as one, and Portia felt like she was finally whole again. She touched Joel's stubbly face and kissed him passionately on the lips. Then Portia discovered the dried blood on his right cheek and noticed that he was favoring his left arm. "Joel, you're hurt. You should see a doctor," Portia whispered as she tried to swallow away the rising lump of emotion in her throat.

"No, I'm fine," he said, then kissed her again. "I love you."

"I love you too," Portia responded, taking his hands and kissing them.

"How's Gunther?" Joel hesitantly asked.

"He had double bypass surgery, and everything went very well. He should make a full recovery if he behaves himself."

"Thank God. We almost lost him," Joel said as he shook his head and sighed.

Portia loved that Joel adored Gert and Gunther so much. And she knew that the stress of the last few days had taken a toll on him. Between the stubble on his face and the dark circles under his eyes from the lack of sleep, Portia just wanted to do everything she could to make him feel better.

"You look so tired. I'm so proud of you for taking care of everyone and bringing my dad's boat home," Portia said.

Joel gently caressed her cheek. "I'm okay. How's Nick and Kirk?"

"Nick has a shattered shoulder, but his surgery went well. Kirk was treated for second-degree burns and goes home today."

"I'm glad they will be okay," Joel said.

Suddenly, Bubba and Tanya joined them. "Portia! Joel! Gert just sent me a text; I'm so happy to hear about Gunther!" Bubba exclaimed.

Portia and Joel turned to greet him, and Portia tried not to burst out laughing because Tanya's bright pink lipstick was all over Bubba's face. Meanwhile, Tanya involuntarily puckered her lips and stuck out her boobs as she put her hands on her hips.

"Welcome home, Joel," Tanya said inappropriately.

Portia hugged Bubba, and Tanya turned toward Joel, going for a full-frontal chest hug. Some things never change. Portia tried to conceal her amusement, pleased that Joel was aghast at Tanya's inappropriate mannerisms.

Gert ran up to the boys with her arms wide open. "Joel! Bubba! I'm so happy to see you!" she exclaimed as Bubba hugged her first. Gert laughed as she patted Bubba on the back and kissed him. Then she turned toward Joel and smiled. "You got everyone home safely. God bless you, Son," she said, then hugged and kissed him. She paused, then put her hands up to his face and closely examined his bloody cheek. "You're hurt."

"I'm fine. I just need a hot shower and a band-aid. Don't worry about me," Joel replied as he squeezed her hands and kissed her cheek. "I'm okay."

Gert concernedly sighed and shook her head. She held Joel's hand and then reached for Portia's. "Gunther is asking for you two."

"Hank is overseeing the offload this morning. Come on, Momma Gert. Tanya, and I brought coffee and some breakfast for you," Bubba said as he motioned for her to sit down.

"You are such a darling. Thank you," Gert said.

Portia took Joel's hand, and they went to the ICU and signed in to see Gunther.

"You can only stay for a few minutes. He's very weak and needs to rest," the nurse said as she showed them to Gunther's room.

When she saw Gunther, Portia inhaled a deep breath; she wasn't prepared to see him hooked up to tubes and monitors. She paused in the doorway and put her hand over her mouth as her eyes filled. Joel gently touched her shoulders and whispered in her ear, "The doctor said he's going to be fine. Everything is going to be okay. Gunther is a fighter. He has Gert, you, and me to help him get back on his feet. And he will."

Portia's soon-to-be husband stood by her, supporting her and telling her exactly what she needed to hear. God certainly had blessed her with incredible men—her father, two wonderful uncles, the Alexandria's crew, and now Joel. Portia's heart filled with so much love as Joel held her hand when they entered Gunther's room.

She slowly walked up to the side of the bed. Gunther opened his eyes, and a smile spread across his pale, withered face when he saw them. Portia leaned close to Gunther, kissed him on the forehead, and took his hand. "I love you so much. I have a very important question to ask you. Will you walk me down the aisle?" she asked as her eyes filled.

"I love you too, kid. You too, Joel. I would be honored to walk you down the aisle. Don't cry. Darn it!" Gunther answered as his eyes filled too.

"Oh, all right," Portia said with a laugh.

Joel walked around the other side of the bed and reached for Gunther's other hand. "I'm so glad to see you. The doctor said you will be fine. We're all here to help you get back on your feet."

"You did good, Son. Oh, and by the way, I'm still waiting for that cigarette," Gunther said, then took a deep breath and closed his eyes.

"That is still a negative, Captain," Joel replied.

"Don't talk anymore, Uncle. You're very tired and need your rest. We love you. We will be back tomorrow morning," Portia said, then kissed his forehead again.

The nurse came in, smiling and motioning for them to leave.

Portia looked at Joel adoringly. "Let's go home."

JOEL YAWNED as he parked his truck at the Port House. He was more tired than he had realized, and it was no wonder, considering he hadn't slept since before they pulled the crab pots. However, his heavy yawn turned into a laugh when he saw that the staircase was a popular hangout. While chewing something tasty he had found by the dumpster, Milena the moose majestically stared at two bald eagles perched on the staircase railing. Joel knew he was tired but wasn't dreaming; two bald eagles and a moose were really greeting him and Portia.

"Oh, Milena!" Portia exclaimed as she got out of the truck.

Suddenly, the two eagles flew away together, and Joel watched in amazement as Portia walked up to the moose and scratched his forehead. "Did you find the apples I left by the dumpster for you?"

Joel quietly got out of the truck and slowly approached the moose. And to his complete shock and delight, Milena let Joel scratch his forehead too. Then the statuesque creature bounded into the distance with an apple in his mouth. Feeling a flutter in his heart, Joel looked at Portia and smiled. He loved experiencing new things with her—including meeting the local dumpster moose.

Portia and Joel held hands as they walked up the steps, with Joel being extra careful not to brush up against the railing since the eagles had used it as a toilet.

"I guess it's time to power wash again," Portia said amusedly.

"And I guess that's my job now." Joel chuckled. "Anything for you, my dear."

Joel received another unexpected salutation when they entered the apartment, and he stepped in dog poop on the doormat.

"Welcome home, honey," Portia said sarcastically. "Rhonda took care of the fur kids while I was at the hospital, but I guess Ice still isn't completely housebroken yet. We are working on that."

Joel was too tired to be perturbed, and frankly, how could anyone be upset with this sweet husky pup? He promptly removed his boot and set it and the mat outside the door. "I'll get that later, or just throw the boots away," he said with a laugh.

Like he had done no wrong, Ice pranced up to Joel, so Joel sat down on the floor and let the puppy jump on him. Tiny also joined the reception and climbed up Joel's arm to sit on his shoulder. Then Screech promptly slapped Ice and Tiny out of his way, so he could put his paws on Joel's chest and have Joel all to himself.

"Hey buddy, play nice." Joel chuckled as he scratched Screech's chin while Portia sat down next to them. Next, Joel petted Screech farther down his back, hip, and tail. Screech immediately hissed in Joel's face, hissed at Portia, and then ran away, yowling and growling. Joel looked at Portia with a perplexed expression and shrugged his shoulders.

"Typical cat," Portia said reassuringly.

They stood up, and Portia helped Joel remove his jacket, ending with her lips finding his. She held his hands and enticingly led him to the sofa. After passionately kissing him, Portia turned Joel's head, so she could get a better look at his temple, which had bled down his cheek. She got a wet towel to wipe off the blood and clean the wound; then Joel closed his eyes and enjoyed her loving touch. After cleaning his face, Portia gently rubbed his injured shoulder.

"Does this hurt?" she sweetly asked.

"Yeah, some," Joel shyly admitted. He wasn't used to anyone caring about how he felt. When he had the flu on the USS Roland, nobody gave a rat's caboose other than the nursing staff that was paid to be there.

Portia frowned and continued rubbing his sore muscles. Meanwhile, Joel smiled and closed his eyes, savoring every second of her love.

"You should go see Dr. Sampson. I'll make an appointment for you," Portia insisted.

"Thank you," Joel said as he caressed her cheek. *My God is this woman beautiful,* he thought. Even though she had no makeup on and hadn't slept well, Joel couldn't get over how beautiful she was, no matter what she did or how she felt.

Portia stretched her legs over his, and he pulled her into his arms, holding her close, never wanting to let her go again. He carefully held his face near hers, hoping his stubble wasn't scratching her.

Suddenly, Portia grabbed her cell phone and started typing. After a minute, she asked, "How about we take a hot shower, and I'll rub your shoulder more? And how does this sound for dinner: prosecco and strawberries, Caesar salad, shrimp scampi over fresh linguine, garlic bread, and crème brûlée? I hired a new part-time cook and am eager to try his food. I just sent the order; it should be ready in an hour."

"That sounds perfect. Thank you," Joel responded, then kissed her on those perfectly plump lips he adored so much.

Portia held Joel's hand as she stood up and smiled, motioning for him to follow her to the bathroom. She helped him remove his clothes, and Joel was more than willing to return the favor. Portia turned on the water, and Joel reached for his razor before stepping into the shower with her. They took care of their necessary shampooing, conditioning, and Joel's face shaving. Then Portia massaged his neck, shoulder, and back. For a moment, he thought he had died and gone to the most beautiful place in Heaven. But when Portia embraced him, Joel knew this was his reality; he wasn't dreaming this happiness. It was real. They held each other close and let the hot, steamy water run over their interlocked bodies.

After some time passed, the water went from hot to warm, so they got out before they got blasted with cold water. They dried off and freshened up at their respective sinks. Portia put on her face creams and perfume that smelled like paradise. Meanwhile, Joel smiled and watched his fiancée preen like an exotic bird. After drying her hair, Portia put on her silk robe and led Joel to the sofa. As they sat down, there was a knock at the door, so Portia jumped up to answer it.

"Thank you," Portia said before closing the door and pushing a serving cart.

Joel quickly commandeered the cart and moved it by the sofa, so they could enjoy their meal comfortably with the beautiful view of Eagle Bay. He popped the cork on the prosecco and poured their glasses while Portia set the dinner plates on the coffee table. Joel sat down next to her, handed her a glass, and gave a toast, which was short and sweet, the only words any person would need to hear, "I love you, Katerina." They clinked their glasses together, took a few sips, and then passionately kissed again. Joel pulled his head back gently, immediately feeling dizzy from the prosecco on his empty stomach.

"You better get some food in your belly! Bon appétit!" Portia exclaimed.

They didn't speak for several minutes as they devoured the delicious meal, and Joel couldn't believe how fantastic the food tasted. "Your new cook is a winner," he said before taking a large, delightful bite of garlic bread.

"I agree. I can't wait to try the dessert!" Portia replied as she moved the crème brûlée closer.

Portia and Joel scarfed down the meal like the eagles eating fish at Spithead. Then Joel reached for the prosecco bottle to refill their glasses. He still couldn't get over how wonderful everything tasted, especially since he hadn't eaten since before the arctic storm hit and the Alexandria nearly capsized. Thanks to the grace of God, Joel returned to his future bride. He stared at her, saying nothing at all, just smiling, lost in his thoughts for his gratitude for being alive, just as his father had told him would happen.

Portia sensed Joel's active mind, squeezed his hand, and asked, "Is everything okay?"

"Better than okay," Joel whispered before kissing her cheek and tracing her collarbone with his fingertips.

Portia felt the same surge of passion he did because she stood up and led him to the bed. Joel was tired, but he still had some energy left, especially after that delicious meal. Once again, they lost their clothing and enjoyed being in each other's arms, this time beneath the sheets. The two eagles glided together, showing each other the deepest depths of their love.

At one point, Portia whispered in Joel's ear, "Loving you makes me feel so high. I love loving a sailor."

"And I love loving a hot Alaskan lady with thigh-high leather boots," Joel responded, then kissed her face and farther down to other lovely places.

For the remainder of the afternoon and night, they showed their love for each other, napped intermittently in each other's arms, and shared the details of their time apart. As the sky turned black and mystical colors danced in the atmosphere, Portia and Joel held each other and peered into the cosmic wonder as they lay in bed together. Joel rubbed Portia's back and enjoyed feeling her resting on his chest, skin on skin.

"I heard you singing when the Alexandria fell to her side, the sea waters lit up like melted gold, the hand of God reached down from Heaven and lifted us to safety, and then I saw the Northern Lights form a cross and two eagles flying together. Then God led us home with a beam of light breaking through the clouds, and the Aleutian Hero found us. I saw God at work, Portia. He led me back to you," Joel said as he stared amorously into her blue eyes.

Portia leaned closer, pressing her forehead against his. He kissed her cheek and the delicate place beneath her ear she loved so much.

"I sang to you that night, Joel. I sat in my bar, strumming my guitar. I didn't know what else to do. I hoped the music would be carried on the wind to wherever you were, like an oldie love song that transcends time."

"It did, Portia. Your voice found me and surrounded me with

love. When I think of an oldie song, I think of my parents dancing in the kitchen, and I always wanted to have a love like theirs. And now, I do," Joel said, then kissed Portia's nose.

"You're my favorite song," she breathlessly whispered as she pressed her chest harder against his.

Joel initiated another long, passionate kiss before he and Portia became one again.

Chapter 24. *Loving a Sailor*

The hospital discharged Gunther. Then Portia and Joel took the Alexandria to Alexander Enterprises in Washington State for repairs. Joel enjoyed Portia's company in the wheelhouse and was thankful he had a woman who shared and understood his love for the sea. And to put the icing on the cake, Portia overcame her fear of sailing away from land as Joel steered the vessel across the Northern Pacific.

"I'm looking forward to meeting your Uncle Ralph. Does he have a family?" Joel asked as he stared ahead at the sparkling Pacific Ocean waves. Portia sighed before answering, and Joel immediately wondered if he shouldn't have asked that question.

"Uncle Ralph's wife, Aunt Belinda, died of cancer a few years ago. They never had any children, so he threw himself into his work. And that's all he does. She was very kind and beautiful. They met in kindergarten," Portia explained.

Joel was sad to hear this. The tragedies this family had endured were far too great; however, Joel knew tragedy all too well himself.

Portia continued, "Uncle Ralph couldn't stand being trapped on the island, and working at sea isn't for him. Sometimes, he will work the red king crab, bairdi, and opilio seasons if there's an unfilled deckhand position. But he loves building and repairing these vessels more than being at sea. He is brilliant. He developed the Alexander diesel engines and sells them all over the world. He's wealthy, but that doesn't mean anything to him. I wish we could spend more time with him. He came and stayed with us after we lost Dad and Chris, but we haven't seen him since then. It's all been hard. Ralph is the oldest brother and always cared for Dad and Gunther when they were growing up."

"I always wondered what it would be like to have siblings. Maybe if I had an older brother or sister, I wouldn't have gone to the orphanage," Joel said.

"I love you," Portia responded sweetly.

"I love you too," Joel replied with a smile.

When they arrived at Port Claus, Ralph was waiting for them at the dock. He had the same withered face as Gunther but didn't look like an alcoholic or a smoker.

"There's my beautiful niece, and wow, is your hair darker! What happened to our little blonde?" Ralph inquired as he hugged Portia and then kissed her on the cheek. "I'm sorry it's been so long since we've seen each other. Kyle would be so happy for you and Joel." He extended his hand to shake Joel's. "So you are marrying my niece. You hurt her, boy, and I'll chop you up and sell you as bait at the Port Claus Fish Market. You got that, boy?"

At that moment, Joel immediately saw the personality similarities between Gunther and Ralph. Joel could've been a jerk in return, but that wasn't his style. He knew that Gunther and Ralph loved Portia and were overprotective, so Joel responded appropriately. "Understood, sir."

Ralph cackled like a seagull and then slapped Joel on the back. "I like you! You seem like an okay kid." Then he reached for Portia's hand to look at her engagement ring. "Getting married! Wow! May you be as happy as Belinda and I were," Ralph said as his voice became somber. "Hey, have you heard from Lizzie and Elijah?"

Portia sadly sighed. "No, but I sent them a wedding invitation. I really hope they come. I didn't tell Uncle Gunther and Aunt Gert. I didn't want to get their hopes up. I know it would do their hearts good to see them."

Ralph frowned, then promptly changed the subject as he looked at Joel. "Captain Layton, I understand you need a temporary deckhand for the opilio season since Nick is down. I'm available if you will have me."

"That's right, Joel. You're the captain now. You make those decisions," Portia said as she took his hand.

"We will be thrilled to have you, and I request that you be co-captain also," Joel gratefully replied.

"I would be honored, Joel. Thank you. Well, let's get you two settled at my place, and I've got dinner reservations for us tonight," Ralph said.

Portia and Joel stayed in Port Claus for a few days, enjoying their time with Ralph and touring the shipyard, which was a real treat for Joel. Since the repairs on the Alexandria would take a few weeks, Portia and Joel flew home. The plan was for Ralph to bring the Alexandria to the Port of Aleutia after Christmas and stay for the wedding, not returning to Washington State until after the opilio season in January.

FOR THE FIRST TIME IN NEARLY 30 YEARS, Joel spent the holidays with family. He and Portia enjoyed Thanksgiving Day at Gert and Gunther's house, and of course, Tiny, Ice, and Screech were also in attendance. Joel enjoyed drinking espresso and watching the parades with everyone while the scents of apple and pumpkin pies filled the house. After that, Joel helped Gert put the hefty turkey into the oven. Then he and Portia sorted cranberries for cranberry sauce and relish.

Gert, Joel, and Portia did their best to make Gunther rest for the day as he was easily winded and had sternum pain from the surgery, so he watched TV with the critters while Portia and Joel helped Gert in the kitchen. And the hard work certainly paid off. Joel hadn't had a homemade Thanksgiving meal since he was a child. He enjoyed the mashed potatoes, stuffing, turkey, gravy, greens, yeast rolls, cranberry sauce, and pies. Gert's cooking would make a skinny man fat in no time, especially with another holiday less than a month away.

Joel thoroughly enjoyed a new Christmas tradition, retrieving a Christmas tree by boat. To kick off the day, Portia and Joel blared 80s music, drove like rock stars to Spithead Dock, fed the eagles their chum, fired up the purse seiner, and went to the Orlov Bay black spruce tree forest. After an hour of thoroughly inspecting every tree in a 500-foot radius, Portia finally settled on the perfect tree, which Joel had to climb and cut off the top. Once he carried the tree, loaded it onto the boat, and powered on the engine to leave, the mighty brown bear Brutus/Joe/Apollo majestically stood on his rock and watched them sail away.

On Christmas Eve, Portia and Joel spent a quiet evening together at the Port House. While listening to carols and hymns, they made Christmas cookies and trimmed the tree as the Northern Lights swirled over Eagle Bay. Joel watched his fiancée sing and dance with Ice as she held him close. Then Joel gently brushed her cheek with the back of his hand and took her in his arms. He cupped her face and kissed her passionately like this was the last kiss of his life. Joel pulled Portia into his arms again as they snuggled up on the sofa with the critters. They enjoyed watching the reflection of the Christmas tree on the windows as the aurora borealis treated them to a spectacular celebration of the Lord's birth while the universe delighted in His holy presence.

On Christmas morning, Joel brought Portia coffee in bed and handed her a small, wrapped box as he sat down next to her.

"Thank you. Merry Christmas," Portia said as she sat up. Meanwhile, Screech rubbed his head on Joel while Tiny jumped on Portia's shoulder, and Ice pounced on the bed before proceeding to shake like a chihuahua.

"Go ahead and open it. Merry Christmas, my love," Joel said as he stared adoringly at his fiancée.

Portia smiled, gently untied the bow, and removed the wrapping paper. She opened the box, which contained a pair of diamond stud earrings and a handwritten note that read, *Honeymoon in Hawaii?*

"Yes, I would love that! I have always wanted to go there. And the earrings are so beautiful! Thank you, Joel!" Portia exclaimed before passionately kissing him to the point his entire body tingled.

"Since I have to leave for the opilio season in January, I thought we could go on our honeymoon when we get back," Joel replied before wrapping his arms around her and kissing her on the cheek.

"Loving a sailor is tough sometimes, but it's definitely worth it. That sounds perfect. Thank you," Portia answered appreciatively as she gently caressed the back of Joel's head, making him feel like the luckiest man alive.

They covered each other in kisses to the point they reconvened beneath the sheets, again showing each other the deepest depths of their love. Joel had never known love like this, and he had never held a woman in his arms who made his body react so passionately.

Portia gave Joel his presents, which were a satellite phone, so they could easily communicate while Joel was at sea, and a photo album of pictures from their adventures. Then Tiny got a new sailor's suit, Screech got a new bed, and Ice got a squeaky toy. All was right with the world. After a light breakfast, Portia, Joel, and Ice enjoyed a lovely hike on Mount Ballyhoo, which ended with a light picnic lunch on the Panama mount, where they saw two eagles flying side by side on their way to Humpy Cove.

At three o'clock, Portia, Joel, and all three critters piled into the truck and went to Gert and Gunther's house for Christmas dinner. Gunther was doing exceptionally well, and his doctor was incredibly pleased with his progress, as were his family members, who were so grateful to keep their patriarch in their lives. Joel grew to love Portia, Gert, and Gunther even more with each passing day, if that was even possible. With two back-to-back holidays with family, Joel was a happy man, grateful beyond words.

After Christmas, wedding preparations were in full swing, for the big day was right around the corner. Soon, Portia and Joel would stand beneath the great golden chandelier with the smiling face of Jesus, watching them say their vows.

As Joel drove into the airport parking lot, he flashed back to the night he spent in Rota with Adoncia, when she had found the job advertisement for a deckhand on the Alexandria, and Gunther's drunken, cigarette-saturated voice had answered the phone. Then Joel laughed as he recalled seeing Gunther for the first time. "Welcome to damn Unalaska, Alaska," Gunther had said with a cigarette in his mouth as he leaned against his filthy, trash-filled pickup truck. At that time, little did Joel know that this scraggly, unkempt man would lead Joel directly to his one true love, which was all thanks to Adoncia, overstepping her bounds and planning his life for him.

Oh Adoncia, if only you truly knew what you have done for me, Joel thought as he walked into the airport waiting area. He recalled the unforgettable day 10 years ago at the Gypsy Market when Adoncia pounced on him like a cat, pressed her perky-bosomed chest against his, and kissed him passionately while Spanish guitar music provided the perfect ambiance. Joel wondered if Unalaska, Alaska, was ready to experience the one and only Adoncia of La Cabaña de la Prostituta. He looked out the waiting room window, and there she was, glowing like a fairy in the Alaskan sunlight as she walked across the tarmac.

Adoncia, you never disappoint, Joel thought as he watched her sashaying hips. As always, she was naturally sensual in all her movements and had a charisma that followed her like a trail of pixie dust. Unlike her Rota attire, Adoncia wore a sweater, jeans, and a winter jacket. Her hair was the same as always though—long, curly, and glowing in the sunlight. She wore large, white-rimmed sunglasses and pushed them on top of her head as she entered the building. Adoncia smiled when she saw Joel. Then she promptly skipped up to him, and they reached for each other's hands.

"No flamenco dress?" Joel asked while his eyes delighted in her beauty.

"No, too frío for that aquí!" Adoncia replied as she hugged him.

"It's so good to see you. Thank you for coming. Please let me take your carry-on," Joel insisted as he took the bag.

"Gracias! Well, I cannot kiss you now, no? You will be a married man, but this makes me so happy. Where is your bride?" Adoncia asked.

"She went to the bakery to finalize the details for the wedding cake. We will meet her at the Port House in a bit. We have a room for you at The Harbor Inn. We can go over there first, and I'll wait while you get settled. That's where I stayed when I first came here, thanks to you," Joel said.

"Gracias, Joel. You look muy feliz!" Adoncia exclaimed.

"I am, very much so."

A buzzer sounded. The baggage carousel began running, so Joel and Adoncia moved closer to it, waiting for her suitcase. A few people crowded around them to grab their bags as well, so Adoncia switched to speaking in Spanish. While Joel wasn't completely fluent, he knew enough to understand what she said.

"Gracias, siempre un caballero. Me retiré y ya no soy una prostituta," Adoncia proudly said, letting Joel know that she retired from being a prostitute.

The woman beside them gave them a disapproving look when Adoncia said, "prostituta." However, Joel and Adoncia continued talking while the bug-eyed woman blatantly stared at them and eavesdropped.

"That makes me very happy. What are you doing now?" Joel inquired.

"Trabajo remotamente. Lo siento, I work remotely doing social media and websites for travel agencias," Adoncia explained as she pointed to a floral-print suitcase, which Joel promptly grabbed.

Over the years, Joel adored how Adoncia spoke. Even though her English was rather good, she always incorporated Spanish words, adding the perfect amount of Indo-European charm, accentuating her accent that drove Joel and countless men wild.

"That's great! You were always tech-savvy. Let's get you settled at the inn," he said.

"Oh, a shower sounds divine! It took me two days to get here," Adoncia replied.

"I know that feeling." Joel laughed, remembering how disgusting and airsick he had felt when he landed in Aleutia.

As he drove to the inn, Joel was amused by Adoncia as she excitedly looked out the window. Just a few short months ago, he was the one relishing in the beautiful Alaskan scenery for the first time. But unlike Gunther's rat trap, Joel's truck was clean, and Adoncia wasn't sitting in a pile of rubbish, nor was there a tiny monkey throwing poop at her. Like Gunther, Joel acted as a tour guide, telling Adoncia about the places they passed as the sun sparkled like gemstones on the bays.

Once they arrived at The Harbor Inn, Joel remained the perfect gentleman, opened Adoncia's door for her, and carried her suitcases. He rang the doorbell, but no one came to the door, despite Tanya's and Bubba's trucks being in the driveway, making Joel increasingly concerned that they were popping tie wraps on the sofa again. His suspicions weren't far off, which became extremely evident when Tanya finally opened the door.

She was wearing a tight, naughty maidservant costume, including a mini skirt that was so short that it should've been illegal, not to mention the plunging top that revealed way too much of her cleavage. Completely bewildered by Tanya's appearance, Adoncia's mouth flew open.

"Oh, hi Joel!" Tanya said as she involuntarily puckered her lips, stuck out her chest, and threw her hands on her hips.

Then suddenly, Bubba's lewd voice bellowed from upstairs, "Where are you, darling? The whipped cream is starting to melt!"

Adoncia's eyes opened so wide that Joel thought they would pop. She became severely agitated. "¿Me trajiste a una casa de putas? ¡Ya no soy una prostituta, Joel!"

Tanya unpuckered her lips, pulled back her chest, and looked at Joel and Adoncia perplexedly. By this point, Joel felt sweat beads forming on his forehead because he knew what Adoncia was thinking, which couldn't be further from the truth.

"Oh, darling!" Bubba's smutty voice bellowed from upstairs once more.

"Just one minute!" Tanya yelled before going up the staircase.

"You brought me to a brothel? I told you I retired!" Adoncia proclaimed in a yelling whisper as she whacked Joel on the arm.

"Ouch! And no! That's just how Tanya is. This is not a brothel. I assure you," Joel replied, doing his best to sound convincing.

Adoncia gave him a skeptical look. "Then why did she do those things with her lips and chest?"

"That's just how she is. She's raunchy, and her boyfriend is upstairs. He's going to be my best man," Joel said, wondering if he should've saved Bubba's introduction for later.

"He's what?" Adoncia asked.

Trotting back down the stairs, Tanya was now wearing a robe, and Joel was exceptionally thankful that she covered her obscene outfit.

"Sorry about all that. Welcome to The Harbor Inn, Adoncia. I'll show you to your room," Tanya said as she motioned for Joel and Adoncia to follow her upstairs.

Adoncia couldn't contain her disgust. "¡Es una vagabunda rubia decolorada inapropiada con labios falsos y tetas falsas! ¡Sus labios y pechos son falsos!"

Joel almost choked on his own spit and did his best to contain his amusement over Adoncia's summation of Tanya as an inappropriate, bleached-blonde tramp with fake lips and boobs.

Utterly ignorant of what Adoncia had just said about her, Tanya continued, "Adoncia, there are other bedrooms down the hall, but you have the bedroom on the right."

That was the final straw, and Adoncia lost it. "¿No es un burdel, sino el dormitorio de la derecha? ¿Y un hombre cubierto de crema batida derretida? Joel, dime que esto no es un burdel. ¡Pero definitivamente está perdiendo una buena oportunidad de serlo!"

Joel was thankful that Tanya had no clue that Adoncia had said, "Not a brothel, but the bedroom on the right? And a man covered in melted whipped cream? Joel, you tell me this is not a brothel, but it's definitely missing a good opportunity to be one!"

"Thank you, Tanya," Joel replied as he ignored Adoncia's outburst, even though she was correct.

"You're so welcome," Tanya began as she puckered her lips and stuck out her chest once more. "Well, here's a key. Breakfast is at 7:30. Please make yourself at home. If you will excuse me, I have work to do."

"Thank you, Tanya. Your house is beautiful," Adoncia sarcastically responded.

Tanya curtsied, then trotted down the hall to the bedroom where Bubba and the whipped cream eagerly awaited her arrival.

Joel shook his head. "I'm sorry about them."

Adoncia threw her head back and laughed. "No worries. I'm just muy cansada! I'm not usually this cranky. This was my first, uh, uh, primer vuelo," she said, not knowing what the English translation was for *first flight*.

"Flying isn't my thing either. Take all the time you need. I'll wait downstairs, so I don't hear them." Joel chuckled as he pointed toward Tanya and Bubba's room. "I'll see you in a bit, huh?"

"Sí," Adoncia said before kissing him on the cheek. Then she closed the door to the bedroom on the right.

As Joel walked down the staircase, he heard giggling and crude sounds wafting from Tanya and Bubba's lair, so he picked up the pace. Once in the living room, he promptly turned on the television to drown out the raunchy utterances. Then he sent Portia a text.

Joel: Hey, beautiful. How's it going at the bakery?
Portia: Uh bakery?
Joel: You said you were checking on the wedding cake?
Portia: Oh yes, the cake is all good. How's Adoncia?
Joel: We are at the inn. She's freshening up from the long flight. Tanya and Bubba are feeling frisky. Tanya was wearing a maid costume, if you know what I mean & Adoncia thought Tanya was a prostitute… and that I had brought her to a brothel.
Portia: LMAO!!!!!!
Joel: It wasn't funny at the time ;-) She's retired now.
Portia: Oh, that's good. … Big surprise tonight! Looking forward to seeing you both. Love you, bye!
Joel: Love you

He scratched his head. What was his bride planning? She obviously had fibbed about going to the bakery, so he was intrigued to see what surprise lay in store.

Joel took a deep breath as he opened the Port House door for Adoncia. Everyone stared at him and the infamous prostituta, no doubt recalling the night Portia first saw Adoncia's cleavage selfie on Joel's phone, Ted appointed himself the moderator, and Joel told his story to the townsfolk. While there may come a time that he would look back and find humor in that memory, this moment didn't fit that criterion.

Joel took Adoncia's jacket and hung it on a hook by the door. He was blown away by her evening attire—a tight, long-sleeved blue dress with a circle on her chest, revealing her substantial cleavage line. Momentarily, Joel was entranced, yet again, by an oval of flesh worn by another influential woman in his life. He certainly had a knack for chesty ladies gravitating to him.

Joel smiled and whispered in Adoncia's ear. "I shall call this your Alaskan flamenco dress, no?"

"Sí, señor. I bought it at the Gypsy Market for my trip," Adoncia replied.

"One of my favorite places," Joel said, remembering the fateful day Adoncia gave him her business card. "Come on. Let's grab a seat at the bar."

Nearly the entire town was there, and for whatever reason unbeknownst to Joel, the Port House was the place to be. Zac had a table with Captain Karchagin, Captain Babanin, Donald, and Captain Smith, no doubt discussing the upcoming opilio season. Meanwhile, Ted, Rhonda, Nick, Polly, Hank, Kirk, and Old Al enjoyed a few pitchers of beer and each other's company, as much as anybody could enjoy spending time with Kirk and Hank. On a positive note, Kirk's burns had healed nicely. Nick wore an uncomfortable shoulder brace, but he was out on the town with Polly, who saw to his every need.

Speaking of flirtatious couples, Tanya and Bubba glowed like the sun on Eagle Bay. They still sickened Joel, and unfortunately, he knew that their giddiness resulted from the whipped cream rendezvous he and Adoncia encountered at the inn earlier.

Love continued blossoming at the Port House as Blade and Leonard sat together at one of the high-topped tables where they enjoyed white wine with a cheese and grape platter. Blade's mohawk was particularly spiky, and Leonard was entirely captivated by Blade's British accent. In addition, Lora sat close to Dr. Sampson, while Alicia and Denny were more snuggly than they'd ever been.

Gert was serving Gunther, Ralph, and Pete root beer as Joel and Adoncia approached the bar. Joel was a tad nervous about this but knew he had no reason to feel ashamed. He held his head high and pulled out two stools for him and Adoncia. When Gert saw Adoncia, her mouth flew open, and then she quickly closed it, which prompted Gunther, Ralph, and Pete to look in Joel and Adoncia's direction.

"Good evening, Gert and gentleman. I want to introduce you to Adoncia. This is Gert, Gunther, Ralph, and Pete," Joel said.

"This is the darndest thing I have ever seen in my life," Pete roared. He burped and reached for his antacid bottle, sitting on the bar top next to him. After taking a generous swig and wiping his wrinkled mouth on his sleeve, he went up to Adoncia and took her hand. "Have you ever heard of a Muscovy, my dear?"

"The bird?" Adoncia inquisitively asked.

"No gorgeous, it's an airplane. I'd love to take you on a sunset flight. Get to know you a little better," the old man said as he stumbled to the point that Joel grabbed his arm.

"You're so kind, Pete," Adoncia began, then kissed the old man on the cheek, giving him quite the thrill. "It's a pleasure to meet all of you. I've heard a lot about you, and I'm happy to be here."

At first, Gunther and Ralph looked at Adoncia in complete shock at her gorgeous physique. Other than Portia, there weren't too many drop-dead gorgeous women on the island, so Adoncia's exotic, movie-star appearance was a complete delight to their eyes. Gunther attempted to articulate a greeting, but his mouth hung open so far that Gert reached over and pushed his lower jaw back into place.

"Wipe up that drool, honey!" Gert exclaimed as she threw a napkin at him.

Subsequently, Gunther gave his wife an annoyed look, took a sip of root beer, and regained his composure. Then he turned toward Adoncia. "So, you're the reason Joel came here. Thank you for sending him our way."

"May I get you two a drink?" Gert asked.

"Root beer for me," Joel said.

"A sangría would be divine. Thank you," Adoncia replied.

"Smart lady! That's my favorite drink too!" Gert responded.

Suddenly, Tiny jumped across the bar and landed in front of Joel and Adoncia.

"Oh, is this Tiny?" Adoncia asked. "¡Él es tan lindo!"

"Watch out! He throws dung and will pick bugs out of your ears. Not that you have any, but try convincing him of that!" Pete warned.

"That's what he did to me when we first met." Joel chuckled.

"He threw mierda at you?" Adoncia inquired, then smiled at the exotic creature.

"All over my Navy suit," Joel replied.

Tiny slowly crawled over to Adoncia and onto her bosom shelf. Then he sat on her shoulder, wrapping his arms around her neck and snuggling his cheek against hers. Adoncia giggled and gently rubbed his back.

"I'll be darned," Gunther began. "This confirms you are part of the family, Adoncia. He doesn't do this with everyone."

"There's a lot of people here tonight. Where's Portia? She would love to see this," Joel asked, looking around the room for her.

Gunther and Ralph huffed and got pissed-off expressions on their faces, so Joel looked to Gert for an explanation.

"She put out a post today that she has a new song. She's been working on it all day," Gert explained with a big smile.

Gunther slammed his fist down on the bar. "That kid pisses me off! She's gonna come down here all scantily clad, exposing things she shouldn't, dancing inappropriately. Gert, I need a real beer!"

"What did you say? You're recovering from heart surgery. You get root beer!" Gert shot back at him.

He patted his shirt pockets like he was looking for something. "Where is my darn cannabis vape?"

"Not in your pocket. I took it out. You can't smoke that in here!" Gert retorted.

Gunther looked at Adoncia and shook his head. "She never lets me have any fun."

"No, she loves you and wants what's best for you. You need to let your body continue to heal," Adoncia said.

"Hence, the cannabis," Gunther replied while Gert gave Adoncia a high five.

Suddenly, Bubba ran up to Adoncia, with Tanya following closely behind him. "Oh Adoncia, I'm so happy to meet you! I'm sorry I didn't see you earlier at the inn. I was, uh, uh, uh, taking a nap. Joel has told us so much about you! Well, not too much…"

Gunther reached into his pocket and threw a tie wrap at Bubba. "Where is your belt, boy?"

"Captain, I had one on today, but I left it at the inn." Bubba chuckled, then blushed.

Tanya took the tie wrap and tightened Bubba's britches in front of everyone and God. Joel glanced at Gert, who shared his mild embarrassment for Adoncia having to witness these shenanigans during her first night in Aleutia.

Then the unimaginable happened. Kirk saw Adoncia and stood up from the table where he and the rest of the gang sat. Never taking his eyes off her, he walked up to her and chivalrously reached out his hand to shake hers. "I'm Kirk, and you are?"

He immediately enamored her, and she eloquently placed her hand in his. "Mi nombre es Adoncia," she replied with her sultry accent.

Kirk smiled, and Joel thought he was watching a bad movie. Then Kirk gently kissed Adoncia's hand and charmingly said, "It's a pleasure to meet you." And Adoncia couldn't stop her cheeks from blushing.

Joel fumed like a freshly fired Tarantula Boss Cannon. Then Gunther stood up like he was going to deck Kirk in the face, but Ralph intervened and gently pushed him back onto his seat.

Kirk quickly sat on the empty stool next to Adoncia, which upset Tiny, who jumped onto Joel's shoulder instead.

"Welcome to Alaska. Perhaps, I could show you around? Show you the sights. Interest you in a mountaintop picnic for lunch tomorrow? I can guarantee that once you have seen Mount Ballyhoo's view, you will want to stay in Aleutia forever," Kirk inquired as if his voice dripped with honey.

"A mountaintop picnic sounds maravilloso. Gracias," Adoncia replied sweetly, completely beguiled by Kirk's charming spell.

Meanwhile, Joel fought back the urge to chunder.

THE PORT HOUSE LIGHTS FLICKERED, which meant the risqué, decked-out bar diva would soon make her grand entrance, and Joel's heart thumped with anticipation to hear another original song by his talented fiancée.

"It's show time!" Gert unexpectedly yelled as she pulled off her apron and frumpy, button-down shirt—revealing a tight, long-sleeved, black sequin top with a V-neck that would stop traffic. She also ripped off her baggy, ankle-length skirt, which revealed skintight black pants and a pair of Portia's thigh-high leather boots. Next, she put on a generous amount of red lipstick before topping off her rock-star appeal with a pair of aviator sunglasses. The crowd went wild because Gert was smoldering, and Gunther thought so too.

"Momma looks good tonight!" Gunther exclaimed as he stared at his gorgeous wife.

"You know it, darling!" Gert blew him a kiss before sashaying her hips to the stage, reclaiming her place at the keyboard.

Joel, Adoncia, Kirk, Gunther, Ralph, Pete, Bubba, and Tanya claimed the front row as the rest of the townsfolk gathered behind them. Joel smiled as he watched Gert, full of life and ready to unleash her inner rock star. *I wonder what my bride has written now,* he wondered, excited to hear the new song.

Suddenly, the loud gong sound permeated the bar, and Joel felt the boom in his chest as if fireworks had exploded. Gunther pretended he had another heart attack, and Gert lowered her sunglasses and glared at him before grinning and winking at Joel. The rest of the band also wore aviator sunglasses and joined Gert on stage, this time with Rhonda on acoustic guitar. Rhonda wore a sequin top that matched Gert's. Ted smiled at Rhonda as he and Leonard took their places, looking extra dapper in their black dress suits with white shirts and black ties.

The gong sounded once more, and the disco ball began spinning. All the men cheered for Portia, which was hard for a man to take, but Joel took it like a champ. He knew he had to share Portia's beauty with the world, and he was okay with that. Meanwhile, Gunther and Ralph appointed themselves the stage bodyguards, standing at ease and ready to take action if necessary.

The song started with soothing sounds of wind swirling, eagles singing, and water splashing the shoreline. Rhonda began some light finger work on the acoustic guitar as the splashing continued, and like a breath of fresh air, Portia entered the bar with Tiny sitting on her shoulder. The wee lad was wearing the new mini sailor's suit Portia had given him for Christmas. When Joel saw them, his heart filled so full of love, feeling so much gratitude for being alive and so thankful that God had saved the Alexandria during the arctic storm, bringing him home to experience moments such as this one.

And oh, is Portia looking glamorous tonight! Thank you, God, for this dazzling woman! Joel thought as his eyes indulged in her lush beauty. A black leather outfit adorned Portia, just as scantily clad as Gunther had so cantankerously predicted. She wore a tight, mid-drift vest that cupped her bouncy bosoms. A mini skirt covered her taut tush and went perfectly with her thigh-high leather boots. She also wore aviator sunglasses, which perfectly complemented Joel's Navy hat on her head. The final touches to her provocative attire included her new diamond earrings and Joel's and Kyle's bracelets. She was voluptuous and ready to rock the Port House.

Portia set Tiny on a stool next to Gert, and then she picked up her infamous, sparkling silver electric guitar. Instead of using the microphone stand, she wore a headset mic. This chick was smoking hot, and Joel almost felt drool forming on his lower lip, like Rufus before biting someone in the arse. The crowd cheered, and the men whistled while Gunther and Ralph looked at the other men like they would pound them into the frozen Alaskan ground.

Rhonda's light guitar picking, along with the peaceful sounds of wind swirling, eagles singing, and water splashing, continued as Portia entered center stage. She held her guitar to the side and lovingly stared into Joel's eyes as she softly sang.

A Navy sailor
Grew up on a bay

Crabbing the summer
Oystering the cold away

Portia pulled the guitar into position and strummed two downstrokes, then moved the guitar back to her side. Meanwhile, Ted and Leonard quietly kicked in on the drums and bass, along with Gert on the piano, as the tempo picked up while Portia sang.

Oldies on the radio
Bring him right back
To a time long ago
Back to his mom and dad

Once again, Portia smiled her sexy grin and pulled the guitar back up and strummed two downstrokes. This time, however, she kept playing while she sang as the guitar ramped up more with each line.

But he went and traveled the world
Lots of people under his command
From what I see staring back at me
I'm marrying one heck of a man

To transition into the chorus, Portia went crazy on the guitar while Ted hit the gas on the drums, and Gert pounded the keyboard. Portia tossed her sunglasses to the side; then she strummed the guitar, singing like an angel on steroids.

A happy wanderer
Found a permanent harbor
Each time he leaves
Yeah, he sails farther

Well, I'm in love
With a sailor
Yeah, times get tough
Loving a sailor
But it's all right
Loving a sailor
Coz he must flow
With the tide

Joel was awestruck, mesmerized, and astonished by his fiancée's talent and the fact that she had written the song about him. He never in a million years thought a woman would love him that much. To be her muse was indescribable.

After hearing the chorus, Joel remembered Christmas morning when Portia had said, "Loving a sailor is tough sometimes, but it's definitely worth it." He smiled, completely blown away by how Portia took moments they had shared together and turned them into a work of art. *This may be my favorite song yet*, he thought. However, he was biased, for every new song of hers would be his favorite, until the next one came along.

"Loving a Sailor" was only halfway through, and Joel eagerly awaited the second half. The tempo slowed slightly as eagle and seagull sounds, along with wind swirling and water splashing, provided the perfect accompaniment to the second verse, which Portia sang as she stared deeply into Joel's eyes and played the electric guitar.

An eagle sitting
Alone by the bay
Watching the water
Just fishing the time away
Water's slapping the shore

Seagulls sing loud
How I long for his touch
Oh how I want him back
But I know he's living his dream
Floating on the waves and with the wind
So I'll wait here waiting patiently
I'm loving one heck of a man

Joel's astonishment continued. Just when he thought he had been blown away by the first verse and chorus, the second verse may as well have been a tornado. He was so thankful to have a woman who understood him and knew he needed the open water like he needed air to breathe. But the reality was the other way around. Joel needed Portia like he needed air to breathe, and he would give up the sea in a heartbeat. However, she would never expect him to do that.

"Joel, I like her a lot! She's fantástica!" Adoncia exclaimed. Then, much to Joel's dismay, she continued dancing with Kirk.

The musical masterpiece continued as Portia sang the chorus again and broke into a wild guitar solo, keeping the dance party going before singing the final section.

Been up all night
Loving a sailor
The best kind of high
Is loving a sailor
He's an old-fashioned heart
He's like an oldie song
That I sit right here and play
While my sailor is gone

The crowd went wild for this song because not only were the

lyrics provocative, but the tune was incredibly catchy as well. *Did she just sing that? Oh yes, she did,* Joel amusedly thought as he felt the eyes of the room on him.

Then he recalled his first night home after the Alexandria returned. The Northern Lights were splashing the sky with wonder, and Joel's arms were around Portia when she whispered, "Loving you makes me feel so high. I love loving a sailor."

My God, this woman is so incredibly talented, Joel thought. He was so stunned that Portia had written this song about him. She described his life perfectly. And thanks to Portia, everyone now knew that she and Joel had *done it.*

"Is she going to wear a white dress?" Pete asked.

"Job well done, bro," Hank sarcastically said as he patted Joel on the back.

Meanwhile, Gunther gave Joel a look from hell, jokingly shook his fist, glared at Portia, and agitatedly crossed his arms.

Portia sang the chorus two more times as she sashayed her hips, moved to the rhythm, and tossed her hair like a supermodel. All the while, the townsfolk danced like it was their last night on earth. Portia wrote catchy tunes, and this song would undoubtedly play in their minds long after it ended because the melody was that darn good. Joel looked around the room as the people danced, knowing that Portia was the reason they were having a ball.

Even though Nick wasn't up for dancing, he was content sitting with Polly, who clapped and moved with the beat. On the other hand, Alicia and Denny swayed like kids at a middle school dance. And then there was Tanya and Bubba, who did many things they shouldn't have. Thinking she was sexy, Tanya danced with puckered lips, shuffling her feet and bobbing her head forward and backward.

Kirk delighted Adoncia and twirled her around like they were doing the tango at a yacht club. Who knew that Kirk had rhythm and could do something other than be a complete jerk? Meanwhile, Blade and Leonard's love blossomed as they danced like there was no tomorrow. In addition to being a gourmet cook, Blade was also a superb exotic dancer, which became evident when he broke it down on the floor as everyone watched in amazement.

"The insect has got some moves!" Gunther exclaimed.

Then "Loving a Sailor" ended with a wild guitar solo—fading into Rhonda's acoustic guitar picking, above the soothing eagle and seagull sounds, along with wind swirling and water slapping the shore.

After the applause and lots of cheering from the crowd, Portia skipped off the stage and jumped into her sailor's arms. Joel felt like he had won the lottery as he held her tightly and breathed in her perfume, where she had strategically dabbed the pleasing aroma beneath her ears. She stared deeply into his eyes and said, "I love you, Joel Layton." And at that moment, Joel knew it was possible to fall in love with the same person—over and over again.

EVEN THOUGH GUNTHER AND RALPH were displeased that Portia had sung about her intimate love life, they smiled at her and Joel, saying at the same time, "Those silly kids!"

Eventually, Joel's embarrassment faded.

"Hey, when are you gonna quit referring to me as a kid?" Portia asked as she hugged her uncles simultaneously.

"When I'm dead! That's when," Gunther replied.

"Not funny!" Portia retorted, then went up to Adoncia and hugged her. "I'm so happy to finally meet you!"

If the townspeople were expecting a catfight, they didn't get it. Instead, Portia and Adoncia hit it off and gushed like two BFFs, complimenting each other on their hair, outfits, and other girlish accouterments. Seeing his best friend meet his fiancée did Joel's heart good. This meeting really could've gone either way, and Joel was beyond thankful that these two starlit ladies were in his life and were beginning a friendship.

"Portia, you are muy bonita and so talented! Cantas como un pájaro cantor. I'm so feliz to finally meet you too!" Adoncia exclaimed.

"Gracias!" Portia cheerfully replied.

"These two voluptuous ladies speaking in a foreign language, it's almost hard for a man to take! This would make a great movie!" Pete said as he held up his phone to record a video. "I'm posting this online."

"Pete, behave yourself! You post that, and I'm gonna sue you," Portia joked.

Pete chuckled, knowing he could get away with murder. Then the old dodger took Joel's Navy hat from Portia's head and put it on. "How do I look? I used to have one of these."

"Suits you perfectly," Joel answered.

Suddenly, Joel squinted as Ted turned the bright lights back on, and Rhonda chose a few oldies on the jukebox to keep the party going. After watching Portia and Gert rock the house, the townsfolk had developed quite the appetite, and Portia's new chef didn't disappoint.

"Okay, friends! Let's head back to the bar! I need some tequila!" Portia loudly announced before kissing Joel on the lips. She swayed her leather-kissed hips from side to side, hammering the floor with those delicious thigh-high leather boots, before climbing one of the poles and jumping over the bar top.

"Joel, she's so much fun!" Adoncia said.

Before Joel could reply, Kirk quickly extended his elbow toward Adoncia to escort her back to their seats. Adoncia graciously smiled and wrapped her arm around his, as if he had cast a spell on her. Joel watched them walk away and shook his head, and Gunther sensed his disconcertment and patted him on the shoulder.

"What did you think of the show?" Gert asked as she stepped off the stage with Tiny sitting on her shoulder.

"You were phenomenal," Joel said with a smile.

"It's so good to see you playing again! This was a wonderful surprise. You look beautiful," Gunther said as he wrapped his arms around his wife, then kissed her on the lips. He picked up Tiny and put him on his shoulder.

"You look tired. Please go sit down. I'll get you another root beer," Gert said, then kissed him again.

"Oh, will you two get a room?" Pete shouted. "Gert, you look ravishing tonight. I'm so happy to see you in the band again. Gunther, once you've recovered fully, you better get your skinny butt up there again too!"

"All in good time, Pete." Gunther chuckled.

Gunther and Pete weren't the only ones thrilled to see Gert in the band again; Bubba could hardly contain his excitement. "We love you, Momma Gert. You look gorgeous! I'm so happy to see you back on stage. Can we have a group hug?" he asked with wide-open arms.

Gunther and Ralph yelled "No" simultaneously as they stepped to the side.

However, Gert wasn't a brute, and she promptly hugged the podgy lad. "I love my boys!"

Bubba's excessive need for human contact aggravated Gunther. "Tanya, you need to hug him more!"

"I did more than hug him this afternoon!" she retorted, then puckered her lips and stuck out her implants.

JOEL RECLAIMED HIS SEAT at the bar next to Adoncia, but she and Kirk were busy, talking and staring intensely into each other's eyes. Joel loathed seeing her with Kirk and would wait for the perfect moment to threaten Kirk within an inch of his life. Joel had already slammed him against the wall twice, and he'd gladly do it again.

After Gunther and Ralph sat down, Tiny jumped on the bar and climbed onto Portia's shoulder. Joel watched his future bride in amazement as she poured a shot of tequila and knocked it back like it was nothing. Meanwhile, Tanya and Bubba wormed their way between Adoncia and Joel, and Bubba struck up a conversation.

"Adoncia, please tell us about when you and Joel met!" Bubba insisted as he stared at her oval of flesh while Tanya licked her lips and looked at Joel.

Joel grimaced, not just because of her gesture, but because of the risqué meeting he had with Adoncia; plenty of details should remain confidential.

Adoncia looked at him and winked before she began. "Well, it was about hace diez años. I was shopping at the Gypsy Market on a hot June day. There's always a lot of fun shopping there, great food, and música. I heard a guitar playing and went to listen. And that's when I saw Joel. He was a strapping young lad at 28 years old in his white Navy suit. Portia, you should've seen him. I even snapped a photo of him!"

"You what? You never told me you took a picture!" Joel replied with a laugh.

"Oh, I want to see! I want to see!" Portia exclaimed as she jumped up and down while her spiky thigh-high boots hit the floor like a jackhammer.

"Yes, I had a camera phone then too. Look at this stud," Adoncia said as she held her cell phone up, waving it around so everyone could see.

Joel looked at the photo and knew it was from that fateful day. The memories came flooding back; he recalled how Adoncia smelled like sugared guava and how her lips felt as they pressed against his, while a warm breeze swirled around them, and exceptional guitar music provided the perfect accompaniment. Joel smiled and thought about how that day at the Gypsy Market led to this moment in Unalaska, Alaska. Every moment of our lives is interconnected, all part of His divine plan, and Joel wouldn't change any part of his life story thus far because it led him to Portia.

"Oh, yes. Please send me that. I love it!" Portia exclaimed as she took Adoncia's phone and goggled over the picture of Joel. "I'm gonna print this and hang it here in the Port House."

Joel did his best not to blush, but it was hard not to do with both leading ladies in his life ogling over his handsomeness. It was hard to deny that kind of attention and pleasure. While on the other hand, Kirk rolled his eyes, and Joel did his best not to slam Kirk's face against the bar top. Fortunately, Adoncia was oblivious to this. She tossed her head back as she laughed, threw her luscious curly hair over her shoulder, and continued telling the story.

"After I took the picture, I went up to Joel," Adoncia began, then paused as she looked at him and grinned.

Joel's heart thumped as he gave Adoncia a discerning look in return. *Please don't share all the details, especially about our passionate kiss,* he thought as he apprehensively smiled.

Like Adoncia had read Joel's mind, she winked at him before continuing and completely omitted the juicy details of that oh-so-passionate kiss and her pouncing on him like a cat. "We had dinner that night. We became good amigos. Joel came to see me once or twice a year for the last decade. When he came last agosto, he told me that he was retiring, and while this made me muy triste, it also made me worry since he had no familia. I got on the laptop, typed away, and found the opening on the Alexandria! Alaska sounded exciting! So, I convinced Joel to call the captain on speakerphone."

"Oh, so you two had me on speakerphone that night! Well, that's just great," Gunther said as he rubbed his temples like he was getting a headache, recalling how drunk and rude he was that night since he was hungover after Gert had left him.

"Oh, Adoncia! Thank you so much for finding this job and insisting that Joel call Uncle Gunther. I will be forever grateful to you. And I love the bracelet you found with Joel's name at the Gypsy Market. I'm so honored to be wearing it," Portia said as she extended her arms.

"Oh, you have two bracelets!" Adoncia observed as she closely examined the jewelry.

"One is my father's, and one is Joel's," Portia explained.

"¡Quiéralo!" Adoncia responded as she squeezed Portia's hands.

"Adoncia, how about I give you a tour of the Port House?" Portia suggested.

"Sounds great!" Adoncia agreed as she jumped up, and the townsfolk watched the ex-prostitute with the oval of flesh and the bar queen with the thigh-high leather boots strut their way to the back hallway.

Joel waited until Portia and Adoncia rounded the corner, and he promptly took this opportunity to have a little chat with Kirk. He slid down to Adoncia's seat and gave Kirk a look from hell. "I'm only going to say this once. You hurt her, and your body will never be found. You got that?"

Joel expected a witty, retaliatory comeback, but one never came. Instead, Kirk nodded his head. Joel returned to his seat by Gunther, who looked at Kirk and shook his fist. Kirk took a deep breath then looked away.

After 20 minutes, Portia and Adoncia returned, and even though they were not trying, they entered the bar like two supermodels strutting down a runway. Even though Joel was sitting, he felt weak in the knees and short of breath as he watched the ladies in all their sensuality. Once again, he was overcome with gratitude for being alive, for God had certainly blessed him by bringing these beautiful souls into his life. Never taking his eyes off Portia, Joel reached across the bar, and she gently placed her hand in his.

Adoncia sexily walked back to her seat and winked at Kirk, yawning as she sat down. "The jet lag is getting to me. I'm muy cansada."

"Okay, I'll give you a ride back to the inn," Joel responded as he quickly stood up, intending to get her jacket.

"You stay here with Portia. Kirk offered to give me a lift. It was such a pleasure meeting everyone. Thank you for being so kind," Adoncia said.

Being the perfect gentleman, Kirk got Adoncia's jacket and helped her put it on. After that, he held the door open for her as they left the Port House. Joel was dumbfounded, and unfortunately, he couldn't do anything about it. The person he despised most was seducing one of his closest friends.

"There's nothing we can do about it. She's a big girl," Gunther whispered in Joel's ear as he patted him on the back.

Blade and Leonard approached the bar and then sat where Adoncia and Kirk had been sitting.

"Hey guys! You two make me so happy! You make a lovely couple!" Portia exclaimed as she reached for their hands.

"They sure do!" Gert added as she cleared away empty glasses and wiped off the bar top.

"Thank you, Portia and Gert! I'm so happy to be in Aleutia now. Leonard and I have some very exciting news to share with everyone," Blade began. "We just bought the Aleutia Bake Shop! Our first order is Portia and Joel's wedding cake. It's going to be scrummy! And I've written a new menu to include sandwiches, cottage pie, jellied biscuits, cranberry-orange scones, caramel shortbread, and Welsh cakes!"

Joel smiled and welcomed this wonderful news. While they were at sea, Blade had prepared some of the most delicious meals Joel had ever eaten, and he knew that if Blade and Leonard were making the wedding cake, it would be delectable, indeed.

"Blade, this is fantastic! I'm so happy to hear this!" Bubba said.

Gunther smiled. "Blade, you're still appointed the cook on the Alexandria! If our team doesn't have jellied biscuits with tea and honey, steamed milk for our coffee, and garlic-basil aioli for our sandwiches, there will be a kerfuffle!"

"Scrummy treats for everyone!" Leonard shouted.

"Scrummy?" Gunther asked as he scratched his head.

"That's how we say yummy in England, mate! Oops! I mean, sir. Uh, Captain!" Blade nervously twittered as his monstrous eyes pulsated.

"Oh, Leonard, don't you just love his accent?" Portia asked.

"I most certainly do, Portia. He makes my heart flutter. Speaking of which, it's time to go. We have to take care of a few things at the shop, and it's getting pretty late," Leonard said. Then he and Blade stood up and put on their matching jackets.

Suddenly, thunder clanged, shaking the sturdy Port House, followed by a nasty downpour mixture of snow, sleet, and rain.

"Oh, that didn't sound good. You two be careful going home," Portia insisted.

"It's really chucking it down out there!" Blade exclaimed as he reached for Leonard's hand; then they skipped out the door.

EVEN THOUGH IT WAS A COLD WINTER NIGHT, young love burned like a yule log throughout Aleutia. Another memorable day had come and gone, and Joel grew happier with each passing moment, if that was even possible. As he sat across the bar from the woman he loved, Joel stared into Portia's blue eyes, still blown away by the incredible song she had written about him, and he couldn't wait to get her upstairs to lovingly thank her.

After the bar closed, Joel took Portia by the hand and led her up the staircase. He slowly unzipped her thigh-high leather boots and gently pulled them off, revealing her tightly toned legs. Not long after, the rest of their clothing fell to the floor, and they again found themselves beneath the sheets, skin on skin, bodies entangled. And just like the lyrics to Portia's latest song, she stayed up all night *loving a sailor*.

Chapter 25. *Twinkle*

J oel had planned on spending time with Adoncia, showing her the island and catching up; however, she didn't need his tour guide services. She and Kirk went on their Mount Ballyhoo picnic, which ended up being much more than *just* a picnic. Tanya was all too willing to share that Kirk had stayed the night at the inn and joined her, Bubba, and Adoncia for breakfast the following morning. When it came to Bubba and Adoncia, two of Joel's best friends, dating two of the most obnoxious people on the planet, he couldn't help but think that Tanya and Kirk should be together instead.

As Joel lay in bed with Portia in his arms, she whispered in his ear, "Perhaps Adoncia was sent to Kirk and is who he needs to turn his life around. Kirk can be a great guy when he chooses to be. Maybe Adoncia will help him reconnect with his daughter too."

"Kirk has a daughter?" Joel asked.

"Yes. She lives in Juneau with her mother. Maybe Kirk and Adoncia will be good for each other like you and I are."

"And that's why I love you so much. You see the good in people," Joel said before snuggling closer and kissing her neck. "I love you," he whispered before his lips slid across her cheek. "Well, I should get up before I show you how much I adore you."

"Are you denying me?" Portia asked with her sultry grin.

"Just heavily anticipating New Year's Eve night," Joel replied as he went in for one more long, passionate kiss.

AS EXPECTED, the last few days leading up to the wedding were a blur while everyone scurried around Aleutia in a frenzy, wrapping up the final details. On rehearsal day, the men decorated the Port House while the women went to the spa. Portia had batted her long, luscious eyelashes and requested that Gunther, Ralph, Joel, and Bubba hang 3,000 white twinkle lights inside the Port House for the reception. Since these men adored Portia, they went along with her outlandish request.

"It's a good thing she's my niece, and I love her. Why does she need 3,000 lights? A few strings would do it. I say we line the room with those icicle lights and call it good," Gunther pontificated.

"Or those netted lights you yank out of the box and throw on your hedges. Botta bing, botta boom, finito!" Ralph added.

"Best invention ever!" Gunther agreed.

"With all due respect, placing each light in its special place will make this room sparkle like a fairyland," Bubba expounded as he yanked up his pants.

Joel shivered and fought back a heave because Bubba had probably just left another whipped cream party, leaving his belt at the inn again.

"Oh here! Fix your britches, so we don't have to suffer!" Gunther exclaimed as he handed Bubba a fistful of tie wraps. "I hope you wear a girdle with your tux!"

Bubba ignored the smarty pants comments, took the tie wraps, and continued making his point. "Captain, I respect your opinion, but those other lights look fake and manufactured. It will look magical in here when we're finished."

Gunther and Ralph looked at him and shook their heads while Bubba used two tie wraps to tighten his waistband.

"Oh, you know what else? We could serve scrummy scones, jellied biscuits, tea cakes, and blood pudding in this fairytale room!" Gunther yelled sarcastically in a fake and embellished

British accent. Suddenly, he got fatigued and placed his hand over his chest.

Even though Gunther was a jerk, this didn't faze Bubba or affect his demeanor. He was never offended by Gunther's sarcasm and occasionally foul moods. Instead, the thoughtful lad had pre-planned. "Hey, Captain, I brought you my camping reclining chair, so you can kick back while we work. You're in charge. You get to tell us if we're doing a good job or not." Bubba promptly set up the chair for Gunther and pointed for him to sit.

Joel was amused and ultimately impressed by Bubba's responses. Bubba knew how to handle Gunther, and it worked like a charm. Meanwhile, Gunther was perplexed but did as requested.

A terrible commotion occurred on the back staircase as Joel, Bubba, and Ralph unpacked the multitude of light boxes. Suddenly, Ice crashed into the room, Tiny tore after him, and Screech ran behind both of them, growling and hissing along the way. Ice frantically put the brakes on, slid across the room, faceplanted onto the floor, and jumped up on Gunther's lap, where he shook like a chihuahua.

"Joel, I hate to tell you this, but your dog is a wimp," Gunther said as he patted the pouty pup. Gunther was only so much of a brute because he pulled Ice close and whispered, "It's okay, buddy. That monkey can be a turd sometimes, and I don't like that cat either."

Screech continued growling and hissing as he ran to the middle of the dancefloor, puffed up his fur, arched his back, and let out several loud, disgruntled meows that made Bubba shiver.

"Heck, I'd be running from him too," Bubba began as he backed up against the wall. "I'm not scared though. I'm cool."

Joel rubbed his temples like he was getting a migraine because he was obligated to do something about the belligerent feline. This cat was no match for Navy Captain Joel Layton of the USS Roland, the vessel that fired Tarantula Boss Cannons, so Joel promptly put on the gear to handle this situation. After putting on his winter jacket and a thick pair of gloves, Joel carefully picked up Screech and took him upstairs as he hissed and yowled the entire way. Once inside the apartment, Joel set down the agitated feline, removed his winter apparel, and tossed it on the floor. Screech promptly went over to the jacket and pissed all over it while Joel watched.

"I don't believe you just did that!" Joel yelled in disgust.

Then Screech frantically rubbed all over Joel's legs, purring and meowing like he had done no wrong. Of course, Joel did what every animal lover would do in this situation. He picked up the jacket, threw it in the washer, and gave the cat some canned food. He told Screech, "I love you, but I don't like you very much at the moment," then went back downstairs to hang the blasted twinkle lights.

I must really be in love to tolerate what just happened, Joel thought, then chuckled. He knew Portia would get a kick out of this, so he sent her a text.

Joel: Your cat peed on my jacket.
Portia: He did it because he loves you. How's the light hanging going?

Joel returned to the bar room, took a picture of Gunther sitting in the chair with his feet up and Ice on his lap, and sent it to Portia, along with a kissy face emoji.

Meanwhile, Tiny climbed up Ralph's leg and sat on his shoulder to assist him with opening the twinkle light boxes.

Thirty minutes later, Joel, Bubba, and Ralph finally unpacked all the lights and removed the annoying sticky labels by the plugs because Portia specifically requested that they come off.

"I'll hang lights around the bar area and polish the poles, so they sparkle and shimmer," Bubba announced with a rascally grin.

"Hey, how about we remove those poles? They piss me off!" Gunther exclaimed as he took a long draw on his cannabis vape.

"Joel, please put lights on the fir trees and place them in front of the windows. Ralph, you get to hang lights on the ceiling," Bubba instructed.

"Okay, deck boss, I was hoping you'd ask me to do that," Ralph said as he took Gunther's vape pen and enjoyed a hit for himself.

Bubba played Rock & Roll oldies on the jukebox, and the macho sailor men decorated the Port House while Gunther sat back and snuggled the pup. He said to one of them every five minutes, "A little to the left—a little to the right. Uh no, that's not right. Move it over a few centimeters."

After four hours, the twinkle light installation had finally concluded.

"Oh, you guys! This is going to be perfect! Ain't that right, Tiny?" Bubba asked as the little punk rocker jumped from Ralph's shoulder and onto his.

"Portia is going to love it. Thanks for your help, everyone," Joel said as he looked around the bar, more than satisfied with the outcome.

"We have one thing left to do. Portia requested that we set up the memory table too," Bubba said as the smile left his face, and he pointed to an empty table next to the jukebox.

The tone shifted from amusement to one of sorrow as a gentle quietness filled the room. Gunther set Ice down on the floor and stood up from the reclining chair while Joel carried a box of memorabilia Portia had prepared.

Gunther reached into the box, sighed, and carefully placed the pictures of Kyle and Chris on the table. He handed Ralph a picture of Belinda, and Ralph somberly placed the photo of his late wife.

"There's one more," Bubba said as he reached into the box and handed it to Joel.

Portia had found Joel's family album, made a copy of his parents' wedding picture, and put it in an antique frame. Joel stared at the photo for a few moments before setting it on the table with the others. Portia never ceased to amaze him. Not only did she include pictures of her father, cousin, and aunt, but she also included the in-laws she never had a chance to meet. Joel fought back the lump in his throat and stared at the table. He loved this woman, and he knew his parents would've loved her too. And Joel solemnly wished he had met Kyle, Chris, and Belinda as well.

Bubba set a Russian Orthodox cross in the center of the table and a candle next to each picture. Joel, Gunther, Ralph, and Bubba stood in silence, looking at the photos and reminiscing about their loved ones, a somber moment indeed for the bravest men on earth.

"Looks real nice, gentlemen," Bubba said, then loudly sniffled.

And this moment certainly tugged at Joel's heartstrings, for his eyes glistened to the point he couldn't see. Gunther and Ralph were emotional as well, so Bubba knew it was up to him to lighten the mood and keep everyone smiling. He promptly went behind the bar and filled four frosted beer mugs with root beer.

"Gentlemen, this calls for a toast. To Kyle and Chris, Belinda, and Mr. and Mrs. Layton! You are always in our hearts. And to Joel, you are the reason we are all together now. To the newest member of the Aleutian family."

"Thank you, Bubba. I'm so happy to be here," Joel gratefully replied.

The four manly men slammed their mugs together and drank root beer as Ice howled like a snow doggie and Tiny squeaked.

WHILE THE MEN SLAMMED ROOT BEERS, the women enjoyed their spa day at the Aleutian Resort, which was Portia's *thank you* to her best friends—Gert, Adoncia, Rhonda, and Tanya. Their morning included a facemask, mud bath, facial, massage, manicure, and pedicure. Then the ladies enjoyed a private lunch with strawberries and champagne on a heated patio overlooking Unalaska Lake, before topping off the spa day by getting their hair styled.

Portia held up her champagne glass for a toast. "To good friends and family, thank you for being here today and always. And a special thank you to Aunt Gert. You have been a mother to me for my whole life. I love you."

Her words deeply touched Gert's heart, and she reached for a hanky inside her purse. "I love you too, my dear."

Portia continued, "Adoncia, thank you for being here and sending Joel to us. I am forever grateful to you. Tanya and Rhonda, thank you for your friendship."

The ladies clinked their glasses and indulged in expensive champagne and sweet, juicy strawberries.

"So Tanya, you and Bubba's relationship is moving along quickly," Rhonda noted.

Tanya cackled. "You're one to talk! You and Ted! But we must get all the spicy details about Adoncia and Kirk!" This prompted a plethora of oo's and ah's from the ladies. "Do tell, Adoncia! Kirk is definitely easy on the eyes," Tanya said.

"¡Sí, hombre muy guapo! He's such a gentleman. I don't know why he's still single," Adoncia replied.

"Because he's been a varmint for most of his life!" Rhonda jokingly retorted.

Portia did her best to contain her amusement because she remembered the lover's quarrel between Rhonda and Kirk long ago. All these years later, Rhonda was still pissed.

"I'd have to agree with you on that one, Rhonda. Kirk was relief captain when Kyle and Chris died. I do have some issues with him on that," Gert added.

Portia understood Gert's opinion and wanted to blame Kirk for not stopping the crabbing as well. However, the Alexandria's crew members were risk takers and decided to pull the pots, despite the bad conditions. Portia had spent the last year being angry with her father and his decision to go to Satan's Expanse. With Joel's help, she realized she needed to forgive Kyle and allow herself to grieve.

"That was a tragedy beyond anyone's control. This way of life is not without its risks. My brother died the same way 20 years ago," Tanya sadly explained. "I was angry for a long time, but nothing could've been done. And we cannot predict how bad the weather is going to be. A rogue wave could come out of nowhere on a clear day, whether or not you're in Satan's Expanse."

"I know," Gert's voice quivered.

"Kirk told me about that night," Adoncia began. "He is devastated over what happened, and he blames himself. But he and Kyle had talked and thought they would get the pots up before the storm hit. Kyle thought the fax machine malfunctioned because the weather update came in later than it should've. Kirk said he didn't think anyone would believe him, so he didn't say anything. Kirk says that's why his drinking has gotten so much worse over the last year, and he has promised me that he will stop and drink only root beer from now on."

"I had no idea about the fax coming in late," Portia emotionally said, then placed one hand over her mouth and reached for Gert's hand with her other. They both took a deep breath, feeling the sense of closure they had desperately needed.

"You know, we all have a past. I was a puta for nearly 30 years. I'm not proud of it. It paid the bills, and it led me to meet Joel. Then Joel led me here to meet you and Kirk. It's funny how things work out," Adoncia said.

"Oh, Adoncia, I hope that you decide to move here. You're Joel's family and part of our family now too. We need you. Kirk needs you. Please stay. I'll help get you a job with the tour agencies here," Portia pleaded.

"And you can stay at the inn until you get settled in your own place or Kirk's..." Tanya kindly offered.

"Oh, you're all so maravillosa!" Adoncia graciously replied as her eyes glistened.

The five beautiful ladies joined hands, each ever so grateful for this time together, celebrating friendship, happiness, and love.

Kyle had always told Portia, "When friendship comes along, hang onto it, treasure it, and protect it with all your might." And that's what she did. Portia looked around at her dear friends and her Aunt Gert. "God is good," she whispered. God is good, indeed.

AFTER A WONDERFUL DAY of hanging twinkle lights for the men and a relaxing spa day for the women, the wedding party met at the cathedral for the rehearsal, then went to The Harbor Inn for a delectable meal prepared by Blade and Leonard, their gift to the bride and groom. Joel had experienced Blade's cooking expertise on the Alexandria with limited specialty-food options, and he could only imagine how excellent Blade's meals would be with all the ingredients at his fingertips.

Joel smiled as he parked his truck at the inn, in the same parking spot where his truck had been waiting for him when he first arrived in Aleutia. So much had changed since that day. He turned and looked at his fiancée, whose hair was lifted high onto her head in a circular bun ornamented with elegant rhinestones. Portia wore a black velvet, button-up jacket with a belted waist and a red strapless dress. And Joel was as handsome as ever in a black suit with a red tie to match Portia's attire, for she had chosen red as part of the holiday wedding palette.

Joel gently lifted Portia's chin before kissing her red lips. "Guess what?" he asked, leaning his head toward hers so their foreheads touched.

"What?" Portia replied seductively.

"I'm marrying you tomorrow," Joel said as he gently caressed her cheek with the back of his hand and then down her neck and chest.

"Is that what we're doing tomorrow?" Portia giggled.

"Mmm hmm," Joel muttered as his lips found their way to that sensitive place beneath her ear where Portia always dabbed perfume. "Well, I guess we should go inside," he whispered.

"Yes, we should," Portia breathlessly replied.

Always a gentleman, Joel opened the passenger door for his lady. He extended his hand to help her climb out without wrinkling her dress or twisting her ankles in the stimulating high heels that adorned her feet. As Portia and Joel entered the inn, they were blown away by the exquisitely decorated hallway, embellished with small fir trees elegantly decorated with white twinkle lights like the ones at the Port House.

"Bless their hearts. This is so beautiful," Portia said in awe at Blade and Leonard's effort.

"You're beautiful," Joel responded as he helped Portia remove her jacket. He hung it on the hook next to the door and continued staring at his stunning lady.

Joel extended his elbow, and Portia wrapped her arm around his. He escorted her to the dining room, which was fit to bedazzle royalty. Pre-lit, white twig trees provided an elegant winter scene that outlined the room. The sound of crackling flames from the fireplace eloquently complemented soft instrumental Christmas carols, and the orange glow from the fire reflected on the glasses sparkling on the flawlessly decorated and preset dining room table. Blade used his favorite red velvet tablecloth, on which he placed a white runner down the center where he scattered red rose petals between four antique silver candelabras holding 20 white burning candlesticks. Antique silverware and clear glass plates shimmered beneath the flambeau light.

To add to the gentility of the evening, Blade and Leonard wore matching tuxedos and greeted the guests as they entered. And much to everyone's surprise and delight, Blade no longer sported piercings or a green mohawk; his head was now bald.

"The décor is so beautiful, Blade and Leonard!" Portia exclaimed as she hugged them at the same time. "Thank you! It's so perfect! And don't you both look handsome!"

Joel expressed his gratitude as well by shaking hands with their hosts. "Thank you, gentlemen. This is amazing. The food smells incredible."

Portia took Joel's hand and led him in front of the fireplace, where she twirled in a circle before pulling his arm around her for an intimate dance. Joel held her close, savoring this tender moment, a lovely memory for the years to come. A few Christmas carols later, Gunther, Gert, and Ralph quietly entered the room, hoping not to interrupt the dancing couple. But of course, Portia and Joel paused the dance to greet their family and friends.

"Oh, please keep dancing. You're such a beautiful couple!" Gert said joyfully. She was all decked out in a green sequined dress, complementing her fiery red hair, teased to perfection. A huge smile was plastered across Gunther's face, for he was delighted to have his beautiful wife on his arm again.

Now that more guests had arrived, Blade went to the kitchen and returned with a silver tray filled with flutes of homemade root beer.

"I like your style, Blade," Gunther said as he reached for a glass.

The wedding party enjoyed root beer flutes and hobnobbed by the fireplace, soaking in the warmth from the roaring flames. But the chatter halted when Adoncia entered the room with Kirk. She was stunning in a light silver dress with long sleeves, an open back, and a slit up to her right thigh. Joel beamed when he saw her; she was still like a fine wine, getting better with age.

To everyone's stupefaction, Kirk kissed Portia on the cheek, shook Joel's hand, and even said, "Congratulations!" Then he turned toward Gunther and Ralph, and the room quieted down to the point one could hear a carpenter ant fart beneath the floorboards. Without uttering a word, Kirk nodded as he shook hands with Gunther and Ralph, which meant, *I'm sorry about what happened last January and for being a jerk…my entire life.* Also without speaking, Gunther and Ralph nodded their heads in return, which translated, *We don't blame you for what happened, but we still think you're a jerk from time to time.* Meanwhile, Gert had a mother's heart, and she hugged Kirk, letting him know she no longer blamed him. Then he smiled and gently kissed her cheek.

Joel was perplexed but knew Kirk was coming out of his ugly shell and was trying to be kind. Joel hoped Kirk would be as good for Adoncia as she was for him.

"Oh, you guys! How about a group hug?" Bubba jovially asked as he and Tanya entered the dining room.

The wedding party was quick to let out a collective, "No!" Then Tanya hugged her rotund fellow, all 175 pounds of him.

"Tanya, you need to hug him more, so we don't have to!" Gunther exclaimed in a yelling whisper.

Now that all the guests had arrived, dinner was ready to be served, and as expected, Blade and Leonard prepared an ambrosial feast. The creamy basil dressing on the spring salad delectably complemented freshly baked rosemary bread with garlic butter. Red skin garlic potatoes, broiled filet mignon, and sautéed broccolini comprised the second course, followed by decaf cappuccinos and caramel shortbread, a traditional dessert from Blade's hometown.

The rehearsal dinner was an evening to be cherished. A celebration of love, life, and family was something Joel had been missing in his life. Now that he had it, his heart was so full that it could've burst into a sea of crystals, like the sun sparkling on Eagle Bay the day he arrived in the Port of Aleutia. Joel smiled as he recalled seeing God's artistry in the sky that fateful day when Gunther first showed him the Aleutian Russian Orthodox Cathedral, and he saw two eagles together for the first time, perched on the Domes of Heaven. This memory prompted Joel to reach for Portia's hand, and he gently kissed her porcelain skin. Tomorrow on a most blessed New Year's Eve, they'll stand beneath the great golden chandelier, joining as two eagles forever.

THE NEXT MORNING AT GERT AND GUNTHER'S HOUSE, Portia opened her eyes just as the sun rose in the east. She was sad that her father couldn't walk her down the aisle, but she had her doting Uncle Gunther to do it. Portia smiled and felt tingly inside as she remembered last night when Joel had said, "I'm marrying you tomorrow." Tomorrow was now today, not just any day, but New Year's Eve, the start of a new life and year as Katerina Layton. So much had changed in the last three and a half months since she and Joel met. And as she lay in bed on the morning before their wedding, Portia reminisced about their time together thus far.

The night she met Joel, Portia was dark and lonely, singing "You Lied" and "On and Off," still reeling from her relationship with her ex-husband. Recovering from divorce was an awful experience for Portia, but it was a necessary bump in the road. Not long after, her father and cousin perished because of the Bering Sea, and a tidal wave of immeasurable grief submerged her. The Northern Lights no longer made her smile, and darkness permeated the brightest days. She changed her name to Portia, dyed her hair, bought some thigh-high leather boots, rolled some joints, and drank a lot of liquor, burying Katerina beneath a glacier of pain, forgetting who she truly was.

Then Joel Layton walked into the Port House and saw right

through the disguise. He didn't see Portia, the Port House bar queen. He saw Katerina, the angel within, and he helped Portia realize that she was still Katerina Alexander and needed to face her anger and grief from losing Kyle. Portia picked up the guitar and wrote "More Than Me," where she faced losing her father and how angry she was with him for going to Satan's Expanse.

Not only did Joel encourage Portia to face her grief, but he also helped her learn how to be happy once again. Portia smiled as she recalled the day she took Joel to Spithead to feed the eagles and how driving on that bumpy road prompted her to write "Country Rock & Roll," where she honed in her style of music, a country theme with a Rock & Roll motor, "a plow that breaks pavement with just one note." She could get down with that country twang, but she could also rock it like a rock star. And who could forget the chair dance when Portia debuted this song to Joel?

Portia recalled the momentous night she discovered Adoncia's text messages, and she and Joel had their public blow-up at the Port House. The next day, she sang "Sail On" before she and Joel made up with everyone listening in the hallway. After that, she and Joel continued spending time together, traveling and learning about each other's interests, passions, and desires. When Joel proposed to Portia in the ice cave, she thought she had died and gone to Heaven. She loved Joel so intently that she couldn't imagine her life without him, which was evident the night before the crew departed for the red king crab season when Joel asked Portia to write him a song. In "Our Last Night," she pleaded with the Bering Sea to bring him home safely.

After the Blessing of the Fleet Ceremony, Portia grabbed a bottle of brandy and her electric guitar, then drove like a mad woman to the Panama mount on Mount Ballyhoo, where she wrote "I'd Rather Die." Despite the emotions she felt, this was a therapeutic experience because she faced her fear of loving a sailor—fearing for

Joel and the crew's fate during the red king crab season. The anguish of loving a sailor was unbearable some days, but Joel's love was worth it.

An arctic storm reared its ugly head shortly after that, putting the Alexandria in jeopardy. Portia and Gert understandably feared the worst when all communications with the vessel were lost. During Portia's darkest hour, Joel's words echoed in her mind, "When in doubt, write." On the Port House stage, she wrote "Strumming My Guitar," praying that the wind would carry her music to the Bering Sea to Joel, who was in a capsizing vessel. The good Lord was watching out for them that night and brought the two eagles back together again.

Once her fiancée was safely in her arms again, Portia wrote "Loving a Sailor." She sang about Joel growing up as a fisherman's son and reminisced about his parents dancing to oldies music. While showing her love for Joel and how she would never take his love of the sea away from him, she also noted that loving a sailor was "the best kind of high" and that Joel was the most incredible song she would ever sing.

"Wait!" Portia exclaimed as she sat up in bed and counted on her fingers. She had sung nine songs since she had met Joel, which was one song short of an album; she needed one more to complete the first installment of their love story. Portia wanted to write one for the wedding reception but honestly hadn't had the time or the big moment of creativity to do it.

Suddenly, inspiration hit her like an avalanche. She jumped out of bed and ran down the hall to Gert and Gunther's music room. The bar-dancing queen grabbed an electric guitar and a notepad, spent two hours writing a musical masterpiece, and then texted it to her band members along with the following message, *Start practicing for the reception. The disco light will be spinning tonight. We are gonna rock everyone with a Port House show. All right!*

Completely satisfied with her newest magnum opus, Portia skipped downstairs to join Gert and Gunther for coffee in the living room.

"Well, hello there. I got your text. The song is amazing! I'll be sure to practice a few times before we leave," Gert said as she stood up from the sofa and hugged her niece. "I'll get you a cup of coffee."

"Thank you," Portia gratefully replied.

"I heard from Joel this morning. Your tomcat pissed all over the pant leg of his Navy suit, so Joel is at the cleaners right now," Gunther said amusedly. He attempted to laugh but ended up coughing instead. Since the heart surgery, he had quit smoking, and thankfully his coughing fits were becoming less frequent and less intense.

Portia and Joel weren't having contact until they saw each other at the cathedral, so this was the first time she had heard of the cat-piss-pant debacle. "Well, at least Ice didn't poop," Portia said.

"Oh, he did. Joel stepped in it on his way out the door to the cleaners," Gunther explained.

"I hope he still shows up at the cathedral," Portia jokingly said.

"Honey, he will be there," Gert reassured as she handed Portia a coffee mug. "That man loves you to the moon and back. A little cat piss and a pile of puppy pucky won't deter him."

"Thank you," Portia responded, then laughed as she took the coffee. She savored her first sip because Gert always made coffee exactly right. Portia enjoyed the warmth of the mug on her hands and looked down at her beautiful engagement ring, which twinkled in the morning sunlight beaming in from the large living room windows overlooking Captain's Bay. Then Portia looked up, noticing that she was standing in front of an antique mirror on the wall. She looked back down at her ring and then back to her reflection in the mirror. The brunette woman staring back at her wasn't *her*. Joel would be marrying Katerina today, not Portia.

"Aunt Gert!" Portia exclaimed.

"What is it, honey?" Gert asked as she rushed over to her.

"It's time to go back to Katerina," she said as her eyes filled.

Gert gently ran her hand down the back of her head. "That makes me very happy. I'll mix the dye."

Gunther couldn't contain his enthusiasm. "Finally! And get rid of those leather outfits and those inappropriate boots!"

"Not a chance, Uncle. The boots are here to stay!" Portia retorted.

AFTER A FEW HOURS of panicking over the cat-piss-soaked Navy pants, Joel returned from the dry cleaners, only to find another gift from Ice, and Tiny shrieking on top of the fridge while Screech paced like a panther. Joel took it like a champ though. His life was changing forever, and for the better, even if it did include cat, dog, and monkey excrement from time to time. After he cleaned up Ice's dog pile, Joel promptly took a shower and shaved his face.

He threw on a pair of jeans and a flannel shirt until it was time to get dressed and head over to the cathedral. Joel's stomach growled, and at that moment, a knock at the door brought a welcoming surprise; Bubba was there with subs and root beer.

"I thought you would be hungry and need some company, passing the time until the ceremony," Bubba said. Then Tiny immediately ran up, climbed his leg, and sat on his shoulder.

"Thank you, man. You read my mind and my stomach!" Joel said appreciatively.

Joel was so thankful to have such a good friend, for Bubba certainly lived up to his title of best man. They devoured their subs while Ice begged for scraps, Tiny squeaked because he wasn't the center of attention, and Screech paced around the table, glaring at them all. After a couple of hours, Bubba returned to the inn to get dressed, and Joel put on his Navy uniform for the final time.

Chapter 26. *Golden*

Joel smiled as he parked his truck at the cathedral. Even though he had been there many times, he was still blown away by the beautiful simplicity of the Byzantine structure. He always felt God's presence when the sunlight celestially shimmered on the golden crosses where two bald eagles were perched. A gentle breeze caressed their majestic feathers and simultaneously filled Joel's lungs with vitality as God welcomed him to holy ground. Joel had always loved seeing eagles, but since he moved to the Port of Aleutia, whenever he saw two eagles together, he immediately thought of Portia. And he remembered what Portia had told him about Kyle and Penny seeing two eagles together as well, and Joel knew that this was most definitely a sign from God. And here Joel was on a most blessed New Year's Eve getting ready to be bound to his eagle forever.

Joel arrived early, so he could pay his respects to Portia's father and cousin, then spend some time alone in the nave. As he entered the cemetery, celestial hues glimmered on the Watermen's Memorial, and he felt a calming peace as a presence joined him. He read through the names on the plaque until he saw *Kyle Alexander*. "I promise I'll take good care of your daughter. I'll never hurt her. I'll love her until my last breath," Joel said. Then suddenly, a bald eagle landed on the memorial stone. The regal creature had a loving expression in its eyes, and Joel knew that God was letting him know that Kyle had given Portia and Joel his blessing. "God is good," Joel whispered as he and the eagle shared this exceptional moment. Not long after, the exalted bird took flight, gliding with the wind toward the snow-capped peaks sparkling beneath the sun. After the lone eagle flew away, Joel walked through the rows of Russian Orthodox crosses until he found Chris's grave. He paused and said a prayer for the Alexander family, who would undoubtedly be missing Chris and Kyle on this momentous day in Portia's life.

"Well, it's time to get married," Joel said as he walked toward the cathedral doors. A quiet peacefulness greeted him when he entered the nave, where magnificent sunrays illuminated swirling plumes of incense. Joel inhaled deeply, letting the heavenly scent invigorate his soul as he looked around, so pleased by the eloquent setting for the ceremony, with no flowers or embellishments other than candles flickering beneath the icons and on several floor candelabras. Rows of antique wooden chairs were on both sides of the room, leaving an open aisle leading straight to the icon of Jesus beneath the great golden chandelier where Portia and Joel would exchange vows.

The quiet peacefulness continued, with the only sound being Joel's footsteps on sacred ground. When he approached the icon of Jesus Christ, the holiness of the silence was indescribable, for Joel had never felt God's presence as intently as he did at that moment. There is just something about the blessedness of being the only person standing before the altar of God that causes a deep reflection into one's soul. Joel relished in this moment of worship and reflection while he venerated the icon of Jesus and kissed His holy feet.

As he stood in Unalaska, Alaska, getting ready to embark on his most incredible adventure yet, Joel's life flashed before his eyes, beginning with his upbringing as a fisherman's son on the Chesapeake Bay, where his love for the open water began. Joel recalled his fondest memories of his parents dancing in the kitchen and his father quizzing him on the books of the Bible. And finally, the saddest memory of all flooded Joel's mind like a tidal wave as he recalled the day he was picked up from school by a social worker after his parents died during the oystering accident. A lump formed in Joel's throat as he relived the devastation of living in an orphanage for the remainder of his childhood and teenage years. He took a ragged breath as he once again felt the sorrow of being a young man without a family and whose only chance for succeeding was to join the service. Despite the sadness that led to this career, Joel thoroughly enjoyed his Navy years, traveling the world and climbing the ranks to become the revered captain of a guided-missile destroyer.

Everything ends eventually. He needed to find out who Joel Layton truly was, not Captain Joel Layton of the USS Roland, so he chose retirement to see where life would take him. Joel smiled as he recalled his visits with Adoncia over the past 10 years. He chuckled when he remembered that pivotal night when he visited Rota for the last time and bought himself a one-way ticket to Alaska, where he met Portia. Adoncia led Joel to his new family, and he would be forever grateful for the blessings this retired prostituta brought into his life.

Suddenly, the cathedral doors opened, and the sound of high heels click-clacked down the aisle. Joel turned to see who had joined him and was greeted by Adoncia's smiling face. She was magnificent as always, such a delight and such a blessing to all who knew her. Wearing a tight, navy-blue, turtleneck dress with a matching lace scarf covering her brunette curls, Adoncia walked up to Joel with her hands out, and Joel placed his hands in hers, then kissed her on the cheek. "Thank you for coming," he said, then motioned for her to sit with him in the first row.

"I brought you a gift," Adoncia said as she reached into her purse and handed Joel a golden box, which was adorned with a heavenly portrait of Jesus's smiling face, closely resembling the painting inside the Dome of Heaven. Joel opened the box and was pleasantly surprised to see pure white sand glimmering beneath sunrays shining in through the windows.

"I bought this at the Gypsy Market. I went to the beach near the Rota base and filled it with sand for you," Adoncia explained.

Joel was overcome with gratitude, such a sweet gift from the woman whose name meant the same. "This is so perfect. Thank you, Adoncia. I will treasure it forever."

At that moment, they heard footsteps in the choir loft, and sacred chants echoed throughout the nave as swirling incense danced in the sunlight. Joel's heart thumped with anticipation because the ceremony would soon commence.

PER PORTIA'S REQUEST, the wedding ceremony followed some Russian Orthodox traditions in addition to incorporating modern customs. Joel didn't know how Portia had talked Reverend Thomas into this mixture of rituals. Nonetheless, the holy man graciously included the requests, and Joel knew a wedding blending these two traditions would be incredibly special. To stand before God with family and friends in attendance, joining this woman in the sacred union of marriage, would undoubtedly be the most momentous day of his life.

Eloquent Russian Orthodox chants glorified God from the choir loft while the guests arrived, and the wedding party assembled. Joel and Bubba enjoyed the holy music in the altar room as they eagerly waited for their cue to enter the nave. Bubba became so emotional at the sound of the angelic voices that he wiped his eyes with a hanky, then abruptly hugged the groom.

After fleeing Bubba's embrace, Joel peeked through a crack in the door and saw that all the guests were seated. Reverend Thomas took his place with the Holy Bible and the icon of Jesus Christ beneath the great golden chandelier, and the chanting continued as the sacred ceremony began.

Joel's heart raced with anticipation. "Okay, it's time!" he exclaimed in a loud whisper.

In all his fuddy-duddery, Bubba uncoordinatedly skipped up behind Joel, accidentally bumping into him and almost pushing him through the altar door. "Sorry! I'm nervous, and I have to pee," Bubba replied as he frantically wiped sweat off his forehead. "I'm okay. I can wait."

"Are you sure?" Joel asked.

Bubba nodded and then nervously pressed his lips together.

Joel chuckled, then took a deep breath, for the highly anticipated moment had finally arrived. Looking more handsome than should be legal in his well-decorated Navy uniform, Joel gallantly departed the altar room and took his place next to the reverend. Bubba followed and then stood next to Joel.

Wearing a long-sleeved, red velvet dress that complemented her fiery red hair, Gert gracefully glided down the aisle as incense drifted through the air while chants filled the cathedral with sacred beauty. Joel smiled at this remarkable woman he viewed as his mother-in-law, a true gem—the epitome of who every great mother-in-law should be.

Now that Gert had taken her place as matron of honor, the choir chants transitioned, and the reverend raised his hands toward Heaven, instructing the audience to rise. In one fluid motion, everyone stood and turned toward the narthex as the choir intensified the chants with vibrato and ethereal elegance. The doors opened, and Joel's astonishment was unparalleled. The young woman Gunther escorted into the cathedral wasn't Portia, for she had golden-blonde hair. No trumpets accompanied the intoning choir, yet Joel could've sworn he heard a fleet of brass because she looked like an angel. At that moment, Katerina and Joel locked eyes, never breaking their connection as she walked down the aisle, and Joel smiled at his breathtakingly beautiful bride.

With wavy blonde hair shimmering beneath an elegant veil embellished with sparkling crystals, Katerina looked like a fairytale princess. She wore a stunning ivory dress with a tight strapless bodice and a puffy tulle skirt, accentuating her tiny waistline where a red velvet bow was tied, with long ribbons hanging all the way to the floor. The power of God and love was overwhelming, and Joel's eyes glistened as his bride joined him beneath the chandelier.

Gunther kissed Katerina on the cheek and gently placed her hand in Joel's. Then he smiled at Gert and sat in the front row with Ralph, Adoncia, Kirk, and Tanya. The rest of the Alexandria's crew was in the first couple of rows as well, along with Katerina's bandmates.

After a moment of silence, the reverend began the Betrothal with a blessing. Then he gave Katerina and Joel each a candle and lit them. After that, in the Russian Orthodox tradition, the deacon intoned an ektenia with assistance from the choir and the audience. All the while, Joel kept his eyes on his bride as the angelic voices filled the cathedral with holiness. Glory to our God, indeed.

After the ektenia, the ceremony continued with the exchange of vows and rings. Joel had put a lot of thought into the exquisite ring designs. The bride's ring was a gold band of twinkling diamonds with a ruby in the center, and the groom's ring was a gold band with engravings of a Russian Orthodox cross between two eagles.

Joel patiently waited for Bubba, who searched four of his pockets before remembering where he had placed the bride's ring, unlike Gert, who promptly handed the groom's ring to Katerina. Then Katerina gave her candle to Gert, and Joel gave his to Bubba. The bride and groom held hands and stared deeply into each other's eyes as the reverend led Joel through the exchange.

Joel peered deeply into Katerina's blue eyes and said, "I do." Then he gently slid the diamond and ruby wedding band onto her left ring finger, forever. Little did Katerina know that Joel had planned an exceptionally thoughtful surprise. Bubba handed Joel a golden locket with an etching of a Russian Orthodox cross between two eagles, perfectly matching Joel's ring. Katerina's eyes glistened as she lifted her veil slightly for Joel to put the braided chain around her neck. After he closed the clasp, Joel reached for his bride's hands, kissed them, and held them tightly as the reverend led Katerina through her portion of the exchange.

"I do," she said, then carefully slid Joel's band onto his left ring finger, forever.

Joel looked at their hands, then looked into Katerina's eyes and adoringly whispered, "I love you."

She smiled and whispered, "I love you too."

Now that the exchange of vows and rings was complete, the ceremony continued with the Russian Orthodox tradition of the Crowning. Gert carefully removed the crystal veil from Katerina's blonde hair while Joel handed his Navy hat to Bubba. With the veil no longer covering Katerina's head and face, Joel stared at his bride and saw the first day of the rest of his life. Her hair was golden, and her eyes were a deep, natural blue, just like Eagle Bay.

"You're an angel," Joel whispered as he stared at his lovely bride.

Katerina blushed while Gert finished preparing her hair for the family crown.

Katerina and Joel were blessed to use the same crowns that Gert and Gunther had used for their wedding many years ago. The crowns were gold with a red velvet lining, perfectly matching Katerina's locket and red bow, and each crown beautifully and ornately displayed an icon.

The Crowning began with the deacon intoning another ektenia. Once again, heavenly and angelic voices filled the nave as incense swirled and candles flickered vibrantly. Following the sacred chant, the reverend offered another prayer. Joel relished these repetitive acts of Russian Orthodox worship, appreciating each sacred moment as much as the last, each full of so much devotion and holiness.

Reverend Thomas picked up Joel's crown and blessed him. Then the reverend held it in front of Joel so that he could kiss the holy icon of Jesus Christ. After that, the reverend gently placed the crown on Joel's head. The reverend continued the same process for Katerina by blessing her and holding her crown at eye level for her to kiss the holy icon of the Virgin Mary before placing it on her head as well. By and by, the candles reflected on the golden crowns, Katerina's locket, and Joel's buttons and medals. Joel and Katerina glimmered as if they were illuminated by celestial light. With Katerina in her ivory tulle dress with the red bow, standing next to Joel in his uniform, they certainly resembled royalty as they wore the Alexander family crowns.

The bride and groom held hands and looked deeply into each other's eyes as Reverend Thomas gave the sermon. "Every day, a lone female eagle would perch on one of the cathedral's crosses, basking in the celestial light, peering into the sun. For the last year, I've been admiring this eagle's strength and resilience, for she could have flown toward the stars, perched on a mountaintop, or perched on a building. But this eagle chose the Dome of Heaven as her fortress. What has this eagle been through in her life? We don't know. We all do our best to persevere through adversity, but I can tell you; be the eagle on the cross. Show the Lord your courage by remaining faithful through difficult times. I've been seeing this eagle a lot over the last year. You may argue that all eagles look the same, and they do; but this eagle is recognizable in that she has a passion for life and love, and this eagle trusts in the Lord.

"God gave us the gift of courage. We must choose joy and remain faithful by being courageous, and the Lord will bless us. And He most certainly blessed this lone eagle. One day in mid-

September, I came to the cathedral and was delighted to see two eagles, one perched on each cross. God had blessed the lone eagle with love. And now, I see these two eagles together daily in the sunlight. They are going through life together. Trusting the Lord together. Katerina and Joel are much like these two eagles. The Lord takes care of those who trust in Him. Katerina and Joel, you have been crowned with love and joined as two eagles before the presence of God. May God bless you in your new life together."

After the sermon, the deacon offered another short ektenia and a prayer, for one can never glorify the Lord too much. In continuing with Russian Orthodox tradition, the bride and groom drank from the Common Cup of Wine. Then Katerina and Joel joined hands, and Reverend Thomas wrapped his stole around their hands, leading them on a walk three times around the lectern where the Holy Bible rested, a walk that symbolized their new journey of marriage. They returned beneath the great golden chandelier and stood next to the icon of Christ, where the reverend unwrapped the stole. Hand in hand, Katerina and Joel stepped closer to the icon of Jesus and took turns kissing His holy feet. As another plume of incense wafted through the nave, the reverend ended the ceremony, letting Joel know that he could now kiss his bride.

Joel looked into Katerina's beautiful blue eyes and gently caressed her cheek. Then he placed his hands around her tiny waist, resting them on the elegant red bow. They carefully tilted their heads and kissed for the first time as husband and wife—standing beneath the great golden chandelier—with the smiling face of Jesus watching them from the Dome of Heaven. Incense twirled in the sunlight, and the choir's angelic voices praised God Almighty. As Katerina and Joel kissed, a loud applause echoed throughout the cathedral.

Once the applause ended, the matron of honor and best man assisted the bride and groom with removing the crowns. With a smile on his rotund face, Bubba handed Joel his Navy hat, and Joel smiled as he put it on his head. He reached for his wife's hand, and they walked down the aisle together as incense plumes swirled above them, candles flickered beneath the icons, and the choir sang like angels bursting forth from Heaven's gates. Behind the newlyweds, Gunther escorted Gert, and Bubba escorted Tanya, with Ralph following closely behind them.

Katerina and Joel waited in the narthex, beginning the receiving line with the rest of the wedding party lining up accordingly.

THE GUESTS ON THE LAST ROW began departing. With a two-year-old little boy clinging to her side, an eloquent young woman with brunette hair and sad emerald eyes was the first person to approach the wedding party. Joel immediately recognized her from the family pictures at The Harbor Inn and in the Alexandria's wheelhouse.

"You're here. You're really here!" Gert exclaimed as she placed both hands over her heart as if she were keeping it from leaping from her chest. With joyful tears streaming down her face, Gert picked up Elijah, holding him close to her heart and gently rubbing his back as the little lad snuggled close to his granny. Gunther wrapped his arms around his wife and grandson, savoring this moment with his family. Meanwhile, Katerina hugged Lizzie, who was trembling and doing her best to maintain her composure.

"Thank you so much for coming. I could only imagine how difficult it is coming here, but I am so thankful that you and Elijah did. We love you so much," Katerina graciously said.

Lizzie took a deep breath and opened her mouth to speak, but no sound came out. Gert placed her hand on Lizzie's shoulder, so Katerina took Elijah while Gert had an emotional reunion with her daughter-in-law.

"I know Chris would've wanted me to come. I'm sorry it's been so long. It's been so hard without him," Lizzie said softly.

"I know it has been, honey. We are here for you. Please remember that, but I know you are in good hands in Anchorage with your momma," Gert replied.

Katerina held Elijah close, and Joel loved seeing her with this precious child. Watching this interaction confirmed that he had chosen the perfect woman to be his wife and mother of his children. With his heart so full of love, Joel wrapped his arm around Katerina and gently rubbed Elijah's cheek, which made the little boy giggle. When Lizzie heard Elijah laugh, she turned and looked at Joel like she had seen an apparition.

"You look so much like Chris," Lizzie said in astonishment.

"And that is the greatest compliment I have ever received. Thank you," Joel responded, then kissed Lizzie on the cheek. "Thank you so much for coming. I'm so happy to meet you and Elijah."

"Don't I get a hug?" Gunther humorously asked as he wrapped his arm around Lizzie. "It's so good to see you."

Lizzie chuckled because Gunther had a gift for making people laugh. "It's good to see you too, Gunther," she replied, then kissed her father-in-law on the cheek.

Katerina motioned for Gunther to hold his grandson. He gratefully smiled and took the little boy in his arms. "You remember me? I'm your grandpa. You lucky little man!" Gunther exclaimed as he tickled Elijah's tummy, and the little boy giggled to the point that everyone laughed at his cackle.

Lizzie smiled, then took a ragged breath. "The last time I was here was…"

"The funeral. We understand, sweetie," Gert empathetically said.

"We certainly do," Ralph concurred as he wrapped his arm around Lizzie, then kissed her on the cheek.

This tender moment tugged at Joel's heartstrings, for he was once a little boy without a father. As he watched the Alexanders interact with their daughter-in-law, Joel's thankfulness for joining this family deepened because of their love and empathy for Lizzie. He certainly admired Lizzie's strength for attending the wedding, returning to the cathedral where she and Chris were married and where her husband's grave was, in the town where they lived and started a family. Everything about Aleutia undoubtedly reminded her of Chris.

Joel wrapped his arm around Katerina's waist, letting her know that he was there for her always. And that was just what Katerina needed, for she leaned into her husband's embrace.

"Well, we should probably get going. We're holding up the line. We will see you at the Port House," Lizzie said.

Gunther smiled, hugged Elijah, and kissed him on the cheek. Then Gunther gave his grandson to Lizzie before kissing her on the cheek as well.

"See you soon, buddy," both Ralph and Gunther said simultaneously, and then Lizzie laughed as she and Elijah walked outside.

"Our daughter and grandson are here. They're really here," Gert said, placing her hands over her heart again.

"They certainly are," Gunther said, then kissed her cheek.

AFTER HALF AN HOUR, the receiving line concluded, and the wedding party returned to the nave to pose for pictures. Following Russian Orthodox tradition, the photo shoot continued as the wedding party visited local landmarks. To begin, they took pictures in front of the cathedral with the two eagles perched on the Domes of Heaven. While the bride and groom walked to the parking lot, they suddenly heard melodious eagle songs jubilating from the golden crosses shimmering in the winter sunlight. Katerina and

Joel turned around just before the two eagles took flight. The photographer captured them watching the regal creatures fly toward the bay, sparkling like gemstones from an illustrious sunray breaking through a magnificent cloud as if it were bursting forth from Heaven.

The photo shoot concluded at Mount Ballyhoo's Panama mount and at Spithead, two places near and dear to Katerina's heart, and now near and dear to Joel's heart as well.

Following that, the wedding party returned to the Port House for the reception and a hot performance by a blonde-haired, blue-eyed rock star with voluptuous leather boots.

Chapter 27. *Rock You*

T he sun beautifully tucked itself behind the mountains when the wedding party arrived at the reception. The Port House was brilliantly adorned with twinkle lights, stunningly complementing Blade and Leonard's meal table decorations, which included candles, red velvet runners, and red and white roses. The guests were already there, keeping it classy, enjoying champagne flutes and frosted mugs of root beer while Ted played a mixture of Christmas carols, oldies, Rock & Roll, and country music.

When Ted saw the bride and groom approaching the door, he grinned and then played the infamous gong sound to let the guests know that Katerina and Joel had arrived. He grabbed the microphone and announced, "Ladies and gentlemen, may I introduce to you, Mr. and Mrs. Joel Layton." The townsfolk applauded as the newlyweds walked inside, and Ted flipped a switch on the soundboard, playing the chorus from "Loving a Sailor." This was the perfect song choice because Joel had most certainly found a permanent harbor to begin the next chapter of his life.

While Katerina's exceptional voice echoed throughout the building, the townsfolk continued cheering and clapping as Katerina and Joel entered the Port House for the first time as husband and wife. Amid the jubilating crowd, Joel looked at his beautiful bride, glowing like an angel as her gown shimmered beneath the menagerie of twinkle lights. Feeling butterflies in his stomach and his heart racing with joy, he slid his arm around her waist, pulling her close, and then lovingly kissed her.

Meanwhile, Pete snuck up on stage, abruptly seized the mic from Ted, and loudly sang along.

Been up all night
Loving a sailor
The best kind of high
Is loving a sailor
He's an old-fashioned heart
He's like an oldie song
That I sit right here and play
While my sailor is gone

Pete's voice was intensely raspy as he sang tremendously off-key to the most provocative part of the song. In addition to the wicked singing, he shuffled his feet from side to side and wiggled his skinny, old-man butt in front of the crowd. Then he mutilated the chorus, sounding like a moose that had gotten its antlers stuck in a dumpster. As the song ended, Pete spun in a circle and shook his keister at the crowd again.

Since he was so beloved by the town as the oldest living resident, in addition to being a decorated war veteran, Pete smiled as the crowd clapped and cheered like he had given an award-winning performance.

Then he stumbled as he stepped off the stage. "There must've been something in that beer they gave me because I'm feeling tipsy!"

"Careful there, Pete. You didn't have a real beer. You had a root beer in a frosted beer mug. Perhaps, you've taken too much antacid tonight," Gert suggested as she grabbed his arm to steady him.

Pete acted like he was holding in a burp. "Oh, you silly young people. I know what beer tastes like, and that was beer for sure."

"It was root beer!" Gert and Gunther yelled at the same time.

"Nope, it was beer," Pete fervently insisted.

"Well then, someone will need to drive you home tonight since you're under the influence," Bubba added.

"Well, Jonathan Timber believes me," Pete replied as he patted Bubba on the back.

"Oh, Pete, you're so funny!" Katerina exclaimed, then hugged him.

By this point, everyone gave up and went along with it.

"Pete, why don't you sit at the bar with the boys until this buzz wears off? We will get you a big plate of food to soak up the alcohol," Gert said.

"Just don't give me any beans, or you'll be sorry," he responded as Gert and Gunther walked with him to the bar.

Katerina and Joel looked at each other and laughed, for there was never a dull moment in the Port of Aleutia. Joel would be forever grateful for his new friends and family—most of all, the beautiful woman with whom he would share his most remarkable adventure yet. And once again, Joel pulled Katerina close for another passionate kiss, never feeling so happy in his life and never wanting this feeling of newly wedded bliss to end.

"I love you," Katerina breathlessly said.

"I love you too, Mrs. Layton," Joel sappily replied.

"Oh, you two!" Bubba exclaimed as he abruptly hugged them.

"Step to the side!" Gunther bellowed from across the room.

FLICKERING CANDLES AND FRAGRANT ROSES welcomed the guests as they sat at the exquisitely set dinner tables. Adoncia was already sitting with Lizzie, each lady going out of her way to make the other feel welcome. All the while, Elijah giggled and pointed at Tiny, wearing a miniature Navy suit that perfectly matched Joel's.

"Where did he get that outfit?" Joel inquired as he sat next to Elijah.

"I brought it for him. ¿No es precioso?" Adoncia asked.

"Yes, that's pretty darn cute," Joel replied as he gently scratched Tiny's head. "I know what you want." Joel took off his Navy hat, laid it on the table, and Tiny immediately crawled inside of it. "Adoncia, I have no idea how you found a small Navy suit that fits him perfectly."

"Hey, you know I'm good with the Internet. I got so good my clients came to me. It was much more work back in the day recruiting them at the Gypsy Market!" Adoncia exclaimed.

Lizzie's eyes bugged out, and Joel decided that this wasn't the best time to divulge the details of Adoncia's previous occupation. Meanwhile, Katerina joined them at the table, almost tripping and falling as she sat next to Joel.

"Careful there," Joel said as he helped his bride sit down and stuff the puffy tulle skirt underneath the table.

The rest of the wedding party joined them, including Kirk, Tanya, Bubba, Ralph, Gert, and Gunther. As they took their seats, Tiny squeaked to greet everyone, and Elijah giggled.

"Do you think Tiny is funny?" Joel asked as he leaned his head down to the giggling boy and draped his arm across the back of Elijah's chair.

The little boy laughed again and then stood up in his booster seat, so Joel reached his arm around Elijah's waist to steady him. Then Elijah turned and reached his arms out for Joel.

"He wants to sit on your lap," Lizzie explained.

Joel felt honored, so he picked up Elijah and gently put the youngster on his lap. After that, Tiny hopped out of the Navy hat and jumped into Elijah's arms.

"I need a picture of this!" Gert exclaimed as she took her phone out of her purse.

Joel felt Katerina wrap her arms around him and Elijah before whispering, "I love you so much."

Joel smiled and rubbed his cheek against hers. "I love you too. I'm so happy."

Suddenly, Bubba let out a loud, obnoxious, and overly emotional sob. "Oh, you guys! This is so beautiful!" He reached into three of his pockets before locating his overused hanky.

Tanya rubbed his back. "Oh, J.T. You're so sweet. You're so in touch with your feelings and everyone else's."

Like the sound of her voice was an aphrodisiac, Bubba embraced his fake blonde and sloppily kissed her for much longer than was necessary, leaving everyone at the table with the sudden urge to chunder. Joel was aghast at Tanya and Bubba's public promiscuity. As if the whipped cream incident at the inn wasn't enough, Joel now had to endure this impromptu make-out session at his wedding reception, which certainly wasn't anything for an impressionable child to see, so Joel immediately covered Elijah's eyes.

"Will you two get a room? Come on. There's a child present. You're gonna pop your cummerbund. You nasty!" Gunther pontificated in disgust as he pulled out his cannabis vape and then took a deep, splendid draw.

"Put that thing away!" Gert insisted. "How many times do I got to tell you that you can't smoke that in here?"

"Hey, sorry, Captain," Bubba began. "I love everybody at this table. I especially love you," he said, then abruptly grabbed Gunther's face and kissed him on the cheek.

"You're fired! I'm getting a new deck boss!" Gunther exclaimed as he wiped his face off with a napkin. "Gert, get me a sanitizing wipe! Quick!"

"Actually, Joel's the captain now," Kirk nonchalantly added.

Katerina put two fingers in her mouth and whistled like she was breaking up a brawl. "Hey, people! Joel and I own the Alexandria, and no one's getting fired!"

"Three cheers for Captain Layton! Hip, hip, hooray!" Bubba exclaimed, then took a messy gulp of root beer before loudly hiccupping.

Slightly embarrassed, Joel looked at Adoncia to see how she was digesting the interactions among his Aleutian family. Not fazed by it the slightest bit, Adoncia winked at him and smiled. Breathing a sigh of relief, Joel laughed, then amusedly shrugged his shoulders.

Elijah tugged at the medals pinned to Joel's well-decorated Navy suit. "Shiny," the little boy said to him.

"Yes, they are shiny," Joel replied as he rubbed Elijah's cheek. Joel had never experienced the love of a child before, and now that he had, he adored it. A warm, fuzzy feeling overtook Joel's entire body as he looked at Katerina, seeing a glimpse into the future—a vision of her holding their baby one day, then Joel walking up to them and wrapping his arms around them both.

Like she was telepathic, Katerina leaned over and whispered in his ear, "You will make a great dad someday." Then she kissed him on the cheek.

"And you'll be a wonderful mother," he replied, then kissed her in return.

While the wedding party hobnobbed at the head table, the rest of the gang gathered around the bar, gabbing and slamming root beers. Zac chatted it up, discussing the bairdi and opilio seasons with Captain Karchagin, Captain Babanin, Donald, Captain Smith, and their wives, along with Old Al, Pete, Ted, Rhonda, Hank, Nick, and Polly. On the other side of the bar, Lora sat between Dr. Sampson and her balding husband while they socialized with Alicia and Denny. Eagerly waiting for dinner to begin, the rest of the townsfolk, including Blade and Leonard, were perched at the stunningly decorated high-topped tables. Meanwhile, Reverend Thomas sipped hot cider, trying not to look displeased with all the root-beer-slamming sinners around him.

THE RECEPTION DINNER was a decadent meal of salad, sourdough bread, prime rib, king crab legs, fingerling potatoes, green beans with bacon, and of course, the exceptional wedding cake prepared by Blade and Leonard. The six-tiered cake rested on a gold stand near the jukebox and memory table where the candles vibrantly flickered. With eight layers of yellow cake with white chocolate icing, raspberry filling, and almond flavoring, the cake tasted as beautiful as its decorations looked. The white chocolate icing provided the perfect backdrop for eloquently placed red and white decorative roses crafted from thick icing by Blade, the master chef extraordinaire. Both decked out in matching tuxedos with red bow ties and cummerbunds, Blade and Leonard sliced the cake, serving it first to the bride and groom and then to the fine folks of Aleutia.

As everyone enjoyed the scrummy dessert, Ted walked up to the stage to make an announcement. "It's now time for the best man speech. Bubba, the spotlight is on you, my friend."

Patting sweat beads from his forehead with his tremendously overused hanky, Bubba walked up to the stage. "For those who don't know me, I'm Jonathan Timber, but everybody calls me Bubba. I am truly honored to be Joel's best man and to call him my very best friend. Joel is a Navy captain with a Navy Cross because his navigation skills saved a guided-missile destroyer from sinking during a hurricane. And, during the arctic storm we faced during the red king crab season, he did it again. He saved the crew members' lives. He saved my life. He's a darn good captain and a good man on top of that. I've known Katerina my entire life, and I am so pleased that she and Joel have found each other. I know he will take care of her and everyone around him because that's what Joel does. That's the kind of man he is. To Katerina and Joel, may your marriage be blessed with happiness and love! I love you both and hope your love inspires everyone! God bless you both!" Bubba said emotionally as he wiped his eyes before loudly sniffling.

"Tanya, go over there and hug him before he comes over here and hugs us! Please!" Gunther exclaimed as he sunk into his chair, bracing for the impact of an impending Chubby Bubba hug.

Luckily for Gunther, Bubba didn't initiate a group hug. Instead, he sat down and wiped his eyes for the umpteenth time.

Even though Bubba's overly emotional sensitivities made Joel uncomfortable, he leaned across the table and shook Bubba's hand. "Thank you, man. That means a lot," Joel said.

"I love you, man!" Bubba boisterously replied.

Meanwhile, Gunther scooted away from Bubba and took another toke on his vape, shaking his head somewhere between amazement and disgust.

TED WENT BACK UP ON STAGE. "It's time for the first dance between Katerina and Joel as husband and wife. Will the bride and groom please come up to the dancefloor?" he asked and then turned on the mirrored disco ball and dimmed the lights.

Joel's heart fluttered as he turned toward his bride, who took his breath away with her smiling face, golden-blonde hair, and ivory gown shimmering beneath the twinkle lights—making her sparkle like a princess. He extended his hand, and she gently placed her hand in his. They carefully stood, with Katerina taking extra care not to trip on her puffy gown. Joel led her to the dancefloor, where the disco ball's spinning lights made her dress glimmer with even more vibrancy while also reflecting on the gold buttons and medals on Joel's Navy suit.

Just like he did the night they met, Joel went to the jukebox and selected the oldie song from their first dance, the same song that his parents danced to in the kitchen the last time he saw them, the song that ended their chapter, but began Katerina and Joel's—the song that had the power to transcend time.

As the music softly began, the guests gathered around the

dancefloor, and Joel slid his arm around Katerina's waist, pulling her close, never feeling a moment in his life that was as magical as this one. The flickering candles, twinkle lights, and disco ball along with the melody of this old, familiar tune made this moment so surreal, and all Joel could do was feel love. He caressed Katerina's cheek with the back of his hand, then gently lifted her chin before kissing her perfectly desirable lips, the last lips he would ever kiss.

No face was without a smile, and no eye was without a sparkle as the guests watched the bride and groom dance cheek to cheek, swaying to the music while the world around them melted away.

Joel felt the presence of angels surrounding him and Katerina. Then he saw the silhouettes of his parents; Penny and Kyle; Lizzie and Chris; and Belinda and Ralph, dancing next to them, sharing in this momentous day and giving their blessings for Katerina and Joel's new life together.

Overcome with emotion, Joel pulled his bride close, and she whispered in his ear, "They're here with us, Joel. I can feel their presence."

"They certainly are. I see them too," Joel replied as he and Katerina stared into each other's sparkling eyes.

At that moment, Katerina and Joel looked out the windows, just in time to see the Northern Lights splash fantastical colors across the night sky—reflecting on Eagle Bay's shimmering ripples.

"God is good," Joel whispered. God is good, indeed.

The song picked up tempo with a beautiful symphony, providing the perfect accompaniment to the swirling Northern Lights. Joel smiled as he stared into his bride's blue eyes and held her hand, lifting it high before gently pushing her outward. Katerina spun a couple of times, smiling like a princess in her glistening dress, and Joel carefully pulled her back into his arms. He held her for a few seconds before gently dipping her toward the floor, pulling her back up, and kissing her passionately. All the while, the disco ball spun, the angels danced around them, and the Northern Lights pirouetted a light show that's only explanation could be the hand of Almighty God.

Gert bawled her eyes out, but nothing could compare to the emotional impact this dance had on Bubba.

"This is so beautiful!" he sobbed, then promptly stuck his head between Tanya's tatas, which was all too easy to do because of her low-cut, hot pink dress.

Considering the intense emotions surrounding them, Gunther took another long draw on his cannabis vape before offering it to Ralph, who took a hit as well.

Katerina and Joel danced slowly, cheek to cheek, and Joel savored every second. When the song concluded, the townsfolk clapped and cheered while the newlyweds shared one more passionate kiss beneath the spinning disco ball.

Katerina held Joel's hands but pulled back slightly, sexily raising one eyebrow and grinning her naughty grin that made Joel weak in the knees. "I have a surprise for you, sailor. I will be back soon."

Joel laughed. "A surprise, huh? You have a new song, which means you're changing out of your dress."

"I'll put it back on later, so you can take it off," Katerina promised.

"Deal," Joel replied. He smiled as he watched her lift her dress and scurry off to the back hallway.

LIKE THE GUESTS, Joel returned to his table to continue socializing and enjoying the reception. He scooted down a seat next to Adoncia, so Kirk took this as his cue to join the others at the bar. Kirk took off his dress coat, hung it on the back of his chair, kissed Adoncia on the cheek, and then swaggered his way up to the bar to slam root beers and shoot the breeze.

Meanwhile, Elijah laughed, and everyone looked at him as he

sat on his Uncle Ralph's lap, holding Tiny in his arms, and cackling the cutest little boy giggles while Tiny squeaked at him. Joel smiled at Elijah and then at Lizzie, so thankful she chose to attend the wedding and spend this time with her family. Suddenly, just over her shoulder in the distance, Joel noticed a fluffy blur scampering low to the floor, coming down the hallway, and surmised that Katerina had left the apartment door open, causing Screech to escape. Joel didn't let anyone know that the cat was there and just watched to see what he would do.

With his tail fur fluffed, the feline entered the bar like he was on a mission. At first, Joel thought that the cat was coming to see him, but his balloon burst when Screech trotted past his chair. Instead, Screech backed up to Kirk's jacket, spraying piss all over it like the jacket was on fire and he was the fireman. The indignant feline moved his head from side to side, twitched his whiskers, and meowed like he was singing a rock song. He shook his tail, lifting his hind feet up and down as if he were pumping the piss out of his bladder. The smell of cat pee hit Joel's nose like a slap in the face, yet everyone at the table watched Ralph play with Elijah, not noticing the pee scent coming from Kirk's jacket or the pee dripping on the floor, creating a giant puddle.

Screech ended his pissing session by arching his back, kicking up his hind feet, and zooming into the hallway and up the staircase, no doubt sneaking back into the apartment like he had done no wrong.

Joel couldn't contain his amusement and burst out laughing. "I love that cat!"

"You love what cat?" Adoncia asked.

"We have a huge tomcat, and he was just, uh, sneaking around down here," Joel said, not telling her that the cat had just urinated all over her bloke's jacket.

"¡Amo a los gatos!" Adoncia exclaimed.

"Did I mention how happy I am you're here?" Joel asked, wondering if she could smell the stench.

"Well, you may see a lot more of me…" Adoncia began.

"Do tell."

"I am going to stay until the crew leaves for the opilio season. Then I'm going back to Rota to clean out and sell my house. Kirk will fly to Rota when he gets back from crabbing, and we will come back here together."

"So, you're in love with a sailor," Joel said.

"All you sailors are the same, but I can endure loving a sailor if I knew I had one coming back to me. And Kirk will," Adoncia responded with love in her eyes.

"I'll always come back to you," Kirk said as he sat down, unknowingly stepping in Screech's puddle.

Joel put his hand over his mouth, containing the laughter.

Suddenly, another fluffy blur caught his eye, coming down the hallway. This time, Ice swiftly trotted into the bar, making his way toward their table. The pup slid into the puddle of cat pee, slid under Kirk's chair, jumped up in Kirk's lap, and ran up his chest with his piss-covered paws.

"Dude, you're wet!" Kirk exclaimed as he squinted his eyes. Then the squint morphed into a smile, and he scratched Ice's back.

As if that wasn't bizarre enough, Tiny squeaked, jumped across the table, and landed in front of Kirk, where the monkey stood up tall, crapped in his paws, and threw it, splattering the remnants all over Kirk's freshly shaven face. Following that, Tiny crawled up Kirk's arm, sat on his shoulder, and looked for bugs in his ear. To everyone's stupefaction, Kirk handled this exceptionally well, even leaning his cheek into the monkey, scratching his back, and saying, "Dude, you're nasty. That's not cool."

"I still don't understand how a monkey so small can have poop so big with an astronomical splatter range," Gunther amusedly said as he watched Kirk nonchalantly wipe the excrement off his face.

"Right?" Gert concurred as she tried not to laugh.

Joel was astounded by his fur kids' antics and surmised that even the animals could tell Kirk was turning a new leaf because they only pulled these stunts with people they liked. Kirk's change of heart was all thanks to Adoncia's influence, for she was the reason they were all together, celebrating life, happiness, and love.

EAGER TO SEE HIS BRIDE decked out in her Port House attire, Joel looked at the clock, knowing that Katerina would soon make her grand entrance. Meanwhile, the happy reception banter grew louder, for a great time was being had by all. Polly and Nick had one of their infamous make-out sessions, and Tanya sashayed across the dancefloor to Bubba. On the other hand, Lora's husband had his arm around her as he glared at Dr. Sampson; perhaps the poor ninny finally figured out that more than adjustments occurred on the doc's chiropractic table. Then there were Alicia and Denny, who were snuggled up like snow bunnies on a glacier, while Kirk whispered sweet little ditties in Adoncia's ear, and Blade and Leonard held each other close as they danced to Christmas carols.

Suddenly, the infamous gong boomed from the Port House speakers, so the townsfolk knew to quiet down. Ted flickered the lights, played the gong again, and turned on the mirrored disco ball, making Joel's heart pound with anticipation because his voluptuous lady of the bar was on her way. He couldn't stop a magnanimous smile from overtaking his face, for Katerina had a hold on him unlike any other. *What will she be wearing? What will she sing?* Joel wondered as he walked to the dancefloor and stood in front of the microphone, along with Gunther, Ralph, Pete, Adoncia, Kirk, Hank, Tanya, Bubba, Blade, Polly, and Nick in the front row. The band members took their respective places on stage, Gert on the keyboard, Rhonda on acoustic guitar, Ted on drums, and

Leonard on bass while Katerina's sparkling silver electric guitar waited for her to rock the house.

The sexy sound of high heels click-clacked on the staircase, announcing that the Port House queen was on her way. Katerina entered the room, climbed up onto the bar, and strutted the length of the bar top. Then she naughtily slid down the pole on the right. She sexily swayed her hips as she walked across the room and onto the stage, where the spotlight illuminated Katerina Layton in all her decked-out leather splendor.

Once again, his tantalizing lady's supermodel attributes left Joel weak in the knees. With a tight, shiny black leather bikini top and matching high-waisted leather shorts, accentuating her curvaceous assets, and providing the perfect complement to her infamous thigh-high leather boots, Katerina's outfit didn't disappoint. To top off the seductive ensemble, she wore Joel's Navy hat, the golden locket, the diamond earrings, and both ID bracelets. And her blonde hair was sassily teased to perfection and was offset by bright red lipstick on the lips that Joel would be kissing for the rest of his life.

And just like the first night they met, Katerina was on stage, and Joel was in his Navy full dress white uniform, looking more handsome than should be legal. Everything had miraculously come full circle since that fateful night just three and a half months ago; all thanks to God Almighty and His goodness. He worked spectacularly—bringing Katerina and Joel together through the influence of an attractive prostituta.

Katerina looked into Joel's eyes and smiled, making him feel like the luckiest man alive. Never breaking eye contact with her Navy man, she picked up the electric guitar, put the strap over her shoulder, and then lightly strummed as Leonard kicked in on the bass. The disco lights reflected on the starlet's shiny leather outfit, and the golden locket drew attention to her perky chest. Joel admired her beauty and watched Katerina's gorgeous red lips as she flirtatiously sang the first verse.

> I said hello
> Tell me what's your style
> Do you like it slow
> Or do you like it wild
> You're hot
> Gonna show you what I got
> Strumming my guitar tonight

The band kicked in full force. Katerina powerfully slammed the pic down the strings, raising the electric guitar to a new level, and Joel felt the vibrations rattle the floor beneath his feet. As she moved her leather-kissed hips to the rhythm, she sang the pre-chorus and wildly strummed like a rock star.

> I've never felt like this before
> Till my Navy man came through my door
> You've got my temperature running high
> Burning right up to the Northern Lights

The bar queen pounded the strings while Ted rocked the heck out of the drums, leading to a kick-butt chorus where country met Rock & Roll.

> I'm gonna rock you baby
> All night long
> I'm gonna rock you baby
> Till the break of dawn
> Gonna strum my guitar
> And wear these leather boots

Gonna play so loud
Blow a hole in the roof
Are you ready
Hey, hey
Are you ready
A little bit of country
With some Rock & Roll
You wanna let me rock you
With a Port House show
All right

And oh, did the crowd go wild, for Katerina had done it again; a sexy outfit and song was the perfect recipe for another bang-up Port House performance. Perplexed but having a great time, Gunther shook his head and laughed at his overly provocative niece. And he couldn't deny how ravishing and full of life Gert was as she put the pedal to the metal on the keyboard.

Gunther leaned over to Joel. "We're two lucky men, Captain Layton."

"We certainly are," Joel replied as he watched Katerina and Momma Gert bring down the house.

Everyone was having a blast because it wasn't possible to listen to a Port House original song without being affected by the beat. Ralph danced with Lizzie and Elijah, Kirk twirled Adoncia, and Alicia and Denny bopped like high schoolers. Lora swayed with her husband, peering over his balding head to catch a glimpse of Dr. Sampson, who preppily sat at the bar with his sweater tied all too perfectly around his neck. Of course, leave it to a few folks to be lewd and crude. Pete broke it down with his old-man-butt wiggle while Tanya and Bubba danced inappropriately, sucking face one minute and spanking each other the next, leaving Ralph with no choice but to cover Elijah's eyes.

The tempo slowed slightly for the second verse, and Katerina foxily swayed her curvaceous hips from side to side as she stared deeply into Joel's eyes.

Some disco lights
Dancing on the floor
Time to strike the gong
And let's begin the show
It's hot
Gonna knock back a shot

Suddenly, the music stopped, except for Ted banging the drumsticks together while Blade came up on stage and handed Katerina a shot glass.

She winked at him. "Thank you, darling," Katerina said with a sultry grin. Then she promptly slammed the shot, making the crowd go wild. After that, Katerina strummed the guitar and sang the final line of the second verse, "Slamming some tequila tonight." And with the rest of the band accompanying her, she sang the pre-chorus and chorus once more.

Gunther and Ralph disapprovingly shook their heads while Joel grinned, amused by his naughty blonde bride.

After singing the chorus for the final time, Katerina took off the guitar while the rest of the band continued playing. The disco lights shimmered on her shiny leather outfit as she flitted off the stage and sauntered up to Joel, making his entire body quiver. He debonairly grinned and placed his hands on her sexily swaying hips, while Katerina slowly slid her hands up his chest, gliding them over the gold buttons and medals that shimmered beneath the lights. She stared deeply into his eyes while she draped her arms over his shoulders and flirtatiously sang the final section.

Oh you love the leather boots
While I sing
Gonna rock with you forever
Be your bar-dancing queen
All right

All the while, the pirouetting hues of the Northern Lights showcased God's artistry in the sky over Eagle Bay as the disco lights spun inside the Port House. And Joel couldn't contain his love for his lady, so he slowly reached his hands up to Katerina's beautiful face and passionately kissed her lips.

Then she wrapped her arms around him, whispering in his ear, "I love loving a sailor."

Joel held her closer until he felt their beating hearts touching like two eagles taking flight.

Portia's Songbook

You Lied

You lied
You didn't tell me you lied
You had me hanging on your words
When you walked through the door
You lied
You didn't tell me the truth
Told me that you needed space
Not that you found somebody new

CHORUS:
And you would come
And you would go
And hold her hand
And I would be alone
You lied
You didn't tell me you lied
Why did you marry me
Then you left me here alone
You lied
You held me then you shut me out
The flame was hot
The flame was out
Am I just a sweet memory
What about the years you spent with me
Oh, you lied
You lied
You lied
Oh, you lied

You lied
Why did you tell me I'm loved
I was so sure that we would last
But you held another girl
You lied
So I will tell you the truth
Now I'm the one needing space
And I will find somebody new

CHORUS

On and Off

I am getting tired
I've been waiting here all night
Hoping that you might
Come back in and change your mind
Oh, how you loved
Oh, how you lied
Just like a lightbulb
From dark to bright

CHORUS:
How did you turn it on and off
You said you loved me
Then you turned and walked away
How did you make up in your mind
What you're thinking
And what you really meant to say
You are a thief in the night
An awesome swindler
With a con artist's appetite
How did you turn it on and off
I've heard your lies all before
Don't come back through my door
Goodbye on and off

Funny how the sun
And the moon they seem to fight
The sun hurts my eyes
And the moon it fills them up
Oh, how you cried
Oh, when you lied
You'll be a trickster
For all of your life

CHORUS

More Than Me

You said
It's what you needed to do
You went farther north
It was a war zone
It was an arctic storm
The waves they claimed you
Yeah, they claimed you

CHORUS:
You took away the sun
You took away the light
I'm living in the dark
Like every day is night
The Northern Lights
No longer make me smile
Something I haven't done
In quite a while
Coz you loved the sea
More than you loved me
Yeah, you loved the sea
More than me

I'm here
Without you singing with me
You were my hero
And I've been so mad
Better than being sad
Sometimes I hate you
But, I love you

CHORUS

I can't take it
So I drink
And I smoke
Don't wanna think
Maybe I'll forgive you
For going away
Maybe I'll forgive you
Someday

CHORUS

Country Rock & Roll

I love a fiddle; I love its sound
I love electric guitars too loud
I love a violin's do-si-do
I love a bass real deep and low

PRE-CHORUS 1:
I'm sitting here in my pickup truck
I'm staring at the radio; my finger's stuck
Do I want some country or Rock & Roll
No, I want country and Rock & Roll

CHORUS:
I want a motor with a thunderbolt
A plow that breaks pavement with just one note
Roll the two together; let's light a smoke
Together we'll get high on Country Rock & Roll
On Country Rock & Roll

I love a cowboy's tight dark blue jeans
I love a rock star's shiny stud seams
I love a cowboy's snakeskin boots
I love a rock star's leather suit

PRE-CHORUS 2:
I'm sitting here in my pickup truck
I'm staring at the radio; my finger's stuck
Do I want a cowboy or a rock star
I want a cowboy who's a rock star

CHORUS

Take a big draw of that smoking, smoking
Ooo, a chair dance, dazzling high
Take a big draw of that handsome, handsome
Cowboy rock star delight

CHORUS

Sail On

You said you'd love me forever
That's when I gave you my heart
But you threw it in the harbor
And now we're drifting apart

CHORUS 1:
So, sail on, sail on, my sailor
Looking for fish in the sea
And when you don't catch one
Don't come crying to me

You are no longer my captain
I'll no longer be your mate
Sailor please chart a new course
Coz I'm not biting the bait

CHORUS 2:
So, sail on, sail on, my sailor
Looking for fish in the sea
And when you don't catch one
Don't come crying to me
So, sail on, sail on, my sailor
Sail across the earth
Well, it's too bad the earth ain't flat
Then you wouldn't be a'coming back
Yeah, you'd be falling off the map

Now you're drifting out the harbor
Headed to the sea of tears
Oh yeah soon you will be drowning
Lonely and drinking some beers

CHORUS 2

Our Last Night

Oh here you are
Looking into my eyes
But tomorrow
You'll be out of sight
On your way
To your other love

PRE-CHORUS:
Oh Bering Sea
Please bring him home to me

CHORUS:
It's our last night
Before you go away
It's our last night
For you and I to stay
In each other's arms
Until the morning light
It's our last night
To love

You said to write
That's what I'm doing now
Kinda strange
I'll do it anyhow
Coz I love you
To the moon and back

PRE-CHORUS

CHORUS

Wherever you are
My song
Will travel with the wind
Wherever you go
My love
Will follow all the way
Because I love you
To the moon and back

PRE-CHORUS

CHORUS

I'd Rather Die

Ever since that night
In my crowded harbor bar
You came in like rolling thunder
From a fallen-down storm cloud
And I was drinking brandy
And you had a beer
You criticized my lyrics
You, criticized my fears

PRE-CHORUS:
And ever since then
I've been trying to defend
My love for this Navy sailor man

CHORUS:
I'll give you a million reasons why
You know I'd rather die
Than live without your breath
Mingled in with mine
I know it's morbid
But it's true
The way that I need you
If love can't stand the test of time
I know I'd rather die

Ever since the day
That we went to Spithead Dock
The eagles were flying crazy
And I told you to stay back
You wrapped your arms around me
Gently kissed my face
Oh you made my heart flutter
Oh, you made my heart race

PRE-CHORUS

CHORUS

OUTRO:
Oh, I need you by my side
Ooo, I'm losing my mind
To this fever that's called love
Oh, I'm so drunk
Oh, I'm so drunk on love
Ooo, whoa, ooo, whoa, ooo, whoa, ooo,
whoa, ooo, whoa, whoa
I said ooo, whoa, ooo, whoa, ooo, whoa,
ooo, whoa, ooo, whoa

Strumming My Guitar

The sea, yeah she'll take you away
But I won't beg you to
Stay away from the lady with your love
Well, that's okay
I'll be waiting on the shore
Till you're coming back for more
I'll be your lady of the bar
Where I'll be strumming my guitar

CHORUS:
Let the chords find the stars
Shining above the ocean tide
Know what it's like to love a man
Who hates his feet on the sand
So I'll strum my guitar
Till the chords kiss the stars
Reflecting on the ocean waves
Home to lost sailors' graves
My heart prays you'll be safe
Till I'll kiss your face
So I'll be strumming my guitar
So you won't seem so far
Away

You're lost, in a storm on the sea
I'm so worried 'bout you
Felt my heart stop I'm barely breathing at all
But I look up
To the dancing Northern Lights
Oh I'm singing all my might
I am your lady of the bar
Where I am strumming my guitar

CHORUS

You got the stars
You got the moon
You'll be home soon
This I know
I know
You got the sun
You got the light
You'll put up one heck of a fight
And come home
Come home

CHORUS

Loving a Sailor

A Navy sailor
Grew up on a bay
Crabbing the summer
Oystering the cold away
Oldies on the radio
Bring him right back
To a time long ago
Back to his mom and dad
But he went and traveled the world
Lots of people under his command
From what I see staring back at me
I'm marrying one heck of a man

CHORUS:
A happy wanderer
Found a permanent harbor
Each time he leaves
Yeah, he sails farther
Well, I'm in love
With a sailor
Yeah, times get tough
Loving a sailor
But it's all right
Loving a sailor
Coz he must flow
With the tide

An eagle sitting
Alone by the bay
Watching the water
Just fishing the time away
Water's slapping the shore
Seagulls sing loud
How I long for his touch
Oh how I want him back
But I know he's living his dream
Floating on the waves and with the wind
So I'll wait here waiting patiently
I'm loving one heck of a man

CHORUS

Been up all night
Loving a sailor
The best kind of high
Is loving a sailor
He's an old-fashioned heart
He's like an oldie song
That I sit right here and play
While my sailor is gone

CHORUS

Rock You

I said hello
Tell me what's your style
Do you like it slow
Or do you like it wild
You're hot
Gonna show you what I got
Strumming my guitar tonight

Oh you love the leather boots
While I sing
Gonna rock with you forever
Be your bar-dancing queen
All right

PRE-CHORUS:
I've never felt like this before
Till my Navy man came through my door
You've got my temperature running high
Burning right up to the Northern Lights

CHORUS:
I'm gonna rock you baby
All night long
I'm gonna rock you baby
Till the break of dawn
Gonna strum my guitar
And wear these leather boots
Gonna play so loud
Blow a hole in the roof
Are you ready
Hey, hey
Are you ready
A little bit of country
With some Rock & Roll
You wanna let me rock you
With a Port House show
All right

Some disco lights
Dancing on the floor
Time to strike the gong
And let's begin the show
It's hot
Gonna knock back a shot
Slamming some tequila tonight

PRE-CHORUS

CHORUS

About the Author

Jamie Grangier graduated *summa cum laude* with a Bachelor of Arts in English from the University of Maryland Eastern Shore's Honors Program and with a Master of Arts in English with a concentration in Composition, Language, and Rhetoric from Salisbury University. Her favorite area of interest is English Romanticism. When Jamie isn't writing, she enjoys traveling and spending time with her family and beloved pets. She currently resides on Maryland's Eastern Shore near the beautiful Chesapeake Bay.

www.ingramcontent.com/pod-product-compliance
Lightning Source LLC
Chambersburg PA
CBHW030907300726
48970CB00001B/51